# VINCENT

*and*

# PABLO

*The Revised Version*

# VINCENT
## *and*
# PABLO

*The Revised Version*

## Tony Warner

Matador
9 Priory Business Park
Kibworth Beauchamp
Leicestershire LE8 0RX, UK
Tel: (+44) 116 279 2299
Fax: (+44) 116 279 2277
Email: books@troubador.co.uk
Web: www.troubador.co.uk/matador

ISBN 978 1783064 052

British Library Cataloguing in Publication Data.
A catalogue record for this book is available from the British Library.

Typeset in Bembo by Troubador Publishing Ltd
Printed and bound in the UK by TJ International, Padstow, Cornwall

**Matador** is an imprint of Troubador Publishing Ltd

*For Lizzie and Harry Kirman*

# November 1941

## *London*

Distracted by the searchlights and continuous ground fire, the pilot of the Dornier bomber panicked and turned south over the river before reaching his destination. Realising his mistake and not wishing to make a perilous landing at his home airfield, he dropped his whole bomb load at random. Wiping out most of Hackford Road, Lambeth. What had been a smug and tidy street was reduced to complete rubble, leaving only the odd wall standing here and there.

At the time, Eugenie was vaguely considering what Paul had said and done, as well as what Vincent had said and not done. Although still mobile at 84, she had no time for, or patience with, bomb shelters. "I'd sooner die in my bed," she said. Which she duly did. Her body was not recovered until three days after the raid, partly because it was assumed that all the local residents had been safe in the communal shelter. Only when some boys eager for lumps of shrapnel for souvenirs uncovered a foot beneath the rubble were the local police informed. In the course of clearing up and removing the body, one volunteer came across a charming pastel of some irises still in its frame but with the glass broken. Against all regulations he removed the remaining shards and tucked it inside his jacket in order to take it home to his missus who was partial to pictures of flowers and would fancy this one for her kitchen.

Little was known about the victim except that she was a widow and had children somewhere. Daughters it was thought, though a son who was 'right posh' was also mentioned. A burial was duly performed though it was a few months later when the arrival of Eugenie's eldest daughter from Dorset, concerned that she had not heard from her mother, sparked a family gathering and memorial service. There could be no possibility of an exhumation but in due course the memorial service was finally held, attended by all three daughters and a man who was undeniably 'right posh'. It was he who organised the purchase and erection of a headstone for the grave. Despite this generosity the daughters were not happy. A family row disfigured the exit from the graveyard. Why, demanded the youngest daughter, was her mother's name so small on the stone? Why was she only given second place to her husband, dead these twenty years?

For a couple of years flowers were left at the grave by the few neighbours who remained in the area and by various relatives for as long as they remembered. But memories are short and the death of one old lady when millions are perishing in the midst of a world war is easily forgotten. If her death was sudden and unmarked, her life took her down unusual pathways, intertwined with the leading artists of the age. Lying beneath the rubble of Hackford Road, partly destroyed by fire, rested her crewel-work motto, which hung above her bed from the day on which she married, her husband's favourite Biblical quotation: "And we know that all things work together for them that love."

*Brixton, London 1941*

# Goupil and Company

## *Paris 1872*

Goupil and Company is now well established in the art world; established enough to believe that it has traditions and old enough to realise that it has become staid and needs to move with the times. New young artists have begun to make a reputation for themselves. Claude Monet has made a bit of a splash, even if his main buyer is the husband of his mistress. Manet has calmed down a bit after painting a prostitute with dirty toenails and a suggestive devilish cat. Degas is at least a gentleman, whose fascination for scantily clad washerwomen and scrawny adolescent ballet dancers is shared by other gentlemen of his class. What Goupil and Company needs is an enthusiastic young salesman who can market the up-and-coming artists to its existing clients, develop new, younger clients and encourage promising artists to enter the Goupil stable, even if returns from them might be a trifle slow.

One of the directors has recently retired from active participation in the company, although his investment remains as an important part of its working capital. He has two nephews who he sees as taking his place in the company; perhaps the elder of those would be the ideal person? As far as he is concerned, this nephew has the added advantage of carrying his uncle's full name. The nephew, though, is given to strange enthusiasms. His father is a preacher and the son has inherited hell-fire and self-sacrifice. Alongside that he has 'got art'. Art, he believes, brings God's work into the salons and into the city. Art shows the human condition and persuades us to ameliorate the lot of the poor.

The Goupil directors are not totally convinced. Their business is concerned with selling paintings, not adopting a social and artistic crusade. Can such a person present the company in the right light? Might he not frighten off their existing clientele? On the other hand he has the backing of someone with a considerable financial stake in the company, he is young and enthusiastic, speaks excellent English and may be just the person to expand their fledgling London operation. It is well known that the English know nothing about art; they only buy two sorts of paintings. Their favourite is story paintings, preferably told in an Italian or French accent, which remind them of their year spent on the Grand Tour. The other is sporting scenes. George Stubbs is pretty well sold out but Goupil is doing great business with Heywood Hardy. His time studying in Paris has obviously taught him how to paint in a serious manner, which he is applying to English hunting scenes and pictures of sweet young girls with appealing dogs. He is the star of the Goupil London firmament.

However, one artist does not pay the way for the Southampton Street premises. A young enthusiast might be just what is required to get these cold Anglo-Saxons interested in real art. Some of the Salon nudes might do the trick; these English are so decadent that they can always get excited over a naked body or a suggestion of flagellation or other hidden delights. Goupil and Company will take a chance. The young Mienjeer van Gogh will be hired and sent off to the London office.

Vincent himself is not so convinced. He would rather be a priest and bring the starving and toiling masses back to God. He has seen them in their disgusting atheism. Men and women both, sunk into drunkenness, anaesthetising themselves after hours of punishing labour. Women selling themselves rather than breaking their backs labouring in the fields, filleting and packing herrings or hauling trucks below ground in the mines. A return to God would cleanse their lives, help them to live for the eternal future, not just for today.

Father is not happy. He does not believe that Vincent can contain himself, maintain the distance that is required of a priest. Either he

4

will fall into the vice and poverty that he condemns or become a latter-day Savonarola, leading a campaign against vice, breaking up the barrels outside breweries, burning down drinking dens and dismantling brothels with his bare hands. The church elders do not regard Vincent as an appropriate candidate for the priesthood.

Uncle Vincent is more helpful. Nephew Vincent's excesses are merely the excesses of youth. Who is not charged with moral righteousness at eighteen? The lad will settle down once he has an occupation suitable to his talents. The boy is already sketching the countryside and wild storms on the beaches, some of which his uncle has collected in an album, not for their quality as much as to show how much he appreciates Vincent's direction. Art as a means of bringing people back to God is a ridiculous romantic fantasy although it might be a good way of bringing Vincent back to commercial reality. Let us get him a profession, something he can throw himself in to, a cause that will overwhelm him. Goupil and Company will transform him into a sensible member of society.

Despite his reluctance, Vincent enters Goupil and Company. And is transformed. Suddenly he has become a respected, if lowly, member of society. His status is slightly higher than that of a footman and certainly higher than a salesman in one of the new department stores. Goupil only deals with those who have plenty of capital to spend on luxuries and this reflects well on its employees. Vincent will also receive a wage, though at the moment he is living on a small starting gift from his uncle, much of which has been spent on new clothes. For the time being, he has to spend up to three months in Paris learning his trade. Paris after rural Brabant is astonishing; it is the centre of the civilised universe. Great men live here. Buildings are imposing and beautiful. Baron Haussmann has done away with the slums and built wonderful boulevards leading to the main railway stations. There are beautiful women, though he is too shy to approach them, and new art exhibitions almost every day. But it is lonely. He knows no-one. His French is good if heavily accented and at this stage his vocabulary is scanty and academic, with none of the street argot that is the currency of the cheap restaurants and cafés that he spends so much of his time alone in. Few wish to engage him in conversation on the purity of the religious life or the redemptive nature of great art.

Days are marginally better than evenings. He rises at nine after a solid sleep, nailed to his bed by an excess of anise. Breakfast is yesterday's bread and a few scrapings of cheese. (Jesus would not have had as much, he tells himself.) Careful ablutions in cold water, dress in his only work shirt, still wet from last night's wash. To the gallery, to arrive by eleven. The worst hour is ahead: a peroration by Monsieur Obach on the qualities of his artists and on the manner in which a member of Goupil and Company will behave and the terms in which he will present the art to its customers.

Fortunately Monsieur Obach has a modicum of taste. For special clients he will repair to his inner room and reappear with a pair of Corot landscapes, their paint twinkling in the saleroom's lights, mirroring the anticipatory light in Monsieur Albert's eyes at the thought of a lucrative sale. Vincent loves the Corots: their exquisite finish, the clouds which drift across the northern sky like guardians of the fields below, each touch of light *impasto* perfectly placed to catch the light and the eye of the viewer without destroying the naturalism of the scene. Besides which, Corot is a man of the people; he has established a day centre for poor children and has bought a house for the blind and indigent Daumier. Art and philanthropy: an ideal combination. There are always several Corots in the inner room. Vincent is still sad when any of them is sold.

For a short while watercolours become fashionable in Paris. Much as he loves Corot and Millet, Vincent is overwhelmed by four watercolours that he sees by the English painter Turner. They have the subtlety and assertiveness of an autumn sunrise, in washes of lemon, orange and leaf green. Now, if that could be translated into oils! (One day Vincent will come face to face with Turner's oils and be struck, in turns both dumb and, later, incoherently verbose with his enthusiasm and admiration.)

By now Vincent has become recognised as a full member of the company. Uncle Vincent has sent him fifty guilders and he is earning fifty guilders a month, enough to buy him a second shirt and to enable him to buy food as well as absinthe. His French has improved, too. Though still quite guttural, he has acquired the polite vocabulary used by the others around him when wheedling customers into a purchase. It is time for him to be promoted.

This cannot happen all at once and is not without a certain amount of pain and dismay on his part. He is to be transferred to London, a growing base of operations but has to spend a couple of months first at the gallery in The Hague developing an expertise in the company's holdings of Dutch paintings. This is a lucrative area for Goupil in London, where genre scenes by Overcamp and Hals have been steady sellers, reputedly much admired by Her Majesty. A salesman with a good knowledge of both French and Dutch painting, including some of the up-and-coming tigers, as well as an admiration for Constable, Turner, Dore and Millais, could give generous returns over and above his generous salary.

# London

## *Ruth*

At one time Ruth Loyer was petite and charming. She is still shorter than average, only just over five feet tall but she has spread out in every direction as a result of a diet heavy on bread and cream cakes. Nor has her character improved over the years. Her girlish chatter has elided into a shrewish whine, except when she is greeting a new paying guest or commenting on the morals of a neighbour. To Vincent she is polite but not effusive. His company pays well and on time. He is a good Christian gentleman. However, he is known to take hard liquor and he is, after all is said and done, a foreigner.

Ruth's father, Elisha, arrived one spring morning in South London with his horse and gaily painted cart, looking for work. Elisha had drifted slowly southwards from his native Lincolnshire, picking up bits of work wherever he could. Rumour was that he was a gypsy, a judgement reinforced by his swarthy complexion and jet black hair. It was said that he had left Woodhall Spa precipitately when a farmer discovered who had impregnated his fourteen-year-old daughter and had come looking for the culprit armed with his shotgun.

Elisha established a thriving business supplying the markets in London from the fruit farms in Kent, as well as doing general removals in the spring and winter. After his marriage to a young widow he would take her and the children off to the hop fields in summer while he continued to ply his carter's trade and carry on whatever dalliances he could in town.

Ruth was the third and last of Elisha's three children, the only girl and the apple of her father's eye. Her father was good with his hands and made her toys and rag dolls in the dull hours when he was waiting for a load to be prepared or for an obstruction to be cleared from the road. At home he would sing to her and tell her stories of travelling folk and olden times. When she was old enough Ruth was sent to the local dame school where she learned to read and write and embroider. Elisha also wished her to be taught to paint in watercolours or to play the piano like a real lady but the cost was extra, one that even this fond father could not afford.

Even so, Ruth grew into a presentable young lady able to read her Bible and write a neat hand. Besides these higher accomplishments she could also sew, cook and help clean the house. Although the whole family expected her to 'marry well', they could not possibly conceive of a life where servants would be employed to carry out the household chores.

By the time she was ten years old Ruth was the only child remaining in the household. Benjamin, her eldest brother, had moved to Plymouth where he was apprenticed in the naval dockyard as a rigger. This was regarded as a safe and fulfilling job for life since we would always have a navy and even the new steam powered ships had supplementary sails and rigging. The second brother, Jacob, had been mad keen on horses since he had first sat on the one that pulled his father's cart at the age of two. Elisha had thought that this would mean Jacob would enter the business with him but one horse was insufficient for Jacob. Instead his passion led him to apprentice himself to a farrier in Surrey who had a thriving business looking after horses for the army and needed extra hands to exercise and feed them. Elisha was concerned about the military connection as he had little truck with any form of authority, especially authority in a uniform. He consoled himself with the thought that the boy was not actually in the army. Not being able to see into the future Elisha was unable to foresee that the army's horses, including their civilian minders, would be shipped out to Sebastopol during the disastrous Crimean campaign, where Jacob would die of typhoid.

Once the boys were well set the question remained of what to do with Ruth. It was obvious that she would marry. Until then she would need an occupation. Elisha was determined that she should not go into service. His free spirit baulked at anything that put you at another's beck and call. Besides, it would mean the girl moving away and he could not bear that. He toyed with the idea of letting her work for one of the market traders though neither he nor Ruth relished the prospect of her being out in all seasons and in all weathers.

Time was moving on and Ruth was already fourteen and had no steady employment. It was her mother who found the solution. Working class women of that era largely made their own clothes or decorated bought or handed-down pieces with extra flounces or ribbons. Ruth's instruction at the dame school and her mother's natural dexterity had given her a fine grounding in clothes making, which Ruth herself had extended into an elegant line in hat decoration.

One afternoon she was marched off by her mother to an expensive clothing establishment in London's West End. The shop owner was shown samples of Ruth's hats and asked for her opinion. Too polite to express her revulsion, the owner still recognised that here was someone who was both fastidious and had an eye, albeit one that would need a lot of training. A deal was made. The girl would be taken on, initially in the back room to add 'finish' to the hats and would be paid a few shillings a week, sufficient to pay for her food and transport.

Adding 'finish' for ten hours a day was dull work and was hard on the fingers, which were pinched, pricked and scraped by needles and materials. Dull it might be but it was warm and dry. The other few workers were quiet and did not swear at you like they did in the markets. Nor did the husbands of the customers pinch your bottom, though she suspected that some of the other girls eked out their meagre wages after expensive dinners with those same husbands.

Ruth kept away from temptation, spoke quietly and politely and was soon allowed to be present when the owner dealt with her customers. Sometimes she even made suggestions herself. These were naive at first, though she gradually began to acquire what passed in millinery circles for 'good taste'. By the time she was eighteen she had progressed full time into the shop itself and was a firm favourite with the clients.

All through Europe at that time was a spirit of rebellion, of demands for better wages and extension of the franchise. Nor had religious antagonisms died away. In England both Catholics and non-conformists were discriminated against and religious riots were not uncommon. Whether it was during one of these or during the suppression of a Chartist demonstration that the windows of the millinery were smashed and an amount of structural damage caused to the building is uncertain. Workmen were called in, including a handsome young craftsman called George Loyer. Both Ruth and George were shy with one another at first but they soon overcame their shyness and were married some six months later.

George was not the abstemious paragon of virtue that Ruth later made him out to be. He both drank and gambled. Ruth was too wise in the ways of the world to try and change him over night. Instead she gave thanks that he was not as wayward as her own father and merely put a stop to his gambling. George's drinking was of the sort to be expected of a young man in his trade: a pint of porter to wash down his lunch, a couple more on his way home from work and a big binge on Saturday night after being paid. Erosion is a slow and subtle process. Engagements were made for a certain time on a Saturday that would cut short the pay-day celebration. Evening meals were served spot on six in the evening in winter and nine in the summer. Sometimes the doting wife, by now with babe in arms, would meet him straight from work, an ecstatic smile on her face at seeing her man appear before her. Though George never forswore alcohol completely, even when they moved from church to chapel, his weekly consumption declined steadily towards zero.

George was a good worker, always in demand with the speculative builders so rife in London at that time. Increasingly often he was able to do small jobs on his own account, which paid better than working for somebody else. Ruth encouraged this independence and complemented it by establishing a small dressmaking and millinery business of her own catering for the middle and lower classes of South London, where she was much in demand for weddings and festive occasions.

They had only one child, Eugenie, named after the wife of Napoleon the third, Emperor of France, who George greatly and erroneously admired as a representative of true democratic monarchy. A single child in Victorian England was unusual. Ruth put it down to complications during Eugenie's birth. George would acquire a sour face when enquiries were made as to the reason and would imply that perhaps not enough effort was made – or allowed to be made – for a familial increase. In a way this was hugely advantageous to all three Loyers. George was able to put money aside, Ruth dressed in better quality cloth than her neighbours and there were no problems about sending Eugenie to school. The family was all set when a plum job fell into George's lap.

With the coming of the railway, Brixton had expanded steadily like a gently filled balloon, attracting ever more speculators into the local housing market. As the Loyers were leaving chapel one morning after Sunday service they were approached by a rotund man of florid complexion who they knew by sight as one of the elders of the congregation and an occasional preacher. (Ruth found his sermons tedious but was too polite to say so.) "Jonathan Gould," trumpeted the man, thrusting out a well manicured hand by way of introduction. "Mr and Mrs Loyer, I believe? If you wouldn't mind sparing me a few moments of your time, I'd just like to introduce myself to you and arrange for us to meet at a later date. I'm about to embark on a large and prestigious building project and Mr Loyer has been recommended to me as a hard working, sober and honest man who I can trust with the supervision of the works."

George tried to explain that he now only worked independently. His objections were brushed aside. "I don't want a foreman, I want a man who can raise a team of builders in his own right, a master builder who can share in the effort and share in the profits." Despite George's unwillingness, Ruth arranged for a meeting at a later date, for one should not conduct business on the Lord's day.

So it was that a few days later the Loyers were admitted to an imposing four-floor house overlooking Clapham Common. Ruth noted that not only was there a maid in attendance but also the sounds of at least two other domestics downstairs. Although the room that Gould described as his office was sparsely furnished, with plain white walls, Ruth's quick eye caught a glimpse of well upholstered furniture in the front room surrounded by the newly fashionable green and gold flowered wallpaper.

Gould himself was ill at ease. He had obviously expected George to come alone. Discussing business with a woman was not what he was used to. As he warmed to his subject his unease vanished, to be replaced by an air of excitement and a look of pure avarice. "I have bought some land," he began. "Good land, just off the road between Brixton and Streatham. Walking distance from the station. My architect tells me that I can easily put twelve houses on that land. Not rabbit hutches, mind but good, solid, independent houses for professional people. Looking at the plans, they could easily sell for as much as 200 pounds each." George and Ruth looked suitably impressed at such a large sum.

"Now, I have laid out a lot of money for that land. I cannot afford out of my own resources to completely fund the building of twelve properties, so I need a partner that I can trust who also knows the building trade. People have told me good things about you, Mr Loyer, both as a person and as a craftsman. No, don't object, just listen to my proposition. First, I do not intend to pay you personally any money at all. Second, during the construction work you will pay your men out of your own pocket. Now, why should any man in his right mind agree to that? I'll tell you why…" Gould's corporation expanded and his cheeks turned a violent shade of puce. "This is why. I'll pay for all the materials and arrange for the sale of the houses. As each one is sold I will reimburse you for your expenditure on the labour up to an agreed amount. Finally, the only cost to you will be your own labour. That is still a considerable loss of income, I know but when we finish, the twelfth and last house will be yours! You will have earned yourself a whole house for one year's work, or eighteen months at the most. How does that seem to you?"

George coughed and spluttered and searched for a polite way of turning Gould down flat. Why should he take such a risk with his savings, paying a gang of labourers and getting nothing in return? Ruth silenced him with a look, stood up and picked up her bonnet. "Well," she said in her best upper class shop girl manner, "that is certainly an interesting proposition, Mr Gould. We will need to consider it carefully and let you know our decision this day week. I'm sure that any arrangements can be subject to a properly drawn-up legal document? Thank you for your kindness and confidence in thinking of us and I bid you a very good day and compliments to your good lady."

The following week was one of constant hum in the Loyer household. George was not at all impressed by Gould or by his proposition. He had seen too many fly-by-night speculators drive good builders into destitution to have any confidence in such a tricky customer with his outlandish proposals. Ruth had constantly the view of her own new house before her eyes. Security at last and a considerable move up the social scale. Some women would have sulked and mooched around in angry silence at George's obstinacy. Not so Ruth; silence was never her style. Every second he was at home George was subjected to a constant disquisition on why getting a brand new house was such good business and how advantageous it would be for her and little Eugenie. There are few men who can resist the constant drip of their spouse's verbiage and George was not one of them. By the end of the week he had agreed to Gould's terms and set about raising a team of dependable men. Ruth accompanied Gould to the lawyer who drew up the articles of association under her guidance and direction. The only person she trusted in the whole arrangement was herself.

As any builder or developer will tell you, there are a whole host of things that can go wrong with such a project. There can be unforeseen problems with the site. Materials can be overpriced, of poor quality, fail to turn up at the required time or fail to turn up at all. Workers can be unsuitable, down tools for no reason, demand extra pay or go on a drinking binge for weeks at a time. A severe winter can bring all work to a halt for months on end and destroy work that has already been done. Worst of all, a decline in the housing market can mean that houses are not selling when all has been expenditure and nothing has been income. Miraculously, none of these problems arose. The houses were completed to as good a standard as was feasible,

14

while still allowing a decent profit margin and were snapped up by enthusiastic buyers who had bid the price on the later ones up to an astronomical 220 pounds.

Some times were harder than others. Whilst waiting for a house to sell, George had often to borrow a few pounds to pay his workmen at the end of the week but he was soon able to recover and to repay the loan. In the end he, Ruth and Eugenie were able to move into the best-built house in the road, still with much of their savings intact, thanks to careful phrasing of the articles of association. Gould donated a portion of his profits to a political party and was later elected to Parliament for a safe northern seat, which enabled him to increase his speculations and become very rich indeed. Many donations later and under a different Prime Minister he was even able to gain a title and enter the House of Lords.

Ruth set about her new house with a will. The parlour walls suddenly came to life with brilliantly coloured birds and flowers. It was a good six months before she dared reveal to George the actual cost of the wallpaper. Then there was the carpet bought new, not second hand from the market, furniture, crockery and knick-knacks, the purpose of which left George scratching his head. "I don't understand what you use half of your tools for," Ruth told him. "Don't you bother yourself about what I use in my kitchen." George shrugged and surrendered to superior logic.

Becoming householders had moved them several steps up the social scale. Instead of renting a couple of rooms for six months or a year at a time, they were now settled in their own home. Not for them the regular loading of their possessions on to a hand cart to move to the next damp set of dingy basement rooms or even the surreptitious 'moonlight flit', leaving the landlord to fume over several weeks of unpaid rent.

Their status was compounded by the installation of a maid in the tiny attic room, which Vincent was later to occupy. A trained maid was expensive and would cost as much as twenty pounds a year plus her keep. By contrast Susan was merely a skivvy, a young country girl in her first position who did all the hard and dirty jobs around the house

15

for a princely five pounds a year, for which she and her impoverished family were profoundly grateful.

George never ventured on another risky venture. Nor did he need to. His reputation for honesty and hard work was such that he was in constant demand, either in his own right or as a gang master on larger works. It was as the latter that Mr Scott recruited him.

Gilbert Scott had made his way in the world by designing workhouses for the indigent poor, not all of whom were grateful for his efforts. Posterity knows him as the designer of the Albert Memorial and the Midland Grand Hotel at St Pancras Station. Northerners and the deserving poor remember him more fondly for his epic Leeds General Infirmary, which they consider to have done more for the sum of human happiness than all the hotels and monuments in Christendom. By the time his path intersected with George's Mr Scott had become the pre-eminent restorer of churches in Britain. Naturally a successful architect did not have time to personally supervise all of his commissions and often left the day-to-day oversight to a trusted foreman or master builder. Despite careful vetting the architect-builder relationship did not always prove a great success. Refurbishments to Westminster Abbey were not going to plan. The builders had proved to be lackadaisical and the foreman more interested in the local tavern than in inspiring them to labour for the love of God and a few pounds a week.

As a chapel man, George was known to be abstemious and even erroneously thought in some quarters to be teetotal. That and his reputation for hard work and good quality had brought him to the attention of some of the minor clergy who were happy to employ him despite his irregular religious views. They in turn recommended George to the Chapter, from whence he was drawn to Mr Scott's attention. Despite being the son of a clergyman Scott was more interested in his employees' ability to do the job in hand than their religious observance. He was impressed by George's quiet and sober demeanour and his understanding of design principles as well as his obvious ability to handle his workforce. Even royal cathedrals are not always awash with funds and Mr Scott's fee included an obligation to pay all labour and material costs. After much haggling George was engaged to put together a gang to carry on with the restoration of the cathedral to Mr Scott's original plans and to his satisfaction as to quality.

Another step up the social ladder for Ruth. According to her, George was the chief builder of the cathedral and Mr Scott's right-hand man. A double exaggeration but who could blame her in the midst of her pride? To the congregation she was able to swell herself up in the knowledge that her husband was working for the greater glory of God, even if it was in an idolatrous neo-Gothic format. The cathedral had been there for hundreds of years and it was only right that it should be maintained for future generations and as a witness to the Word. George was particularly proud that he was usually left in charge at the cathedral whilst Mr Scott busied himself with the design of the monument for Her Majesty's deceased and ostentatiously mourned husband.

Working so far from home meant that George was often late for supper, so Ruth was not too concerned when one January evening she did not hear anyone at the door until nearly seven o'clock. Instead of her husband it was an impeccably turned out bobby standing there with condensation from the fog dripping from his neat cape. No police training on how to deliver bad news in those days. Just a curt: "Your husband is dead. You'd better come along and identify the body." It was a long and mournful carriage ride and an expense that the new widow could ill afford. George had at least been neatly laid out, a task simplified by the multiple bone fractures which he had suffered in his fall from the wooden walkway high in the roofing of the cathedral.

Grief takes people in different ways. Not for Ruth weeping and wailing and gnashing of teeth. Hers was a hard, stoical, withdrawn grief, one that she kept huddled up inside and which never left her. She spoke of it to no-one, not even to her own daughter, and it soured her life until the day she died. The whole world was viewed through the distorting mirror of her grief. Bad news was to be expected. Good news merely the smoothing of the path to eventual oblivion and a reunion in heaven in anticipation of the day of resurrection. If she had been a lukewarm Christian before, she was a severe and judgemental

one now. Few escaped her moral rigour or her biting tongue. Her
cleanliness was next to fanatical, her carefulness with money bordered
on the miserly. "I am but a poor widow," she declared, "and I must
guard my mite as best I can for myself and my darling child."

Not that she was totally without means. She and George had been
careful to save against a rainy day and she had her own house with no
encumbrances. Yet the savings would not last forever and some way of
earning a living had to be found. Eugenie was evicted from her
bedroom and her bed moved in with her mother's. The maid was given
notice, not so much to save money as to have another vacant room. In
her place a 'daily' was employed to wash, clean and make beds. All this
in order to make way for paying guests of the better sort, mainly
commercial travellers who had no wish to be bitten to death in flea
pits or woken in the dead of night by drunks and loose women.

Business was slow at first, what with being new to it and slightly
further out from the centre than was ideal. Ruth's idea of a good
supper was meagre, which put off several gentlemen. Slowly she built
up a portfolio of regulars, mainly ones who missed the comforts of
home and relished the genteel atmosphere. The smiling charms and
ministrations of Eugenie, delighted now to have men about the house
to look after, did the business no harm at all, entertaining the eyes of
the customers as she did.

*Brixton Road*

# Brixton 1873

## *The White Horse*

lready the lights are lit in the kitchens of the houses below as Vincent's train pulls into Brixton station. He has a feeling of superiority looking down on the village from the raised platform of the station, poised at roof height above the bustling streets. Many of the residents of this middle class suburb can afford to keep a small carriage, though the regularity of the new railway makes it an unnecessary luxury for the majority. There are even a few Hackney carriages mixed in with the flow, though it is a well known fact that most cabbies refuse to take a fare south of the river. These must be charging their fares a pretty penny, Vincent thinks.

His day has been a great success. He has managed to sell a small Constable landscape to a client and, despite the haggling, has sold it for the asking price. Monsieur Obach has noticed this achievement and the polite but firm manner with which Vincent has conducted himself. Time for a celebration, perhaps? Mrs Loyer will be out shopping still with Eugenie, leaving it late so that she can get a discount from the market stall holders desperate to palm off the last of their wares, so there is no point in returning yet to his lodgings. The walk up Brixton Hill has given him a thirst, which he needs to assuage with more than water.

Half way up the hill is a public house, the White Horse, whose illuminated interior beckons Vincent to a haven of jollity and good nature. Even the crudely carved and painted white horse on a pillar outside chimes in with his mood of release and success. The frontage is imposing in a brash English manner, with just a suggestion of mock

Tudor crossed with hints of Gothic enhanced by the stained glass windows on the door.

Vincent pushes ahead, to be greeted by a fug of tobacco smoke as thick as one of the famous London 'pea soupers'. There is a hush. He feels dozens of pairs of eyes turned towards him. Why should this be? Nothing like this happens in cafés in Paris or The Hague. But this is not a café, this is a pub and a working man's pub at that, or one for those who pretend to work. Vincent in his smart clothes sticks out like a sore thumb. This is no time to retreat. He approaches the bar and orders a beer, which is slopped onto the counter in front of him. To his surprise he is asked to pay immediately, a cultural quirk that he finds appealing. Appealing also is the price of the drink: merely a few coppers. Not so appealing is the taste of the beer. It is flat, though he had been told to expect that. It is also bitter and sharp to the taste. He wonders if he has been given something the barman has been trying to get rid of. He looks around. Most of the other men are drinking something similar, except for those who are sat in front of some dark beer that he soon learns to call porter.

A group of labourers is playing dominoes in one corner with a great clashing of the cards on the table top and occasional shouts of 'Knock!' or 'Out!', often accompanied by a blasphemy or two. Almost out of sight another group are playing a card game unfamiliar to Vincent. Despite notices which proclaim that gambling is forbidden, they are obviously playing for money. This group is, next to Vincent, the smartest dressed of all the drinkers and smoke ready-made cigarettes rather than the roll-ups favoured by the others. Pipes are popular everywhere, mainly the new imitation wood pipes, though a few old men are puffing on clay pipes, some of them with broken stems.

Vincent takes a seat and tries to look casual. A couple of workmen enter, their clothes spattered with paint, and sit down with their drinks at Vincent's table.

"You alright here, guv'nor?"

Vincent is taken aback. He knows the word 'governor', someone who is in charge of an area or a province. Perhaps this shortened version means something similar, perhaps a tone of respect, like calling someone 'sir' or 'my lord'.

"I'm fine, thank you."

"We ain't seen you here before, specially in those posh clothes of yorn. And you a foreign gent, too, by the sounds of it."

"Yes, I'm Dutch. I just moved into lodgings in Hackford Road."

"Ah, old Missus Loyer. She's a funny old stick she is. Really thinks she's a cut above everyone else, though her father was only a carter like my old man. Makes out her daughter is a debutante or somfink. Stuck up old cow. She keeps a good clean house, though, I'll say that for her. Me and him is painters, as you can probably tell. What sort of line are you in, then?"

"I work for an art gallery in Southampton Street."

"Cor, that's a good skive that is. We put on paint every day and get paid just enough to get by. Them posh painters charge as much as a hundred guineas just for a portrait of some fashionable bit of stuff no better than she ought to be. Now, those guys over there, they're the ones what makes the money round here." A twitch of the head indicates the card players. "Never out of here but always rolling in dosh. Wait, here comes somefink. You just watch this."

A scruffy urchin has sidled through the door and moves over to the card players. One of them holds out his hand and the boy drops a rolled-up paper into it, then gives a longing look at the glasses on the table before sidling off as scruffily as he had arrived.

"See that?" asks the painter. "There's as much as a couple of florins in there."

"But what's it for?" asks Vincent, rather confused by the transaction and by the references to florints, which he knows to be the currency of part of Austria.

"It's a bet, see. That feller's a bookmaker, runs his book from in here. 'Gainst the law, of course. He slips the local coppers a bob or two and the publican's happy that he spends so much in here, so he just grins and bears it."

"They can't all be bookmakers, though, can they?"

"Nar, the other fellers, they're not so nice. Those two at the back, they run a couple of girls. You'll see them later if you stick around when they come in to pass on their money. Always trouble that pair. If it's not a punter getting drunk or claiming he was robbed, it's the girls trying to hold some money back. The fights we've had in here some nights! Old Joe, the publican, he lets 'em use a couple of rooms upstairs for the better payers and charges them a good whack an' all. So he don't care about the fights driving away the posh trade 'cos he gets more money out of the tarts and the pimps."

"I'm 'Enry, by the way, 'Enry Kirman but everyone calls me 'Arry. Pleased to meet you." Harry sticks out a grimy paw, which is covered in flecks of dark blue paint.

"Vincent van Gogh," replies Vincent, "but no-one in England can pronounce my name so you had better call me Vincent." The pair shake hands tentatively, much to the amusement of the other drinkers. "How is it that you know all about the people in here?"

"I'm a bit of a regular, see? My missus, now, she's what's called 'strict and particular', which means that she don't hold with drinkin' and smokin' and suchlike. So when I wants a drink or two after work I have to come up here, not down in Stockwell where I live. 'Cos I'm not really from here they tells me all the gossip, as they know it's not going to get around. Like I know who's got a girl in the prison up the road or who's carrying on with who. A great area for carrying on this is, as well. Those pimps over there, they never go short of a bit of ready, though they'd dearly like to get some of the nobs from the other side of the river down here. They just want a bit of jam on their bread, or even some caviar, if you see what I mean?"

Vincent is not so sure that he does see but nods sagely all the same and offers to buy Harry a drink, an offer which is seized on with alacrity. The flat English beer is not really to his taste but absinthe is unheard of and the drink that is called gin here is nothing like the *genever* of his homeland. It does have the advantage of filling up a large amount of space which would otherwise go unoccupied by Mrs Loyer's meagre suppers.

Harry is intrigued to find that Vincent is a fellow Methodist, though obviously not a 'strict and particular' one. "The Methodists round here, they aren't as heavy duty as the Welsh ones or the ones up north. Most of us men like a quiet drink but we don't overdo it like some do and we're all hard-working types. We goes to chapel on Sundays and reads the Good Book as we should. Most of us don't even swear, or not very much anyway. Me and the missus goes to a very friendly chapel over in Isleworth. Come and join us one Sunday, we'd be glad to have you. Only don't tell anyone that we met in a pub, eh?"

The White Horse has begun to fill up and some of the clientele are becoming increasingly rowdy, though careful to give the card players a wide berth. Harry and Vincent's table is no longer theirs alone, making conversation difficult. Harry is getting worried that his wife will begin to guess where he is and Vincent is apprehensive that Mrs Loyer might feed his supper to one of the commercial gentlemen. Before they part they arrange a meeting for the following Sunday in order to attend the Methodist chapel in Isleworth, a journey that Vincent regards as something of an adventure.

On arriving home Vincent is disconcerted to find not one but two commercial gentlemen already seated at the dining table, looking more like a comedy double act from the music hall. One is long and thin with a drooping nose and a moustache to match. Throughout the meal his conversation is limited to 'Pass the salt' and 'Nice bit of meat, that', as if his vocabulary has been totally drained by a hard day of salesmanship. The other, corpulent and puce, seems not to have wound down from his exertions, or to have made it part of his sales routine never to allow the customer a second for speech or reflection. Both Mrs Loyer – no stranger to the uninterrupted monologue herself – and Eugenie seem to find this amusing. Although he finds the man tedious, Vincent is happy not to expose either his ignorance of English life or his accent to the assembled company, rightly certain that the corpulent one would readily make fun of both to Vincent's embarrassment.

*White Horse Corner*

# Brixton

## *Eugenie*

Eugenie, or Jen-Jen to her father, was a happy and bubbly child. Spoilt by her parents and grandparents alike, she was overweight enough not to be able to walk until she was two years old. This did not stop her talking 'six to the dozen', as her father said. As soon as she could she was out and about in her grandfather's cart and delighted in being trundled across building sites in a wheelbarrow. Like many only children she was both secretive and wilful, unwilling to share favours or friends with others.

Although she loved both of her parents, it was her father that she idolised. From the day that she started to talk he would treat her like an adult, having long, grown-up conversations with her as if she were his sister or his wife rather than his baby daughter. His monologues may have been a form of compensation for having been obliged to sit at home for so long. Whatever its cause, it cemented their relationship and convinced Eugenie that bearing the name of an empress confirmed her importance in the world. Whilst her mother bought her pretty things and put ribbons in her hair, it was her father who took her to work on houses and churches and even Mr Scott's new government ministry in Whitehall. Coming home they would stop at wayside stalls for sweets or fruit, both of them catching hell from Ruth when Eugenie arrived home covered in plaster dust and sticky sugar.

School came as a horrible shock. Eugenie was no longer the sole centre of attention and played the clown to compensate. The attention thus attracted was not of a kind that she relished and it took many long conversations with her father to convince her that laying low might be a better policy. Although school was not yet compulsory for all, the Methodist tradition of thrift and hard work also encompassed a respect for education as a means to earning a respectable living and multiplying one's talents, as well as enabling a good Christian to be fluent in the reading of the Bible. Other children had books and money. Thanks to her father, Eugenie had another great advantage: language. She already had an adult vocabulary by the age of five and was able to read books and religious tracts with no hesitation. Quite what she made of them is difficult to say but at least it was only her age and lack of experience that impeded her understanding.

In a class-based society such as Victorian London, those who aspired to social mobility had at their disposal a range of important signifiers. The Loyers already had a house of their own and a maid. They had a certain standing and a reputation in the community such that Ruth was looked upon locally as a 'superior person', albeit one who gave herself airs and was most high and mighty. Their daughter was always well dressed and went to a school where she learned 'extras' such as drawing and painting in watercolours. Both George and Ruth agreed that something was missing and that lack had to be urgently rectified. They bought a piano.

None of them could play but soon Eugenie's lessons began to bear fruit and she could manage to accompany her parents on some of the simpler hymn tunes. Although she never became accomplished Eugenie progressed on to Handel and Beethoven, though Mozart was considered too frivolous for a young girl. Her father secretly encouraged her to try out some of the more genteel music hall songs, playing by ear. Hymn tunes were a duty, Handel was for showing off, the music hall was fun and enjoyment. In essence she became the polished and educated young lady that her grandfather had wished Ruth to be, with the prospect of a favourable marriage ever before her.

Eugenie was a child of her time. As a builder's daughter she would be expected to work for a short time in a clean and undemanding environment before marrying a young man of her own social class, perhaps a jobbing builder 'on the rise'. The idea of establishing herself in a career was inconceivable, any more than a descent into the realms of the streetwalker or the *habitué* of public houses.

*Elfra Road, Brixton*

# Brixton, London

## *1873*

*My honoured uncle*

*I have at last arrived in London, where Monsieur Boussod has introduced me to the new business. As a recent establishment we are not yet in the forefront of the galleries here though we do have a good clientele among the cognoscenti of the city. This week has been a trifle slow but I am informed that such is normal at this time of the year. I am pleased that there are not too many demands on my time in the front office, as it has given me leisure to become acquainted with the holdings in the stock rooms.*

*Most interesting for me is the collection of English painters. Reynolds, Constable, Gainsborough and Turner are well represented and you are already apprised of my admiration for them. My admiration doubles when I imagine them painting 'en plein air' in the English weather!*

*I have not yet formed a view on the contemporary painters. For the most part they appear to be technically accomplished, having often studied at the French ateliers, whilst their subject matter appears to me to be rather retrograde. They love knights in armour, tales from ancient British and Greek myths and scenes from Shakespeare. What can all this mean? Is there an allegorical aspect that I am missing? Certainly there are some allegorical paintings which seem to have a moral message: fallen women are reprieved or have their consciences awakened, Biblical scenes and so on. These have excited the critics but are not what sells from the gallery and certainly not what excites me. They have no genuine morality to them; so many exercises in producing what the artists believe the public admires. In fact what sells from the gallery are hunting scenes and pretty women, the more scantily clad the better.*

*However, we are making waves with some of the contemporary French artists we have introduced. Degas is particularly popular with his ballet scenes and we have managed to sell two small paintings by Manet, though he is regarded as rather daring, so that it is only the younger crowd who express admiration for him, mainly to annoy their elders I believe.*

*My first innovation here was to exhibit a Monet landscape and a river painting by Renoir. They caused such a furore and even laughter in some quarters that Monsieur Boussod ordered that they should be taken down and replaced them with a van Ruysdael seascape (which sold almost immediately) and an Overcamp, which is currently under consideration by a titled gentleman. I obviously have a lot to learn about the art business in London.*

*Monsieur Boussod's clerk has found me lodgings in Brixton, which suit both my pocket and my station in life. Brixton is a quiet village, which has only recently become annexed to London itself. It has a charming green centre and some impressive four-storied houses for the better sort. I am lodged in the attic room of a smaller establishment, which is both warm and clean, so that I find myself happy both in my work and in my domestic situation.*

*Your affectionate nephew*
*Vincent*

# Brixton, London

## *1873*

*Dear Theo*

    *London at last. I was beginning to expire of boredom in The Hague. Such a bourgeois place; I'm ashamed to admit that it is the capital of our country. After Paris it was such a trial; no decent cafés and not a brothel in sight. Perhaps that was good for me; I managed to save some money, which will come in useful in London.*

    *The crossing itself was terrible. Although there is now a regular steam packet, we were tossed around for nearly eight hours. Most of my fellows were violently ill and I was exceeding glad to be able to reach dry land at Harwich. I had a long wait for the train connection there and did some drawing, none of it any good. I'll need to apply myself more if I am to improve. Mauve says that I show promise but he probably only says that to impress Uncle Vincent and to pacify Father.*

    *We got into London in mid-afternoon. Smoke everywhere, like Monet's paintings of railway stations or a Turner with the colours toned down. A cab took me off to my lodging and violently overcharged me for the privilege. This lodging is in an area called Brixton. From the look of it, it was once a pretty little village but is now being built up to be just another part of London. There is even some talk of building out the metro that far one day. All that remains of the village is the green, which is a home for beggars, tramps and women of the worst kind.*

    *I have an attic room in one of the better houses of the village. The house is behind the main street. It is on three floors with a front* door which opens straight onto the road. My room is sparsely furnished with a bed which is barely large enough for my bony frame, a washstand, a cane-seated chair and a wardrobe. Since I have so little to put into the latter it is a waste of the limited space. I have to draw in my breath in order to navigate around it and get to the washstand.

My landlady is around forty, though she tries hard to make herself look younger. She is very loud and talks all of the time. Her idea of a good breakfast is what she calls 'bread and dripping', which seems to me to be just animal fat. Supper is tripe or a pig's head. I am desperate for a good Dutch herring. Fortunately I can buy a meat pie or some jellied eels in town for lunch, which reminds me of our childhood. For all that, the lodging is clean and tidy, not like some around here which are crawling with vermin. Being clean explains why it is popular with what are called 'commercial travellers', men who make a living going from town to town selling their proprietor's wares. I'm told that these men make an excellent living from their profession and are very choosy about where they stay. As it is, I'm no different to them, going from Paris to The Hague and now to London to sell my proprietor's wares.

The landlady has a daughter who is very well built, almost in the Dutch manner but much shorter. She is very jolly and makes fun of her mother's loquacity and of my accent. She says I have a 'lisp' and must therefore be a gentleman. This is not much of a compliment in Brixton. Apparently young aristocrats affect this 'lisp' in order to demonstrate their superiority, which the London working classes find to be an abomination. My landlady and her daughter feel themselves to be above the labourers and cab drivers despite sharing their prejudices. They also share their accent, which is nothing like the English that we learned in Holland. It is as different as Frisian is from Brabant.

Sad to say, I am working hard at being a good art dealer, which consists mainly of being deferential and keeping quiet for as much time as possible, even when the customer says something crass. I have *done nothing yet from a social point of view, except for attending a small Methodist church (they call them chapels here to differentiate them from the state religion) where the people have been quite welcoming.*

*I remain*
*Your loving brother*
*Vincent*

*Electric Avenue, Brixton*

# Brixton

## *Autumn 1873*

*My Dear Theo*

*This has been a most exciting week both for the company and for me personally, as I shall relate to you later.*

*On Thursday, towards mid-afternoon, a carriage drew up outside the premises and an imposing person alighted, accompanied by a lady and two gentlemen in military uniform who were obviously his subordinates. The personage in question was large in every direction. Not fat but strongly built like a Prussian guardsman, if not quite as tall. He sported a magnificent set of whiskers, bushy and well trimmed by some fastidious barber. Though smartly dressed I noticed that he had failed to fasten the bottom button of his waistcoat and that there was no ironed seam to his trousers, which I felt to be most unusual. Because of his whiskers and his size it was difficult to tell his age; somewhere between thirty-five and forty-five, I would imagine. From a cursory glance at his face you could easily take him for an elder statesman of some sixty summers, it held such gravity. By contrast, his comportment was that of a young man barely out of his teens, though somewhat slowed by his massive build. Neither his hair nor his beard showed any touch of silver. Nor did his pockets, as you shall see later.*

*The English staff obviously recognised both his person and his quality. With much genuflection they escorted him into the main salon where he was plied with wine and the best cognac, reserved only for the most important customers. The military gentlemen stood either side behind his chair, whilst the lady floated around the room for a while before taking a seat. Monsieur Boussod looked rather shocked at this, that someone should seat themselves in such august company and began to address himself to our visitor in the most sickeningly fawning manner, with a 'Your Highness this' and a 'Your Highness that'. From this I gathered that this was a member of the Royal Family, no less! The lady's position seemed somewhat less distinguished. Monsieur Boussod referred to her merely as 'Madam', whilst the Prince addressed her as 'Soo-Soo', a particularly terrible appellation, which made her sound like some kind of pet dog. Although the lady wore a wedding ring it appeared that she was married, though not to the Prince.*

*We were all reminded later to maintain the utmost discretion about the Prince's visit, a discretion which I also urge upon my dearest brother, especially as I am sure that British gossip has little interest in my native country. Having said that, I am certain that both my uncle and our dearest Mama will be delighted to hear that I have met, though not been introduced to, the Prince of Wales. Our Papa, however, may well feel that this is merely one more occasion for falling into the sin of vanity.*

*The visit lasted some forty minutes, at the end of which the Prince purchased two sporting paintings by Heywood Hardy and a rather racy painting of women in a Roman bath. He left without attempting to pay or to carry off any of the purchases. One of the equerries took Monsieur Boussod into the office where he paid out of his own pocket book, though I am sure that the money came from the Prince in the first instance. I thought I caught a look of relief on Monsieur Boussod's face; dukes and princes seem to have a bad habit of not paying their debts. Who would dare to dun the heir to the throne or fight a duel with him? I am told, though, that there was some talk of a parliamentarian citing a royal personage in a divorce suit last year.*

*The two hunting prints were packed up and I was despatched with them to Marlborough House, an imposing building in a rather dull Georgian style. English architects are like we Netherlanders: they want to be gay and amusing but really their hearts are not in it. I was directed round to the back entrance to deliver my parcel so that all I saw were flunkies and cooks, no more royal personages. I am told that the Roman bathers were delivered elsewhere by someone else even if Monsieur Boussod was not prepared to divulge their destination to the rest of us.*

*Well, that was my public excitement. Now to my private one.*

*On my way home from the gallery a week or so ago I met a working man called Harry Kirman. Harry is a member of an evangelical congregation in the western suburbs of London, in a village called Isleworth. On parting he invited me to go with a member of his family to a service at his church. I mentioned this one evening at supper and, much to my surprise, Miss Eugenie asked if she could accompany me. As always I hope it is the power of my love of mankind and of the word of God that attracted her but really I think she feels constrained and smothered by her small world and always being at her mother's beck and call. Be that as it may, our small party made a friendly excursion out to Isleworth last Sunday.*

*The priest is a Reverend Slade-Jones, a man of Welsh extraction. As you know, the Welsh are famous for their singing voices and their fiery tempers. Slade-Jones has both. His sermons are extraordinary: full of invocations of hell as a fiery furnace in which sinners are burnt to ashes again and again through all eternity. Such a view ought to repulse me, who is full of the love of God for all humanity but what makes it more humane is his insistence that sin is not just a negative 'Thou shalt not'. A good Christian, says Slade-Jones, has positive virtues, the virtues of the true pilgrim. He helps others, particularly the poor and the downtrodden; he refrains from sin and the vices of the body whilst he also helps his fellow man, however far into sin and degradation he may have fallen. Hell is not just for those who have done evil but also for those who have failed to do good. You can imagine that this has moved me considerably as one who has succumbed too often in the past to the sins of the flesh and failed to help those in greater need than I. Well, dear boy, I am confirmed in my former resolution to bring the Word to all in our society by teaching and through my actions.*

*I mentioned this to Slade-Jones, as well as my thoughts of becoming a priest like Father. He was delighted by my enthusiasm and determination to avoid henceforth the sins of the flesh but cautioned me against the priesthood. "You are too single-minded, my friend. Being a priest is an administrative post, you know. All I do is to look after the chapel and co-ordinate the congregation's activities, be they good works or the annual outing to the coast for the orphans from the home. You need to be more like Henry here. He goes about his business and proclaims Christ's message by his life and by his good works. One day I will persuade him, and by God's grace you as well, to preach before our congregation. Priests do not have a unique view of the heavenly wisdom. Read the scriptures carefully. Apply them to your life and work, then show us in your sermons the way to eternal life." Such is the way of these Methodists. It is a way that I shall endeavour to follow, though I believe it is a hard and narrow road.*

*Poor Harry Kirman was much embarrassed by these comments for he is a reserved man and not much given to analysing his life, never mind standing up in front of over a hundred people and lecturing them on the Way. Miss Eugenie paid little attention to the reverend's comments, being more engaged with studying the hats and dresses of the ladies around her. Still, she is yet young and it bespeaks good character that she is happy to spend her day with us in this manner.*

*Our journey home was much quieter than the earlier one. The ladies were obviously tired by the service and the travelling and had little to say to one another. Harry's wife did not look too well though I attribute this to the possibility of what the English term 'an interesting condition' rather than to any positive illness. Harry himself was unusually quiet, which may have been his way of reflecting upon the sermon or his concern about his wife's health. The Reverend Slade-Jones had thrown me back upon reflections of my own life: on how I*

36

could best help my fellow men, whether it be through good works, by entering the priesthood or even by artistic endeavour. I just cannot imagine that I can do it by selling reproductions of hunting scenes to rich patrons.

Nevertheless, your brother has been moved to much excitement by this wonderful week and wishes you both joy and good health.

*Vincent*

*Brixton Railway*

# Southampton Street, London

## Autumn 1873

*Dear Tersteeg*

*You asked me in your last letter to give you some indication of the progress of young van Gogh. I assume that you would like to give some sort of verbal report to his uncle and in consequence beg you not to show him this letter so that I may be entirely frank in its writing.*

*As far as a knowledge of painting is concerned, he is excellent in the main areas. Whenever a customer is specifically interested in Dutch art I am perfectly content to leave him to van Gogh, even when it is a question of a living artist such as Mauve or Israels. He is perfectly well acquainted with the stock that we hold in London alongside our holdings in Paris and The Hague.*

*Although he admires much English painting, his knowledge here is not quite as comprehensive. On the 'classic' artists such as Gainsborough, Reynolds and particularly Constable he is very sound, though he does display an incomprehensible passion for that man Turner, who could never seem to manage to finish a canvas in his latter days. Of the rest, including the best of our modern English artists, he is quite dismissive, of which more later.*

*I know that one of your objects in employing such a young man was to find someone with a knowledge of, and an enthusiasm for, the current crop of French artists. This, van Gogh usually displays. He speaks well about the Barbizon school and of Millais, who chimes well with his Huguenot views. Of Manet, he is admiring both of the man's technique and of his grimy view of humanity, which to me is quite repulsive. At least the fellow knows how to paint, which is more than can be said for that clochard Cézanne, who seems to think that blobs of paint on the canvas are sufficient. I have refused to have any of his daubs, be they consigned even to the farthest reaches of our dampest basement.*

*According to van Gogh, the coming young men are a group who just paint 'impressions' of landscapes. Turner has a lot to answer for here, since these people seem to be followers of his of some kind and equally unable to finish a painting. One exception is a Monsieur de Gas – obviously a gentleman from his name – who has a series of charming, if sketchy, pastels and paintings of deshabillées washerwomen and of ballet dancers. I allowed van Gogh to have some of these sent over from Paris and they are proving a qualified success with the louche younger set, though he was unable to persuade the Prince of Wales into a purchase.*

*So, you can see that from the point of view of knowledge the young man is perfectly acceptable. However, from the point of view of personality and business acumen he is not yet as one would wish. Young Mienjeer van Gogh is a man of enthusiasms, which he must learn to curb. His religion tends towards the evangelical and what the English call non-conformism, specifically a sect called the Methodists. You know more of protestant religion than I but this group seem to take everything to extremes. Anyone can deliver a sermon, even women. They take their instruction solely and directly from the Bible and even argue theology and morality with their own priests. Besides that, they also proselytise wherever they find themselves. Van Gogh has got into the unpleasant habit of lecturing his fellow workers on the nature of God. The other day he even had the temerity to tell me that original sin is a myth and that bishops, popes and priests are unnecessary. I can't imagine what his father would say to that! In the end I had to warn him not to discuss religion at the gallery and that any mention of religious matters to customers would result in instant dismissal.*

*Nor do his enthusiasms end there. Van Gogh has decided views on art, on what is good and what is bad, as well as a belief in a social and redemptive function of art. This is all well and good. One would expect an art dealer to be able to make judgements about the quality* of a work, to have his own favourite pieces and artists and even to see it as an important part of society. Unfortunately this to van Gogh is overwhelming. He forgets that he is a dealer and a businessman whose job it is to sell paintings to our customers rather than to lecture them about what they should be buying and telling them that certain items, among them our most popular and lucrative sellers, are a waste of the canvas on which they are painted. Several times I have had to detach him from harried and embarrassed customers anxious to escape with an inoffensive painting of which van Gogh does not approve.

Now, I hope that this is a callow young man's lack of experience. Certainly there has been a lot less of it over the last few weeks and I believe that my strictures have had some effect. Certainly I will persevere with his business education in the expectation that if this can be allied to his knowledge and visual perception he could well be a great asset to the company. During the visit of the Prince of Wales and Mrs Pelham-Clinton he was properly deferential and kept his own counsel, even when the Prince purchased some paintings which, I have to admit, were not of the highest quality. I only wish he could be so with all of our customers, then he might rise to the highest ranks of the company.

Your friend and colleague
Boussod

# Brixton

## *Autumn 1873*

### *Job*

"'Ere, Vince, you're a student of the Good Book, ain't yer? What do you make of this Job story, then?"

"What do you mean, 'what do I make of it'?"

"Well," says Harry, "it all seems a bit mean to me. Here's old Job, never did no harm to no-one, brought up his kids proper, made himself a bit of dosh. Not by screwin' no-one, not like any of those bastards over there." Harry indicates the pimps and the bookie at their interminable card games at the best table in the White Horse. A quick drink after work has become a regular ritual with Vincent and Harry.

"So Job, he does good by hisself. Builds up his flocks, gets the kids a nice house, praises God as he should, then he gets shafted. It just ain't fair."

"Well, that can happen to anybody," objects Vincent. "Your house can burn down or you can lose your job or even get run over by a Hackney carriage."

"Yeah, well, that's luck, innit? What was it you said the other day about something Shakespeare said about luck?"

"Well, it's not really luck," objects Vincent, "but what he says is: 'there's a Providence that shapes our ends, rough hew them how we may'." Vincent is delighted to show off his learning, especially quoting an English poet to an Englishman.

"That's it, that's exactly what my old grandma used to say: man proposes but God disposes. We do what we can. It's like playing cards. You just make what you can of the cards that luck deals you, or

41

Providence if you are posh and clever. If you've got a better hand than the other feller or you can bluff well, you win. Maybe you can even get on by cheating, faking the cards. On the other hand, if you are walking down the street and someone does you over, that's just bad luck. I suppose that when God gave us free will he knew that some of us would do evil things that would cause the rest of us to suffer. That's alright, I understand that. Take the rough with the smooth, says I. But that's not what happened with poor old Job. It weren't no accident nor nothing; God just stitched him up. The Devil turns up and he bets God that he can make Job turn against him. So God lets the Devil kill off his wife and his children and his sheep and his goats. And if that's not enough, what does he do then?"

"Smites him with sore boils," says Vincent, for a change far less happy quoting the Bible than he was in quoting Shakespeare.

"Yeah, and those boils is no fun, I can tell you. I had some on my bum and it was horrid. But the point is, it ain't no accident, no Providence or nothing. It's just God and the Devil playing a game."

"But Job wins out in the end. He discomforts the Devil. He proves his love for God, he never curses him. Then he gets his goods back."

"Yeah but his wife and his children are still dead and he's had a really hard time of it. Neither of us would of stood up to that. Imagine you were in love with a woman, your wife even, and she treated you like that."

Vincent's eyes light up for a moment at the thought of having any woman at all, never mind a wife. Then his situation depresses him. "The Lord giveth and the Lord taketh away," he says in his best solemn manner. "Blessed be the name of the Lord."

"Well," says Harry, "it ain't so much the Lord what giveth but my Lizzie. In about four months' time, I reckon." They are both tempted to celebrate with a large gin abstaining for their individual reasons, neither connected with their church's view on abstinence. Harry knows that the smell of it on his breath will force his wife off to vomit in the commode. Vincent fears his landlady's disapproval and the withering remarks she would make to him in front of Eugenie.

42

Vincent has spent a long time recently studying the Bible with Harry Gladwell. Gladwell has views on the priesthood despite having neither Latin nor Greek and Vincent is coaching him in a manner in which he would have loved to have been coached by his father. The study has not been good for his faith. Or rather it has changed his faith, moved it on to another track. The God of his father and the Old Testament have disappeared, his figure subsumed into the *Urreligions* of the world, a dark and oppressive figure ready to wreak judgement upon the just and the unjust alike. Vincent does not care about the unjust. On the other hand, the Jobs of this life speak to him from their misfortune. Now only Jesus Christ is his excuse or his exemplar for religious observance. The archetypal pilgrim through the 'slough of despond' and sin, Christ gives to Vincent a promise of love and forgiveness, not a doctrine of vengeance. His faith has not been lost; it has been transmogrified from the iron-clad remonstrances of his father into the love and shelter that he can see in the relationship between Harry and his wife. If God is to test him he will not refrain from the curse; he will shout and struggle against the divine will.

# Brixton

## *Autumn 1873*

### *Eugenie*

Since Father died this house has become a prison. All my time is spent in cleaning or making beds. Sometimes Mother takes me with her to the market. I think this is because the market men give me extra measure when I smile at them. Never mind, it is an outing and far better than struggling with the washing or peeling potatoes. My hands are red and chapped like any skivvy. They don't slide across the keys of the piano as they used to. That is not so important. I no longer play hymn tunes. The gentlemen guests can take a little bit of Beethoven if it is romantic enough but they much prefer the music hall songs.

I miss the piano much more than I miss school. Most of the girls were younger than me, or should that be 'younger than I'? I never could tell the difference. So we were constantly going back over things I had already done, which were never very interesting the first time around. Still, it was something out of the house and other people to talk to. Mother never talks to me about getting married now. She wants to keep me slaving here until I'm old and shrivelled like the sad old women who sit around drinking gin outside the White Horse.

At least we are not poor. Terribly poor, I mean. We have the house, which is more than most people have, and an income from the commercials. I have a new dress at least twice a year, as well as hats and even stockings. Mother thinks it is good for trade that I am well dressed in front of the customers. I could do with a new pair of shoes but they will have to wait until the spring.

The thing is, we never go out, never go anywhere. I don't count chapel, of course. That isn't really 'going out'. With Dad we sometimes went to the music hall. Mother thought it was a bit low but I loved it, especially the singing when everyone knew the words. Dad liked the comics. You could tell from Mother's expression that she thought them quite disgusting. She should have heard the jokes and the language on the building sites sometimes when I went there with Dad, though the men tried to calm it down a bit when I was around but some joker always forgot himself. I do miss the men stroking my hair and calling me their fairy princess. Fat chance of that now.

We don't eat as well as we did when Dad was alive, either but I've got quite plump despite that. Too much bread, potatoes and suet pudding, I suppose. Being stuck in the house all of the time doesn't help either. I got so desperate the other week that I even went off to the chapel in Isleworth with that weird Mister van Gogh. It was quite fun, I suppose. The bus ride was good, getting into some greenery and along the river. I don't reckon the chapel was any better than ours though Slade-Jones, the minister, was quite fun, jumping about like a jack-in-the-box and miming the devils pushing the damned back into the fires of hell with their pitchforks. Funny, but he was quite jolly afterwards and not at all serious.

Watching the other women was best. Most of them were quite well dressed, just like the women up town, though some of them did not wear bustles and I swear that there were one or two who did not wear stays at all. That's what they call 'bohemian', I suppose. Mother would have died at the hats and bonnets. Some of them were so plain that they looked like over-sized frying pans or coal scuttles. One woman had wrapped coloured ribbons around her hat so that they hung down like so many multi-coloured icicles. I couldn't help staring. The other women ignored her even though they were very sober themselves in black or in dark colours. During the service she would stand up and shout things from time to time. Obviously she wasn't quite right and I felt very sorry for her. The other women coddled and petted her like a little baby. I'd quite like to go back there again, if only to get some fresh country air in my lungs.

I'm not sure I'd want to go there with Mister van Gogh, though. He is so intense and quotes the Bible all of the time. Can you imagine him singing along in the music hall? Harry Kirman says they meet from time to time in the White Horse so I know he likes a good drink but Harry says they talk about religion most of the while. No doubt they eye up the loose women there as well. Lizzie Kirman would kill poor Harry if she knew.

Anyway Mister van Gogh has been to Paris, so I guess he has had his share of drink and loose women, young though he is. You should see the way he looks at me sometimes. Looks like that would make your petticoats shrivel, as Granddad used to say. For all that, he's a perfect gentleman. He never makes a crude suggestion or laughs at the naughty jokes that some of the commercials tell. Perhaps his English isn't good enough to understand them. Anyway he just looks and is very polite in his funny accent and, oh, so serious! Imagine marrying a man who is that serious! And his ginger hair. You could end up with half a dozen ginger babies. Wouldn't that be awful! Marry Mister van Gogh? No, never, not ever.

*Caldharbour Lane*

46

# Isleworth

## *1874*

### *Joanna*

Two hundred years before, Joanna would have been lauded as a wise woman or burnt as a witch. Some members of the congregation regard her as both sad and frightening. Her unkempt appearance causes amusement among the children but they are too wary to mock her openly. Many of the adults regard her as just plain mad. The eldest women respect her as one of God's fools, a priestess, a prophet even. They remember her namesake, Joanna Southgate, who made so many astonishing prophecies before being gathered into heaven. This Joanna may be another such.

Reverend Slade-Jones does not believe in prophecies, at least not in those that do not emanate from the Bible. Revelation ended with Christ; modern life is a time of sin and decadence. Joanna is merely mad, child mad in a harmless manner. Her revelations are those of innocence. Of someone who has no understanding of politeness or what is acceptable in public. He tolerates her interjections in the service, her unintelligible outbursts and cries of enthusiasm often leading to frothing fits among the pews, which cause her to be removed. Some call this 'speaking in tongues'. Reverend Slade-Jones has yet to recognise any real language in her babblings. Whether she is possessed by angels, by the Devil or is just plain mad, he is unsure. He just wishes that she would take herself off to the Quakers where she belongs.

This evening Joanna is wearing her best dress. What was once a perfectly respectable black dress with a modest bustle and short train has been added to over the years with patches where the cloth has worn thin. No attention has been paid to matching the colours, in fact the gaudier the better, although she has at least stuck with plain colours rather than the stripes and flower patterns that were recently in fashion. To match she wears her favourite bonnet. Again, this was once a calm and respectable black to which she has added multicoloured ribbons, which must originally have been wound securely round it and fastened with pins. Over time they have become adrift and now hang down like a circular veil or the fly excluders that housewives hang over their open front doors in the summer.

Her attire brings murmurs from the congregation. Of consternation among some, anticipation among others. Joanna in her finery is frequently a prelude to an excruciating outburst of meaningless babble, either sent by God or a product of her disordered mind. On the other hand, Joanna herself is on her best behaviour and evinces her most ladylike behaviour. "Yes," she exclaims in little more than a loud whisper, "tell us the gospel story. Alleluia!" Very mild by her normal standards, almost as if she is gathering her strength and mental resources for one great final assault.

For the first time in his life this is Vincent's turn to preach, to deliver a sermon in a real church, made of wood though it be. In recognition of this significant event his friends have gathered round from Brixton. Ruth Loyer has on her blackest and most severe costume, buttoned to the neck and wrist with no sight of any lace or furbelows. Eugenie, younger and unmarried, sports slightly more decoration; her eager young face is the equivalent of several yards of pure white lace. Lizzie Kirman is beginning to resemble the ball that she will become in later life. Only five feet tall, this third pregnancy is blowing her out even further than the others. If she knew of the other four to come she would be horrified. Harry has been carefully dressed by Lizzie in his Sunday best, which is already becoming too small for his expanding figure.

As might be assumed, their level of attention varies, almost in inverse proportion to how much Vincent wishes that they were engaged. Eugenie manages the first five minutes or so before drifting off wool gathering, dreaming of the handsome commercial who has taken to bringing her flowers each time he arrives at Hackford Road. Her mother, on the other hand, is much taken with the sermon, repetitious though it is. She sees herself as the pilgrim fighting against the sins and backsliding of a sinful world, a bulwark of purity holding back tides of evil. For Harry there are not enough down-to-earth examples and those that there are have already been rehearsed to him by Vincent in the public bar of the White Horse. Lizzie is totally absorbed in the new life inside her. She tries to talk to it, to reassure it that the delivery will be fine. She has always had easy deliveries. Life in the Kirman household will be cosy, tight even, but it is a loving household. The child will be surrounded by kindness and attention. 'Laura', Lizzie decides, if it is a girl, 'Laura Elizabeth'. Lizzie knows that it will be a girl and dismisses the whole idea of cudgelling her brains over a boy's name.

Meanwhile Vincent is cudgelling the idea of the pilgrim, the fruit of Paul Bunyan's imagination in Bedford gaol. "We are strangers and pilgrims on the earth," he declares. "Feel with me the storms of life. Listen, we might compare our life to a journey. Each one of us passes through many phases. The great poet Shakespeare shows we move from one part of our lives to another, from mewling and puking brat, to schoolboy walking tardily to school, to lover and husband, and finally to bent and broken old age. Not all of us will complete the journey. It is a pilgrimage, not a race. How quickly we arrive, or whether we arrive at all, is not important. It matters not how long we remain on this earth but how we conduct ourselves during our sojourn. Our life is a long walk, a journey, a pilgrimage from earth to heaven."

"Tell us about the journey," sings out Joanna, "tell of the trials and tribulations." Many are astonished; this is unusually coherent for a Joanna utterance.

"That is a long journey, brethren," Vincent says in response. "Does not every one of you feel with me the storms of life? The Psalm tells us of those who go down to the sea in ships. We are all mariners on the sea of life. We have all sailed happily in calm waters. From time to time our puny barques have been rocked by storms and tempests. There have been doubts, backslidings. Emotions of which we are not proud now that we have navigated safely back to dry land. You have listened to Job's comforters telling you to curse God. Your souls have shrunk and melted with your troubles. But let me tell you, there is more joy in heaven when a spirit has passed through great tribulation than when an angel is born."

"Speak of angels. Conjure the tribulations," cries Joanna.

"The heart of man is very much like the sea itself. It has its storms, it has its tides and in its depths it has its pearls, too. At our best we love our neighbours as ourselves." (Vincent darts a covert glance at Eugenie, who is considering a lady in a deep purple gown and wondering whether the colour might suit her own pale complexion.) "Remember those in deep waters, who consider the stormy winds which lifteth the waves thereof. Their souls melt in them because of their trouble. They mount up to heaven and they go down again to the depths. Friends, has that not happened to all of us, that we have sunk into the 'slough of despond' because of troubles that we thought we could not bear?" Ruth sniffles ostentatiously into an expensive silk handkerchief.

"Those that cry out unto the Lord in their trouble will be relieved of their distress. He brings them into their desired haven. To reach that haven we must love God with all our strength. O Lord, we suffer great things for thy sake."

"And you too, you too," sings out Joanna.

"Remember the words of the Psalm:
These raging winds, this surging sea
Have spent their daily force on me
They bear no breath of wrath to thee
'tis I, be not afraid.

It is Christ who says, as he said at Gethsemane, 'It is I, be not afraid'. If you are beset, be not afraid. If you are in sin, do not lose heart, be not afraid. If you are at an impasse in your life or in your souls, do not despair, be not afraid. We change in many respects, we are not what we once were, we shall not remain as we are now. All will change and all will be well. We will dwell in our father's house, where there are many mansions, as long as we keep our faith and believe."

"And you too, you too," sings out Joanna. She is standing in the aisle, her arms outstretched as if at a crucifixion, swaying gently forwards and back. A muttering as of the gentle sound of waves on a shingle shore comes from the congregation. They have never seen her like this, possessed yet supremely calm. Slowly she floats forwards towards the pulpit chanting "Amen, amen to you" over and over again as she progresses. In front of the pulpit she stops, raises her arms towards Vincent as if imploring something of him or of the heaven that lies beyond. "Alleluia," she cries. "Listen to the words of the righteous man. Listen to the Word."

All is silent behind her. No longer does she sway but stands stiffly as if turned into an icicle or a pillar of salt. "Listen to the Word. Een van ons komt bij een splitsing van wegen. De ene weg leidt naar hitte, pijn en vernietiging. Vallen. Een scheiding van God.

Geloof in hemzelf als een bovennatuurlijk wezen. Groot ongeluk en teleurstelling. Een neergang voor zijn ziel terwijl zijn herinnering beter dan ooit is.

De andere weg is die van de goede Samaritaan. Van het redden voor God van de gevallenen Van het Woord verspreiden.

Hij kan verzwakken, de strijd opgeven, maar hij moet de zondaren verheffen, diegenen die gevallen zijn redden van het kwaad."

And, as if she is a balloon that has finally expelled all of its air, she collapses motionless to the ground, a yellow froth around her lips which bubbles foully as she gasps for air and grasps and pulls at her clothes, which seem to be throttling her as she lies otherwise dead to the world.

Vincent is nonplussed. He cannot finish. He cannot stand. Harry helps him down from the pulpit. For the congregation his reaction is incomprehensible. One or two have been themselves down to the sea

51

in ships or seen military service in the low countries and recognise Joanna's outburst as being in the language of those lands even if they do not understand what is said. Vincent is helped out and into an omnibus. He is silent all the way back to Brixton. Harry undresses him and puts him to bed, where he is to remain, in silence, for the whole of the next week.

*Brixton Road*

# Mayfair, London

## *1874*

### *Susan*

**M**rs Susan Pelham-Clinton is bored. Her husband has declared that he will spend the afternoon at his club before attending a late night sitting in the House of Commons. Susan finds this male fascination with politics unfathomable, particularly since both Mr Disraeli and that vile, common Mr Gladstone seem consumed with providing bread and circuses for the lower classes. But what can one expect of a Jew and an evangelical, both of whom deceitfully pretend to be scions of the Church of England? "A policy of sewage," she snorts dismissively, though she cannot for the life of her remember which of the two contending prime ministers this refers to.

Nurse interrupts her revelry by presenting baby in its finery prior to the afternoon walk. Despite the mild weather, the child is buried beneath layers of blankets, wrapped in thick woollen over-clothes and covered by two delicate shawls. Susan believes that the baby looks the spitting image of its father, down to the suggestion of an imminent paunch. Her husband, however, believes that the child has his nose. Susan knows that this is impossible, unless it is the result of some form of osmosis or transference. She coos over the baby briefly before dismissing the nurse with a wave of her hand and a cold stare. Recently she conceived the notion that there is a growing attachment between nurse and Mr Pelham-Clinton. Not that she would care if her husband were to take a mistress (*another mistress*, she corrects herself mentally) but she would be mortally offended if he were to take up with a mere servant. Actresses and flower girls are bad enough but such a *bêtise* would only be suitable for romantic adolescents who know no better.

It is not that Mrs Susan Pelham-Clinton is a snob. Far from it. Her belief is that social classes are ordained by God: "The rich man in his castle, the poor man at his gate, God made them high and lowly and ordered their estate." Such is the teaching of the church and it is this that gives England its power and its stability, uninfected by continental Jacobin-ism. *Thank heavens for the Constitution and the Royal Family*, she thinks, though she knows far more of one than of the other.

Which reminds her why she is so bored. Eddie has not been near her since that day at the art dealers when he sent her those naughty paintings. Ten years ago she would have blushed at the thought. Today she just giggles. She can hardly just drop round to Marlborough House to see if Eddie is free. That would be fine for a chambermaid (*or for a nurse*, she adds fiercely) though not for a lady in her position. Perhaps a note, or even a letter? No, that would not do either. She should not seem to be at all importunate. A man should not be chased, he must always feel that he is the hunter and the woman his frightened quarry. No, she should go out, somewhere where she can meet Eddie by mistake. A drive down Piccadilly or through Hyde Park.

The carriage is ordered. Her morning dress is exchanged for something a trifle more fashionable.

Parading in the carriage produces mixed results. Susan Pelham-Clinton is, after all, a respectable married woman. Her husband is a Member of Parliament and a Conservative one at that. But behind that respectability lies scandal. It is well known in all of the stately homes in England and Scotland, with the possible exceptions of Osborne House and Balmoral, that she is the mistress of an important person. This alone produces mixed reactions. Elderly ladies in particular contrive to ignore her whole existence. A younger set eye her with excitement. Some giggle behind their fans. These are caught in an agony of indecision. Can they wave and smile or should they copy their grandmothers and ignore her completely? The result is a childish squirming on seats together with a flurry of adjustments to clothing.

Social climbers and those with ambitions towards court circles are even more embarrassed but better versed in the niceties of protocol and in ways of hiding their true feelings. This woman could, after all, be the mother of a future king of England. Conceived on the wrong side of the blanket, maybe, though not the first one to accede for all that. The old Queen might be strange and querulous but no-one can conceive of her having Susan Pelham-Clinton's head chopped off. Victorian society can handle angels and whores. Respectable adulterers are a much more difficult proposition.

Susan has shown off her face and her equipage. She has been hailed by many and pointedly ignored by some. She has not seen Eddie. Perhaps a return to where she last saw him? Orders to the coachman to drive to the picture dealers. Not that she is interested in art, she just wants to revive her last memories of Eddie. She is received at the dealers by a strange, angular young man with a peculiar accent. He has not shaved that morning, possibly in an attempt to avoid aggravating his acne. There is a weird light in his eyes. They flash like gaslights with a faulty wick, highlighting the ginger in his hair and stubble. Susan finds him disquieting. He is obviously doing his best to be polite and civil, obsequious even, as befits a mere shop assistant. No, he says, he has not seen His Royal Highness, not since the day he was there with Madam. Would Madam care to look at the latest acquisitions? There is a delightful Alma-Tadema that Madam might care for. No? Of course, Madam, we will inform His Royal Highness that Madam has been here. He will no doubt be desolated to hear that he has missed Madam. The young man refuses a delicately proffered tip and escorts Madam to the door and into her carriage.

He re-enters the gallery at the moment that a royal personage emerges from an inner room. A loud sigh and a large wink to the gallery assistant. Vincent watches as he walks off down the street. Two equerries in day dress follow at a discrete distance before helping him into an unmarked carriage, which then drives off at a sedate pace. Vincent wonders how he can admit to his brother and his parents that part of his new duties appears to be sheltering the Prince from importunate mistresses?

Mrs Pelham–Clinton returns home dissatisfied. No, not dissatisfied, in a raging temper. The day has been wasted. She has been cut by ageing countesses and giggled and pointed at by young honourables and youngest daughters. Beyond all else, she has not had sight of Eddie. No doubt he is off to some theatre to ogle a teenage actress or flirt in his box with some floozy of an old flame. She hurls a cigar box at the empty fire grate and immediately regrets it as Eddie's favourite cigars spread out all over the floor. "Throw it all away," she orders the maid as she sweeps out of the room in her temper. The maid's young man will have an unexpected present on her day off, as long as he performs adequately first.

*Hyde Park*

*To: V. v. G*

*Sir*

　　*We were most gratified with your tact and discretion on the occasion of our last meeting. We would be further gratified if you were to show your love for our person by acting in the same manner should any like event arise in future.*

　　*In the meantime we assure you of our firm regard. As an overseas national you may perhaps have some difficulties in the future, in which case we assure you that you may call upon us for assistance.*

*A. E.*

# Brixton

## *1874*

### *Eugenie*

Mr Cunningham is a very smart sort of gentleman. His cravat is always neatly tied, even at the end of a hot summer day. Although his boots are not new, they always sparkle and the heels show no signs of wear and tear. When he speaks there is a trace of the north in his voice, which he keeps low and 'well modulated' as my old piano teacher would say. I suppose he is quite old really, getting on for thirty probably. Still, he must be twenty years younger than the other commercials that we get here. They are very hairy, with great heavy side whiskers and huge scratchy moustaches. Mr Cunningham has a moustache but it is black and delicate looking. His side whiskers are cut back and his hair is always neat and tidy. Mother is not too happy about this because he uses macassar oil which she says gets all over the furniture.

Most of the commercials work for companies in Yorkshire selling woollen goods or fancy gloves. Mr Cunningham 'represents' a group of cotton manufacturers (a 'consortium' he calls it) around Manchester. They have become increasingly worried by cheap materials from India, so they have got together to make clothes as well as just making yarn. Most people I know make their own clothes or send out to the dressmaker, though I must say that some of the dresses I have seen in the department store in the high street do seem quite nice. But would you want to wear the same dress that everyone else is wearing?

I have put the flowers that Mr Cunningham brought me in a vase in the front room. I think he is rather disappointed about this. "They were bought just for you," he said. I told him it were best if they were enjoyed by everybody. Really, I thought it would be extremely indelicate of me to take them into my bedroom. And what would Mother say?

She is not best pleased with me as it is. Mr Cunningham invited both of us to go with him to the music hall. Mother came over all sniffy and turned him down flat, as if he had invited us to dine with the Devil. It is ages since we have been to the music hall. Not since Father died. I did use to enjoy it so. In the end I couldn't contain myself and clapped my hands and said I should be delighted to go. You should have seen the look on Mother's face! She couldn't say anything, of course, since Mr Cunningham is such a good regular customer. And she couldn't change her mind, either! Not sure what was worse: having turned it down when she really wanted to go or to see me going off to enjoy myself. Unchaperoned at that! Her face would have turned milk sour.

Anyway, off we went. The Palace of Varieties is not far, just down the hill, on the green. I had on my best burgundy dress with the subtle grey stripe. I got the idea from a woman at chapel. The grey stripe makes it look more interesting and fashionable and stops the burgundy making me look like I am in half-mourning. Mr Cunningham said it was most fetching and that he would suggest the idea to the consortium next time he was in Manchester. Then he bought me a corsage of red paper roses, which he said set off my complexion. Usually with Father we sat in the stalls but Mr Cunningham had got us tickets for the gallery, which I know cost threepence more, where we could see all the people below as well as having a good view of the stage and the orchestra pit.

What a raucous evening it was! The magician started it. Once he had made the doves fly out of his hat and lines of flags appear from his assistant's ear everything went wrong. When he tried to make coloured balls come from nowhere they dropped out from under the tails of his coat instead. Then he lifted his hat and a pack of cards fell out. We didn't know whether to laugh or jeer. A singer came next and made a rotten job of something by Mozart, which I used to play on the piano. She couldn't hit the top notes and only managed an approximation to the others. The audience obviously wasn't too keen on Mozart in the first place. By the time she was half-way through you could hardly hear her for the boos and cat calls.

During the interval Mr Cunningham apologised to me as we sipped our lemonade. I told him not to worry, that I had found the magician amusing, as well as the performing dogs, even the one that made water on the stage. "A good job it was only water," he said, which made a woman behind me titter. The second half was much better, even if the audience was still just as loud. A comedian made us all roar with laughter pretending to be an inventor. Many of we ladies pretended not to understand some of the broader humour. My favourite was a lovely boy who sang a song about losing both of his parents. I couldn't help but weep and Mr Cunningham lent me one of his elegant cotton handkerchiefs and held my hand for the remainder of the evening, to stop me getting too upset, he said. On the way home he proffered his arm and I took it as seemed right and proper. What Mother would say to such forward behaviour I cannot imagine. But what a lovely evening!

Today is Mr Cunningham's last with us this week. He says he will be back soon and has booked with Mother for the week after next. Brixton will be very dull without him. Some of the other commercials are very loud and boisterous but not much fun behind all their false jollity. 'Whistling in the wind', Mother calls it. Singing loudly to keep their spirits up when underneath they are miserable at being away from home. Some of them don't even seem to have any home at all; they spend all of their time on the road like those artists in the music hall. What they do on a Sunday when the shops are shut and the buyers are at church I cannot imagine, especially in the winter when it is too cold to spend the day in the park. Even the White Horse closes during the day on a Sunday.

About seven o'clock Mr Cunningham came down to breakfast with his luggage. I was in the kitchen putting some things on a tray so that when I came out I did not notice his sample case, huge though it is. Suddenly it was just there in front of me and I nearly fell flat, tray and all. Then an arm reached out and held me round the waist to stop me falling. What a fool I felt, half holding the tray in one hand while Mr Cunningham held the other, his spare hand holding me up. I blushed so hard I thought my whole face would burst into flames. Of course I thanked him, even though his arm lingered around me longer than I thought proper. And he thanked me too and apologised for putting his bag in my way. Quite what he was thanking me for I can't imagine. After a while he let me go, rearranged the things on my tray, gave me a slight bow and went in to breakfast.

I was all of a flutter. Fortunately Mother did not seem to notice, so I was able to go on serving. As usual Mr van Gogh had made a mess, dropping food all round his plate and spilling tea on the table. We do not put out the tablecloth for breakfast, so all I had to do was to wipe up. Every time I looked up Mr Cunningham was watching me, so I started blushing again and got all of a fluster once more. Luckily this time I didn't have a tray in my hands.

Around ten past eight there was the sound of a cab on the cobbles and a great shout of "Cunningham! Cab for Cunningham!" Mr Cunningham flew up from the table and manhandled his sample case outside and into the cab. "Don't forget your Gladstone," I shouted to him, spying that bag still standing in the hallway. He grabbed his bag and guess what? He turned to me and kissed me full on the lips! I was astounded. Then he ran his hand down my face, turned about and rushed into the cab.

Perhaps I should have objected but it was all so quick. Maybe I will object next time? There I go, being naughty. Of course there should be no 'next time'. But it was rather pleasant. His lips are soft and quite full. His moustache is soft. Feeling it on your face is like being brushed by a butterfly or like those butterfly kisses I used to exchange with Father when I was little, just barely touching one another with our eye lashes. And having your face stroked is wonderful. My father used to do it to send me to sleep. Not that I went to sleep this time of course. Quite the opposite. For the rest of the day I was like a jack-in-the-box, bouncing about all over the place before stopping dead for minutes at a time. Mother kept worrying that I was sickening and dosing me with Dr Collis Brown's Chlorodyne, which made my 'away times' even longer. Well, what a day!

*Streatham High Street*

# Brixton

## *1874*

### *Ruth*

Being a widow is a hard life. I have to manage the house and the business, keep the gentlemen guests in order, ensure the hired helps and the stall holders don't cheat me. Then there is Jen-Jen. Not that Eugenie is any problem, not like some of the girls around here. There are one or two I could name; if they sat down in my parlour I would wash all the cushions afterwards. Jen-Jen is clean and proper. Every morning she is up to help me with the breakfasts and in the evening waits at the table like a complete butler. Mid-times she tidies and cleans and helps me with the shopping. When she's with me at the market I can usually get things cheaper. She smiles and chats with the stall holders. Nothing improper, mind, just her natural charm.

But what am I to do with her? She can't go on like this forever. One day she will want to be married, like all good girls. On the other hand, how could I do without her? I would need to pay someone to do all the things that she does. How could I find anyone so reliable? And if I had to pay someone I would have to put my prices up, so no-one would come here and I would starve. That would serve her right for running off and deserting me. Ungrateful girl!

Some of my gentlemen have eyes for her as well. That Mr Havard who calls himself a major, though I don't think he has ever even sniffed an army barracks, trimmed yellow moustache or no. He's always making eyes at her, lecherous old sot. You can see what he is thinking, even if he is even older than me. I did think at one time he was going to make me an offer. Looking for a quiet, cosy billet to retire to probably. I cut him off before he could even get started, gave him one of my looks, the sort that used to shut poor George up for the rest of the day. No trouble with the major after that.

Then there's that Mr Cunningham. He's a fly one, that one. Much younger than the others, hasn't been worn down yet, still has his sharp edges on him. Sharp dresser as well. "Can't expect my customers to believe in my goods if I don't dress well myself, can I?" I expect he is right. I always wear a smart bonnet to go out in just in case I meet a prospective client. Now, Mr Cunningham, he is the sort to turn a girl's head. Good looking, too. He'll need watching I dare say. Jen-Jen seems to like him. She even went to the music hall with him. I must have a word with her. Commercials are not reliable, they don't make good husbands. One minute they are selling stock left, right and centre, the next they can't even shift a peanut. Besides which they are never at home. Just like sailors, they have wives and babies in every port. No daughter of mine will be treated like that. I certainly must have a word with her. Next time they want to go to the music hall, I'm coming too.

Then there is that weird Mr van Gogh, good Christian though he is. Too fierce for my liking. You can see him walking across fiery coals or throwing himself in front of lions. Fancies himself as a pilgrim for Christ. Certainly not the sort for an elegant and independent girl like my Jen-Jen. Good job he's got, mind. Up to town every day in his Sunday best. Quiet job, out of the rain, meeting all the nobs, steady money. They say his uncle owns part of the company. That can't be bad. Means he's got good prospects. If the uncle got him the job, he might leave the company to him when he snuffs it. Imagine him as a son-in-law! All righteousness and indignation. Never a joke or a bit of fun. He'd drive all the customers away. And the children with all that nasty red hair. No, never.

# Brixton, London

## 1874

*Dear Theo*

*How long it is since I wrote to you last! We should struggle to keep in touch as closely as we can, each a staff upon which the other could lean.*

*I have been prostrate this last week or two as the result of a nervous illness which beset me whilst in church. Whether it was the result of the tension and excitement of delivering my first sermon or the encounter with a prophetess afterwards, I cannot say. Whichever it was I have been so disturbed that I could hardly talk, or even think.*

*My sermon, which I have enclosed with this letter, was very well received by the general audience. Unlike Rev. Slade-Jones I concentrated on how a good Christian should act in the world for his own sake, not out of fear and damnation. Job did not behave as he did out of fear of God but out of love of God and in the security of his own righteousness. As you know, I am no Job. I have doubted God and I have done things of which I am not proud. We have both disported ourselves with grisettes in Paris in a manner that I would not care to have reported to our parents.*

*Speaking of which, dear boy, now that you are also working for the company and in Paris, no less, I expect that you are contemplating misbehaving yourself. You mentioned a certain seamstress in your last letter and I assume that you are setting your cap at her. Do I remember someone of the same name modelling for Lautrec at one time? The girl was rather tubercular. She didn't seem* long for this world. Perhaps she has calmed down and given up her rackety existence.

As far as young ladies are concerned, I have finally determined to make my feelings known to Miss Eugenie, perhaps in a month or so. She is such a charming creature and was so good to me when I was ill that I'm sure she would be an excellent wife and mother. Of course she is still young. This makes her seem a bit flighty and a trifle fluffy. Her concern at the moment is for bonnets and dresses, though that is true of most young ladies of her age and situation. Given her background she is quite sophisticated. I heard her playing some Bach on the piano the other day. It was absolutely delightful. Not that she knows anything of painting, or of architecture either. Despite that, she knows all of the building terms and all of the parts of a church, things that she learnt from her father.

My problem is that I barely earn enough to support myself, never mind a wife. If I got some preferment within the company it might help. Ideally I would wish to work as a minister somewhere. The church is always looking for ministers for the counties of Nottingham and York, the coal mining parts of England, which are also receptive to the word of the gospel. With the help of a good wife I can see myself evangelising those poor benighted parts of the country. Harry Kirman tells me that the miners are concerned only with dogs and drink. As a southerner Harry is not to be relied upon. He looked at me askance when I first told him that I work north of the river. Yorkshire must be an unintelligible foreign country to him.

Which brings me back to my sermon. When I had nearly finished a mad woman, who often declaims at these meetings, strode up to me and began to prophesy. In Dutch of all things! She suggested that I should 'rescue those who have fallen', which suggests to me that my place is to be among the miners. That wasn't all she said, of course. Much of it was quite gnomic and I didn't understand it all. The upshot of it was that I was horribly upset, my mind was completely shot and I could not control myself. Her words, or indeed her prophesy, were not that severe or outlandish. But they were in Dutch! This from a creature who *can barely master her native English. Who babbles in incomprehensible gibberish when she falls into her fits. The Lord save us from fits and incoherence.*

*Anyway, dear boy, I am proud to have been listened to attentively by God's people. Whatever happens, may God's will be done.*

*Your ever-loving brother*

*Vincent*

*Clapham Common*

# Deptford, London

## *Autumn 1874*

*Dear George*

 *These winter days are quite depressing. I am round the local shops and department stores all day until they close at six, lugging my great big samples trunk from one to the next. Luckily the take-up here is quite good. Mainly for tat, it is true but enough to keep up my commission level. The new cotton bloomers are a huge success, probably because they are so cheap. Old man Murgatroyd seems to have got it right. He pretends to run a mill but most of his cotton is bought in from India and then made up in the factory. Next month he says he will have a range of cotton dresses as well for me to push. Can't say that they will be very smart or last more than a week or so. Knowing Mr M they will be dirt cheap.*

 *Once the shops and the stores close there is nothing to do here. I'm in a bed and breakfast place, which is outstandingly dreary and damp with it. I've no idea how the paper manages to hang on to the walls and the bed feels like it is stuffed with Pennine rock. I shan't stay here again. There's not much to do in the town, either. No music halls, just low drinking dens where you might get either murdered or poisoned. They say that the playwright Christopher Marlowe was killed in a pub brawl here in Deptford. More likely he just died of boredom.*

 *Life is much better at Mrs L's place in Brixton. The food isn't up to much but the place itself is clean with no bugs or rodents to worry about. And then there is the little Eugenie, Mrs L's daughter and her pride and joy. She really is the most delightful creature, nicely padded, if you know what I mean, and most presentable. Like Mrs L she's a bit above herself, thinks she's better than she actually is. That's the result of her father having been connected to the church, I suppose, even if he was only a builder. And she's not shrill and sassy like the mill girls back home. Anyway, she is very lively and likes a good outing. Even plays the piano, though I wish she weren't so keen on that dreary classical stuff.*

*Went with her to the music hall at the end of last week. The money that has been spent on the place! Locals reckon that it is all of 30,000 pounds but I think that it was nearer 40,000. The first half was rubbish, it was embarrassing to be there. Any crowd in Manchester would have torn the place down, 40,000 or no. Good job the second half was better. Do you remember that skit we saw last year about an Irish wedding? Well, that lot were on, the Leno family, doing an hilarious thing about an inventor of explosives. And then there was Champagne Charlie in his top hat and tails staggering all over the stage. For me the best bit was a young singer called Charles Chaplin. His piece was a terribly mushy song about an orphan. Abominable stuff. Miss Eugenie, on the other hand, was quite affected so that I had to lend her my best Heywood and Co. handkerchief and hold her hand for the rest of the performance. You can imagine how upset I was about that! She was happy to take my arm on the way home, too.*

*Next morning I confess I was a bit naughty. I deliberately left my bags in the hallway in front of the kitchen door where I knew she would fall over them. Which she did. Of course yours truly was on hand to catch both her and the tray. You can imagine that I was in no hurry to let her go! By the time I did she was the colour of an autumn apple, all blush and no paint. Mind, I don't think she was in any rush to get away either. Once I'd loaded my samples case into the cab I had to go back for my Gladstone. There was Miss Eugenie standing over it like a guardian angel. I couldn't let an opportunity like that go missing, now could I? So I dived in, gave her a quick goodbye kiss full on the lips, stroked her cheek, made my exit. When the cab pulled away she was still standing there, her hand on her mouth and the* front door still wide open. I'm back there in a couple of weeks, which should be entertaining.

Now, there's something I must educate you about. Young ladies who are properly brought up often baulk at one stealing a kiss or two. You have to be sure to stroke their cheek at the same time. For some reason this calms them down and stops them putting up too much resistance. I think it has something to do with their grandmothers stroking their heads to send them to sleep. Whatever, it puts them in a fine mood to accept intimacies and I counsel you to try it with that little Emily that you are so keen on.

Your devoted friend
Paul Cunningham

# Southampton Street, London

## *Autumn 1874*

*Dear Tersteeg*

*We appear to have become fashionable all of a sudden. Perhaps that is the result of out latest visit by the Prince of Wales. Not that he has bought anything since his first appearance. The possibility of his presence seems to have encouraged the faster set into dropping into the gallery on the off-chance of meeting the Prince. This has caused something of a personnel problem within the company. The Prince himself is most taken with young van Gogh and even asks for him by name when he visits. By contrast the young set still find him most off-putting. The seriousness of his demeanour, the strength of his passions and the heat of his religious views they find disturbing. His piercing eye unsettles the ladies who seem to feel that it is an attempt upon their virtue.*

*None of this is to denigrate the man who, apart from a recent nervous illness, has been most diligent and useful. I have the feeling that he is at last settling down and has begun to accept that picture dealing is a business, albeit one where it is possible to become emotionally involved with one's stock. I must admit that it pains me whenever we sell a Corot, the more so that I wish that I could have them all in my private collection. Now that van Gogh has proved himself I suggest that we reward him at the same time as making use of his talents and experience for the company. His younger brother Theodore has been working for the company in The Hague for some time and is due to be transferred to Paris in the near future. Would it make sense if we used Vincent as the lad's mentor to initiate him into the Paris business, to 'show him the ropes' as the English say? They could have two weeks together first in Holland as a kind of working holiday before* moving to Paris. By then, Theodore should be well prepared for his new position and Vincent could reacquaint himself with the younger artists.

Oh, how I wish that I was able to spend time in Paris! London is a dreary sort of place full of rain and fog. The streets are filthy and the traffic is abominable. There are none of those beautiful wide new boulevards that one finds in Paris, except for those which lead to aristocratic mansions. All the Thames seems to do is to provide a conduit for the coal from downstream, which creates all the fog and the dirt and the effluent from upstream, which adds to the perpetual stink of the place. The better sort of people are bearable, as they are everywhere, but the lower classes give themselves airs. Even when they say 'Yes, sir' or 'No, sir' they do it with a malicious look and intonation as if they are waiting for you to turn your back before they pounce on you and beat you to death. Every day one hears of dockers refusing to work or of agitators and anarchists being arrested. I am fearful that one day this will all spread to my beloved France. Now that we have suppressed all of the Communards, France can grow strong again and wrest its rightful possessions from the Huns. Not that I expect these dreary republicans to be able to apply themselves to the task. We have always had our greatest glory under a strong leader such as Charles Martel, Louis XIV or the Emperor Napoleon.

And the women here! So badly dressed. Except of course for those who have the good sense to buy their dresses from the best houses in Paris. Such a waste, since English women have a brazen strength and nobility to them, not affected or sly like some I could name at home! English women and English horses, a wonderful gift to the world. Not that I would tell my wife that. We took in a pair of paintings recently by Albert Moore. Full of naked young women, obviously English. They all look like they are bathing and changing their clothes after spending all day in the open air chasing the fox. Quite delicious.

Anyway, dear colleague, let me know your thoughts on the van Gogh brothers. If you are in agreement I will make all of the necessary arrangements in London.

Yours,

Boussod

# Brixton

## *Winter 1874*

### *The White Horse*

"Have another pint of this porter, Vince. It will set you up a treat. You look like you lost a pound and found a penny. Everything alright at work? Problems at home? What is it?"

"They want me to go back to Paris."

"Well that's ok, innit? I'd love to have a week or so in Paris. All them gorgeous girls showing off and doing the can-can and things. Can't see my Lizzie doing that."

Vincent is not so enthusiastic. "I'd rather stay here. Paris is terrible in the winter, cold and damp. And they want me to babysit my brother. He's a good lad and we get on well but he is rather young and he does manage to get himself into all sorts of scrapes from time to time."

"Not like you, eh, Vince? My feeling is that you don't want to be too far away from a certain young lady."

Vincent grimaces. Maybe the porter is too strong or he has yet to acclimatise himself to the taste of warm English beer. "You could be right there. I'm going to do something about it before I leave."

"Don't rush in, old lad, there's plenty of time and plenty more fish in the sea. How old are you now, twenty-three? She can be no more than seventeen. Plenty of time yet for both of you. Lizzie and me, we rushed into things and look at us. I'm no older than you and already I have a house full of children and have to work all hours to feed and clothe them. Not that Lizzie isn't a good girl and I love her dearly but it would be great to be able to go out with the lads of a weekend, go down the palais or to the music hall. And how would you feel having old Ma Loyer as your mother-in-law? Staring at you all the time with that disapproving look of hers, as if no-one in the world is good enough for her. She'd grind you down inside of a week. Home spot on time of a Saturday, pass her over your pay packet, unopened and untouched. You hang about, my lad, no good will come of rushing."

Harry sips his beer. Vincent gulps down more than he intended to and splutters half of it over the table. His expression segues from grim to glum to embarrassed in a couple of seconds. Harry merely grins. He is obviously in high spirits, despite his house full of children.

"Look here, Vince. What do you think of these?" A rolled bundle of papers appears from his knapsack, slightly stained by the remains of a brawn sandwich. He mops the table with his neckerchief, spreads them on the table, holds them down with an array of empty beer mugs that the barman has been too idle to collect and wash. "Been trying to draw the children. Looks a bit like them but they don't seem to come out right. You're in the trade. Got any tips?"

The drawings are by an amateur and not a very talented one at that. Harry is obviously more at home with a paintbrush than with a pencil. Vincent is perplexed. How can he start? What can he say that will not offend his friend?

"Well…" Long pause. "First thing is, a soft pencil or even some charcoal. The hard pencil you are using is all very well for marking out when all you want is a faint line that will disappear under the slightest touch of a brush. You've been trying to get a darker tone in places and nearly gone through the paper. Use a softer one and rub it down to get softer tones. Just dab it off with some bread pellets. Has anyone ever told you how to draw a face? I thought not! Most people's faces are an oval, some a bit longer or a bit rounder than others, but start with an oval. Then draw a cross on it. A cross piece about a third of the way down, then a vertical straight down the middle. In principle our faces are symmetrical: ears on each side, two nostrils, mouth half and half. Even old Seamus over there. One ear is bigger than the other; despite that, they are both on the same line. His nose is all over the place, though."

74

"He used to work the fairground booths," puts in Harry. "Took on all comers. His nose has been broke more often than a brickie at the end of the week. Mind, I see what you mean. We must all have started off more or less symmetrical. Doesn't work top to bottom, though."

"Quite right." Vincent is in his element now. "That's why we put the horizontal line about a third of the way down. That's where the eyes go. Now, you have to be careful with that one. No-one has their eyes exactly level. You just take it as a rule of thumb and adjust it bit by bit, like you do when you are mixing paint colours. Start off by following the rule, like how much red you add to the blue, then change it as your eyes tell you. Look, like this."

Soon the backs of the drawings are covered in lines and measurements. The existing drawings are altered and overdrawn into a state of incoherence. Cigarette packets are destroyed, opened up and scrawled across, leaving the cigarettes themselves to dissolve in puddles of stale beer.

"'Ere, is you eyeballin' me?" Seamus is tired of their scrutiny and unkind comments on his physiognomy. Harry and Vincent pacify him with a half pint of porter and he adds his comments as if joining in some obscure kind of parlour game. Despite all efforts the portrait of Seamus resembles a Cruikshank cartoon rather than an honest likeness. Not that either Seamus or Harry is at all dismayed, for Seamus it undoubtedly is on the cigarette packet before him, while Harry's optimistic drawings of his children do not resemble them at all. *I'm making progress*, he thinks. *I could get quite good at this.*

Vincent is amused by all this as well as being excited by an unwonted intake of beer. Perhaps he should try out some sketches in his own right. So much more fun that trying to sell boring prints to ignorant aristocrats and bourgeois. Maybe he and Theo could go on a painting holiday to Scheveningen or along the Seine once they are established in Paris. Some little *grisettes* might be persuaded to pose for a few francs and perhaps stay the night into the bargain. He pulls his thoughts up short. After all, he aspires to be a man of the cloth and one that is soon to be married into the bargain. Quite where he is to find a parish or what he and Eugenie would live on has not yet presented itself as a real problem outside of the pearly mists of his dreams. Now is not the time to confront inconvenient issues.

He and Harry leave the White Horse, each somewhat unsteady on their feet. Both are steeling themselves to confront withering female reproaches whilst congratulating themselves on an amusing evening well spent. At the corner they doff their hats to one another in mock salutation and turn their individual ways, Vincent with more of a spring to his step than when he arrived, Harry with a resigned shrug as he totes his bag of tools and brushes over his shoulder.

# Streatham, London

## *Winter 1874*

*Dear George*

*What a magnificent week this has been! I can't seem to go anywhere without they give me massive orders and not just for tat, either. That old sod in Camberwell, who would hardly give me the time of day last month, was all over me the other day and just couldn't get enough of my samples. He wanted to take the samples off me then and there to display and I almost had to fight him off. In the end he ordered enough of the flannel drawers with the fake lace edging for every woman in Camberwell. To my surprise he also took twenty of the grey dresses with the purple stripe that I'd drawn up from what Eugenie was wearing last month. That looks like it could be a nice little earner. I must see if she can spot something like that again.*

    *As for Eugenie herself, I got a dress made up for her by one of the women in Oldham. It's a bit of a cracker and she will look super in it if her mother ever lets her wear it. In a way it is very modest, right up to the neck with some extra ruffles then down to the wrists in the same. There's a bit of a train, which is fastened back to the right wrist. All with a gauzy effect, in the palest grey with a tinge of blue to it like the autumn mist rising off the Thames. Doesn't that sound lovely? What mother could object to that? The point is, dear boy, that it touches everywhere. It really is skin tight, all round and all the way down. Eugenie would fill it magnificently. I'm dying to see her in it. Her eyes lit up when I produced it on the hanger. Though she said she could never wear it, I could see that she was dying to get her hands* on it. The feeling is mutual! She says that she can't wear it until she has made a bonnet to go with it. No-one is going to go to all that trouble and refuse to wear the dress, now are they?

Talking of Eugenie, you'll notice that I'm not at my usual base in Brixton this week despite its attractions, not least the little miss herself. All part of the plan. If I stay in Brixton Mrs L knows where I am and what I am doing. As it is, I can 'accidentally' meet Eugenie in the street or at the market and we can spend some time together. Not only that, she can make an excuse that she is going out to meet friends or to attend a prayer meeting. You can imagine what form my prayers are taking when we are meeting! Instead of going back to Manchester with my orders, I've sent them off by post instead, special delivery, so I can stay here over the next week. That means we can go off somewhere on our own, to the park perhaps or even to the Cremorne Gardens. They say they are a bit rough nowadays but it can't be too bad during the day or anything like Oldham on a Saturday night.

★

Guess what? I'm engaged! There are certain ladies up north who will be furious to hear of it but I couldn't pass up the opportunity.

I arranged to meet Miss on Sunday afternoon when she had told Mrs L that she was going to help out at Sunday School at the local chapel. Instead of which she came over here, new bonnet, sunshade and all. She was a bit funny at first about coming to my room until I told her that it was the most private place to change her dress. Of course, I offered to help. She wasn't having any of it and told me to wait outside. Imagine my surprise when she called me to go back in. I may have had the dress made a trifle tight; anyway she had squeezed herself into it but couldn't manage all the hooks and fastenings.

At first I was ham-fisted as if I'd never handled a lady in or out of a dress before. Naturally I took the opportunity to trace out the lie of the land as I was doing it. A touch here, a stroke or a pat there. After much struggling and squealing she was nicely tucked away. Didn't she look *smart! All the girls in Streatham High Street gave her venomous looks and more than one gentleman was stopped in his tracks and had to turn to stare. Like a vanilla ice with chocolate and cream topping she was.*

*We made slow progress. The hem of the skirt is tight, so you can't take normal-sized steps or walk very fast. Fortunately there was an omnibus stop quite close by. Miss had to lift her skirt a little to get on and I was happy to have a good look at a pair of well turned ankles. An old gentleman was behind us and he absolutely turned purple. "You disgusting hussy," he shouted, "showing off your legs like that. You should be taken in charge for immoral behaviour. On the Sabbath, too. Aren't you ashamed?" Miss turned a becoming tone of scarlet and hurried up to the top deck of the omnibus. I was too engrossed in studying how tightly the dress wrapped around her rear end as she mounted the stairs to worry about some old religious maniac shouting and screaming.*

*Have you ever been to Cremorne Gardens? It's a most astonishing place with all sorts of people strolling along the alleys. There are trees and bushes everywhere like a regular wood, with little nooks where you can pause for private conversation or to arrange an assignation. During the day the better class of people predominate, plus a sprinkling of shop girls, mechanics and the like. The older folk sit and listen to the bands, the quartets and the singers while the more rowdy element dance, laugh and sometimes drink too much. We had a rare old time. Miss was quite taken by the various attractions and the opportunities afforded by the odd shady bower. I was happy to introduce her to your favourite saying: that kissing a man without a moustache is like eating an egg without salt or beef without mustard. Except that she doesn't like eggs. Fortunately I was able to persuade her to appreciate moustaches more!*

*Even before dark the night birds appear. The gentlemen are absolutely not short of a pound or two in their Sunday best suits and brushed toppers, no doubt straight from afternoon service. Not a bowler or a five-shilling suit like the rest of us. Their quarry is the brightly feathered birds of paradise in their flounces and furbelows wandering the alleys as if lost in some romantic reverie. Sadly the dream is shattered when, like peacocks, they open their mouths in a shattering* screech. Despite this the hunters are happy to have found their quarry and take the opportunity to ensnare them in their nets, taking them off for food and liquid refreshment before trussing and stuffing them.

Less conspicuous are a number of young lads in very tight trousers and rakish caps. Some of the older gentlemen feel the need to look after them, alone and abroad as they are. I was amazed that Miss knew all about them. Of course there must be such as these in Brixton and louche women too, I dare say, though they must be of the lowest sort. At first I was all for leaving when it got dark but she was quite jolly by then and demanded to stay for the fireworks. That gave me the opportunity to hold her hand and even slip my arm around her waist from time to time. Which I did almost continuously in the dark on the way home.

By that time Miss was a bit frisky, having had a nip or two of gin more than she was accustomed to. We kissed and cuddled all of the way up the stairs and I stroked more than her face, I can tell you! But she had to get home, which meant changing her dress… Now, if she couldn't do it up on her own there was no way she could unfasten it. I was forced to assist.

Even then it peeled off with some difficulty. She does have such milky shoulders! Like any well brought-up young girl she was firmly resistant. Like any girl of her age she was excited and compliant. Suffice to say that in the course of the next hour I was forced to make many declarations and promises in order to smooth the path to my ultimate goal. Well worth it, they were as well! Such a luscious, tender morsel, smooth and tasty as new churned butter. Everything in the right place and plenty of it. With luck I will revisit that pleasure soon and often thereafter. Once a right has been granted it cannot be refused. All much better than Saturday nights in Oldham when we would slip the mill girls some coppers to do it standing up with them behind the pub. Yesterday cost me a lot more than a few coppers, I can tell you but I certainly got my money's worth.

Your engaged friend
Paul

# Brixton

## *Autumn 1874*

### *Ruth*

Now here's a turn up for the book. What a day! That girl will be the death of me.

I'd had a hard day anyway. The house full, the help off sick and Jen-Jen moping around like love in a mist. Must be her time of the month. And the butcher refusing us any more meat until we pay him for the last lot. "I'm not paying," I said to him. "Them kidneys were off and the liver looked like someone had taken a green paintbrush to it. If you don't like it, I'll take my custom to Robinson's instead." "And much good it will do him," he said and stomped off.

So I was left doing everything on my own. Good job it wasn't cleaning day. Anyway, I'd finally settled down in the parlour with my embroidery when he sidles in, all smarmy and smirky like. He knows I don't like anyone in the parlour of an evening and I tells him so. Well, that doesn't put him off. He just carries on regardless, like I'd never said anything. He goes on about how lovely Brixton is at this time of year, the weather clement, the leaves still on the trees turning wonderful shades of red and orange and brown. No wind, great weather for sitting outside in. Not like where he comes from, he says.

Then he starts talking about what a difficult life this must be, running the house and bringing up Jen-Jen all on my own. Now I'm not going to be pitied by the likes of him. "Not at all," I tells him. "There's plenty has it harder than me. Thanks to my dear George I have this house, which gives me a roof over my head and some regular money coming in. Then Eugenie helps me. She's a good girl. Brought

81

up proper, not like some. George and me, we gave her a good God-fearing education. She can read and write and figure and knows the difference between right and wrong. She goes to chapel regular on Sundays. Twice sometimes."

I could see he was impressed. It had wiped the smarmy grin off his face, in any case. So then he starts on about how well the house is run, always clean and that, especially compared to some around here. Although he says Brixton is a good place to live, close to the countryside and not too built up. He likes rambling in the country, he says, and does it a lot where he lives, though the mists and the weather make it difficult to do much. Besides which, his job keeps him indoors a lot of the time when he would rather be out rambling. Then he goes on about his job, how it gives him the opportunity to meet so many interesting and important people. Plenty of prospects. A steady income and always in demand. At that he catches me looking a bit sour. "No," he says. "People like what's new, what is fashionable. As long as we keep up with that, we'll never go out of business." At which point he tells me how much he earns, which after all isn't that bad, even if he has to spend more than most on his clothes. A bit put by, he says, with always a little left over at the end of the month.

By this time he is turning bright red and looking like he doesn't know where to put himself. 'Does he need the toilet?' I ask him. Shakes his head. Goes even redder than a ripe tomato, blustering on about his work and how well they think of him. So much so that he is taking on extra responsibility and bringing in new products. I'm getting impatient with him. Time is getting on, which is more than my embroidery is. Burning the lamp is costing me good money. There's still something he wants to say, maybe for me to give him tick or give him steak with his supper. I begin to fidget. At last he comes to the point.

"Although I'm still quite young," he says, "I have a settled position in a respectable company where I am well thought of. I work hard and enjoy what I do, with the prospect of progressing further, perhaps even having my own company eventually. Being away from home so much I get lonely and long for some real companionship. The time has come for me to think of marriage. You have told me yourself what an excellent wife and mother Eugenie would make. She is hard working, well brought up, educated, pious and respectable. As well as that she is very beautiful. She is just the sort of girl I could introduce to my mother and my sisters with no compunction whatsoever. As she has no father living, I apply to you as her mother to give me permission to address myself to her with a view to a formal engagement and marriage."

This last comes out all in a rush as if he has learned it all by heart, which I suppose he has. I'm all in a fluster. What to do? What to say? What would George have done? No, that's no use. He would just have come to ask me. For nearly five minutes I am completely silent. He sits there wringing his hands and looking anxious. "Well," I say at last, "Eugenie is very young, as you know, and may well not be interested in marriage at her age. I was some years older than her when I married and, despite the fact that darling George was the best of all husbands, there have been times when I thought that I was too young to be a wife. Still, it is not for me to decide. She has a mind of her own and there is no denying a young girl when she has set her heart on a man, however unsuitable he may be." (I give him a sharp look at this point and he winces.) "You can have my permission to make your proposal to my daughter but I want no long faces or tantrums if she turns you down. Is that understood?"

He turns red again and stammers out his thanks and apologies. Nearly knocks over the lamp as he rushes out of the room like a madman. There is no way I can get on with my embroidery now. I just can't pay it enough attention. Wanting to marry my daughter for heaven's sake! Who does he think he is? With luck she will turn him down. I just couldn't bear having that weird Vincent van Gogh as my son-in-law.

# Brixton

## *Autumn 1874*

*Dear Theo*

   *I may well reach you before this letter can. Nevertheless, it is imperative that I write to you or I shall explode with my own anger and anxiety. "No, never. Not ever," is what they said to me. Not ever! Such is not a way to be dismissed. I shall fight. I will resist 'Not ever'!*

   *Let me tell it to you as it happened.*

   *First, I went to see the mother. Since the father is dead it is only right to approach the nearest relative. Perhaps it would have been better to have started with the grandfather as the closest man in the family. But then living in the mother's house, to avoid her does not seem correct. Anyway, I go in to see the mother. She is embarrassed and nervous, as if she already knows why I have come. In preparation I have learnt my speech so I can come straight to the point. "I want your permission to pay my addresses to your daughter," I say. Immediately I can see that the mother is flattered and impressed. She knows that I have a steady occupation and meet many important people, as well as being a God-fearing and stable man. For some time she was struck dumb with joy at her daughter's good fortune. After the customary warnings about the girl being too young or unprepared (something that she has no doubt taken from the penny novels that she reads in secret), she finally gives me permission and pushes me out of the room so that she can hug her good fortune to herself.*

   *Not wanting to let the iron grow cold, I approached the young lady straight after supper the next day. Perhaps that was a mistake? After all the running around serving and clearing away, she appeared red and flustered and tried to avoid speaking to me. I blocked her path and would not let her pass until I had had my say. As I spoke her redness receded to be replaced by a cold pallor. Out of the corner of my eye I could see the mother sneaking away behind the door jamb, desperate to avoid being seen, but equally desperate to catch every word. The girl tried to push past again. I moved over to deny her an exit. For a while we danced opposite one another, she insistent on moving past me, I determined that she should not. "I do not demand an immediate reply," I said. "Marriage is a serious matter that should not be entered into lightly. Take your time. Consult your mother and your priest. Only then should you decide whether or not we should be married."*

*"No, never. Not ever," she says and bursts into tears. At which I am flabbergasted. What is this sudden rejection? Why has she not at least considered my proposal, discussed it with her family? "'No, never. Not ever!' What kind of a response is that?" I ask her. I reason with her. She no longer tries to push past me. I no longer stand in her way. "Give me a reason," I implore her, "for your sharp and categorical rejection of my offer." At which she prevaricates. Cites my foreign nationality and her unwillingness to leave either London or her mother's house. How could she speak to my relatives when she knows no Dutch? They are educated people, I tell her; they all speak English, and French, too. Besides, we would live here in London. No, she couldn't take me away from my family and my homeland. We go on like this for some time, her reasons becoming weaker and ever more far fetched.*

*At last I catch a movement out of the corner of my eye. It is the mother creeping away, having heard all that she needs. Miss is well aware that we are now alone in the passageway. She at last speaks freely. Recently she became secretly engaged to a young man without her mother's knowledge or consent. One of the commercials by the name of Cunningham. 'Fly' as they say in Brixton. Loose of foot and loose of morals. A young man on the make, ready to do anything to 'get on'. Certainly not to be trusted, neither with your purse nor with your sister. None of this can be said. All I can do is to persist, suggest that I would make a better husband, that she should throw him over in favour of me.*

"No, never. Not ever," is all the response that I get. She rushes off to her room, leaving me dazed and perplexed. Naturally I taxed her mother with the matter. She gave me that hard basilisk stare of hers, as if she knew nothing of the whole affair. Totally unlikely. Mothers and daughters are always locked in a female conspiracy as we know from our own mother and Anna. Can you imagine Mother not knowing that Anna is engaged, 'secretly' or no?

Forgive me. I am not at my best. That 'Never, not ever' has completely disconcerted me. I am glad to be leaving in a couple of days to the comfort of Holland and the love and support of my faithful brother. And from there to Paris, where I can forget faithless London and we can be once more two young bachelors with never a care in the world.

Your desolate brother

Vincent

# Brixton

## *Autumn 1874*

Well I never! And I thought Mr van Gogh was just interested in God and art. There he was, bold as brass, stuttering along about how good his prospects are and what an excellent husband he would make and how much he values me and so on and so forth. At some point he even told me that he had spoken to Mother about marrying me and she had agreed. She might have spoken to me first! What a cheek! She'll be running off with that nasty greasy Major Havard next, just to spite me. Anyway, I turned Mr van Gogh down flat. "No, never, not ever," I told him. At first I tried to be polite, made all sorts of excuses, but he wasn't having any. Like a dog with a bone he just wouldn't let go. Standing there in front of me like a lame horse, not letting me pass. In the end I just told him flat "No, never, not ever" and that completely deflated him. To some extent I felt sorry for him. I'm glad that I cut him off so that he won't ask me again. When I pushed past him he looked like he would never move from the spot, just vanish in a puff of smoke, like the magician's assistant in the music hall.

Paul was very amused when I told him about it. Mr van Gogh and him never got on so I'm not surprised. I was rather hoping that he would name the day himself, especially when he suggested that we might go somewhere on our own. Instead he took me to Cremorne Gardens. I love going there but I wish that he had made a proper declaration instead. As it was, we were not alone even there. We met Maud, who had her new gentleman in tow. Now Maud is not what Mother calls 'fast'. Rather, she is always stepping out with one beau or another. This one is a bit special. Maud's type is always rather flash. Someone who will spend a lot to impress her, whether he has the money or no. Once he runs out of cash she is off, no promises made or taken. Mr W she calls this one. A real toff, even if he is an American. He tries to hide it with a posh voice but the American sound is still there.

Not that he wasn't perfectly polite, calling Paul 'Mr Cunningham' and me 'Miss Loyer'. Maud is thoroughly smitten. She positively melts when he looks at her, blushes all the time and stares at him with those big brown calf eyes of hers. If he suggested they lie down in the bushes she'd have her dress off in a second. Not that he did, of course. Gentlemen don't do that sort of thing. Instead he invited us to walk across the bridge to his studio, which we happily agreed to do. Maud looked a bit peeved at this. No doubt she was expecting a cosy evening there with Mr W all on her own. "Come and watch the fireworks," said Mr W. "They are twice as brilliant from the other bank. Above are the explosions and below are the reflections in the river."

What would you expect of an artist's studio? I thought it would be some vast space with paintings stacked around the walls and pots of paint all over the place. Mr W's studio was not like that at all. Certainly there were paints: they were neatly set out in jars on the shelves as powder. 'Pigment' Mr W called it, and talked about mixing it with various oils and varnishes to get different effects with the right tone and consistency. Can't see Harry Kirman doing that. He'd just open a tin and slap it on. The space itself is quite long and narrow, divided into 'rooms' by work benches, some covered in materials, others with picture frames that had been painted with butterfly motifs and were drying out and some with lots of sketches on paper.

Pride of place was a large easel about a third of the way down the room. On it was a long oblong canvas of a scene with five figures. They looked very old fashioned to me, like the carvings my father used to show me on ancient monuments, Roman or Greek or something. Except the Roman ones usually had no clothes on, whilst these seemed to be dressed in today's fashions. I didn't care for it at all, too static, dull and boring. Imagine my amazement when Mr W said it was a view of Cremorne Gardens! If I'd seen the painting first I would never have bothered visiting the gardens, Paul or no.

Looks like it could be dusk. The sky is a strange green colour as if it might have rained recently. Instead of being dark as well, the ground is a pale red or peach colour, like the sun is going down. On the right, a group of people lounge around the table, half asleep if you ask me. Three ladies and a gentleman stand talking in the centre, looking bored, which is perhaps why the other is taking her leave. Now, Cremorne is nothing like that. Always lively with something interesting going on: jugglers, actors, music, all kinds of things. Not to mention the goings-on among the visitors.

Paul was quick to point out a *chaise longue* at the end of the room and said that that was where the models posed naked. Then he winked and cast a meaningful glance at Maud as if to suggest that she did more than just pose there to be drawn. Perhaps I shouldn't say it, but wouldn't it be wonderful to be drawn by some great artist so that when you are old and fat you can look back and say "How beautiful I was". Not that I'm that beautiful. Though I've got quite a good figure. At least Paul tells me so. Wouldn't that be something to show the grandchildren? Can't you just imagine them in an art gallery giggling over Granny's naked bottom!

Well, in the end we did watch the fireworks, while Mr W scribbled away with a scrubby bit of charcoal on scraps of paper. I suppose he meant it to be the fireworks but since it was all in black it looked more like the cat scratches on our chimney after the sweep has been. Maud thought they were wonderful. Paul and I preferred watching the fireworks themselves. One thing Mr W was right about: they looked twice as good reflected in the dirty old Thames.

Maud stayed behind 'to grace the posing couch' as Paul put it, while we made our way back to his lodgings in Streatham, where we adopted our own version of the posing couch. I must stop doing that. It is very nice though certainly not proper. Mother would be furious if she found out and would call me all sorts of names. Yet it is so very nice and Paul does it so well and tells me so many nice things and calls me so many lovely names.

# Paris

## *Winter 1874*

Theo and Vincent are both the worse for wear. After two weeks sketching and painting at Scheveningen on the Dutch coast, they arrived in Paris late yesterday. The more respectable bars and places of amusement had already closed. Nevertheless, the two brothers found plenty of the lower sort to amuse them until the early hours. Although the gallery does not open its doors until midday, they still find considerable difficulty in presenting themselves on time and suitably attired.

They have taken lodgings in a student area so far untouched by Baron Haussmann's rebuilding schemes. Vincent rationalises this choice by pointing to the number of artists who also live in the area. These are not the sort of artists who would ever be permitted to cross the portals of the Goupil gallery. Despite this the brothers relish their conversation and the repartee in the bars and cafés Followers of Gustave Moreau attack proponents of Manet for his lack of colour and decoration. Bougereau and Watteau are dirty words here, pandering to bourgeois sentimentality. Vincent's championship of Corot and Millais is roundly challenged, even by those who have pretensions to exhibit in the official salons. "Why doesn't Millais just write sermons? Corot's landscapes may exist somewhere in the Jura or in his head but not within a hundred kilometres of Paris!" Vincent is strong in their defence: the quality of tone, composition and brushwork in Corot, the moral certainty of Millais and his empathy for the poor peasantry. As usual, neither side is moved or convinced. Debate continues until early morning or until the bar owner gets fed up, ejects his noisy clientele and puts up his shutters.

This first morning, Theo is directed to the stock room where Vincent is to instruct him on the prints and paintings that they contain. Both are well versed in contemporary Dutch painters and French art of earlier in the century. Living French painters are a different matter, there are so many to choose from. Chardin, of course; what of Perroneau or Beraud or even Edouard Detaille? Account books are consulted for prices and past sales. Some artists fall into, and then out of, favour. Their prices remain on hold. Their paintings cannot be sold for less for fear of alienating previous buyers, so that the paintings moulder for months or even years among the stacks in the stock room. Other paintings, usually by dead artists, are held back to increase their rarity value. Only now after a gap of fifteen years have the three Turner landscapes begun to be shown to clients, alongside a couple of paintings of the Basque coast by an American follower of his.

Despite the urgings of Monsieur Tersteeg, the brothers spend an inordinate amount of time discussing the merits of the various painters and proposing ones who should be included. Theo is all for Israels who he regards as a thoroughly modern and 'elegant and delightful' artist, as well as a captivating person. Vincent has stumbled across Monticelli, an artist from Marseilles who he claims to be a supreme colourist. Again, neither can convince the other, leaving them to agree on Delaroche and Gérôme (Ingres having been rejected as a government slave who should be left with his *seraglios*). By the end of the day, they have worked through most of the stock and conquered the worst of their respective hangovers.

After their early excesses the days and nights settle down to a steady routine. Though alcohol remains a central part of their diet it is taken in more moderate quantities, allowing the brothers to be both bright and becomingly servile with the gallery's clients. Gradually Theo replaces Vincent as the face of the company, while his older brother makes the rounds of various artists' studios, particularly the artists who had participated in this year's independent exhibition sneeringly referred to by one critic as 'Impressionists'. Vincent's preference is for the leader of the group, one Edouard Manet, who he regards as the most serious, and for Mary Cassatt, who he finds the most delicate. On a more commercial level, he finds an interesting source in Monsieur de Gas' lighter works and takes several of them on consignment for the firm, his application to purchase them outright having been refused by his superiors.

Theo is finding his new profession most congenial. Day in day out he is meeting the cream of French society. Unlike in London the Parisian aristocracy regard an interest in the arts as a divine duty, even if they are no more likely to part with hard cash. Paradoxically British visitors are more extravagant and less conventional. A radical art purchase has become a badge of sophistication for the young, titled Victorian gentleman in the same way that the acquisition of sub-standard fake Venetian renaissance art had been for their Georgian grandfathers. Some of these visitors even know Theo by name, so that it is no surprise when he is told that an English 'milor' is asking for him. Both parties are confused at the meeting. The strongly built Duke ('portly' if one is being less polite) is obviously expecting someone else. Theo has never met his grace before. Some twenty minutes' conversation ensues, by the conclusion of which the Duke of Lancaster is pleased to instruct Theo to convey his compliments to Mr Vincent van Gogh. With that the Duke wishes him 'good day' and strolls off along the boulevard, followed by the stares and whispers of the passers-by.

Consequently another encounter two days later comes as no surprise to Theo. An elegantly dressed lady stands in the middle of the gallery demanding to see 'that lick-spittle van Gogh'. Theo has no idea what a 'lick-spittle' might be, though the word is evidently not meant to be complimentary. "Where's that horrible carrot head? He's hiding my Eddie from me, just like he did in London. I'll tear his eyes out if he is at it again. Where is he, the cowardly rabbit?"

Theo introduces himself, to be met with shouts of incredulity. "Why are you trying to pass me off with this child? He's not the one. Have you a production line of fake van Goghs waiting to mislead and betray a poor wronged woman? I know he's here. They told me in

London. He's here and keeping my Eddie from me. I demand you bring him here to me this minute."

Monsieur Obach, the general manager, is called. He tries to pacify the irate woman, with no success. "Mienjeer van Gogh the elder is not here. He is visiting an artist's studio. He will be here later in the week, should Madam care to call." Madam will have none of this. She shouts even louder, demands that Vincent should be sent for, waving her umbrella as though she means to thrash both Theo and Obach into submission. At the height of her tantrum the flailing umbrella catches a Japanese vase, which is in pieces even before it shatters on the floor. Undeterred she continues to vent her temper on the glass of a Turner watercolour on the rear wall. At this point a *gendarme* forces his way through the small crowd that has gathered outside to watch the performance within. Before he can attempt restraint or even speak he is pushed aside by a veritable Amazon, possibly a female weight lifter or wrestler (should such perversions actually exist).

"Come now, Susan, we'll have none of this. You know how it upsets you. These gentlemen will report this to your husband if you are not careful. He will take away all your privileges. How would you like it if you couldn't see your baby again or walk out in the grounds? Come now, it is time to calm down and go back to the hotel." This last is accompanied by the clasping of massive hands upon Susan Pelham-Clinton's upper arms, rendering her immobile and causing her to lose her grip on the dangerous umbrella.

"The poor lady is not herself," explains the Amazon to Monsieur Obach. "She has had a difficult time with the birth of her child and her kind husband has been good enough to organise a restful stay for her in a residential home in Kent. For some reason she took it into her head to visit Paris, just took off on a ferry one evening. The exertion has been too much for her, poor thing. There, dear. We'll just take a Hansom back to the hotel. You can take some of your relaxing medicine and tomorrow we will take the boat train and get you back to England."

With this the pair push their way out through the crowd, leaving an abashed Monsieur Obach and a mystified *gendarme* who has been totally unable to follow the rapid cockney flavoured explanation since he knows not a word of English. Monsieur Obach explains to him that the lady is ill and that there is no need for him to take any action. To save face the *gendarme* disperses the spectators in his most forceful and officious manner.

Vincent has a typically male disdain for gossip. As a result his explanation of this event to Theo is totally unsatisfactory. He tells him that the lady is one that he has mentioned in his letters and that the relationship has obviously come to an unfortunate end, as such things do. Nor can Vincent elucidate further on the Duke of Lancaster. He has no recollection of such a personage and no idea why he might wish to pay his respects.

The mystery is solved a few days later towards the end of the afternoon when the two brothers are left guarding the empty gallery. Both Theo and Vincent recognise the current toast of Parisian society, the Princesse de Sagan and pay her due courtesy with the lowest of bows. Her portly companion is similarly known to both. "Your Grace," says Theo. "Your Royal Highness," says Vincent. "No, my dear van Gogh. In Paris I am the Duke of Lancaster and you must address me accordingly. I'm afraid that my poor Soo-Soo caused a bit of a to-do here recently. Poor thing, she has become somewhat unhinged since the child's birth and her husband has had to have her locked away in an asylum somewhere down in Kent. My Alix never really took to her and one can see why. Never mind, one is here to buy presents, my dear van Gogh and I know of no-one better to assist me."

The 'Duke's' friend Edward Langtry has announced his engagement to a Miss LeBreton, the daughter of the Dean of Jersey. A domestic present is in order. Nothing seems to suit until Vincent produces some of his latest acquisitions, the collection of pastels delivered on consignment from Monsieur de Gas. "Charming," proclaim both Duke and Princess in unison. Miss LeBreton would no doubt love one of the representations of ballet dancers at the *barre*, especially as she is reputed to be a great lover of the stage. Edward would also be happy with viewing so many under-dressed young women. However, this is to be Miss LeBreton's present; Edward requires something more personal. A view of the races is declared to be perfect, with the horses parading in the ring and the jockeys in their brilliant colours (including those of the Prince de Sagan and Monsieur Rothschild with whom the 'Duke' is to dine that evening), the horses delicate and excited in their pre-race anticipation. The Duke is so taken with this purchase that he chooses another, to be despatched to Lord Arthur Somerset, his racing manager, as a Christmas present; quite fitting in its way and one is certain that he would not be interested in paintings of nubile young women in tutus. "Wonderfully well observed," is the Duke's comment. "Wish this chap would come over to Ascot or Newmarket some time. Well done, van Gogh."

"Thank you, Your High…, Your Grace."

Vincent's gracious effusions of thanks are interrupted by the entrance of an elegant young man. Although nearer the Duke's age, his erect carriage and brisk manner allies him more with Vincent, with whom he is obviously acquainted. He and the 'Duke' stare at one another for some moments with that awkward social uncertainty when people know that they have met before but cannot put a time or a name to the occasion. Vincent is able to dispel the fog by making formal introductions. "Mr James Whistler, the Princesse de Sagan and His Grace, the Duke of Lancaster."

"Ah, Your Grace. I believe we have met a couple of times at the Gardens, although we were never formally introduced and you were sailing under different colours on those occasions."

"Whistler, yes. The painter chappie. Studio over the water in Chelsea, I believe. Lots of slash and dash they say. Never seen any of your stuff but my people are not very keen on it. That's no matter; they are almost as ignorant of painting as I am. If it weren't for young van Gogh here, I would be totally lost and splashing out on all sorts of rubbish. Still, delighted to meet you. Let me know if you have an exhibition in London and I'll be sure to drop in."

With an elegant bow, Mr Whistler shakes the two fingers proffered to him and in return delivers the Duke a calling card. "What's this? Oh, your address in Paris. Most amusing. Do look at this, my dear."

Leur rire avec la même gamme
Sonnera si tu te rendis
Chez Monsieur Whistler et Madame
Rue Antique du Bac 110

"It's a *jeu d'esprit* of a schoolteacher friend of mine," says Whistler. "He has a penchant for sending letters to his friends in rhyme and I thought it would be amusing to adopt it for my card."

"Not sure that Alix would go with that. Never mind. I bid you good day, gentlemen." The brothers bow the couple to the door, elated with a lucrative sale at the end of a dull winter's day, leaving Vincent to negotiate with Whistler about handling some of his prints in between trying to explain to Theo that the Prince had appeared so much more imposing on first encounter in London to invite comparisons to 'a Prussian guardsman'.

# Brixton

## *Winter 1875*

How dreary it is here! All of the commercials have gone home for Christmas and New Year. It is raining cats and dogs outside and I haven't seen Paul for over two weeks. Mother is in a strop because there is no money coming in and even Grandpa hasn't been around for ages. Rheumatism, he says. I just think he doesn't want Mother moaning at him all of the time. He'd rather be down the pub playing dominoes with his mates.

Then, my bosoms are getting sore. They seem to be growing again. Paul says it is quite normal to have a growth spurt at my age and that a certain amount of stroking might have helped this along. Not to mention some kissing, pinching and nibbling! There I go, getting all red and flushed again. Anyway they are certainly getting bigger. I've not been able to squeeze into the dress from Paul for weeks. Maud is delighted with that. She has been pestering me to lend it to her for a painting Mr W wants to do of her. He seems to like girls in white dresses; there was a painting of one on an easel when we were there that time with Paul and Maud. I suppose that I will have to lend it to her now that I can't get into it.

I wish I knew where Paul is. I've tried writing to him at his company but I've not had a reply. He did say that he would be very busy at this time of the year and that he would have to take on a colleague's area as well as his own, the colleague having been taken sick. I do miss him, though. I wish he would write. Perhaps he has written and Mother has hidden the letters from me? Just the sort of thing she would do. Not that I could come right out and ask her in case he hasn't written. She would want to know why he would be writing to me. I know, I'll just ask her if I've had any letters. After all, following his declaration Mr van Gogh might well have written, mightn't he?

Maud is just as bored as I am. Mr W is away in Paris with that posh sharp-faced wife of his and he has spoiled her for any of her usual casuals. Like me she is missing her time on the 'posing couch'. She is right. Once you get a taste for it, it is very difficult to give it up. We reassure ourselves that it will only be a short time before our men return. We did try and cheer ourselves up on a dry day last week with a visit to the Gardens. There was a juggler there who was quite interesting but it was rather cold and windy so we kept on the move. Some men bothered us a bit until Maud gave them the sharp end of her tongue and they soon moved on. Then an old gentleman of about sixty accosted us and harangued us about our sinful lives and how we should turn from the paths of wickedness before we were led to eternal damnation. He was near as frightening as the Reverend Slade-Jones. He was a slight man of about moderate height, a bit unsteady on his feet. Looked rather worn down with great lines on his face. Thin lipped, looked half dead. We tried to explain to him that we are not those sorts of women but he wouldn't listen to us, just raised his voice higher and higher. It was so embarrassing! The men that Maud had shooed away stood over by some bushes laughing their silly heads off. In the end he thrust pamphlets into our hands and took off. What a to-do!

At least it wasn't boring. Me and Maud had a good laugh over it later. My, I'm hungry. I always seem to be hungry at the moment. The amount of cheese I've eaten in the last week or so. Obviously the growing bosoms need feeding up. Then I think I'll write Paul another letter and tell him about the old gentleman at the Gardens.

# Paris

## *January 1875*

*Dear Mrs Loyer*

*Now that my brother Theo has been fully inducted into Goupil's business in Paris, I will be transferred back to London later this month. I will therefore need some lodgings for the foreseeable future, my engagement with the company having been confirmed.*

*In the past I have found your establishment to be ideal for my needs, being most convenient and exceptionally comfortable. There is nothing in Paris that can compare in terms of comfort and a general welcoming feeling. Please let me know that you will be happy to accept me on the same terms as those pertaining to last year.*

*Your humble servant*
*Vincent van Gogh*

# Brixton

## *January 1875*

*Dear Mr van Gogh*

*Thank you for your recent letter, which took some time arriving due to the recent storms in the Channel.*

*As it happens your old room is still vacant, although it was occupied off and on over the autumn. I will have it swept and tidied before you arrive. I assume that the same arrangements will apply as last year: that the company will pay me direct each week, one week in advance. I should like to mention that I expect no renewal of your attentions to my daughter. All of that will be treated by all parties as if it has never been.*

*Cordially yours*

*Ruth Loyer (Mrs)*

# Paris

## Spring 1875

*Dear Vincent*

*You remember you brought in a landscape by that creole, Pissarro? And I told you that it was completely unsaleable? Well, I've sold it! To a stockbroker. He fancies himself as a collector and an expert on the new modern painting, knows all of the artists around Manet. Fancies himself as a painter as well. Typical middle class Sunday painter. I found him quite intolerable. He went on for over an hour about how Pissarro's brushwork is superior to Monet's and why landscape painting is inferior to portraits because it is merely recording what the eye sees with no soul or passion. Just the sort of argument that you would use and just as wrong headed, but at what length! Still, he paid cash on the nail, which is more than some of your aristocratic types do and I have a feeling that he will be back. I'll have to hunt out some more paintings by Pissarro and perhaps even a Sisley or two, though they say that Sisley only paints half a dozen canvases a year because he can't afford the paint or the canvas.*

*Anyway, this chap is called Paul Gauguin. He has the face of a prize fighter, with a nose that can't decide in which direction it was broken last. Perhaps it is just trying to keep in touch with his eyes, which have a strange cast to them and are the shiftiest pair I've ever seen. Worse even than that innkeeper who tried to cheat us that time in Scheveningen. Gaugin also has a huge protruding square jaw like the prow of an inland bargee. That's it! He really looks like a bargee who has been in too many brawls. I'll be as polite to him as I can and nod every now and then as he drones on about art representing the infinite. He's not someone I would trust with either my money or my sister.*

*Speaking of whom, Anna wants to come to England to improve her English and to find work. To be honest I think she wants to do anything that will get her away from Mother and Father for a while. No doubt she also thinks that she might find herself a nice English husband. She is certainly good looking and a wonderful housewife, though perhaps she is not forward enough or exciting in her conversation for most men. I wish I could find someone like her, kind and thoughtful, the sort of woman who would spoil you like a mother, amuse you like your best friend and keep you snug and warm in bed.*

*From which you can probably tell that I am infinitely dull and lonely since you went away. I am drunk no more than one night in three and have only visited the ladies at the house once in all that time. Even the bordello is no fun on your own. Never mind, I shall endeavour to make friends in this town like you have in London.*

*The Duke has been in a couple of times since you left but hasn't bought anything. He seems to use the gallery as a place of assignation to meet ladies who may be otherwise engaged. I rather like him. He's not pretentious like that Gaugin chap, quite happy to admit that most art leaves him cold; he'll only buy as presents for friends or if something really excites him. I've not seen either the Princess or the mad English lady. Whenever the Duke is here it is with a different lady. His taste is quite eclectic and he is certainly no snob when it comes to his choice of women. What do you say if I introduce him to Lautrec? They would make a wonderful pair and heaven knows what women they would end up with! Don't suppose it will ever happen, but it is a wonderful thought to amuse*

*your sad and desolate brother*
*Theo*

# Brixton

## *Spring 1875*

"Come in here, Miss. I want a word with you."

*Oh dear,* thinks Eugenie. *Mother is in one of her strops again.*

And indeed Ruth is in full strop. Her face is fiery, her figure seemingly swelled to twice its normal size, hands on hips, a bulldog about to take on a lion.

"I've got a bone to pick with you, young lady. What do you call this?"

"A book, Mother."

"Don't you dare to 'Mother' me! Less of your cheek. I'll have the hide off you as soon as look at you, big though you are. What are you doing with this book?" She holds out a copy of *Out of the Depths.* "Do you know what this is?"

"Dunno, haven't read it. Some old gentleman gave it to me."

"And where might you be that some kindly old gentleman forces such a book on you?"

"Just out walking in the park. With Maud."

"And what park might that be?"

"Well…"

"Come on, girl, answer me. It was no park round here, I'll be bound."

"Well, no." Long pause. "Actually it was at the Gardens."

"And which gardens are they? Ah, I know. That would be the Cremorne Gardens, would it not?"

"Yes Mother, I suppose it would."

"There's no 'suppose' about it! So you and Maud were just strolling along arm in arm, the first time you had ever been there?"

"Well, we were. Not doing no harm to nobody. When this old gent comes rushing up to us, gives us a lecture about mending our ways and returning to the paths of righteousness. Then he pushes this here book into my hands and rushes off."

"And I suppose you do nothing to arouse this old gentleman, never having been there before, never mind in male company! No flashy clothes? No flirting with young men? No saucy looks at older ones? No making of assignations?"

"No, we don't do things like that. We just walk out together whilst Maud's gentleman is away abroad." (*Whoops! Let the cat out of the bag that we'd been there before. Nearly mentioned Paul there as well. A good job I've lent that dress to Maud already, so she can't find it if she goes ferreting around in my things.*)

"So why should he take you for a pair of prossies on the prowl? This is one of the books that them do-gooders hand out to prossies in the gardens. You must have been doing something. Or just looking the part?"

Eugenie makes protestations of injured innocence. Can't two respectable girls take a walk together without some old man with a dirty mind thinking the worst of them?

Ruth is not ameliorated. She is growing ever larger and redder. "So you are oh so respectable, are you? Would you care to tell me when you are expecting your next visitor?"

Eugenie is puzzled at first by her mother's euphemism, despite the fact that she has heard it before many times, her mind being fixed on the possibility of Paul's return. "You mean my period?"

"Exactly. Or have you been cavorting around Cremorne Gardens with a red camellia in your hair?"

"Well, you know I'm not particularly regular. It could be any day now."

"Is that this month's, last month's or even the month before that?"

"Have you been spying on me?"

"Who do you think does the washing around here? Who washes your rags for you while you are out flaunting yourself in public, baring your fat arse for all and sundry? I don't know why you bother wearing those fancy lace-edged drawers of yours, you seem to have been whipping them off quickly enough."

"Oh, Mother, it's not like that. It's just Paul. And we're engaged. He's going to marry me as soon as he gets his new company orders."

"You are engaged when I tell you that you are engaged! What Paul is this? I'll have his eyes out and his ears off not to mention his privates, except that he's done enough damage with them already."

"You know Paul, Mother. Paul Cunningham. From Oldham. He..."

"Yes, him. Used to stay here. Not seen him for months. Not since he got wind of your condition, I dare say. Done a moonlight. You won't see him again, my girl."

Ruth's assertion confirms a fear that had been steadily growing in Eugenie's mind for some weeks. Her defences collapse. She deliquesces into a sobbing bundle, her head in Ruth's lap. Ruth's anger transmogrifies into maternal compassion, though not without its stern edge. An hour of tut-tutting and hair stroking follows, before both women are composed enough to talk rationally about what is to be done.

"I shall write to his company," says Ruth. "Tell them about what he has done and shame him into marrying you. It would serve you right, marrying a commercial but never mind, it's the best that can be done. We could sue him for breach of promise."

"I've tried writing to him several times," sobs Eugenie. "The letters keep coming back with 'not known at this address' on them. I think he must have someone sending back anything he gets from here. You know we can't go to law. We would just get cheated, them lawyers would take our money and we'd never get anywhere."

"Right, so I'd better get on to old Mrs Roberts, see what she can do."

"That dirty old witch. Not on your life. I'm not having her poking around my insides, sticking her used knitting needles up me or poisoning me with her homemade gin. I'd rather die."

"If your father were here he would most likely have beaten you to death for what you have done. I've a mind to give you a good thrashing myself. Well, bad temper won't get the baby a new frock. The only solution if you can't be wed or won't try and get rid of it is for you to take a long holiday, five or six months it looks like. I'll talk to your grandfather, see if he still has people he knows up in Lincolnshire. You can stay with them until it is born, get someone to take it in, then come back here as if nothing has happened."

"Oh, no! I'll be stuck away among the cabbages and all those yokels and pikies. No-one to talk to and nowhere to go. Impossible."

"Very possible. The only choice you've got, my girl. You've made your bed, now you can lie on it, though you've been doing rather a lot of that of late. What cannot be cured must be endured."

Eugenie knows when she is beaten but continues to resist for some time, if only for form's sake. She also silently determines to send Paul one last letter in the hope that he will reappear to whisk her off, if only up north to Oldham.

# Tottenham, London

## *Spring 1875*

*Dear George*

　As you can see, I've now got a new patch up here in North London. I've got the whole lot north of the river, as far out as I care to go. If Tottenham is any measure the further north you go the worse it gets. As far as I'm concerned from now on I'll stick as close to the West End as I can, only coming out this far if I'm desperate for some extra orders.

　This is by way of a promotion for being such a dedicated and successful salesman south of the river. Actually I think it is a bribe. Whichever way, it puts a lot more shekels in my pocket. One drawback is that I have to make my own contacts. Old Ranyard was so furious at having been moved out that he refused to leave any names for me to pick up. Bastard! Still, you can't blame him, having been given the push for no reason after all these years.

　"So what's it a bribe for?" you might well ask. As you know, that dry old stick Murgatroyd has never married. No surprise; who would ever want to marry him, tight old sod? Consequently his heir is his sister's only child, Sarah. Now this Sarah is pretty sharp and more or less runs the business already. She can price up a dress just by looking at it for ten seconds and work out how to produce it cheaper inside ten minutes. As well as that she is in charge of the production line and rules those girls with a rod of iron. Nothing gets past her. Anyone even a minute late or too slow at the work is straight out of the door, no messing. Once she is completely in charge you see how much money that company will rake in. And for some unknown reason she is in love with me!

*"Now what's wrong with that?"* you say. First off I reckon she would turn out to be as much of a slave driver at home as she is at the mill. No smoking indoors or anywhere else if she had her way, and no coming in late after a couple of swift beers down at the Trowel and Hammer. *"Keep your feet off the chairs, don't disturb the antimacassars,"* you know the kind of thing. Rows with the domestics all the time, changing cooks every month and only the ugliest, most downtrodden maids, and even they won't stay for very long. For lots of cash and a pretty girl that would just about be bearable, but Sarah is so ugly! She has a figure like a factory chimney, straight up and down with nary a protrusion to be seen. A nose you could cut down trees with, lips so thin they look like razor blades, thin lank hair that never looks washed however hard she seems to try. She keeps it tied back so tight you'd think there is no hair there at all, just black paint. Oh, I forgot to say, she has a bad case of religion. Her idea of a good time is a Bible reading or a discussion on how to improve the morals of the poor. If introduced to a gentleman she will only shake his hand if she is wearing gloves, which she does most of the time to prevent anyone seeing her knobbly fingers. But as Murgatroyd's heir she will be richer than any posh duke or duchess in the whole of Lancashire. Once the old man dies and she starts squeezing the profits out of the mill and drives all the competition to the wall, she could end up as one of the richest women in the country and her husband could live in style, perhaps even get in to Parliament or end up with a title. Baron Cunningham of Oldham! Wouldn't that be a laugh!

The upshot is that I am engaged to the love-lorn Sarah, though even the thought of the money or the baronetcy was not enough to settle the question. Murgatroyd was the one who clinched it in the end. He said I had a choice: propose to the girl and have the whole territory of North London or refuse and have the sack like Ranyard. Reckon I can put off the wedding for a year or two 'while I get myself established', in which time I can have a grand old time on the extra commission. No need to tell any of these cockney lasses that I am engaged, is there?

To some extent I'm sorry to leave South London and Brixton in particular. Miss Eugenie was quite delightful but the time had come to bail out of that particular vessel. After the first couple of times she had come to enjoy our little cuddles, so much so that I could hardly get in the door without her ripping the clothes off me. And she was so careless! I tried to get her to use the old whore's trick of a bit of sponge with vinegar on it. She was always in too much of a hurry. Nor would she bother with a douche either. Desperate to get at it again. No doubt you can guess the result. Even I can count to twenty-eight and when one gets as far as fifty-six, there you can be pretty certain. So I did a runner. She wrote to me of course but I gave the clerk a shilling a letter to send them back marked 'not known at this address'. No point in reading them and getting all upset, is there?

Well, I don't think that we will be meeting up again for some time. I'm going to set myself up with some little place of my own down here so that I don't have any nosey landlady poking around or checking on who comes and goes. Of course it is all for the good of the company, so that I can sell six days a week and not have any expenses going back and forth to Oldham. My fiancée should be delighted that I am working so hard in her interest. Just to keep me company perhaps you could come down some time. We could have a grand old time and I know just the place where we could go for some light entertainment.

Your soon-to-be-married and soon-to-be-rich friend
'Baron' Paul Cunningham of Oldham

# Brixton

## *Spring 1875*

### *The White Horse*

"Vince, you look terrible. What have you been doing over in Paris? Wild nights of wine, women and song?"

"Some of that, but mainly looking after my little brother, stopping him getting into too many scrapes. Then you don't look too grand yourself. How is Lizzie? How is the new baby?"

"Not baby, but babies. Two on 'em. Twins, as if we didn't have enough already. It was noisy enough at home before. Now it is total chaos. Lizzie has her hands full, what with the two little 'uns and all. Washing everywhere. Not a hot meal or a drop of porter in sight. All six of us crammed into two rooms and lucky to have that much. No time and no money. This is the first I've been in here in six weeks. Good to get out of the house. I'll be sleeping in here next; the only place I can get some peace and quiet without kids bawling at me and Lizzie fussing and shouting. I've told you before, Vince: once kids start arriving everything else goes out of the window. Your life is never your own."

"All the same, you know you love them dearly. I've seen you playing with them, letting them climb all over you. The more the merrier it seems to me." Vincent is silently contrasting this with his own home life, spoilt by his adoring mother and whipped into line by his severe and censorious father, where each new child wore down his mother's enthusiasm and deepened his father's gloom.

"Yes, but they are a tie." Harry sips gently at his pint, making it last as long as he can. "Still, I manage to get out to the life class down at Borough Road every week. It's quite a relief. No boss, no customers, no wife, no kids. All on me own with just a sheet of paper. What do you reckon?"

Harry has splashed out on a proper folder and some paper from an art shop. Not the best quality but far better than the sandwich wrappings Vincent was shown the last time. "Hey, isn't that…"

"Seamus! Yes it is. I must be improving if you recognised him straight away. They had this strip of a man before, no bigger than a pipe cleaner and twice as hairy. They wanted someone with more meat on him, a bit of muscle, you know?"

"I don't think much of that one." Seamus has shambled over from the bar. "It makes me dick look tiny."

"Don't you remember how cold it was that night, Seamus? Half of us were wearing gloves and there you were in the buff. Your goose pimples were bigger than your dick that night."

"Yes, I guess so, but don't show it round the ladies' class, will you?"

"Do you pose for the ladies as well?" Vincent is rather shocked, though he can't say why.

"Yes, they want a real man in front of them. I have to wear this posing pouch though, in case it frightens them. Irritating old thing it is, too. Really digs into your crotch with them strings. Much better without one for the fellers but not so interesting to look at, if you know what I mean?"

Quite what the genteel ladies of Borough Road Art School make of broken-down bruiser Seamus does not bear thinking of. *Too much damn art around here*, thinks Vincent viciously. Despite that, he steels himself to study Harry's work and prepares to make as many bland comments as possible. To his surprise he no longer needs the bland comments. Harry is no Velásquez or Tintoretto even so he is turning into a competent draughtsman. The pencil drawings are precise with careful proportions and a modicum of cross-hatch shading in the approved academic manner. More interesting are a series of charcoal sketches that seem to have been made with the side of the stick rather than the tip.

"I do them in the break," says Harry, a trifle defensively. "Just as a bit of fun. Makes the figure look a lot more solid. Like sometimes in the dark you see someone walking along. They just look like a lump, not a person at all. Those pencil things are too light, unreal, so..."

"Ethereal?" suggests Vincent.

"Yes, I guess so. Ethereal, that's a good word. Prissy is what I'd say. Anyway it's good to play around a bit without having to worry about the size of Seamus's dick all the time. And you can add in extra shapes to give a full picture. They don't have to be real shapes just suggestions, so you have something happening over the whole of the paper not just a figure in the middle."

Vincent is not convinced. This way points to a mad nothingness, filling the page for the sake of it, a child's scribble. Perhaps it is a stage that all amateurs have to go through? A way of creating a composition before they have the technical ability or the intellectual grasp to encompass a whole scene?

The silence does not worry Harry at all; he is too far gone in his ideas of what the drawings might lead to if only he had the time and the skills. He recovers from his brief reverie in time to remember his manners and his duties as a drinking companion. The porter delivered, he returns to the subject of Vincent's absence.

"So, go on, tell us, what were you were doing over there?"

"Not a lot. Lots of talking and drinking in bars. Not a lot different to here, is it? Sold some paintings. Went to a lot of studios and exhibitions. Oh, and I met this American painter with a funny name, Whistler, who says he lives down in Chelsea somewhere. He's coming to the gallery next week with some of his stuff. You might like to meet him; he's also got funny ideas about just catching the essence of a scene rather than bothering too much about the detail. Likes to dissolve his figures into the background until you can't tell where they end and the background begins. He said he was going to start a new painting of 'white on white' when he gets back to London. Can't imagine what he means by that. A snow scene, I suppose. Not that the snow in London stays white for very long."

Vincent takes a long draw of his pipe, which he has begun to affect recently. "My sister is coming over soon. She's trying to find a job as a governess, though I think she might find that difficult. I've fixed for her to stay at Mrs Loyer's for a while, though I'm not sure that she'll stick it there."

"Why? She's no more of a tight-fisted old faggot than she ever was, is she?" Seamus, who is still sitting at their table in the hope of acquiring another pint of porter, nods in agreement having once or twice been on the sharp end of Ruth's tongue.

"It's not that so much, it's just that the whole atmosphere in the house has changed. Before it was sharp but efficient. Now it just feels gloomy, as if everyone is on a knife edge waiting to bite one another as soon as look at them. I just hope I'm not there when the explosion happens. Then there's the problem with Miss Eugenie. You know she turned me down? Well, that has caused all sorts of embarrassment; we can hardly speak to one another and most of the time she just pretends I'm not there, while I can't look at her for more than a few seconds in case she thinks I'm staring at her."

"I have a feeling that you are still sweet on that girl."

"Well, you don't change over night. I know I was angry when she turned me down with her 'No, not ever' but I still felt the same for her. No doubt it was her mother who put her up to it. She has never liked me. Not keen on foreigners, I expect. Perhaps I'll forget it all. Go back to Holland and become a priest. My father would sponsor me. I could take the Word out to the poor and the dispossessed or even become a missionary."

"You don't need to go out to Holland or to the fuzzy-wuzzies to find the poor and the dispossessed. Try the East End, or even Camberwell if you want the rough end of the stick. Listen, Vince. Don't let all this get you down. It's not like you to be put off so easily. Here you are at work, bringing over artists no-one has ever heard of with weird ideas, even stranger than mine, and getting people to buy them despite the snide comments in the newspapers that you tell me about. If you want the girl just go back and try again. Don't take no for an answer. So what if she says she's engaged! How many engagements get broken, or would be if the couple had the guts to tell one another that they have changed their mind? You just get in there and try again. What have you got to lose?"

"Well, my dignity."

"Dignity? Bugger that! When did dignity put food on your plate or a woman in your bed? Persistence is the thing. Ask her at least once a week so she knows you are serious and still interested. Then if anything happens she'll know that it's you she can rely on."

Vincent is not convinced but it's his round so that the topic lapses while he makes his way to the bar. The rest of the evening is spent on Seamus's housing difficulties, the woman he is living with making noises that perhaps he should pay her some rent or make other arrangements. None of the three have had a good week. A good job that you can still get a tasty drop of porter at the White Horse.

*Southampton Row, London*

# Brixton

## *Spring 1875*

Every day for sixteen days Vincent pays his addresses to Eugenie, politely asking her to marry him. Not with any effusions of devotion but in a simple, humble manner. Every day for sixteen days Eugenie shakes her head and turns away. Not a word said. By day seventeen the proposal has become a ritual, so much so that Vincent has ceased to expect any response. All he anticipates is that dreaded 'No, never. Not ever'. Instead Eugenie bursts into tears. "I'm going away," she cries and disappears into the kitchen, only managing the crocks on her tray with the greatest difficulty.

Vincent is mystified. What does this sudden confidence mean? Why should the girl be going away? Major Havard is not much help. He nods, winks and insinuates with much reference to 'happy events' and 'friends up north', leaving Vincent flustered by this combination of English reticence and obscure allusions. What is required is a straight answer from an informed source. Someone who will not 'beat about the bush', or, as his parson father would put it, 'someone who would look you straight in the eye and tell you the gospel truth'. If Eugenie will not do this herself then he must have recourse to the acerbic tongue of her mother.

Little has been well in the Loyer household of late. Ruth's father has asked for time before he can finally arrange a safe haven in Lincolnshire for Eugenie. A family in Woodhall Spa has been mentioned but communications with them are proving both difficult and delicate. A large sum of money has been mooted, which has complicated matters. With the affair dragging on Ruth is increasingly

115

anxious that Eugenie's condition cannot long be hidden from the neighbours or from the paying guests. Her frustration has turned to anger. Her father, daughter and even at times the commercials are subjected to the sharp edge of her bitter tongue. Everyone at Hackford Road creeps about as if treading on particularly thin eggshells. Into this cauldron steps Vincent, sustained only by an evening reading John Bunyan, steadying himself by visions of becoming Mr Strong-in-his-Faith.

Stubborn, if not overly strong, Vincent eschews all elaboration and immediately demands to know the situation with Eugenie. He still wishes to marry her. Is she engaged or not? Why is she going away? Is it to go north to be married? If so, why is she so obviously upset?

Normally Ruth would have turned aside such impertinent enquiries with one of her withering tirades. Now after weeks of having to contain herself, she is ready with the full story, complete with commentary. The stupid naive girl betrayed by an evil seducer, a Lothario from Manchester. Taken in by empty promises, left alone, abandoned and with child. A typical commercial's trick. Damn them all. So Ruth will be left all alone to manage the house. Then the brat to look after if no-one will take it in. More than a poor respectable woman can bear. Men. All the same. Lead you on and then cast you aside. A good job poor dear George is not here to see it.

Now that the dam has burst, Ruth is impossible to stop. Vincent sits for over an hour as the flood of her invective sweeps over him. Only the arrival of the 'daily' stems the flow, allowing Vincent to rush off to the station to catch his train for work.

Fortunately the day is a particularly busy one, beginning with a young lady of quality attempting to sell her watercolours. With the death of her husband she has fallen upon hard times. Receiving no assistance from either her own or her late husband's family she is selling what she can in order to support herself and her children. Vincent is unable to help. Middle class homes are full to the rafters of the genteel watercolours of their daughters whose education has taught them to sew and paint and play the piano, with only mediocre results. The lady

116

will need to try another profession before she finally falls into destitution or worse. Much as he would like to help, Vincent knows that the situation is commercially impossible. A woman on her own with a child has little chance of even the most menial post as a maid or kitchen skivvy. All she has to sell on the open market is herself.

Almost immediately his time is taken up by a young couple who are looking for a centrepiece for the living room of their new house. The husband, inspired he claims by years of learning Horace and Virgil at school, wishes to purchase a Roman scene full of young ladies in the baths, either covered by nothing at all or by the flimsiest of transparent wraps. His wife is horrified. What will visitors think? More importantly, what will her mother think? This may be appropriate for a single gentleman's bedroom but not for public display. She is much more taken by an improving scene by Rossetti or even Holman Hunt (though the latter is somewhat dreary in colour in comparison). The discussion and viewing of appropriate paintings takes over two hours before the couple leave unsatisfied. Only for them to reappear later in the afternoon and finally settle on a Burne-Jones painting of lithe young ladies (this time fully dressed) posing as angels or souls ascending to heaven, the subject fitting both the husband's appreciation of the female form and the wife's aspirations for an improving moral subject.

A collection of gay young things invade the gallery. Despite it being obvious that they are there purely for a social event, to gossip and flirt with one another, it is still necessary to attend to their requirements. Prints and paintings are brought up from the storeroom, to be dismissed as too boring or to be giggled over in mock moral horror. Despite the best attentions of Vincent and the rest of the gallery staff, no sale is made and the rest of the day is spent returning the stock to its proper place in the basement and elsewhere, leading to a particularly late finish.

Finally, in the dark of a winter's night Vincent is able to sit on his train home and think about the revelations in Brixton. Coming out of the railway arches his head is still spinning. He sets off along Coldharbour Lane in the opposite direction to his lodgings. By the time he reaches Camberwell Green he at least has the situation clear in his mind. He cuts back to Stockwell through a maze of backstreets replete with dirty children and noisy dogs. Cold and hungry, he does not return to Hackford Road until nearly midnight, his head completely befugged by the tobacco fumes from his pipe which he has been compulsively smoking and refilling for the last three hours. Ruth opens the front door to him, furious that she has been kept awake until this late hour by a tenant who has no doubt been drowning himself in cheap gin at some low drinking den. One look at Vincent stills the recriminations in her throat. This is a man of black brow who is, if anything, far too sober for his own good. Not a word is spoken. Vincent takes himself upstairs to collapse into a dreamless sleep.

*Streatham Hill*

# Brixton, London

## *Spring 1875*

*Dearest Mother and Father*

*As you can see I have arrived safely in England. The journey here was even worse than I had expected. The captain of the ferry had decided not to sail because the weather was so bad. The owners, concerned that they would be losing money if the ship did not sail, forced him into it. Several passengers removed their luggage and declared that the crossing was unsafe. There followed an almighty row on the quayside as those passengers demanded their money back and the ferry owners refused. If the police had not intervened they could well have come to blows. At one point in the crossing I felt that the captain and those passengers had been right and we were all going to drown. I have never been so ill in my life. As it was we arrived at Margate eight hours late. The port master had to send out two steam tugs to tow us in or we would still be standing off the port waiting for the waves to subside.*

*I was delighted to find that Vincent was there to meet me. He was very anxious by that time, having arrived early so that we did not miss one another. Fortunately the train journey into London was smooth and uneventful, allowing my stomach to recover its equilibrium and me to regain my land legs.*

*Brixton is a very pleasant suburb on the edge of London with several roads of impressive houses and others of well built terraces that house the numerous working people. There are lots of trees and parks giving an impression of a small country town. Vincent says that there was even a small village stream but that has now been hidden underground and incorporated into the sewage system. Not as romantic, although it no doubt greatly adds to the health of the local inhabitants. Hackford Road is one of the newer streets in the village housing a good class of people. Our landlady, Mrs Loyer, says that they were all built by her husband, a noted local builder who died young in an accident when working on one of London's cathedrals.*

*Mrs Loyer herself is a sharp business-like woman. She is very parsimonious and keeps the house spotlessly clean and makes sure that her lodgers respect both the house and one another. I have a pleasant room with a bed, a small wardrobe and a washstand. This is much larger than the one Vincent enjoys. I suspect he has arranged it for me specially and that he pays a little bit extra for it without telling me. As well as the commercial travellers who lodge here the other inhabitant is Mrs Loyer's daughter, Eugenie. She is a pretty girl rather in the Spanish manner, with curly dark hair and a full figure. Her features are good, not sharp like her mother's, though her skin has that typical English lardy look to it as if it is going to turn blotchy and melt as soon as the sun comes out. As far as character goes she seems willing to please. One feels that there is a happy and jolly person there as one would expect of a young lady of only seventeen years, but she appears somewhat downcast at present.*

*I have signed up with an agency in the Strand in order to find employment as a governess. They have already sent me for one interview where unfortunately I was not successful. I was under the impression that my French would be an advantage. Instead the family were most insistent that their children should learn German. The old Queen's late husband was German and the Prince of Wales is constantly visiting his German relatives, including the Kaiser himself, much to the chagrin of his Danish wife who hates the Prussians with a seething fury for their dismemberment of her native country. Still, the agency is optimistic that they can place me with a good family in the near future and I am happy to spend my time improving myself with visits to the leading cultural facilities that London offers. Eugenie has even offered to accompany me to some of them including to the*

*Cremorne Gardens, a favourite haunt of the Prince of Wales, and to the music hall. I'm not sure whether Father would approve of the latter, so I have put her off for the time being. She seems very anxious to have some company and tries as hard as she can to make a friend of me, something which I am quite happy to allow as I know no-one in London and can hardly explore on my own for fear of getting lost or of being taken for a loose woman.*

\*

*Exciting news! Vincent is engaged to be married!*

*This is to Eugenie, the daughter of his landlady, Mrs Loyer. I knew from Theo that he had asked her to marry him before he went away to Paris though she had refused him then. Obviously they have come to some sort of an arrangement since his return. However, I have to tell you that I believe that they may have anticipated their union by a few months, probably before he left London, and that this appears to be the reason for the young lady's change of heart. I will talk seriously to Vincent about this as I do not believe it to be the sort of behaviour that we should expect from him. Since Eugenie is so young it is in my heart to excuse her. Vincent too, for it is obvious that marriage was his objective at all times. He was wrong in allowing his enthusiasm to get out of hand and taking advantage of the girl. But then you know Vincent, always misled by his enthusiasms and getting himself into all sorts of scrapes. I just hope that this time he has landed on his feet.*

*Nevertheless, I shall take Father's part and find as much scripture as I can to show my brother that his conduct was contrary to the laws of God and man. I am certain that Saint Paul has much to say on the subject; all I can remember at the moment is that he declared 'it is better to marry than to burn', so perhaps Vincent has avoided hell fire by his tardy engagement. For propriety's sake the marriage itself will not be long delayed. I'm sure that it would give the young couple the greatest of pleasure if you could both be here for the wedding. Would Father be happy to officiate at the service, or at least deliver a homily*

121

or read the lesson? Although the church is only a wooden building the beliefs of the priest and of the congregation are in complete congruence with our own and Father would feel completely at home there, as would you, dear Mother.

I will write to you again as soon as I can. I will insist upon Vincent for him to tell you the happy news directly himself.

Your obedient daughter

Anna van Gogh

Hackford Road

# Brixton

## *Spring 1875*

*Dear Theo*

 *My mind is awhirl with theology when it should be full of joy at my impending marriage. Reading the Epistles, I find commended to me* **'faith, hope and charity'**. *Reverend Slade-Jones claims this is a mistranslation, where it should be* **'faith, hope and love'**. *I am insufficient of a scholar to decide. Our father seems to dismiss both versions in favour of a misanthropic reading of his own.*

 *Anna invited our parents to the wedding some time ago, at the same time letting slip that Eugenie is with child. Our father scolded me severely for what he termed my licentiousness, utilising the full force of his Biblical learning.* **'Shun youthful passions and aim at righteousness'**, *a quite impossible injunction to follow in one's youth as we both know so well. Even Saint Augustine fully indulged his youthful passions. I could almost hear Father shouting out his injunctions from the page as I read them:* **'Take a wife in holiness and honour, not in the passion of lust'**.

 *What could I do? I could hardly leave him in the belief that I had seduced a young virgin, so I had to confess to him, as I have done to you, that the child is not mine. The thunders of all the earth's volcanoes could not have overborne his vitriolic response! One would have thought that I had plucked a prostitute off the streets. Indeed he implied as much, insisting that I cancel the marriage and have no more to do with my poor Eugenie.* **"The body is not meant for immorality but for the Lord,"** *he wrote.* **"Your bodies are members of Christ. He who joins himself to a** *prostitute becomes one body with her. Your body is a temple of the Holy Spirit.*" Is that charity? Is that love? Father at his most censorious always quotes Saint Paul. Rather he should think of Jesus forgiving the sinner, taking Mary Magdalene into his band of followers. He should remember the ninety and nine that have not strayed and the feting of the sinner that returns to his father's table.

In my last letter to him I tried to reason with him. Even Saint Paul is prepared to forgive the sinner in true Christian spirit. "**If a man is overtaken in any trespass you who are spiritual should restore him in a spirit of gentleness, bear one another's burdens and so fulfil the law of Christ.**" This is the true spirit of forgiveness, of charity. As for love it will redeem us all. What I do for love I do also for the good of my own soul. It is written, "**Make love your aim and earnestly desire the spiritual gifts.**"

What response did I receive? A curt letter of three lines refusing to attend the wedding and refusing admission to his home of me, '**that harlot**' and all of our offspring '**conceived in sin and lust**'. As for his blessing he chooses to throw Saint Paul at me once again: "**Let the marriage bed be undefiled for God will judge the immoral and adulterers.**"

So there you have it. We are cast off, even to the third or fourth generation. Our father can find neither forgiveness, nor love, nor charity in his heart. We, my dear brother, must exercise them for him as much as we are able. Where we see evil we must practise goodness, where there is hate we will douse it with love, where there is backsliding through circumstances we must rescue it with charity. Remember that "**God has not destined us for wrath**".

Anna has said that she will meet you off the boat at Margate. She has conceived a great affection for the English railway system with its numerous curves, tunnels and viaducts. Her recent excursion to Harrogate to enquire about a position with an elderly lady has left her full of excitement for making another journey, if only into Kent.

*I have bought the rings and a new coat for the wedding. Eugenie is having a new dress made (let us hope that it is not already too small before it is finished). She and her mother are spending hours together refurbishing hats and old bonnets in the most modern style possible. To my surprise I am quite calm, especially if I do not allow myself to dwell upon our father's letters. More exciting even than the prospect of the wedding is the arrival of my best man and dearest brother. There is so much that we will have to talk about.*

*My Bible is my best companion for the moment. Reading the life of our saviour has allowed me to feel the certainty of redemption for us all, however hard the road may be. I have a new motto, which I will cleave to with all my strength:* **"Let love be genuine. Hate what is evil, hold fast to what is good. Do not be overcome with evil but overcome evil with good."**

Your dearest brother
in love and charity
Vincent

# Isleworth

## *19 April 1875*

"Brothers and sisters in Christ, we are gathered here today to witness the joining together in matrimony of our brother Vincent van Gogh and our sister Eugenie Loyer. This is one of the most joyful of all the duties that I have to perform, second only to the baptism of a soul into the family of Christ. It was only last year that brother Vincent stood in this very pulpit and proclaimed himself a pilgrim wending his difficult way towards the eternal city. We sat entranced by his words, determining too to join him on that difficult yet happy journey. We sang today those beautiful words of the hymn:

'there's no discouragement
will make him once relent
his first avowed intent
to be a pilgrim'

Marriage is an important step upon life's pilgrimage, where we take into our sole care another who has become dear to us, to love, hold and protect that person as is enjoined in the prayer book of another place 'in sickness and in health'. The blessed Saint Paul has much to say upon the matter of marriage."

Vincent and Theo exchange looks and quiet grunts.

"We all know his injunction to us to marry, the following of which differentiates us from the scarlet woman of Rome: 'the unmarried and the single... they should marry. For it is better to marry than to be aflame with passion'. Now here I differ from the saint. Let all who marry be aflame with passion! Let them be carried away with love and desire for their future partner in life, let love be uncontrolled."

Eugenie has turned a beetroot red. Ruth's look would turn holy water to vinegar. "Alleluia," shouts Joanna. "Za liubov, za liubov na boga." She is noticeably more disturbed than usual, her tongues more outrageous.

"Saint Paul enjoins wives to be obedient to their husbands, to love them in all things and to bow down their heads before them. This is well known; it is a commonplace of our society and the reason why we do not accept women into the spheres of trade and commerce." (Ruth 'humphs' gently in her seat.) "But there is more that he says on the question of marriage. He turns to the husband. He says to him: love your wife truly, shelter and protect her in all things, protect her from evil, for he says 'love bears all things, believes all things, hopes all things and endures all things'. Let us go forth in love of one another and of the word of the Holy Spirit."

"Alleluia slushi na dumata na Cristos."

"Now I say to Eugenie and Vincent as they embark upon the sea of matrimony that they should hold fast to one another, love one another. They should follow the good advice of the blessed Saint Paul: 'Be watchful, stand firm in your faith, be courageous, be strong. Let all that you do be done in love'.

Amen."

The small congregation is grateful for the brevity of the Reverend Slade-Jones' homily despite the embarrassment felt by some and the dispassionate cynicism of others. Eugenie is grateful that her time of nausea appears to have abated; to vomit in the middle of the ceremony would just be too much. Ruth remains stony faced especially after being reminded of her anomalous position as a woman of commerce in a man's world. Contrary to tradition she is not sniffling into her handkerchief but looking determinedly round at the others as if daring them to comment on Eugenie's obvious pregnancy. Joanna is dancing up and down in her best finery augmented by extra bows and ribbons for this festive occasion. She edges nearer to the front as the ceremony continues, her eyes fixed on Vincent whatever her gyrations.

Theo produces the rings. The words are spoken. The couple kisses for the first time.

Joanna rushes forward, embraces them both. "Amen. Alleluia I prophesied ou Van het redden voor God van de gevallenen Van het Woord verspreiden.

Hij kan verzwakken, de strijd opgeven, maar hij moet de zondaren verheffen, diegenen die gevallen zijn redden van het kwaad. Listen once more to the word of God. Fulfil your destiny. Alleluia Alleluia." Chanting her alleluias Joanna is led away out of the chapel by her friends leaving a dazed Vincent and a bewildered Eugenie.

Anna had thought of following the new fashion and engaging a photographer to capture the happy event but this had proved inhibitingly expensive. Instead the wedding party leave immediately for Brixton. Despite the chilly weather Vincent and Eugenie lead the way in an open carriage, its normal use as a fruiterer's cart disguised by swathes of crepe bunting and the draping of one of Ruth's third-best set of white sheets. Behind follows the rest of the family and friends, sitting knee to knee on the benches of Ruth's father's cart, similarly adorned and specially painted with the help of Harry Kirman for this wonderful event.

★

"Like a band of gypsies. And her so high and mighty passing herself off as lady muck and all the time she's just some pikey brat," grumbles one of the neighbours behind her twitching curtains as the wedding party arrives at Hackford Road. "At least Arthur will have some horse manure for his roses."

Despite its ordered appearance, the wedding reception for the guests has caused wide dissension in the household. Ruth had wanted bread and margarine with thin slices of ham washed down with bottled beer for the men and lemonade for the ladies. To her chagrin Ruth is unable to get her way in her own house for probably the first time; Anna and Eugenie have formed common cause to argue for a range of meats and pies. Eugenie is happy with lemonade but Anna has shyly produced a bottle of the best *genever* from her luggage, originally intended to celebrate gaining her first position or else her dreamt-of engagement and marriage. Theo trumps her with a litre bottle of green absinthe. Unaware of the imminence of these two treats, Harry and Vincent have made their own arrangements: jugs of draught porter brought over from the White Horse by Seamus who stays for the rest of the afternoon to drink most of it in the company of Ruth's father.

The old man himself is delighted at the idea of becoming a great grandfather and happily trades his tales of an itinerant carter's life in Lincolnshire with Seamus's reminiscences of the fairgrounds of England and Ireland. "A great life," they both agree. "Plenty of *craic*, plenty of beer and plenty of girls." Harry listens quietly to them for a while before tipsily asking: "Isn't Ireland just rain and potatoes and Lincolnshire just fens and cabbages?" Seamus, used to such ignorance, merely turns up his eyes in disgust. Ruth's father is more militant in the defence of his homeland. "You're a typical southerner, you are. Nothing exists for you north of the Thames, even Tottenham is beyond the reach of the civilised world. There's chalk hills up in Lincolnshire, just like the South Downs here. And there's Lincoln up on the heights, what used to be one of the most important cities in the land. We was ruled from there when King Richard went off to the Crusades. I'm told there's a bright new town called Scunthorpe where they've discovered iron ore. They say it will be rich and famous in no time. But for me the real jewel is Grimsby on the Humber River. Like Rome it is built on seven hills, though not as grand. Full of good fisher folk who go up as far as Scotland and right down here to the Dogger Bank. Lincoln is posh, with the cathedral and all that, but Grimsby is where the work and the money is to be found. Some of them trawler owners are really rolling in it. You should take the kids up on the railway some time. They would love the beach at Cleethorpes and the beer's much better than the piss you get down here."

As nominal hostess, Eugenie has been circulating among her

guests. The day is taking its toll and she has had recourse to holding the back of a chair with one hand and the arm of her new husband with the other. Maud and Mr W have joined her, Maud resplendent in Eugenie's lent dress. "I can't imagine how I ever got into that," opines Eugenie. "You weren't in it for long," whispers Maud to her with a giggle. Vincent and Whistler are surprised at their common connection outside the art world. The social occasion allows them to unwind towards one another, distinct from their formal business personas. Whistler expresses his excitement at the progress of his portrait of Maud in her new dress, a portrait inspired by his friend Manet, as well as by a series of paintings of the Thames inspired by Manet's disciple, Monet, 'but not as loose or unfinished as he allows his work to be'. Vincent and Eugenie are cordially invited to visit the studio in Chelsea, all the others politely hiding from Vincent the fact that Eugenie has already been there once before.

The party is momentarily halted by a delivery: two parcels for Mr and Mrs van Gogh, both labelled 'with the compliments of the Duke of Lancaster'. Whistler, Theo and Vincent are astonished, the others merely bemused. Could this be a mistake or some kind of joke? Eugenie cannot wait. She rips open her parcel to reveal a magnificent Indian shawl, which she promptly wraps around herself and pirouettes in around the room, all her tiredness forgotten. Vincent is prevailed upon to open his own parcel. Inside is a note on expensive notepaper, the heading bearing simply an embossed coronet. "Congratulations on your marriage. Thank you for your help and assistance in London and Paris. I am told that you are partial to these exotic things. A. E." With the note is a pair of beautiful Japanese prints, which Vincent immediately recognises as the work of the great master: a view from Satta Suruga and an exquisite rendering of cherry blossoms. He has long cherished such prints but the popularity of the master's prints in France in particular has put his prices beyond Vincent's reach. Theo and Vincent are ecstatic. Harry loves the landscape. Eugenie is much taken by the cherry blossoms. Ruth turns up her nose in disgust.

Anna enquires of Ruth who the dumpy lady is who is nursing the twin infants in the kitchen. She has been introduced but such has been the excitement of the day that the information has not completely sunk in. "That's Harry's wife, Lizzie. The smaller man over there, he's a drinking pal of Vincent's. Four children in five years and, if I am not much mistaken, another one on the way. Or two, if it turns out like last time. All he has to do is look at her and she falls. That's how they got wed in the first place." Ruth seems blissfully unaware of the inappropriateness of her last remark. Anna sees a fading but determined little woman, ground down by caring for her rapidly growing band of children, resolutely presenting a strong front to the world. A woman who cares more for her children than she does for her husband.

Reverend Slade-Jones has managed to persuade Seamus to top up his glass with porter, which he feels he needs having been captured by Major Havard. The major has managed to join the throng as the only commercial currently in residence, Theo and Anna having taken up the other available rooms. Waxing beetroot red, the Major is unstoppable on the question of the continued establishment of the Church of England and the maintenance of the disabilities for Jews and non-conformists. From those domestic matters he rushes on to the proper government of India and the need to keep civilised the benighted tribes of Africa, by force if necessary. There is an overwhelming suggestion that he prefers force as a first rather than a last resort. Reverend Slade-Jones is stunned both by the flow of verbiage and the intolerant world view that underpins them. He wonders where Christian love and compassion is meant to come into the equation, which seem to be totally absent even in the Major's determination to spread the gospel. Another glass of porter would wash the bad taste from his mouth.

For the last hour a portly gentleman with a magnificent watch and chain spread across his corporation has been gently sipping absinthe in the corner of the room. He now strolls into the centre and booms out a greeting in a thick French accent. "Ladies and Gentlemen, please forgive me for interrupting this merry gathering. I only know a few of you, so I feel that I must first introduce myself. I

131

am Monsieur Boussod, the manager of Goupil and Sons gallery in London, where Mr Vincent van Gogh is an esteemed employee. At the moment our gallery in London is in Southampton Street. I am happy to tell you something that has been a secret so far: that next month the company is taking over the premises and clientele of Holloway and Sons in the Strand." Boussod pauses for effect and is rather confused by the slightly aggressive silence that confronts him. "This has left the company with a dilemma as to what we should do with the Southampton Street premises. Our first thought was to close it down. However, our management in Paris has decided that perhaps it is time for the company to branch out and become a trifle more adventurous. Therefore the existing part of the company dealing with prints and the more traditional works of art will move to the Strand. The Southampton Street gallery will be devoted to contemporary British and French painting in particular, with regular exhibitions by the leading artists of our time as well as more general sales. Since this is a time of celebration and the giving of presents I have one more to bestow. Naturally the gallery will require a manager who is familiar both with the contemporary art scene in France and in England. I have recommended to the management in France, and I am happy to say that they have agreed, that the new manager should be this gentleman here, Mr Vincent van Gogh."

Loud cheers from all assembled, especially Ruth who is delighted at extra income coming into the household for no extra work on her part. More drinks are called for and the party degenerates into raucous confusion, including singing in English, Irish, Welsh, French and Dutch.

★

The long hard day has taken its toll. Visitors have all gone home. Relatives have retired to bed leaving Theo and Vincent together with one last absinthe to wash away the excitement of the day. Vincent has been on the go since four in the morning, organised friends and relations and been 'on show' for hours. The wedding itself would have been enough to tire him but Joanna's reappearance and repeat of her prophecies stunned him almost as much as her first demonstration had done. He has been drinking steadily since mid-afternoon and this has drained the last of his energies. He and Theo drain their glasses and start for bed. Vincent does not make it; he collapses to the floor, writhing in the first of the fits he is to suffer for the rest of his life. The ever-faithful Theo tends to him, rolling him on his side and pressing a cleaning towel between his teeth. Once the fit is over Theo eases him to his feet and helps him upstairs for the first night of his married life.

*Fleet Street*

# Brixton

## *Autumn 1875*

Autumn is drawing towards winter. The days are shorter, the winter fog is gathering its strength before enveloping London in its annual shroud. Despite the depressing aspect out of doors, Hackford Road is settling down to a more joyful winter than it has enjoyed for many years. Eugenie has been safely delivered of a baby girl, a solid eight pounds, who has been christened Cornelia after Vincent's mother. Ruth would have preferred a boy but would have settled with calling a girl Georgina after her late husband. Eugenie, wishing to make the child as much Vincent's as possible and to cement his love for her, was insistent on Cornelia, instantly shortened to Nelly by all and sundry. Vincent requires no incentive to love the child as much as he loves the mother, happy to hold the bundle at any time, even when it becomes soft and damp in his arms.

Despite the young couple's political manoeuvring, Pastor Theodorus van Gogh is not appeased. Not only does his interdiction of his house to them still remain, he also refuses to accept any mail at all that originates in England. Thus he is unable to directly receive the good news from Anna that she has been successful in securing a position as companion to an elderly wealthy widow in Harrogate, where perhaps she may be fortunate enough to meet some equally wealthy eligible young men. Theo has appointed himself post master, passing on the good news to his mother indirectly from Paris. Encouraged by this, Vincent has once more made use of his brother's good offices. In a spare moment when Eugenie was sleeping with the child in her arms he has completed a quick pencil sketch of them, which he has forwarded to Paris and from there to Holland. His mother is both frightened and delighted. After some hours' contemplation of the image she hides it beneath her best linen, a place where her husband will never look. Over the years her collection grows to such an extent that the drawer becomes increasingly difficult to close.

Eugenie finds in Vincent a calm and considerate lover, none of Paul's rambunctiousness or thunderous passion. She appreciates being allowed more time to seek her own pleasure, to be stroked and fondled in a gentle prelude, so much so that she is even able to forget that her mother is sleeping, or maybe not sleeping, in the next room. Now she is nursing she knows that she is safe for a while. Despite this she is taking advice from Maud on avoiding another pregnancy and ensuring that she makes implementing her instructions a regular habit.

As well as being disappointed in the child's name, Ruth has also found that her financial expectations have been dashed. Eugenie no longer shares a room with her and cannot be expected to move into Vincent's attic. Now that Anna has moved to Yorkshire the young couple have taken over her room with a consequent loss of rent, which is only partially compensated by the release of Vincent's old room. Nor can Eugenie be expected to be the unpaid help, forcing Ruth to employ someone full time who is more acute and less slovenly than her previous part-time maid. Vincent's new job has brought with it a small increase in salary, much of which increase goes on clothes and linen for the baby. Taking a cue from her mother Eugenie relieves him of most of the rest, leaving him a modest amount for his train fares with a little left over for the odd pint with Harry at the White Horse. Ruth believes that the money she receives from Eugenie is the whole of Vincent's remaining salary. She is wrong. Eugenie is carefully squirrelling away a small amount each month against a rainy day, for such things as doctors can be expensive. Further, she has heard from Vincent his tale of the desperate woman trying to sell him her watercolours. She has no wish to be made destitute and who knows how long any man will stay around?

Taking on the existing gallery has not been as exciting as Vincent had thought. Most of his time is taken up with accessing, packing and despatching the stock over to the Strand and dealing with the resulting exasperated enquiries. Some pieces have gone missing. Others are not what they are stated to be in the stocktaking sheets. In the meantime the gallery itself is being repainted a very pale shade of Naples yellow, which is replacing the previous crimson alizarin. The crimson refuses to go peacefully and continually bleeds through the layers of yellow to give a dull orange-brown finish. Harry, who Vincent has managed to engage for the job, is worried that he is putting on so many layers of paint that he will soon be out of pocket.

What Vincent would prefer to be doing is visiting artists' studios in London and Paris in order to build up his new stock. For the time being he is reduced to planning a collection of exhibitions that would mark time from an artistic point of view, whilst still advertising the gallery as a leader of the avant-garde. The pre-Raphaelite Brotherhood are hardly new arrivals but they are still viewed as wild and unconventional. Besides, Vincent is rather taken by their use of colour; far less dreary than most of their contemporaries. So they will be his first major exhibition, shorn of the more moralistic products. Then perhaps something French. Perhaps a joint exhibition of Boudin and Jongkind, the English always tempted by maritime scenes. Although his brief is to be ahead of other galleries in London he is also aware that the gallery must make a profit. To do this requires a dedicated clientele and a reputation for having an 'eye' for the next big name or artistic movement. Whistler has promised that he will move his custom from the Grosvenor Gallery to Goupil, a move that Vincent heartily welcomes despite Whistler's slow sales and small reputation. They have agreed that his latest painting 'Nocturne in Black and Gold' should be the first of his pieces to be exhibited once it is completed and the varnish has dried.

The Pre-Raphaelite exhibition is not as easy to arrange as Vincent had first thought. Their painstaking methods and growing popularity mean that unlike most artists they do not have studios bursting with unsold work. Rossetti in particular has a lack of finished work, so that Vincent is reduced to what he terms 'studio scrapings': pencil sketches used as preparatory ideas for larger oil compositions. Four of these can be framed up and look sufficiently finished to be shown. Others are on odd pieces of paper or torn card, whatever came to hand at the time. Vincent despairs of these, but Eugenie has a clear view of what should be done. A 'scrapbook' is made from standard-size mount-board with a drawing glued to each page. Vincent carefully drills a series of holes along the edge of the card and the whole is held together with Veronese green ribbon. The book is displayed in a *vitrine*, a page turned on each successive day. Despite dismissive comments, particularly from other artists and even Rossetti himself, the book is sold along with two of the pencil sketches to a Scot down on business from Glasgow for the week.

Half-way through the show's run Vincent realises that he has a disaster on his hands. There is no follow-up, he will lose momentum and his clients will disappear to other galleries if he has nothing new and exciting to show them. Boudin has an exclusive contract with Durand-Ruel for both France and England. Jongkind is in declining health, besides which his peripatetic life has made him almost impossible to contact. He may be in Lyon or perhaps Avignon. There is a rumour that he could be back in Paris though even Theo's best efforts fail to find him there. A joint Boudin-Jongkind show is impossible. What is to be done?

The remaining Rossetti pencil sketch and a large painting by Edward Burne-Jones are purchased by a shipping magnate from Liverpool looking to furnish his new house in London. "Why have you got no Whistlers?" demands the magnate in his peremptory tone, as if demanding to know why the ship has insufficient ballast.

"Well," replied Vincent, "Mr Whistler has promised us his latest painting once it is completed and we hope to have it on show very soon."

"Not enough. Totally insufficient. Get hold of Whistler and bring him over to Princes Gate on Friday afternoon. Around three before all my wife's cronies turn up for afternoon tea. Here's my card. Leyland's the name. Don't be late." An issue of instructions about the delivery of his purchases and Leyland disappears in a fog of cigar smoke.

It transpires that Whistler is already in conversation with Leyland about a sumptuous redecoration of the main dining room at Princes Gate. He has assistants working on preparing paintings, stencilling and gilding frames with a butterfly motif, constructing ceiling structures and applying fabrics to the master's directions. No price has so far been mentioned. Whistler expects the commission to set him up for life, both financially and professionally. Any further conversation with Leyland and Vincent would be likely to be an added bonus. A bonus indeed, for Leyland proposes nothing less than full financial support of a major Whistler exhibition at the Goupil gallery. He will pay for the redecoration of the gallery to Whistler's specification, all printing and postage costs for invitations and catalogues, private view refreshments, newspaper advertising, framing costs and even the cost of a uniformed attendant on the door to welcome the guests and to keep out the riff-raff.

Time is short and Whistler still has to spend a lot of his time supervising the decoration of Leyland's Peacock Room. Nevertheless he sets to with a will, convinced that his fortunes are at their zenith. He borrows Vincent's Japanese prints, now neatly framed, as an inspiration for a view of the old Battersea Bridge and a painting of three women he has been working on in a desultory manner for some time. Three views of Cremorne Gardens are brought out of storage, refreshed and a light coat of varnish added. Vincent's assistants have to take great care in hanging the exhibition, some of the paintings not being quite dry.

Although the Prince of Wales is unable to see the exhibition himself his patronage is enough to encourage much of his entourage to attend the private view, turning it into one of the most unexpected social events of the year. Vincent spends his time 'working the room', making himself personally known to as many of the visitors as possible and encouraging them to revisit the gallery, and to take an interest in the modern trends in art and the exciting movements in France, of which Mr Whistler, as an artist trained in Paris, is an outstanding example. Whistler corners any journalist he can find, plying him with whiskey and explaining the finer points of his painting and suggesting exactly what the journalist might write in his newspaper the following day.

Vincent is quite successful in his endeavours, selling a third of the exhibition on the opening day. Whistler is less so. His portrait of Maud, which he entitles 'Arrangement in White and Black', does not meet with universal acclaim. "This is a portrait of a night-time streetwalker arrayed in her finery, a dress designed to show off the goods to a prospective purchaser in the best possible light. Her rouged face does nothing to hide her common features, perched upon a disgusting feather boa. We may only guess at her further degradation: her underwear dingy and not quite clean, the dirt between her toes, the unmentionable diseases that she carries within her. A disgusting creature painted in a dull and disgusting manner." Another writer wished to know why all of the subjects were painted at night and why none of them appeared to be finished. A young writer called Oscar Wilde dismissed such criticism: "Popularity is the only insult that has not yet been offered to Mr Whistler."

"All publicity is good publicity," declares Eugenie, anticipating a later-received wisdom by a hundred years. "As long as they are writing about Whistler it doesn't matter what they say. People will still come in to see what all the fuss is about. One in a hundred will love it and one in a thousand will buy something." Not even Eugenie could anticipate the furore that followed the publication a few days later by John Ruskin, the most eminent art critic of his day. After his earlier enthusiasm Ruskin had grown to dislike Whistler's painting in general. 'Nocturne in Black and Gold' proved to be the last straw:

"For Mr Whistler's sake, no less than for the protection of the purchaser, Mr van Gogh ought not to have admitted works into the gallery in which the ill-educated conceit of the artist so nearly approached the aspect of wilful imposture. I have seen, and heard, much of cockney impudence before now; but never expected to hear a coxcomb ask 200 guineas for flinging a pot of paint in the public's face."

# The Times

## London 1877

"Sadly we are in decadent times, in the arts as in politics, religion and society in general. There are leaders of this decadence; one might cite the writer Wilde as a grimy example. In painting the charge is led by the Goupil Gallery on Southampton Street, where all that is most offensive and immoral in the world of commercial art is to be found. Readers will already be aware of the current court case between the painter Whistler and Mr Ruskin, the eminent art critic, around a so-called painting displayed at this gallery last year.

If anything, the current exhibition has surpassed the Whistler exhibition in terms of its determination to insult the intelligence of the public. Rarely have we seen such incompetence gracing the walls of our capital city. It comes as no surprise to learn that these artists have been so oblivious to good taste that they have been driven out of the salons and forced to exhibit in the back rooms of a photographer's premises at their own expense.

Even within this slough, one can still find the odd gem, even if these do not gleam very brightly. Mesdames Morisot and Cassatt have a certain charm, mainly derived from their subject matter. Who could fail to be moved by a scene of a proud mother by her crib or children playing by a pond or admiring the ducks? Our pleasure in these scenes is spoilt by the sketchiness of their execution and by the slapdash application of the paint, no doubt learnt from their male brethren. Of these, the only ones who deserve any attention at all are Messieurs Manet and Degas, who can at least put paint on to canvas in a reasonably tolerable manner. This they ruin by an insistence on obscure and unenlightening subjects: the 'flâneur', that epitome of French decadence and idleness, horse races and scenes of ballet rehearsals attended by malformed females in both the moral and the physical sense of the word.

What is to be said of the rest? Of the incompetent negro Pissarro, the painter of fans Renoir and the visually impaired Sisley and Monet? Renoir needs to return to his fans. He may be able to copy but he is totally unable to create a composition or to choose a colour scheme which is co-ordinated across the whole painting. Pissarro may be excused as a mere savage led astray by his betters but for Monet and Sisley there can be no excuse. There is no calmness or subtlety to their execution, even when they claim to be painting the most bucolic of scenes. All is violent reds, greens and yellows applied in waves of solid pigment, where even the floods outside Paris are rendered as if they are a raging storm at sea. Foliage becomes a tangle of colour where one is unable to distinguish leaf, flower or bough. As an added insult they claim to have derived inspiration from our great artists Gainsborough and Constable, who must be turning in their desecrated graves at the thought.

We believe that Messieurs Goupil and Sons have given their Southampton Street gallery to a young Dutch employee as an experiment in showing the latest in continental and British art. The sooner that they bring this experiment to a close the better."

★

"Look at this," says Vincent. "How can we survive reviews like this? *The Times* is the worst but all the others are in the same vein. We will be forced to close. Goupil will just not let us go on."

"Vincent, darling, this is great! The best thing that could have happened to you. The exhibition is in all of the papers alongside the Ruskin defamation case. Even the penny dreadfuls have something on it though I don't suppose your customers read those. They certainly read *The Times*, even up in the north. If those Lancashire industrialists visit one gallery on their annual visit to London it will be the one they have heard about: Goupil. And here is something that Theo has sent us from Paris, an amusing cartoon about the Impressionists' exhibition." Eugenie waves a copy of a French newspaper under Vincent's nose. A flustered *gendarme* is confronting a pregnant woman outside the exhibition. "Madame," he tells her, "you should not go in there. It would be too dangerous for you in your condition."

"I don't see how that helps us at all," grumbles Vincent. "It only makes the situation worse. People will get hold of that and say that the French hate this painting as much as the English do. This could be the first time the French and the English have agreed about anything in 900 years."

"Don't be so pessimistic. Listen to me, I know what I'm doing. Have you got a good-size drawing pad, one about three feet tall? Good. Now, what I want you to do is to copy the cartoon on to your pad. Full size. Fill the whole page. When you've done that I'll add the writing at the bottom, if you can do me a good translation into English."

Vincent is at a loss, but nearly two years of marriage have taught him to be an obedient as well as a loving husband. The drawing is duly completed to his satisfaction, the feel of the pencil in his hand once more giving him immense pleasure. In the meantime Eugenie has turned up two old frames from the attic. The backs are removed and the glass cleaned of dust and mouse droppings. She mounts the original French cartoon in one of the frames, *The Times* review in the other.

"Now, when you go in to the gallery tomorrow you take everything out of the window and pull curtains across so that nobody can see into the gallery. Then you mount your version of the cartoon on a board and display it on a small easel in the window with these two items either side of it. Leave them there for a week or so and see the results." Vincent is not convinced but does as he is told. After all, Eugenie was right about the effect of the publicity on the Whistler exhibition, which made Goupil a resounding profit and Vincent himself an excellent commission.

# London

## *Autumn 1877*

*Dear Theo*

    *It is one of those beautiful English days outside. The sun is shining, the few clouds are just pieces of fluffy white material ambling across the sky and the trees are turning magnificent shades of yellow, amber, dark green. It is enough to make me take up a paintbrush at last, which I hope to do in the summer when life is less hectic.*

    *I thought that things at home would be quieter once little Nelly was no longer a baby. How stupid of me! After all my younger brothers and sisters I should have realised that once babies start to walk life becomes ever more difficult. Little Nelly is into everything, opening cupboards and putting anything she finds into her mouth. She seems to have inherited my temper and can become completely furious if she doesn't get what she wants. Now she has a few more words it is easier since she can at least demand 'bread' or 'milk'. If you ask her if she wants anything she just says 'No' very loudly, whether she actually wants it or not. Jen-Jen insists that I speak to her in Dutch because she says she does not want the child to learn to speak English with my terrible accent. Really I think that she harbours thoughts of us all being able to go over and stay with our parents at some time in the future but I can't see Father ever allowing that. You will be surprised to hear that I find speaking Dutch very difficult. I speak English all day at work and of course Jen-Jen knows no Dutch, so I speak English at home all the time. Anyway we don't want the child to pick up my terrible accent in Dutch either!*

    *As you know the last exhibition at the gallery here was the 'bande à Manet' plus a few others from the same stable. The reviews were exactly* as you would expect. After all, even in Paris they are not accepted. By the way, thank you for the cartoon from the newspaper. I did a copy of it, which I displayed alongside the original in the gallery window. I have to admit that it was Jen-Jen's idea, complete with blacking out the view of the interior from the road. Never have there been so many people of all sorts in the gallery; it was packed from morning to night. Most of them came to scoff of course, and made the sort of rude comments that only the English upper classes would be crass enough to voice in public. Despite that, there were several who came back again and again, usually with a wife or friend in tow, and bought a piece or a smaller one from the stock room. Many of these people had never bought a painting before in their lives and some even had to borrow money to do so. At Jen-Jen's suggestion I allowed one or two of these to pay in parts and even dropped the price slightly for one man who bought three Pissarros in one go. I'm delighted to say that all of the part-payments have been made and that several of the buyers have been back and purchased another painting. In the end it has been quite a sensation, for the right reasons this time.

Jen-Jen has badgered me into appointing her as a part-time advertising agent for the company. In fact she is just giving me ideas about how to promote things here but I think she has ambitions towards the Strand as well. I don't pay her very much but she seems happy with the situation.

Whistler seems to be getting into difficulties. He is so awkward and litigious at times that it can be a problem to control him. He lost a lot of money over the Ruskin case where he was given derisory damages but the jury refused to find in favour of him over the matter of expenses, so he had to pay his own. Then there is a problem with Leyland. Whistler never signed a contract with him about how much his Peacock Room was going to cost and went merrily ahead designing a room fit for the Grande Porte himself, at a cost to match. Leyland has paid him some money on account and now they are arguing fiercely about how much is outstanding. I fear that Leyland will do something offensive in the end to which Whistler will take offence and perhaps go to court again with all the expense that incurs. If Whistler

145

*does not get back at least what he has spent on this, I fear that it will mean financial catastrophe for him. Furthermore he has some domestic difficulties. I always thought that he was a bachelor but it turns out he is married to a lady who has decamped in a huff to Hastings, leaving Maud Franklin to move in with him in Chelsea. Exactly what you would expect from an artist, I suppose. Jen-Jen further tells me that Maud rather thinks that she might be in the family way. Just girls' talk at the moment and I don't think that Whistler is aware of the situation yet but I'm ready to trust in what Jen-Jen tells me, she and Maud being so close.*

*How are things going with you in Paris? There are rumours here that the economic situation is likely to become more difficult over there. Still, the rich always have money and a few francs a year makes no difference to them, they will just leech more out of their tenants. (There I go, too much time spent listening to Harry Kirman's socialist ideas.)*

*I've also enclosed a couple of little drawings of Nelly for Mother, which I'm sure you will send on to her. I must say that I am rather pleased with these two; I think they have caught her character nicely. Hopefully Mother will be pleased with them. Let me know what she says and if she wants me to keep sending drawings to her.*

*Your devoted brother*

*Vincent*

Streatham

146

# Brixton

## *Christmas Day 1878*

Eugenie and Ruth are cooking Christmas dinner. For a change there is a companionable chatter in the kitchen alongside the rattle of utensils and the bubble of water on the stove. Grandfather Elisha has managed to find a farm-bred goose through one of his old cronies and as a reward is allowed to sit quietly undisturbed with his old pipe in his mouth in a large chair in the corner of the kitchen. The pipe has gone out and his head has drooped onto his chest. Ruth has scolded him a couple of times for falling asleep but the old man has protested that he is just resting his eyes.

Vincent is on his knees in the parlour in front of a steaming tin tub. Cornelia is helping him bath baby Rose, who is squealing with delight and thrashing her legs so that the water is going everywhere. Not that Vincent cares; he is enjoying himself almost as much as the baby. Rose has learnt to float, or perhaps she is young enough not to have forgotten her watery nine months' gestation. Cornelia pushes her from one end of the tub and Vincent pushes her back from his end. From time to time the thrashing legs upset the equilibrium, causing Rose to submerge. She is unfazed by this, keeping her mouth shut but her large brown eyes open.

There is a firm knock on the door. Vincent cannot leave the baby unattended in the bath and Eugenie and Ruth are up to their elbows in assorted vegetables. A good-natured discussion ensues. In the end it is a pinafored Eugenie who answers the door to Harry Kirman in his Sunday best supplemented by a garish neckerchief that the children have bought him for Christmas and which he will probably never wear again. "Hello, ducks," he says, giving Eugenie a quick kiss on the cheek. "How's it all going?" Eugenie does not reply. She knows that this visit augurs no good. "I've just dropped in to see Vinnie, wondered if he'd like to pop round to the White Horse for a quick drink before lunch." Eugenie lets out a grumpy 'humph', one that she has obviously inherited from her mother.

Vincent knows where his duty lies. "I'm bathing the babies, Harry. Then there won't be much time before the lunch is ready."

"Come on, all you have to do is to dry and dress the babies. The bath will knock them out and they'll be off to sleep in no time. The girls are still putting things together by the looks of it. Plenty of time for us to have a quick drop down the pub."

Having made a token response Vincent is now open to suggestions and this seems a pretty good one. "Well, let me get the babies' dresses first. You can help Cornelia button her dress while you wait. She hasn't yet got the idea of matching each button to the corresponding buttonhole."

"Won't be long, sweetheart," calls Vincent as the two men head rapidly for the front door. Ruth hurls them her sour basilisk look, which Eugenie has not quite learnt to imitate. Instead she has developed a smile that is so deceitful, a scowl would be less threatening. "Don't be late. And you, Harry Kirman, make sure that you don't keep him too long."

"Phew, I thought she'd never let you go! Did you see that look she gave you? Give her a couple of years she'll be just as hard as her mother. Well, never mind. She's a good girl and she'll look after you well, whether you like it or not. God, am I glad to get out of the house. There's Lizzie of course and our five. Then there's her mother and sister with the sister's two girls. And my mother and grandmother. Good job they've not brought any kids along with them. It's all wimmin' and kids, kids and wimmin'. And Lizzie's period is late again. That would be the last straw. Trouble is, we just can't keep our hands off one another; that's how we got hitched up in the first place. Still, never mind. Worse things happen at sea."

Vincent is still in the first flush of fatherhood and thinks that six children would perhaps not be so bad. Despite that, it is a change to be back in the old White Horse. "I've not been in here for ages. What with work and the children, there just doesn't seem to be time or a lot of spare money around."

*Like mother, like daughter*, thinks Harry. "Come on, drink up, time for one more at least…"

"Are you still going to the drawing classes at Borough?"

"No, gave them up last month. I got as far as I could and there didn't seem to be any point just going for the sake of it. And Seamus wasn't there any more. They replaced him with some old stick of a feller with no skin on his bones, so there was no mileage in trying to catch the muscle tone with him."

"Why did Seamus give up? He's not propping up the bar here today, either."

"In the nick. He was collecting a debt from a feller and leant on him a bit too hard. The feller ended up in hospital and Seamus ended up in Wandsworth for eighteen months. So no more drawing classes for me. I've done some painting, though. Whistler's been good to me, had me down his studio a few times. Taught me how to prime a canvas, slapping on that egg mixture. Gave me a few tips about mixing oil colours. They're not the same as what we decorators use, you know. All that pigment and stuff. And he went on quite a bit about light and shade. I know about that from the drawing classes but it seems different in oils. Not that he uses much contrast like that, he just seems to paint moonscapes. Now, don't get me wrong. I know he's a good painter but I could never paint like him. Too fluffy, just too tasteful, if you know what I mean? But one thing he's said that really struck me, he said: "What's the good of art if it doesn't show things that you can't see?" I puzzled over that for weeks. At last I figured it out: what he was getting at was that art isn't just a way of reproducing what is out there on to the canvas, it's more than that. What 'more', I don't know but if I keep at it I might find out."

"That's very philosophical of you, Harry. That's what my French painters are trying to do, show things you can't see."

"Yes, but they are still trying to show the world out there even if they do it in a different way. It's just technical, isn't it? It doesn't show how you feel about something, just what it looks like in the morning as opposed to the evening. All very flashy and charming. That's it, just charm! Where's the real world? Anyway the real world looks like it is catching up on Whistler. He's fallen out with that Leyland and they've had a right old barney over payment for the Peacock Room. Good job I made sure that I got paid for my bit of it. Leyland is refusing to pay any more and is demanding back money he has already lent to Whistler as well. The sharks have got wind of it and they are circling. Every tradesman and odd assistant is dunning him for money and it looks like he is going to fail badly, so you'd better get a move on and sell some paintings for him to get him out of the mess."

"Not at this time of the year. We do quite well before Christmas but trade is fairly dead then until the spring when all the nobs pick up the rents from their tenants. Still, I'll see what I can do. Jen-Jen is pretty thick with Maud, so she'll be over there all of the time when Maud's baby is born. I can see the pair of them cooking something up between them. Where did this other pint come from? We'd better drink up quick or there will be trouble."

Too late.

The pub door bursts open and in marches Eugenie. She is carrying a tray covered with a cloth. She drops it down in front of Vincent, hard enough to cause a tinkle of crockery and a general sensation in the room yet not hard enough to break anything. The men grab their beer glasses to prevent unwanted spillages. "Here's your dinner. Get it ate. Don't forget to bring your plates home when you eventually bother to come. And you, Harry Kirman. Your dinner will be ready for you at home. Get off there now before we have Lizzie in here as well." She storms off to a round of applause and ribald comments from the other drinkers. Vincent and Harry drain their glasses and slink off sheepishly, Vincent carrying the tray with his still uneaten Christmas dinner on it.

# Brixton

## *1879*

*Dear Theo*

*Thank you for the presents for the children and most of all for your excellent news about our parents. It grieves me seriously that I cannot see them or even write to them direct. Still, I have my postman who keeps me in touch. Please thank Mother for me for the knitted shawl for Cornelia and the blanket for Rose. No doubt she thinks that the weather here is even colder than in Holland, which isn't true. Winters here are quite mild and if it weren't for the fogs we would be out walking every day. Eugenie and I went to Brockdish Park a lot over the holiday and it was delightful to be out in the fresh air before the fog descended last week. Christmas was one of the best that I have ever spent, except for one little incident when I got myself into a bit of a scrape alongside Harry. I only wish that you could have been here to share the holiday with us.*

*I have been doing some drawing recently and even tried my hand at painting. A total disaster. Apart from the fact that I don't have the technical skill, there is not really enough space here to put up an easel and the children are into everything. Cornelia nearly poisoned herself. She had the top off a tube of Prussian blue and was about to squeeze it into her mouth when I managed to stop her. You can imagine the fuss that would have caused. I got shouted at enough because of the paint on her hands, which she proceeded to wipe all over her pinafore. So I have had to make do with pastels, which are easier to manage and to put away out of the reach of little fingers. We found some tiny spring irises in Brockdish Park, no bigger than fifteen centimetres tall, which Cornelia plucked and brought home with her. Before they could fade* too badly I did a quick pastel drawing of them, which Jen-Jen liked so much that she has had it framed and hung in the parlour. Perhaps I shall do some more flowers when they all come up later in the spring.

There has been one more addition to our circle. Jen-Jen's friend Maud has just had a baby daughter who rejoices in the name of Maud McNeill Whistler Franklin, just in case anyone might be wondering who the father might be. Whistler has got himself into a bit of a mess as I suggested to you that he might. His creditors are after him and he was about to be made bankrupt when Jen-Jen came up with a sharp idea. She has been saving money steadily from my wages and has saved everything that I paid her from the gallery accounts. This was just enough to pay for Whistler and the two Mauds to go off to Venice for a couple of months in order to fulfil a commission that I got for him from the Fine Art Society here in London. In return he has made all of his paintings over to me, so that I can keep them as my own in Brixton. I am to keep any money from sales. I've promised to let him have them back when he is able to repay me the money for the Venice trip. This is all a clever invention of Jen-Jen's, which has at least kept Whistler's paintings out of the hands of the bailiffs, though he has been forced to sell his house and some of his effects have gone to Sothebys to be sold there. All very sad.

Harry Kirman will be devastated. He has been down at Whistler's studio so much that he has almost become a sort of unofficial assistant. He makes up stretchers and frames for him as well as painting them. Besides that, he has done some copies of Whistler's paintings. They are not too bad now that Harry has learnt to control the paint better. I'm surprised that he wants to do it; he is so dismissive of the originals, which he describes as 'vacuous' (a new word for Harry; he has obviously picked up more than painting techniques from his master), whilst still admiring the skill with which they are painted. Lizzie will be relieved. She thinks Harry has been away from home far too much recently and suspects that he has a mistress tucked away somewhere, especially in the light of her advanced condition. She needs to be careful; art can be a much more demanding mistress than any woman.

There are not many good things to be said about sharing a house with one's mother-in-law but one has just presented itself. I have persuaded Boussod to let me go over to Paris for a couple of months in order to go round the studios there. This is only possible because Mrs Loyer will help Jen-Jen with the children while I am away. Jen-Jen wanted to come herself but even grandmotherly affection did not extend as far as looking after two babies for eight weeks. Never mind, I'm sure we will manage to get away together at some time in the future.

So, I will see you in a couple of weeks' time and we can go on studio visits together and spend some evenings on the town. I hope you will not find me too dull as an old married man. I will bring over some drawings of the children, which I will have the greatest delight in being able to send off to Mother direct. You don't think you could persuade her to come and visit you on her own as well, do you? That would be wonderful.

Your loving brother
Vincent

Vincent

# Grimsby

## *1881*

*Dear Vince*

    *I never was much good with a pen, or with a pencil either come to that, but today I am even more ham fisted than ever. The reason being I dropped an otter board on my right thumb. We'd just finished with the last catch of the day and were pulling in the gear. Maybe it hadn't been wound in enough or it was the roll of the sea. The board came down sudden-like before I could get my hand off the rail. All of the thumb above the top knuckle was squashed completely flat. They say there is no point in chopping it off. The nail has just peeled away and the whole thing looks like a squashed walnut.*

    *My fault, I suppose, for being too greedy. There's not much call for house painters up here. Them what has a house are too tight to have someone paint it for them. Landlords here won't mend a window never mind paint the house, so I've taken to the sea for a while as what they call a 'deckie learner'. Really it's just a sea-based labourer: pulling in nets, humping the crates, sorting the fish. With my thumb as it is I don't suppose I'll be doing that for a while, which gives me extra time for my painting.*

    *Mr Ross, who is a big ship owner here, has asked me to paint his latest boat, twice! First I have to paint the boat itself in his company colours with special attention to the crest on the funnel. Then I have to paint it on canvas for him. He's given me some canvas: proper sail stuff, none of your namby-pamby London painter's guff. About two feet by three, so the largest I've ever done. His cook gave me some ancient eggs to use for the primer though I was tempted to eat them despite their age. I don't have any money for oils so I'm going to use* the boat paint, which should do the trick. If this turns out I reckon that some of the other trawler owners will have their boats done as well. It could be a nice little earner and a lot warmer and safer than being on the boats themselves.

In the meantime, here are a few of my latest daubs. Some of them are a bit small, an idea I got from Whistler after he came back from St Ives. The largest is about eighteen inches; to save paint I had to thin it with petrol from the shipyard. If you can get any of your rich aesthetes (there's a nice new word from old Harry) or aristocrats to buy one or two I'd be very happy. Please split the money half and half between me and Lizzie. I'd like to say to give it all to Lizzie but I need some for paint and brushes; it can't all be smuggled off the docks.

You'll see I've been struggling to get down to what it feels like to have to grind out a living. The fishermen here look healthy on the surface. They all have those great ruddy weather-beaten complexions. Look closely and most of them have something amiss. Toes have been frozen off, fingers missing, an eye put out by a swinging block and tackle, backs giving way under the lifting. Their wives are no better: ground down by poverty and the fear their man may not come home from sea this time. Which is worse: the storm that keeps them in port so that they make no money, or the storm that hits them at sea, making them fear for their lives? So lives are short here. There are few grandfathers to be seen, except behind the counters of the shops.

I've taken lodgings in King Edward Street in a row of terraces near the dock gates. My neighbours are fierce, but friendly at the same time. They have easy tempers, with fights breaking out at a moment's notice. Next second all has quietened down and they invite me in for tea while I sketch their heads or a family group. I pay for my hospitality with sketches of their children. Not great drawings but a lot better than that day in the White Horse. You'll see a couple of the interiors on the roll I sent you. None of that 'fisherman's cottage' rubbish – the sentimental stuff that the St Ives gentlemen turn out, all hanging nets and neat tablecloths – but bare walls, threadbare clothes and a single pot on the stove. Can't see that selling, can you?

You might manage to shift some of the seascapes. There is a view of the harbour I'm quite pleased with, all masts and sails. It is getting on for dusk. The light is diffused through the clouds, throwing all sorts of strange colours onto the masts: lilacs, pinks, some heavy blues and even a touch of veridian. I tried not to put too much sky into it else it would get too sloppy. A couple of other seascapes are not too bad and I'm rather pleased with the small oil of a half-eaten fish. How easy it would be just to cut the canvas in three: sand in front, sea behind, sky in the distance. No-one would accept that of course, but I'm experimenting with some charcoal drawings to see how such an approach might work. If nothing else it gives me practice with tonal variations while still concentrating on the essential detail.

It is getting too late to write. I have to be at the docks for the five o'clock tide tomorrow for a day's work unloading and cleaning the boats as they come in. Every day's work down the docks gives one more day of freedom to paint.

Your devoted friend

Harry Kirman

The Grimsby Fish Docks

# The Times

## 1881

"Readers of this newspaper will have perceived that when institutions become so tainted with scandal that it appears they cannot continue, they change their name in order to deceive the public into believing that they have become new and respectable organisations. Thus communists manage to hide themselves as the Social Democratic Federation and socialist trade unions become mere friendly societies. Even in the arts one can see this trend with the renaming of the Goupil Fils Gallery in Southampton Street as the Outland Gallery. The management will no doubt tell you that this merely reflects the change of ownership, but we are not deceived. The management remains the same and the exhibition policy continues in a manner the like of which will no doubt lend to it the soubriquet of 'The Outrage Gallery'.

The artists who exhibit at this gallery are known for their general incompetence. The three so-called artists who share the space for the next two months surpass all that has gone before. Best of a bad bunch is Mr Whistler whose etchings of Venice received such popular and critical attention two years ago. He is known for a series of paintings, which he entitles his 'Nocturnes'; the miniatures that he shows here may well be entitled 'Five Easy Pieces' for their size and complete lack of either detail or interest. He claims to have painted these watercolours on a visit to St Ives, doubtless at a time when it was shrouded in sea mist.

Alongside him is another set of seascapes in watercolour by one V. V. Governor. Such a name strikes this writer as a pseudonym, a 'nom de pinceau'. For who would want to own to having painted these atrocities? The artist appears to be a follower of Turner in his dotage, for much is hidden behind mists and scumbles of paint. Nor can the artist even manage to apply the paint reasonably smoothly but leaves gobbets of it strewn across the paper like random bird droppings. The impression is of someone who has learnt to paint from a correspondence course written by Monsieur Monet.

Worst of a bad bunch is one H. Kirman. Again on a small format, these vary in that they are oils rather than watercolours. Subject matter is the most banal that one can imagine: a half-gutted fish, a hand holding part of a fishing net, a bent old beggar and so on. They are rendered in the roughest manner with heavy black outlines such as never existed in art or nature, enclosing a pot pourri of colours that look like they were applied with deformed fingers or a broken scalpel. Kirman's art is not just outrageous it is also totally asinine and it says much even for the public who frequent this gallery that none of them have been sold.

With luck the Outland Gallery will soon get its quietus and move out of this particular land. Of Whistler, Governor and Kirman all we can say is that between them they would gather enough talent to make one unnoticeable journeyman painter."

# Paris

## *1885*

How wonderful Paris is, even better than I had expected. Even in autumn the sun is shining and it is beautifully warm. Vincent has taken me to see the tourist sites, the Notre Dame cathedral, the Louvre and so on. Next week he says that we are going out to Versailles, which is the French version of Buckingham Palace. What a pity they don't have an emperor any more, that would be really exciting. The roads here are very wide and lined with magnificent trees, which are at their best now with their autumn leaves on. Not like poky old London with its alleyways and twisting streets. Nor very friendly I should imagine with all these big houses and your neighbour fifty yards away. And the waiters are so rude! Vincent said that it is different in the student cafés and then refused to take me there!

Never mind, he did take me around to look at some artists' studios, which was quite a revelation. Those that have money, like the dwarf Lautrec, have big open spaces like Whistler and there seems to be a naked model in every one. Lautrec hates being called a dwarf. He says that dwarfs are not eligible for national service and he is one centimetre above the minimum height. I still think he is a dwarf. Foreign artists don't have such good lodgings. We went to a block called the floating laundry, which was absolutely squalid. One room each, sometimes with three or four sharing a single bed and a smelly stove in the corner which looked like it would poison you instead of keeping you warm. I don't suppose most of them could afford the wood to keep it going, either. One room had four Spaniards in it.

One of them, a Señor Casas (he couldn't have been much more than sixteen) said that they slept and painted in shifts, as there wasn't enough space for them all to paint or sleep at the same time. The room was stifling and probably freezing cold in the winter, with the window patched up with bits of cardboard. There was just a bucket in the corner and I was very pleased that it had a lid on it, even though they said it had been emptied that morning. I don't think that any of them, including this Casas, had enough money for food and they certainly weren't spending any of it at the public baths. I felt so sorry for them that I asked Vincent afterwards to keep an eye on young Casas and to help him a little if he could. Vincent just joked about me picking up waifs and strays but I'm sure that he will do something on the quiet.

I thought that place was squalid until we went on somewhere called 'the beehive'. You go in on the top floor straight from the road then just keep going down about three of four floors. I say 'floors' but these had more holes than floorboards. The rooms were just cardboard partitions and you could hear every word spoken in almost all of the rooms on the same floor, as well as being able to spy on the people downstairs through the gaps in the floorboards. The cardboard was warping from the damp last winter and cracking from the summer heat. Not a stove or a bucket in sight; judging by the smell it seems that the tenants just walk a bit further down the hill to do the needful. No baths here, either. Vincent bought a couple of pieces for a few francs each, for which the sellers were embarrassingly grateful.

Having our own gallery has completely altered the way that Vincent does business. He still takes the majority of the paintings and prints on a 'sale or return' basis. This is his background stock of his regular artists, which he can bring out for regular clients. Increasingly he is trusting his eye and buying work in from unknown artists and selling it at a much higher price. If it doesn't sell he keeps it aside for several months or years before bringing it out again at a higher price. If it still doesn't sell he doubles the price and tells everyone that the artist is now achieving recognition and his work is in huge demand.

Should the artist die in the meantime, so much the better, we can cash in on the sympathy and the rarity value.

Getting the gallery was a huge stroke of luck. I think we deserved it because it came out of our generosity in the first place. When Whistler went bankrupt I lent him all of my savings to take Maud and the baby off to Venice for this print commission that Vincent had set up for him, on the basis that we kept any money from sales until he returned and paid me back. While he was off in Venice Vincent sold four paintings, which set us up nicely. Then Whistler sold the whole edition of his first set of Venice etchings and could pay me back the money I had lent him. That gave us enough to buy out the gallery business, which was purely the 'good will' and the client lists. Payment for thin air if you ask me but that seems the way that business is done nowadays. I told Vincent that it was ridiculous that he made so much profit for the company that all he got was a measly wage; owning the gallery itself was the only way to make some decent money. He was quite resistant at first but I told him the story of my parents and their house speculation, which won him over. We just had enough left over for a quarter's rent on the gallery itself and for the new sign outside. In the meantime Vincent had managed to track down this Jongkind and put on an exhibition with him next to some of the later paintings by Turner. Even *The Times* liked that one; we English are such suckers for sea scenes.

That set us up nicely but the big success was Whistler's second set of Venice etchings, sold out in the first three weeks. Everyone came to the show, or rather they did eventually. Whistler insisted on doing everything as usual but when the opening party was due to begin kept everybody waiting outside. They got quite upset about it until they found out why. Around half an hour after the advertised opening time the Prince of Wales arrived with Princess Alix. She is always late for everything, so the Prince had told her that they had to arrive at a time that was an hour before the actual one. She was still half an hour late. Whistler took them inside, locked the doors and proceeded to give them a conducted tour of the gallery for nearly an hour. You could hear what he was saying outside because he had to shout all the time, the Princess being so deaf. The Prince reserved a couple of pieces though he never bought them in the end, and that set the whole thing off as the place to be seen and be seen to buy.

Now we can put on whatever shows we want without having to refer them to the Goupil management all the time. I must admit that that is not always a success. A while ago we decided to have an unusual exhibition just of small works, about postcard size. Whistler had a set that he had done while on holiday in St Ives, of which we sold a couple. Vincent brought back some small watercolours he did down in Brighton (he walked all the way there and back, would you believe!) and sold one of them. Harry Kirman sent us some of his oil paintings from Grimsby, which were a total disaster. Nobody had a good word to say about them and *The Times*, of course, was absolutely scathing. Using the bad publicity to get the buyers into the gallery just didn't work this time. Out of friendship Vincent is going to persist with Harry's work in the hope that he might be able to channel some money off to Lizzie and the children.

I am still angry with Harry for disappearing off up north and leaving poor Lizzie behind with six children to look after. He did leave her some money that he had saved up from various bits of work he had done on the gallery and for Whistler but not a huge amount. A good job Lizzie is resourceful. She still takes in sewing but really makes a living working with Mother on making hats. Fortunately bonnets have gone out and hats are now in. Although Mother doesn't think much of the art business, she is happy enough when Vincent brings paintings over from Paris because she can copy the hats from them, which are always much ahead of the fashions in London, so she and Lizzie have ended up doing quite well. As far as we are concerned it means that she doesn't need to take in commercials any more, which is a good job as we need the space for us and the girls.

I thought of Harry when Theo introduced us to a couple of artists in a café the other day. One was a really delightful man – half negro – called Camille. I always thought Camille was a girl's name, but never mind, he was absolutely charming and a real gentleman despite being coloured. The other man was despicable, a greasy type who you expect to be selling you shares in a gold mine that doesn't exist. And so opinionated! Anyone would think he was the head of the Académie Française instead of a hard-up painter. His eyes are set too close together, which gives him a shifty look and a great big nose, which would cut you in half if you got too close. He made me think of Harry because this man, Paul, has walked out on his wife and children in Copenhagen so he can go off and paint. Sheer self-indulgence I call it. Theo says he is going to be a great painter and has got Vincent to take some of his paintings. Vincent was reluctant because he can't stand this Paul chap any more than I can. I don't mind us having his paintings to sell as long as he doesn't come over to England and expect us to be polite to him. As it was I was pretty icy and spent most of my time talking to Camille and brushing Paul's hand off my leg while trying not to listen to him droning on.

For the last three days we have had the company of Theo and Vincent's mother. She is a wonderful woman, so friendly and open. I had feared that she would be a dry old stick from the way that Vincent describes his father. She is not like that at all. We got on like a house on fire. I could see how delighted she was to see Vincent again and how disappointed she was that we did not have Cornelia and Rose with us. She talked all the time about how Vincent had been so difficult and inattentive at school and how grateful she was that he has now settled down to be a caring and responsible businessman and father. "I don't want the girls to be like their father," she said. "Make sure that they attend to their lessons and read their Bible every day. Make proper ladies of them. Let them have fun, good food and good table manners." She seems to love Cornelia in particular, though she knows full well that poor Nelly is not Vincent's. Nor does she ever allude to the reason why Vincent and I married so hurriedly. As far as she is concerned we are just like any other married couple who anticipated the ceremony a little, which is very kind of her.

We are back to England soon after our visit to Versailles, back to work and looking after the girls. I have thoroughly enjoyed our time in Paris, seeing the sites, meeting the artists and looking at all the wonderful dresses. I could sit in the parks for hours just thinking about how I could adapt them back at home. Vincent even lent me a small sketchbook so I could jot down some ideas. It's not art, just an *aide-mémoire* as they say. Vincent likes me to be nicely turned out and I don't think I have disgraced him at all on this visit. Perhaps that is why he has been so romantic the last month or so!

# Brixton

## *1887*

### *Ruth*

That girl will be the death of me! Sometimes I wish she had just gone away up north with her fancy man, just like that reprobate Harry Kirman. First she swans off for weeks in Paris leaving me to look after the girls and the house all on my own. Then she comes back and I know she's had a good time because it's obvious she is in the club again, even if she doesn't know it herself. There's a way she has of carrying herself. Her complexion goes all rosy and she smiles all of the time. Must be something in the blood. And the names she gives to the poor girls! Rose isn't too bad. I suggested Martha but she wasn't having that. "Too old fashioned, too Biblical," she said. What's wrong with Biblical, I ask? Then there's Cornelia. What sort of name is that? Georgina after her poor father would have been better and much more respectful. Then the third one: Maia! That's not even a proper name, now is it? If one of them is going to be named after his mother, then why not Ruth? Too Biblical again, I suspect.

She doesn't even look after them properly. It's always "Mother, can you look after the children for a day while I sort out something at the gallery with Vincent?" or "We have to go to Munich for a couple of weeks, you'll be alright with the children, won't you?" It's a good job I have Lizzie round here a lot of the time. She knows what it's like to have lots of children around and helps me out when I start getting too sharp with them. Lizzie has got one less now that young Harry has gone off. Quite a turn up that was. He was standing outside

165

the music hall selling newspapers when he heard they were auditioning for a boys' choir. Next thing Lizzie knows there is the choir manager on her doorstep ready to discuss terms and take young Harry off there and then. So he's off to the West Country with a few shillings in his pocket and some more sent regular to Lizzie every month. I wouldn't want one of mine gadding off like that, but it's one less mouth to feed.

Me and Lizzie are doing rather well at the hats business. Next week we are taking on a new girl. She'll need training. We'll put her with Doris, Lizzie's eldest girl, who can take her through the basics. Hats have changed quite a bit in Paris this last year or two. They started off being mere handkerchiefs hanging on to the hairdo with a miracle of pins. This year it looks like they are getting larger and flatter and some even have brims. I'm making a special one for Jen-Jen as a kind of advertising. She can wear it when she is out and about flaunting herself. I must say that she has become a bit of a flirt. Wasn't that always the case with the little hussy?

There's a Spaniard that I think she is quite keen on called Ramon or something like that. She is always writing to him. She says it is strictly business and she is doing it to save Vincent the trouble. Quite why she gets so excited when she writes I can't imagine, unless there is something going on. Not that there can be with him in Paris and her here in London. She's a bit too close to that Whistler chap for my liking as well. He's a disgrace, moving that Maud Franklin in as if she's his wife when the poor lady is shunted off down to Hastings. These artists are a disgrace. I'm just grateful that there are none in this house. Can't say I miss the commercials, either. That Major Havard even had the cheek to propose to me just after Jen-Jen got married. Soon sent him away with a flea in his ear, I can tell you! What would I want with a man at my age? He was just after a comfortable billet to retire into.

The big scandal at the moment is the Prince of Wales. He is always up to something. If it isn't gambling, it is being mixed up in divorce cases or stories of his latest mistress. He has surpassed himself this time.

Taken up with a Mrs Langtry and put her on the stage! "Lily Langtry, the Jersey Lily." Whistler has done a painting of her as some Grecian goddess or tart called Phaedre, all bright lights shooting out behind her and her boobies half hanging out of her dress. The Prince is said to love it and has bought it for her and Princess Alix is furious. Of course the Prince had to make it up to her, so he has commissioned Whistler to do a double portrait of his two sons, Albert and George. Originally he wanted a group portrait of him and the Princess with all of the children but the Queen said that it was impossible since the children are all so badly behaved. Really I think she was jealous because she thought it would be too much like Winterthaler's one of her and Prince Albert. So the Prince suggested a portrait of the Princess. They say that Princess Alix became incandescent with rage and accused him of 'parading her to all and sundry just like one of his floozies'. In the end they settled for a portrait of the boys and since Whistler is the only painter that Princess Alix can ever remember meeting (he talked to her for over an hour at his Venice exhibition and VERY LOUDLY so she could hear some of it), he was chosen for the job. He'll have a hard time of it. Albert is so flighty he can't sit still for a moment and George is so glum and boring by all accounts, Whistler will have a job making him look like he is not present at his grandmother's funeral. That can't be far off either, the black old witch, sitting in her castles spending our money. At least Edward gives us all a bit of fun reading about his latest escapades. If he can't be properly royal he is at least amusing.

Can't sit about here all day. There are some new paintings arrived from France and I need to have a look at them to see if there are any interesting hats. Keeps us ahead of the mob. That way the customers will always keep coming back.

# London

## *1889*

*Dear Señor Casas*

 *Thank you for the roll of paintings that you sent me. My wife and I have followed your career for some time and we are delighted to see that you have used your time well in Paris to put together a varied and interesting corpus of work. For such a young man you have absorbed your influences well, although there is still some work to be done in that department. 'Au Bain', for example, is much closer to Degas than it should be, while the 'Interior of the Moulin de la Galette' could almost be by Lautrec himself. Despite that, this latter painting has an air of sadness and an otherworldly feel that is all your own. I have had to hang it at some distance from the other painting of the same interior, as the young woman in that painting is done in a much sharper and challenging manner, forcing us to look for whoever she is meeting somewhere outside the picture frame rather than being pulled into her mood as we are in the other painting. Your use of colour is so obviously different and so differently applied that together they would present too much of a contrast.*

 *I have also hung the painting of a young woman in a dark dress slumped on a green chaise longue. There does not appear to be a title for this one so I have called it 'Exhaustion'. To be honest she looks more like she is in a drug-induced stupor rather than taking a well earned rest. Some of my clients will appreciate that, as there is a spirit of decadence among the younger set here at the moment. Next to it I have hung your portrait of Eric Satie, more for the Monet-influenced background than for the rather effete and ill-defined figure of the* composer. I have to say that I think you are much better at painting female figures than male ones.

I return to you two paintings that I am unable to accept. 'Desnudos' is far too much of a study exercise, as if you were assigned to a difficult part of an atelier where you had a poor view of the model and had to make the best of a bad job. The flesh is well done, I admit, but this just does not work as a composition. The other one is the painting of a riot in Barcelona, which appears to side very heavily with the rioters and suggests brutality by the police and mounted cavalry. Although I have much sympathy with it from a political point of view, as a merchant it is impossible for me to display such a work at this time. There has been huge political unrest in England recently with violent strikes by dockers and even by match girls. Fear of anarchists is everywhere. If I were to show this painting I would be immediately closed down by the authorities. Less important is the fact that I would be unable to sell such a subject to my clients. I would advise you to try and show the painting in Barcelona where I am sure it would find favour among Catalan nationalists.

My wife and I will return to Paris some time in the autumn of next year and we would dearly wish to visit your studio and that of Señor Nonell. We both feel that Spanish and Catalan painting has much to offer, especially when it combines the fierceness and delicacy of traditional Spanish painting with the elegance and flow of France, as you have so successfully proved. My wife is particularly glad that you have found a studio of your own and moved out of Le Bateau-Lavoir. I think she has a rather motherly feeling for your welfare despite the closeness in your ages. In the meantime, should you come across any of your compatriots that you feel you can recommend to me, either in Paris or in Barcelona, I should be delighted to visit their studios.

Yours sincerely
Vincent van Gogh
Director, Outland Gallery, London

# Brixton

## *1892*

I'm in the Royal Academy! Twice over!

Whistler has been doing some sketches of me that I rather like. One is of me seated in one of Mother's new hats. She made it for me as a kind of advertisement, with a huge brim and a cute flower decoration on top. He has called it 'Winged Hat' and I must say that it does look as if it might take off at any moment. The other one I like even more. It was done one morning when I was a trifle late getting up and came downstairs in my nightgown and with little Maia wrapped up in a red towel and her little pink night cap on her head. She does look sweet! Good old Mr W has made me look a lot younger than I am, which is quite a feat first thing in the morning. I wanted to buy it but Whistler had already sold it to an American from Chicago. Doing that caused quite a bit of friction with Vincent because it was sold straight out of the studio instead of through the gallery. Vincent thought he had an agreement to be the only one who sold Whistler's work. Fortunately I was there at the time and managed to patch things up. They can both be bad tempered and grumpy at times. I just smiled sweetly at them and talked ever so quietly so that they had to calm down and listen to me, an old trick I learnt from Grandfather who says it is what the gypsies do with wild horses.

That sorted everything out with the boys so that I was able to tell them what I had worked out for Paris. Goupil is to put on a large retrospective of Whistler's paintings and prints, which the 'Duke of Lancaster' has consented to open. After expenses the gallery commission will be split half and half between Goupil and us. Maud is absolutely delighted because Whistler says that if it is a success they will move to Paris where he will open an *atelier* especially for English and American students. Let's hope he has some money put aside as well. He is nearly sixty now and can't last that much longer. The Mauds will need to have something to live on when he goes.

Sorting the men out was fine but now Mother is in a strop. She is convinced that I am carrying on with every man in sight. It is ridiculous. First it's Casas, who I've only ever seen once when he was no more than a boy and once later. She says I'm always writing to him, which is true. I do all of Vincent's correspondence now unless it absolutely has to be in French or Dutch. Then she says I go all gooey when I write to Casas. That's true in a way as well but only because I remember him as a boy and think how nice he was with his great black eyes. With three girls I often think how wonderful it would be to have a son; I know Vincent thinks that way too. After the trouble I had with Maia the doctor says that I can't have any more children, so we will just have to love the girls that little bit more. And Mother says I flirt with Whistler. He's nearly sixty! What would I do with such an old man? What I do is I jolly him along, he is so grumpy and suspicious. Even now after all these years he still hates the English, which is probably why he gets on with Vincent so well. I'm nice to him as much for Maud's sake, so that he doesn't start getting all mean and nasty to her.

I think Mother also harbours thoughts about me and the butcher. He is quite sweet and gives me some of the better cuts of meat. She says he winks at me, which can't be true because he only has one eye and you can hardly wink with one eye, now can you? She says I dress like a tart with my little waist and nice bosoms. That's just the fashion; the wasp waist makes the bosoms look even bigger. More than that, they seem to have expanded like balloons after the children. Just because all of the other women round here go about in tents, it's no reason why I should. Mind, it is getting on my nerves and if it weren't her house I'd ask her to leave. As it is she's always round at Lizzie's working on the hats. A good thing, too. It keeps her occupied and stops her sticking her nose into our business.

Cornelia is seventeen now, the same age I was when I got married. To think it was that long ago! Vincent is all for sending her off to Paris to stay with Theo and Johanna to learn good French and then to work in one of the couture houses. She is certainly interested in the fashion business and we have had some fascinating times together designing dresses for us that are just as good as any you get over here. Perhaps it is inherited from her father (heaven forbid!). I can see a young girl in Paris getting herself into all sorts of scrapes. Johanna is wonderfully level headed but she can't look after Cornelia like one of her own. Mother wants her to work on the hats with her and Lizzie, which is quite a good idea. A bit limiting, I thought. Women will always wear hats but it's not something you buy every day nor is there a huge profit in it. Really, I would like her to stay here with me. Mother says it is not fair on the girl. She is quite right for once. Rose and Maia say that we should marry her off to one of Papa's rich clients so that she can live happily ever after in a big castle. They suggested that Mr Wilde would be a good candidate. I told them that he isn't rich enough. I could hardly tell them anything else, now could I? We will have to sit down together and discuss it sensibly.

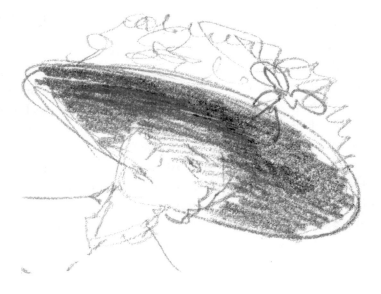

# London

## *1894*

*Dear Theo*

    *First of all, my respects and grateful thanks to Johanna for looking after Cornelia and being such a wonderful substitute mother to her. Eugenie was most apprehensive of the girl starting her working life in Paris where there are so many snares and temptations, as we both know. I am delighted that she seems to be steering clear of them and is making progress in the couture house. I was somewhat worried, as well, that all she would be given to do there would be endless sewing but she tells me that she is now working beside one of the designers and turning his sketches into clean illustrations and then into cutting instructions for the tailors. From what you tell me it appears that I do not need to worry that the designer might himself be a danger to her virtue. She has dropped some hints about how handsome Whistler's assistant Walter is, so perhaps Johanna might cast a caring eye in that direction.*

    *We have had a limited success recently with Gaugin's paintings that he left with us when he sailed for the South Seas. His Martinique paintings caused quite a stir and we have none of those left but the Pont Aven ones have offended our protestant sensibilities. I say 'we' partly because I am now almost more English than the English and also because I find them rather unpleasant. Those acid colours allied to the flatness of the images set my teeth on edge. Perhaps I cannot sell them because I cannot summon up any enthusiasm for them? Still, Jen-Jen tells me that as long as they sell I should continue to try and push even the Pont Aven paintings. She is much better at the business side than I am. She has also developed* quite an eye for a painting, so much so that I can leave her to look after the gallery while I am away.

Now that I am recognised as a lay preacher within the church I often spend my Sundays at various chapels across the country. Last week I preached in a place called Barnsley in Yorkshire. Barnsley is a coal mining town; if the mines ever closed down the town itself would die completely. In good times the miners are wealthy compared to other workers of their class. Unfortunately good times do not last. If the demand for coal goes down the miners are put on short time or laid off completely. There are often accidents, particularly in bad mines where the seams are difficult or where the owners have scrimped on the safety precautions. Many are the miners who have crushed limbs or suffer from 'black lung' from continually breathing in coal dust. The women try desperately hard and keep their houses as clean as they can but many of the men are too addicted to drink and deprive their families of a sufficiency of food. Once in drink they are forever fighting and cursing. Among our Methodist congregation there is great devotion but the community as a whole is a heathen wilderness. I must confess to a crisis of confidence after a day spent in the town. What am I doing selling paintings to rich merchants and aristocrats when I should be spreading the word of God among these benighted people? If it had not been for Jen-Jen and the girls I believe that I would have thrown up everything in London and settled down here to preach the gospel to these downtrodden and unhappy people.

But I did not.

Instead I returned to Brixton to find a letter from my good friend Harry. He reminded me of our evening talks in the White Horse, which I found touching. His son Young Harry has been touring the music halls for some years. Eventually he ended up in Grimsby and Harry has found him a job on the trawlers owned by one of his patrons. I still show some of his paintings from time to time. They are good and getting better. Sadly they have no resonance among my buyers and consequently I have quite a stack of them down in the storeroom. Luckily he has found a way of keeping himself without having to go to sea, as you will gather from this newspaper cutting.

*Grimsby Evening Telegraph*
*"Museum opens with exhibition of trawler paintings*
*Generous donations by local art patrons*

*Grimsby's new museum and art gallery opened Thursday last with its first exhibition, a collection of marine paintings by the local artist Mr Henry Kirman. Mr Kirman specialises in paintings of trawlers and has received many commissions from owners as far away as Hull, Fleetwood and Lowestoft to immortalise their new vessels in paint. Apart from paintings of the vessels themselves there is a striking rendition of the dock tower as it appears against a storm-threatening sky, the tower emphasised by the use of a long, thin canvas. We are happy to announce that this has been purchased by the Freemen of the town and donated to the museum. Mr J. Ross has made two donations in a similar spirit. The first is a painting of his new trawler the 'Emily Jane', which is named after his daughter. The other is a four-feet wide canvas of the fish docks, so crowded with ships that one can hardly see the water beneath. Mr Kirman has beautifully rendered the masts and rigging jostling together against a stunning sunset of rushing clouds. The opening was attended by the Mayor and Mayoress of the borough, Mr and Mrs Newby, as well as by many of the Aldermen and councillors."*

So you can see that Harry has been hard at work. His trawlers are nothing like the stuff he sends to me with their heavy outlines and grisaille work. A combination of Gaugin and Whistler in Harry's strange idiosyncratic manner.

I also have a press cutting to show you. Perhaps not as grand as Harry's, but I am quite pleased with it nonetheless.

*The Lady*
*"Delicate flowers for one's drawing room*

*We recently attended a charming exhibition of flower paintings by*

*V. V. Governor at the premises of Stone and Company in Burlington Arcade. Although we know nothing of the artist we can only assume from the delicacy of the work that they are by a young lady of elegance and feeling. Unusually the paintings are in a form of pastel, with a few in coloured chalks. So many watercolours have a dry and desiccated appearance whilst these, in contrast, leap off the page with an immediacy that is restrained enough not to be overwhelming. Readers are urged to consider these excellent paintings as a valuable addition to their drawing room."*

I love the idea of being described as 'a young lady of elegance and feeling'. They are not great art, I know. They were a wonderful release from the chores of running a gallery, without being too demanding. Sales just about paid for the framing costs, which was as good as I could expect.

Well, my boy, look after yourself. You were looking a trifle peaky the last time we met and we can't have you being ill so soon in your married life. Jen-Jen recommends regular doses of Dr Browne's Famous Chlorodyne if you can find that in France.

Your loving brother
Vincent

# Brixton

## *1896*

ather has been in bed now for the last four days. He is much
worse than I have ever seen him. We are all very worried about
him; he is running a fever. Every now and then he will shout
out things in Dutch, which Mother says sounds like the prophesy the
mad woman told him at chapel. When he is better he mumbles a
jumble of sentences that I recognise from *The Pilgrim's Progress*
alongside Biblical phrases. The Reverend Slade-Jones says these are
from the Revelation of St John. I wouldn't know; that part of the Bible
doesn't interest me, full of hell and damnation and the end of the
world.

The first fit was when Grandma died. Not a bad one. He seemed
to get over it fairly quickly. I don't think he ever liked Grandma very
much and she was going mad as she got older. Poor Mama could not
as much as take a letter from the postman without Grandma telling
her what a brazen hussy she was, having an affair with such a low
person. Maia and I would just sit and giggle but it was hard on Mama
and made Father utterly furious. So he was not taken too bad when
she went. The news about Uncle Theo totally destroyed him. He
collapsed when he read the telegram, frothing and shouting, sweat all
over his face. Usually Mother can handle him; this time it took all
three of us to hold him down and to get the gag in his mouth. It was
hours before he was able to get up and talk coherently.

Mama wanted to go off to Paris with him for the funeral but had
to stay behind to look after the gallery. Not that she was that keen on
going to the funeral. She wasn't sure that Father would be safe on his

own. What if he had another fit like the last one? Father convinced her that Cornelia would look after him in Paris so she let him go off on his own. Cornelia sent us a telegram to say that he had arrived, setting our minds at rest. What she didn't tell us was that he had another fit at the funeral and had to be taken back to Aunt Johanna's in a cab. Cornelia was so worried about him that she accompanied him all the way back to Brixton and she is the one who is sitting with him now. That is really good of Cornelia because I know how much she loves Paris, even after her disappointment with Walter. I think that artists make terrible husbands anyway. Poor Mrs Whistler died all on her own in Hastings. Maud refuses to marry Whistler now because she says that he was such a rotten husband that she is not prepared to take a chance with him. At his age I can't imagine he is much good to her in bed. (Aren't I terrible! Mother would be furious if she heard me saying something like that. She thinks that none of us know anything about what goes on between a man and a woman but living round here you can't but notice.)

Now that Mama is in the gallery all day long we three girls run the house. Very well we do it, too. Cornelia is the nurse. I am the cook. Maia is the cleaner and general maid. When Mama gets home the house is all neat and tidy with a hot meal on the table. We are quite pleased with ourselves despite our worry over Father. What it does mean, though, is that all our plans for the future are on hold until Father recovers. Cornelia says that she has learned enough in Paris and she is going to set herself up as a couturier in London. Grandma left a good sum of money from her hat business that she had with Mrs Kirman. The money is supposed to be divided between the three of us but Maia and I have donated our share to Cornelia. At first she did not want to accept it. Then we had the idea of being business partners. Cornelia will have a half share because she is going to do all of the work and supply the expertise. Maia and I have a quarter share each. If we want to go into the company ourselves, Cornelia says that she will have us on the basis that we start out as the lowest apprentice and only get to do the interesting things once we prove we are assets to the company. Cornelia has obviously learnt a lot in Paris and from Mama, who is much better at business than Father.

That's our plans. What will happen to them if Father dies, I do not know.

# Barcelona

## *1899*

M ost of the people on the Ramblas at this hour amble along
placidly, not wishing to exert themselves at the end of a
long and tiring day. Not so Carlos who hurries along in
a precipitate slouch, head and shoulders perpetually bent so that one
would be amazed at how few collisions he is part of or has narrowly
averted. His speed draws glances and ungracious comments from the
other pedestrians, annoyed by this incursion. At one time his mere
appearance had been enough to cause scandal. By now the other
residents have become accustomed to it, if still disturbed by his general
behaviour.

Today he is sporting, of all things, a top hat, an affectation adopted
only by rich foreigners. Many must have been the foreigners who had
worn this particular piece of headgear, its nap worn almost bare and
its brim sad and crinkled. Carlos is very attached to this top hat since
it hides and partly shades his enormous nose, which one wag had
claimed was so large that his chin had been transposed there by
mistake. In truth his face does appear to decline directly from his lower
lip to his Adam's apple with no protuberance in between. To add
weight to his general appearance Carlos sports the largest set of side
whiskers in Barcelona: great fluffy things, black with an occasional
ginger tinge when the light strikes them at a certain angle. Today he
is wearing galoshes and an overcoat that is several sizes too large for
him across the back, though in length it barely reaches his knees. Pablo
is constantly tempted to draw his friend as a stick insect but feels that
even the good natured Carlos would be insulted by this.

Carlos is not well today. His already long face has fallen by ten centimetres, his hair is even lanker than usual and his complexion is a mixture of mud and acacia honey. The good news is that he is worried about his health, which all his friends know is perfectly fine. According to him the constant wind at this time of year has brought on his neurasthenia. His joints crackle as he walks, his body is stooped so much that you expect that his knees and his chin will come into contact at any moment.

It is Pablo that Carlos is hurrying to meet at Els Quatre Gats, the café that Père Romeu has opened in imitation of Aristide Bruant's Chat Noir in Paris. Both establishments favour art students and their modest clientele as well as poets and musicians. As far as Pablo is concerned anywhere he can discuss art is fine by him and one in imitation of a café owner immortalised by Toulouse Lautrec is even better. Carlos does not talk about art very much. When he is not painting or drinking he is thinking about love. Not like Pablo who would paint all night when he should be out on the town.

"Pablito," Carlos says, "this climate is killing me. My brains are fried by the sun in summer, blown away by the winter winds and whatever is left over of them turned into a soggy mush by the spring rains. Even Malaga is better than this."

Pablo thinks Carlos is wrong about Malaga but then he has no relatives living there. He may well be right about Barcelona, though at least it is a capital city and a much more cultured one than boring Madrid: "As well as publishing our own arts magazines we get copies of ones from other countries. Here an artist is respected, not sworn at in the street for his long hair and English tweeds. Now, there's a place to be! England with its great artists and its wonderful women."

"Pablito, don't you start that again. You know that the climate in England is the worst in Europe. They don't have a climate, they just have weather. And the women! Huge Amazons who spend their time sleeping with their horses and chasing wild animals across the bogs and the marshes. If we go anywhere, we go to Paris."

Carlos has become quite excited. Throwing back his shoulders he

181

resumes his full height, a height which always embarrasses Pablo. Neurasthenia forgotten, there is even a twinkle in his eye. Miraculous how a single word can effect such a transformation. Paris! "Sunyer is in Paris, and Manolo. There are great things happening there. Think of Monet and Pissarro and Degas; they have taken the world by storm. Then there is that dwarf Lautrec whose posters you so much admire. Besides, Parisian women are the most elegant in the world."

"I might have known it," muses Pablo. "Instead of the light of culture that I thought I saw in Carlos's eyes, it is the light of love. He is tired of the brothels, especially the cheap ones that are all that we can afford, and of paying court to young ladies across a drawing room with her *duenna* in attendance. What he wants is a proper love affair with a real woman who will love him for himself, not for the few pesetas he gives to the madam afterwards. Carlos is a romantic. He reads Byron and Shakespeare. He is a veritable Don Quixote of love; he tilts at windmills and widows, rides any ass in the brothel and calls her his beauty. While I, Sancho Panza Ruiz, watch on and try to save him from his idiocies, from proposing marriage to any cunning tart who takes his fancy. How stupid he could be in Paris! What he needs is an English woman. An English woman would look after him and subdue him to her will. Perhaps she would also beat him as she beats her horse. I think Carlos might like that."

Carlos slaps a drink down in front of the ruminating Pablo. For a change Pablo is on his own. His broad brow is furrowed in concentration and his olive black eyes are half closed. He is studying a sheet of A3 paper which is on the table in front of him and which the careless Carlos has almost defiled from the brimming glasses.

"What do you think?" asks Pablo. "Haven't I done the place well? Romeu will be pleased enough with me to clear out my slate."

"Is that meant to be the terrace here?"

"Of course, can't you tell by the building? There aren't many like that in Barcelona."

Carlos is confused. The poster is indeed a marvel; it makes Els Quatre Gats look as exciting and as elegant as Renoir's version of the bar at the Folies Bergère. On the clean and solid tables are spotless cloths on which some dandies and their ladies are leaning, beer mugs in hand. Such a place to which one might take one's betrothed or even one's sister if suitably accompanied. By contrast the real Gats is dingy and smoky. The clientele, if rather romantic in theory, have a tendency to dress in an *outré* manner, as witnessed by Carlos's top hat and overcoat and Pablo's ostentatious black velvet trousers and matching waistcoat.

Pablo has caught his friend's hesitation. "It's an advertisement, it's not meant to be a portrait of the place. You can be as free as you like with an advertisement. You don't suppose that Bruant is as jolly as Lautrec made him look, do you? Or Jane Avril as exciting? Advertising is a game, like art, making you believe anything but the truth. The artist is an out-and-out liar, making you believe whatever he wants you to. Even photographs are at the mercy of the skill of the photographer and the tricks of the dark room. I gave up trying to get as close to reality as I could when I was fourteen. My father thinks that is the end of art. Really it is just the beginning. I want to put something of myself into it, to involve the viewer, not just flatter the subject."

"Well, Père Romeu will certainly be flattered by this piece of yours. Whether it will bring him any more customers I sincerely doubt. That apart, it's a good piece of work. Solid construction, a bit bold with the colours, though that's normal with posters. You've been rather too free with the perspective for my liking and those figures behind look like you've lifted them straight from your sketchbook. Oh! You did! Still, they do look stuck on just to fill in the space."

The discussion continues for some time until subsumed into the normal unruly rout as more people join the table. As the company gets louder and increasingly diffuse Pablo becomes quieter and more withdrawn. Finally, around midnight he slips away to his studio where he paints until dawn.

# Barcelona to Paris

## *1900*

T hird-class carriages are no more comfortable in France than they are in Spain. The same slatted wooden seats, the same filthy windows and dirt-spattered floors, the same smell of ancient cigarette smoke and dirty feet. None of this bothers Pablo and Carlos. Their excitement grows with each significant landmark. The Franco-Spanish border. Perpignan station, not yet christened the centre of the universe. The fort of Salses-le-Château, marking the end of Catalan domination and the entry into France proper. The walls of the Massif Central receding against the great flow of the river Rhône. To while away the time, the boys share their meal of bread and sausage with their travelling companions in the carriage who produce delicacies of their own: pigs' trotters, a rough pâté, a handful of fierce chillies and, best of all, a litre bottle of homemade Collioure wine.

Pablo has borrowed money from his father for the journey, donated begrudgingly after the wanton waste of a year's debauch in Madrid followed by a typical teenage revolt which led to him stalking out of the family house and taking up residence in a brothel in Barcelona's 'Chinese quarter'. After the rail fare all he has left is thirty-five pesetas. Fortunately Carlos is better endowed, paying for their transport to the train and for odd snacks seized at stops at remote rural stations while the train takes on coal and water. The small amount of money he has been paid for some illustrations in *Juventud* has long gone, as have the sausages that the grocer paid him for decorating the front of his shop. With luck his father will soon receive the fee for the patent medicine poster, which he will forward to him in Paris. Never mind, something will turn up.

By rights Pablo should still be in Barcelona. Utrillo has organised an exhibition for him, his second in the city, at the Sala Parés. Instead he has taken the early train in order to avoid the opening party. As a compliment Utrillo has hung paintings by Casas, now the leading artist of the younger set in Barcelona, next to Pablo's. Pablo is furious at being lumped in with someone he regards as old fashioned and bourgeois, an exponent of *passé* styles like impressionism and ignorant of the beauties of the recently rediscovered El Greco. Why should he be lumped in with this old man of thirty-five? He is uncertain whether he is angrier with Utrillo or with Casas, unaware of the great favour that Casas will soon confer upon him despite the newspaper review which describes Pablo's work as showing 'carelessness and a lack of experience'.

Arriving in Paris is a disappointment. The station is wonderful: huge leaping iron buttresses and painted Corinthian columns. Walk outside. This is worse than Barcelona! There are beggars on the dirty streets, whores hanging about the entrances touting for custom, tugging at the boys' jacket sleeves, almost climbing on them in their desperation for even the cheapest encounter. That neither Pablo nor Carlos speak any French seems no discouragement, indeed their youth and their obvious ignorance of the local going rates are a veritable inducement. Even their aggressive sales pitch cannot withstand the dumb tiredness of a two-day train journey on slatted seats. All the boys want to do is to find a cheap bed and sleep for a day. As it is it takes them several hours before they can find a hotel that is cheap enough for them, even in this run-down area with its streets filthy with rubbish. Despite the bed bugs they sleep until well into the next morning, huddled up together under the hotel's thin blankets. Pablo had hated the weather in Madrid. Paris is worse: cold and wet at the same time. Even the autumn rains and thunderstorms of Barcelona are better than this. Perhaps he should never have left Malaga?

Next morning they set out to find Utrillo. No luck. Utrillo is still

185

in Barcelona fuming over Pablo's refusal to attend the exhibition that he has organised for him. They have had to walk all of the way across Paris, from south of the Seine right up to the butte of Montmartre. For the first time on the journey they regard it as fortunate that they have almost no luggage. Other fortune now smiles upon them. Taking a lunchtime coffee in the sleaziest café they can find, they come across Nonell. Particularly fortunate in that Nonell is in funds for the first time in his life. His show at Els Quatre Gats has gone particularly well and Mademoiselle Weill has sold three of his paintings. So enthused is he that he is about to leave his current studio on the rue Gabrielle and move into a larger one that has both gas lighting and a wood stove for heating, the rue Gabrielle having neither. He can arrange with the landlord to let Carlos and Pablo have the old studio at the same rent as he has been paying: sixteen francs a month. Sixteen francs is an enormous sum. Carlos does some arithmetic. To stay in the hotel will cost twice this amount plus they will have to take all of their meals in cafés, an extra expense even if they reduce themselves to one *plat du jour* and a glass or two of absinthe. Deal done!

They go off to view the studio and negotiate with the landlord. He wishes to charge them extra as there will be two of them living there. Carlos wishes to pay less since they are poor young students. Eventually the landlord agrees on fifteen francs, payable in advance. Carlos delves into his *portmanteau*, turns his back on the others, unfastens a hidden compartment and produces a small purse from which he pays the landlord. He turns the purse upside down and a ten-peseta piece falls out. Nonell looks at this piteously and invites Carlos and Pablo back to his new studio for a supper of cold sardines and bread.

Good luck continues. The Catalan clique has decided that if Nonell is moving into a new studio it should be blessed with a party. Cheap red wine from the Corbières, anchovies from Cadaques, bread from the *boulangerie* round the corner, girls from wherever they can be found. A grand night is had by all. Riera forgets his bourgeois origins and sings his collection of dubious songs. Manolo becomes increasingly drunk and wraps his arm around Pablo's neck in order to stay upright, even though both are sitting on the bare floorboards already. Even Casas turns up and turns out to be less of a stuffed shirt than Pablo had been expecting. "I am a true Catalan," he declaims. "An anarchist in politics, a nihilist in philosophy, a symbolist in art. Long live Gauguin and Bakunin!" With which he collapses into a sleep from which he cannot be awoken until the following morning. Carlos is completely unaware of the art talk around him, engrossed as he is with Germaine Gargallo, a whore from Almeria who works the tourist area around the Gare du Nord. Germaine is flattered to be singled out but finds Carlos singularly unattractive. Despite his unappealing appearance Germaine has decided to stick around with him for a while, having been told that Carlos's father is rich and that the lad has high financial expectations, even if he is in financial difficulties for a while.

Cheap Corbières wine is unforgiving, so that it is with heavy hearts and sore heads that Pablo and Carlos turn out of their blankets early the next afternoon. Some time elapses before they realise that their good fortune is continuing. Full of last night's meal and with stomachs revolting against an excess of wine, they have no desire for food. Which is a good job because ten pesetas goes absolutely nowhere in an expensive city like Paris where one needs as much as two or even three francs every day to live on. A day on foot exploring Montmartre with one coffee between them leaves them satisfied but shivering when they return to the studio.

Will good fortune never end? Utrillo has returned from Barcelona. For Carlos he brings money from his father, enough for food and rent for several weeks. Pablo is envious until Utrillo turns out another pocket. Here is the price of two paintings and a drawing sold from the exhibition at the Sala Parés, plus the money for the medicine poster. The boys hurry off to Père Tanguey to purchase his cheapest paints and canvases. They also set aside some cardboard and some broken wood that they have come across for those days when they can no longer afford to paint on proper canvas. Is not Paris a wonderful place to live and be an artist!

# Paris

## 1900

*My dearest Madame van Gogh,*

*The days here have been long and dreary. Winter is bad enough but your absence makes it even worse. However short the days, without you they feel interminable. I spend my time dreaming of your return and only then can I settle down to paint with a clear mind. Even the warm companionship of my compatriots fails to raise my spirits in your absence.*

*Since you have left, I have completed the two paintings that I had started. 'Laziness' is one of those that I enclose with the parcel that I hope you will receive soon after this letter. I am very happy with this one; it conveys nicely those long afternoons when one does not feel like doing anything, even reading, and life drifts away in a pleasant reverie. What I am totally delighted with is the other one, which I call 'After the Bath'. You remember the one I am talking about? Both subject and execution fully delight me. I shall hang it above my bed so that I can gaze upon it every evening. This is one painting that I shall keep close to me for all eternity in memory of the magnificent Madame van Gogh.*

*Now, something that will please you. Two young Spanish men from Barcelona arrived recently. I know how much you like young men, Spanish ones in particular! They wear matching corduroy suits, much the worse for wear by now, which seem to be their only clothes. First is one Carlos. A tall, bent, dry stick who is all of nineteen but looks ninety. They say he paints. How can he when he spends so much time mooning over the local tarts?*

The other is a short, dark-eyed, intense youth with gimlet eyes and the hands of a woman. He rejoices in the name of Pablo Diego José Francisco de Paula Juan Nepomuceno Maria de los Remedios Cipriano de la Santisima Trinidad Ruiz y Picasso. Put all those on end and they are taller than he is! He already has a growing reputation in Spain, or at least in Cataluña. A couple of years ago he showed a big painting ('Science and Charity' I think it was called, a doctor and a nun around a sick woman's bedside) at the Madrid Fine Arts Exhibition and later in Malaga where it won a gold medal. That's not saying much; my five-year-old nephew could win at least a bronze medal in Malaga, which is by no means the cultural capital of Spain. Another painting with a miserable subject called 'Last Moments' was in the Spanish pavilion here in Paris last year. Nothing special, but an achievement to be selected in the first place.

Utrillo saw an exhibition of his drawings at Els Quatre Gats and was very impressed, which means more to me than all the official approval in the world. He was so impressed that he organised another show for him at the Sala Parés where he hung young Pablo's paintings next to mine. I think Utrillo means that as a compliment but I'm not sure to which of us. One thing that may well put you off this young man is certain proclivities that he is said to have. He spent all of last summer in a cave in the mountains with a gypsy boy. You know those gypsy boys will do anything for a few pesetas. I've already seen him edging up to Manolo, who is himself not too choosy about where he donates his favours.

Please, my dear Mrs Van Gogh, come back to Paris soon, when I can show you 'After the Bath' and introduce you to my new compatriots. Life is dreary without your beautiful smile to enliven it. Until then I remain

Your affectionate, loving and obedient servant
Ramon Casas

# London

## 1900

*Dear Señor Casas*

*Much as I value our friendship I am a respectable married woman and I absolutely forbid you to write to me in such terms as contained in your last letter. It is imperative that we maintain a serious and close business relationship, which will allow us both to hold our heads erect in polite society. I know that Spanish modes of address can be more exuberant than those common elsewhere, England in particular but I still cannot believe that such a missive as your last would be permitted even in Spain. I beg you never to write to me in such terms ever again.*

*I have received your roll of paintings. I must say that I am delighted with them and much happier than with the letter that preceded them. As for the 'After the Bath' painting I beg that you will destroy it or at least lock it away in a dark cellar somewhere so that no-one will ever see it, so much do I disapprove of the subject no matter how excellent your execution may be. I dislike it even more than I dislike that fatuous beard that you have begun to develop in imitation either of the young Prince George or that anarchist Bakunin. Rusinol said to me when I was in Paris that it is "better to be symbolist and unbalanced, even crazy and decadent than vile and cowardly". That is fine for art. Yours is the better for it and is certainly not 'vile and cowardly' but real life is different and an unbalanced and crazy anarchist beard is not to be endured. When next I see you I shall come armed with a razor.*

*Another thing... You should move further away from Lautrec. If anyone is unbalanced, it is he. As he gets older his illness troubles him more, leading him into greater bouts of depression and even deeper into the bottle. His company nowadays merely leads to dissipation. As far as your art goes, it is time that you have fully absorbed all that you can glean from him. Fortunately the recent batch of paintings have moved away both from Degas and Lautrec. I warn you, though, that if I perceive any backsliding in this matter I will have no hesitation in returning the offending painting with no qualms whatsoever. If you wish to please me in anything it is in this evolution in your art. I might even forgive the beard!*

*Your young man sounds interesting. As you know I am always interested in young men, particularly young Spanish men for some reason. This is no doubt the result of having three daughters and no son. The dark charm of young Spanish men reminds me of the son that I never had but always wanted. From what you say of him it does appear that he is a young man of much talent. Such a pity that he is a follower of Mr Wilde! Since he is so impoverished I would be much obliged if you could enclose a couple of his paintings with your own next parcel. Hopefully this will not be necessary too soon, as I am planning to come to Paris in the early spring once the weather is milder and the winds in the Channel have ameliorated.*

*Until then, I bid you farewell and assure you of the friendship and affection of your devoted admirer*

*Eugenie van Gogh*

*P.S. I urge you again to be more circumspect in your letters in future.*

# Paris

## *1900*

Pablo stirs sleepily and throws an arm across Gabrielle in an attempt to stop her snoring. With luck she will wake up in time for them to make love again before she has to leave ahead of Carlos's return from whatever overnight debauch he has been engaged in. Their friendship could not withstand Carlos's discovery of Gabrielle in Pablo's bed. Pablo thinks that Gabrielle has consented to sleep with him for free because she believed his story about being a virgin. A complete mistake. Gabrielle is well aware that any middle class Spanish boy would have been introduced early to the local brothels in order to prepare him for marriage, whilst enduring interminable engagements to a possibly unwilling future bride who must herself be kept pure for her wedding night. She has gone to bed with Pablo because she thinks he is rather sweet. A girl should have fun, not be thinking of business all of the time. Nor is she much concerned about Carlos who she thinks is rather a bore. Besides which he is impotent. He can kiss and stroke but that is all he can manage. The refusal of his organ to rise is frustrating to Carlos and deeply insulting to Gabrielle. Pablo has no such problems as she has been told by Rosita and has recently confirmed for herself.

Gabrielle wakes. They make love lazily. They doze. Paris is well awake. There are noises below. Pablo throws back the sheets, dives into some clothes, picks up a drawing pad and pencil. Pushes the protesting Gabrielle onto the chair with the bursting horsehair upholstery, ignoring her protests that the hair is uncomfortable in places so recently made tender. Just in time. A groggy Carlos arrives, still drunk from the night before. "Why are you so late?" demands Pablo. "Where have you been? Gabrielle has been here for hours waiting for you. A good thing, too. She is wonderful to draw." Always facile with a pencil Pablo has already completed one rough sketch consisting almost entirely of a single line. He turns four pages as if to insinuate that these already contain images of Gabrielle.

"Yes, I have waited for you all this time. Now you come in drunk with no word to me. Is this what you call your love for me?" Gabrielle has a whore's facility of being able to dress even faster than she can undress. Before Carlos can know it she has on her coat and disappears through the door.

"Carlos, you drink too much. Look how offended Gabrielle is with you. All you need to do is to stay sober and be nice to her. See how she came here this morning looking for you."

"I don't care. She doesn't love me. She only came here to torment me because she knew I wouldn't be here. I drink to forget her. It only makes me want her more. I can't go on like this. It is alright for you. You just spend half of your time painting then go off to Rosita. She's madly in love with you even though you don't care a fig for her. I think you care more for Manolo than you care for her."

"What are you trying to say about me and Manolo? He is a good friend and a great sculptor. We love one another like brothers, in the same way that I love you. If you are suggesting anything else I think you had better apologise or I will never speak to you again."

"Oh, I don't know. I apologise. He does keep calling you 'my little sister', though. Shit, life is so complicated. Maybe I will get a gun and shoot you all, then shoot myself. I could be famous after my death, have my picture in the newspapers and have a special exhibition of my paintings at police headquarters."

"In that case, you will need to borrow some of mine. You've only finished two canvases since we have been here. I don't think Paris is good for you. We need to go to London or Munich. Look at these magnificent paintings by Klimt in *Simplissimus*. Munich, that's a place where they take painting seriously, without bothering about impressionism, *pointillism* and all that. The only modern French painter worth bothering about is Gaugin and even he has run off to Tahiti. That's what we should do, go east or west it doesn't matter. Somewhere that will get you away from your whores and your absinthe. Let's go to Munich tomorrow and leave all this."

"No, Pablito. We have a nice studio, good friends. And I couldn't leave Gabrielle, she is so wonderful even if she is destroying my mind. She is the woman of my thoughts and the object of my life."

"This is getting us nowhere. Put our coat on, it's your turn. Come with me to Mademoiselle Weill's, she says she wants to see some of my bullfight paintings. Then we can see what is the *plat du jour* at the Arlésienne."

"Damn," says Carlos. "Sauerkraut again."

Mademoiselle Weill is like Carlos in one respect: he is nineteen and looks ninety, she is thirty and looks to be at least eighty. She makes a modest living buying paintings from young artists for little more than the cost of the canvas and selling them on again to *petit bourgeois* and rich tourists for twice the price. It takes her ten minutes to choose three of Pablo's best bullfight paintings and two hours for the two of them to arrive at a price. Pablo's lack of French and Mademoiselle Weill's rudimentary Spanish do not help, though they are merely picadors in the contest. Weill is the matador enticing the poor Pablo to take any amount to alleviate his poverty. Pablo is the bull, fiercely intent on being recognised as a growing talent and determined to assert his true worth. Both participants thoroughly enjoy the contest, which is resolved to the dissatisfaction of both.

Sauerkraut it is at the Arlésienne which, despite its name, is run by a rotund and angry woman from Alsace. Nonell is already there accompanied by an elegantly dressed man in his thirties who greets the newcomers in impeccable Catalan. "My boys, welcome. Come and join me and my good friend Isidore. We have had an excellent morning and he has had the grace to sell me one of his paintings. He is such a sweetheart, you know." Nonell introduces this character as

'Père Manyac', "who is like a father to we poor Catalan exiles. Without him we would all have starved long ago."

Manyac nods, strokes his gingery beard, pushes back his thinning hair, regards Carlos and Pablo contemplatively. "And how long have you two pretty boys been here in Paris? Only a month? What a shame I did not meet you before. I am always looking for some young company." Nonell winks at Pablo and inclines his head. Although Manyac's words have been directed at both of them he has not taken his eyes off Pablo since his arrival. This makes for a difficult meal, especially as the rough red wine makes Manyac ever more effusive. All of the sauerkraut and the odd elusive pieces of sausage ingested, Manyac insists that they repair to the studio to examine the paintings.

Once there he does at last take his eyes off Pablo, picking up canvases excitedly, examining each one with near-sighted precision. Two he rejects, moving them behind him, their faces turned to the wall. "Why are there so few drawings?" demands Manyac. Pablo looks embarrassed. "There were some more but it was so cold last week that we had to burn them to keep warm."

"Don't do that ever again. Keep everything. Those two paintings over there. Paint over them. I don't want to come here and see such rubbish again; too much soul and not enough form. Some more self-criticism would be in order. Now, I have an offer for you. The workers at my factory in Barcelona are on strike at the moment. As soon as they get hungry they will slink back to work. Whatever Casas says, anarchism may be good for art but it is bad for owners and for the workers. As soon as they return I will come here and buy all of these paintings, except for those two over there, for 150 francs. Then every month I will buy all of the work you produce for the same 150 francs. How does that suit you, my boy?" Manyac puts his arm around Pablo's shoulders, causing him to twitch uncomfortably. "I have good connections. Let me talk to Ambroise Vollard. We'll see if I can't arrange an exhibition there for you next year. What do you say, huh? A deal?" He chucks Pablo under the chin and stands back to admire both the paintings and Pablo at the same time. How can a poor boy refuse? He can live easily on seventy-five francs a month, and here he is being offered twice that. Of course he accepts. Manyac is delighted with his deal and exits arm in arm with Nonell. Carlos digs into his *portmanteau*, retrieves his purse, leaves and returns with a full bottle of absinthe which the boys share, taking alternate swigs from their sole glass.

*Pablo*

# Paris

## *1900*

"I'm sick of this. I'm off. I'm leaving."

"Again? What is wrong this time?"

"The weather is terrible, even worse than Barcelona. The sun never shines, the east wind blows through me all of the time. When it isn't raining, it's snowing. And this is supposed to be spring!

You paint all the time like clockwork. All I can do is stand and look at the canvas. I can't think about painting or great themes, all I can do is think about seeing Gabrielle. And when I do see her, what happens? I try to be nice to her, to buy her nice things, take her to bed, get her all excited. And nothing. Then she gets angry with me, shouts at me. Yesterday she even threw her bedpan at me. Good job it was empty but it still hurt. When she's with me now she doesn't even bother to put her sponge in, she knows there's no need. You get all of the girls you want. I just want one girl and I can't have her. It's maddening. So, I'm leaving. Manyac keeps trying to bribe me so that he can move in here instead of me. I might as well take his money and go."

"You mean you've already taken his money? That's betrayal. You know I can't stand him. I only bother with him because he buys my paintings and gives me enough money to live on."

"And then some! He's been a good friend to you. So what if I take his money? I'm going anyway and he might as well pay me to do it."

"But he'll just be here all the time, pawing at me and gazing at me with those lecherous eyes of his. He even has the cheek to tell me how to paint! I can't stand him and you are contemplating abandoning me and letting him live in here?"

"It can't be helped. If I'm leaving somebody has to move in here. I don't care who it is as long as it isn't Gabrielle. I couldn't stand the thought of you and Gabrielle being together. Anyway I'm going to spend Manyac's money right now. Jarry has got something that I have to have, so I'll go and fetch it straight away. You go down to the Arlésienne and order a table for us tonight, about half a dozen of us. And tell her, no bloody sauerkraut!"

"Carlos, don't get anything from Jarry. He's a raving madman. He's as likely to shoot you as to sell you something. He'll see your wish to buy something as a bourgeois aberration and an insult to his anarchist principles. Besides which, he will insist on reciting one of his poems. Even Jacob cannot understand a word of Jarry's poems, and he's French. Neither of us has any chance with them whatsoever."

"No, Jarry knows what I want and what I want it for. He's in total approval because he thinks it is an affirmation of freedom and a blow against French society. You'll see tonight. And don't worry about the bill at the Arlésienne, the rest of Manyac's money will take care of that. Where's my hat? I'm off. Don't forget, no sauerkraut."

Pablo is amused by Carlos's antics. This is the best he has seen him for weeks, finally arisen from his 'slough of despond', up and doing something at last instead of sulking around and getting paralytic drunk. No doubt it is the thought of returning to Catalonia, to the invigorating southern spring which by now has more or less passed into early summer before the buds on the rare bushes in Paris have even begun to burst. Cheered by these thoughts he puts on his new coat and sets off for the Arlésienne. Well, not quite new coat, new to him at least. Bought from a stall on the flea market with some of the detested Manyac's money, without which he would have starved or been forced to return to Barcelona long ago.

The proprietress of the Arlésienne listens to his request carefully, including the interdiction of sauerkraut, and breaks out into a long tirade against filthy foreigners who can't even put together a simple French sentence besides making such impossible demands so late in the afternoon. Even if his French were considerably better, Pablo would still not be able to understand her heavy Alsace accent, which sounds closer to German than to French. An agreement is reached for a price that Pablo finds extortionate. With luck Carlos will pay Jarry less than anticipated or he will be organising a whip-round by the end of the meal.

Next, Pablo sets about rounding up the list of friends that Carlos has left for him. Manolo is at his studio trying to persuade Riera to buy one of his sculptures. Riera is reluctant. The last time they had agreed on a sale Manolo had sold the piece at a higher price to a tourist while Riera was returning to his lodging to collect the money. Then there was the time that Manolo had walked into Riera's whilst he was away on holiday and sold Vollard his entire collection of Gauguins. In lieu of a sale Manolo is happy to settle for a free meal. Riera comes too in the forlorn hope of wringing some of the Gauguin money out of Manolo. Pallares they meet on the street. He has been to the studio to look for Pablo and been redirected by the nosy concierge to Manolo's. Gabrielle and Rosita they find on their usual beat outside the Gare du Nord. Odette is with them so they bring her along, too. Pablo does not think this is a good idea since he has been deceiving Rosita with Odette and is afraid that Odette might inadvertently let something slip, being a total blabbermouth.

The party assembles at the café. Unusually there is an appetising smell of cooking from the kitchen. Two litre bottles of red wine are on the table alongside a collection of almost clean glasses. All of the resident cockroaches have turned their attention to the kitchen, leaving the humans undisturbed. All that is missing is Carlos who appears right on cue, even jollier than when he left the studio. His top hat is at a jaunty angle, his overcoat envelops him entirely, more for effect than for warmth. This is the overcoat that he and Pablo have been sharing on a daily basis since their arrival and prior to Pablo's new purchase. As a result it is now almost transparent, so worn it has become. Carlos refuses demands that he remove these garments. He seats himself at the top of the table as befits the prime mover and launches into song. This is a jolly Catalonian ballad about a man who discovers that his mistress has been unfaithful to him, so he leaves her to go off to his beloved homeland while she kills herself in despair.

To much applause Carlos announces once again that he is going, that between them Manyac and Jarry have made it possible for him to make this decision. He cannot possibly stay because Gabrielle, with her unkind behaviour, has broken his heart. Cheers of agreement from everybody except Gabrielle. This farewell speech is interrupted by the entry of a huge tureen full of spaghetti in a tomato sauce, topped with what look at first to be worms but to the delight of all turn out to be preserved anchovies. Plates are piled high. Manolo tries to make a vote of thanks but nobody is listening and, his mouth being crammed full of pasta, he is incomprehensible anyway. Empty bottles are removed and two more arrive. Eating slows down. Carlos staggers to his feet unsteadily.

"It is too late," he cries, "I am going. I am betrayed and I am going." From under his coat he pulls a French army revolver, points it at Gabrielle. "Traitoress. Deceiver. You have ruined my life. For this you must be punished, for I know that you will not kill yourself for love of me when I am gone." He fires. The gun is too heavy, Carlos is too drunk. The bullet ploughs into the table in front of Gabrielle who screams with fear. Silence. Then a crashing of benches as they all seek to rise at once. "Farewell!" shouts Carlos, pushes the revolver into his mouth and fires. Silence once more. Then pandemonium. An ambulance is called. Pablo and Manolo ride with it to the hospital with the dying Carlos. The café owner wails. She knows that she will never get paid now.

# Paris

## *1900*

The funeral is a miserable affair. All day long the rain has been falling steadily. As the funeral cortege sets out it develops into a total downpour. All twenty or so mourners are completely soaked before the end of the street. The men's hats gush water, the women's dresses cling so close that the fastenings on their corsets stand out for all to see. On they all plod past the local church to a protestant cemetery where the vicar does not object to a suicide being buried in his particular consecrated ground. As chief mourner Pablo leads the procession, eyes down, feet softening in his sodden shoes, his eyes studying the landscape as a setting for his memorial painting. With more luck and determination he could have escaped back to Barcelona to avoid both the shooting and the burial. Now he has to make the best of the situation.

The vicar is no keener than any of the others to stand in the rain longer than necessary. His prayers are particularly short. There is no homily. Two grave diggers shovel the soil on to the cardboard pauper's casket as quickly as they can within the bounds of propriety. Pablo gives them fifty centimes each and a whole franc to the vicar for church funds. The mourning group breaks up, each making his or her way out of the rain with the utmost alacrity, off to change into dry clothes and attempt to get warm before meeting this evening at Casas's studio.

As the most successful Catalan artist in Paris Casas has the largest studio, well able to cope with all twenty mourners, plus others who may turn up. All of the canvases have been stacked against the wall, newspapers spread on the painting table and loaded with food from the local café, as well as whatever the participants have been able to supply themselves. That paint is seeping through the newspaper and on to the food worries no-one since this is the normal situation of their everyday lives. The men have clubbed together to buy demijohns of cheap wine from Auxerre, which is said to be easier on the head as well as on the pocket than their regular Corbières. There are only two chairs, one of which is covered with Carlos's clothes upon which perches his famous top hat, even more squashed and disreputable than it was last year in Barcelona. The second is left vacant for whoever might want to make a speech or to sing a song. Behind them stands Casas's easel. Just for tonight it holds a coloured sketch by Pablo in honour of his dead friend, one which he intends to use as a base for a full-scale painting once the day of mourning is over. Never one to bother with authenticity, he has demonstrably pirated a burial scene from his beloved El Greco and transferred it to the cemeteries of Paris. Instead of a grave Carlos has a full sepulchre, outside which he is about to be received by naked women clad only in their stockings (*Carlos would have loved that*, thinks Pablo) before being translated into the empyrean. To tell the truth this is a terrible sketch, which is to become an equally terrible painting. As with all funerals no-one is prepared to tell the truth. The dear departed is the greatest friend, and most superb painter, considerate lover and generous giver to the poor. And Pablo's sketch is the finest tribute that any artist could have.

The wake warms up. By the end of the first demijohn the babble of conversation and the bursts of laughter are enough to keep the whole street awake, should anyone be bothered. Gabrielle is not amused. She is still annoyed at Pablo and at herself for sleeping with him after Carlos's death. Such behaviour in a friend is inappropriate, especially since he was taking advantage of the poor grieving widow. Not that she and Carlos were married, or even that she cared for him at all. Her survival and status as the girl of the deceased, allied to her added interest as the proximate cause of his demise, has inflated her already hefty sense of self-importance, which the two evenings with

Pablo have seriously diminished to the status of a mere easy tart. Nor can she recognise herself as one of the black-robed grieving figures that Pablo has placed around Carlos's figure.

Gabrielle's moody look and refusal to catch Pablo's eye have infuriated him. He does not like funerals, has a fear of death which may strike at any moment, and awaits hell and damnation, even though he does not believe in it. Processions of hooded Easter figures through Malaga haunt him at these times and to the end of his life. Death is irreversible. So is life! He is stuck. His painting wobbles between Lautrec, Degas and Gauguin. His social life is confined to the Catalan clique and to Manyac in particular. His only French friend is Max whose company, whilst interesting, has also excited comment and stifled smiles among the Catalonians. Even now he is stuck between Manolo and Manyac when he would much rather be sidling up to Gabrielle or even to Rosita if Gabrielle's bad mood were to persist. He is drinking too much too quickly. As he always does when drunk he tells Manyac in the loudest tones what is wrong with impressionism and why *pointillism* is a dead end, fit only for bourgeois intellectuals. And why has Manyac not arranged the promised exhibition with Ambroise Vollard? Unshaven for several days, black eyes on fire, swarthy complexion inflamed by the wine, Pablo is like some swashbuckling pirate about to board a treasure ship.

And here is the treasure ship. Nonell is late as usual. Forgiveness is easily granted as he bears a half-drunk bottle of absinthe in his hand and a striking girl on each arm. Pablo is stricken. This girl is so beautiful, grand and stately, excellently dressed, wearing the most elegant hat to be seen in the whole of Montmartre. A veritable goddess! Nonell introduces the other girl as Marie-Claude, this one as Fernande. Pablo cannot take his eyes off her. Fernande is also much taken with the devotion of this strange young man with the insistent expression and a blaze of fire in his eyes. Deserted by her lover, son and husband, Fernande is desperate for love, excitement and devotion. Perhaps devotion most of all. Manolo sums up the situation in an instant. "Let me introduce you," he cries across the room. "Fernande de Labaume, this is my little sister, Pablo. And his nearest friend Père Manyac with our French acquaintance, Monsieur Maximilian Jacob."

Fernande is confused. *Surely not?* she thinks. But the evidence speaks for itself. Jacob is known as both a poet and a blatant homosexual. Of Manyac she knows nothing except that she has been told by Nonell that he will be moving into Carlos's studio after the funeral. This is a man who wears flowered waistcoats and a yellow gardenia in his buttonhole. She has seen such men in some of the more bizarre cafés and bars in Montmartre, where, as one knows, anything goes. She has also seen the pretty boys who hang about outside such bars waiting to be noticed by the men in their flowery waistcoats and yellow gardenias. There can be no doubt. She turns away from Pablo in disgust to talk to Casas, stroking his beard the while, much to Julia's annoyance. Pablo's face collapses. He seems more depressed by this rebuff than by Carlos's funeral. "Never mind, little sister," says Manolo to him, "these little things happen." If that were not bad enough he strokes Pablo's head as he speaks.

Pablo erupts to his feet, spilling red wine all over the floor. "I hate this. I hate you all. Paris is all whores and homos. It's cold and wet and dirty. Not a moment longer. You can all stay in your shit. Carlos is well out of it. You have killed him but you shan't kill me." There is a shocked silence then a huge burst of laughter as he throws himself through the door. "Poor little boy," laughs Manyac, "never could hold his drink. He'll be better in the morning when he has slept it off. You can't imagine how well I will look after him." There are sniggers across the room. Fernande turns up her nose in disgust.

Pablo is not at the studio tonight. Nor is he there tomorrow. His clothes have gone. Likewise his paintings, despatched back to his father in Barcelona. Gone too is the rent money which has not yet been paid for this quarter and the whole of the 150 francs that Manyac had paid him that day. He has left no note or forwarding address. No-one knows where he has gone. Only Casas has any idea, an idea which he is keeping strictly to himself.

# London

## *Spring 1900*

Father seems much happier since the wedding and in much better health generally. I think all of the funerals recently depressed him. It all started with Grandma and Uncle Theo, which saw him in bed for weeks. Then there was Millais and William Morris the same year, followed by Burne-Jones some while ago. Each piece of bad news brings on one of his turns, so much so that Mama virtually runs the business now. She is the one who goes off to view the salons in Paris and talk to the artists, as well as doing all of the selling work in the gallery. She has turned into such a flirt! You should see her with the male customers, especially the young ones. She smiles, flounces up and down the gallery and gives them such looks! "Mama, you should be ashamed," I tell her. "Some of these men are young enough to be your son."

"Exactly," she says. "It's lovely having you three girls, but it would have been wonderful to have had a son as well. Anyway don't exaggerate. I'm not that old. Besides, whatever you might say I sell more paintings than your father ever did."

Which is true, I suppose. Anyway the only death which didn't bother Father was Ruskin's last week. He never did care for Ruskin after the court case with Whistler. By then, of course, he was much stronger and the wedding picked him up as I said. That wasn't his first reaction, though. When Cornelia came in with the news he went as white as a sheet and deathly quiet. We all thought he was going to have another fit; Maia was already standing by with the gag. Then he let out a great rush of air as if his lungs were going to burst and broke into the biggest smile you have ever seen. "My darlings," he said, "I never thought I should live to see this moment. I thought the Lord had deprived me of all my strength so that I should be the sooner with him. Now let us put this last century with its deaths and tribulations behind us and rejoice in this joyous news!" Father does forget sometimes that he is not speaking from a pulpit. He would have been much happier as a preacher than as an art dealer.

So we all went off to Leeds for a week to see Cornelia wed. Aunt Anna and Uncle Jacob had all five of us in their big house in Harrogate. It turns out that Uncle Jacob is some kind of cousin to Cornelia's intended, Simon and they are both Jews! What a kerfuffle that was! All sorts of comings and goings about where they were to be married until Cornelia put her foot down. They got married twice! Once in the largest Methodist hall you have ever seen and then again in the synagogue. Cornelia has also determined that the children will be brought up in both religions, though I can't see how that will work in practice. She has also told Simon that she is not going to change her name. His relations, especially his mother, are furious. Father thinks it is wonderful. Cornelia says that her name is what sells her fashions and it would be bad business to change it now. I don't know what Simon thinks. I don't suppose anyone has bothered to ask him.

Mother was most shocked when Cornelia told her about Simon. His family owns a wool and cloth company, which he represents in London. "A commercial," shrieked Mother. "No daughter of mine is going to marry a commercial!" Father managed to pacify her somehow. I suppose he pointed out to her that Simon was not in the travelling line. Indeed they have bought themselves a pretty house on four floors in Chelsea, no doubt with the family money, which is hardly what one would expect from a mere commercial. The idea of a marriage completely set our parents off on the moral homily track. Father kept quoting 'a virtuous woman is a jewel above price', while Mother kept going on about used clothes. "You wouldn't want to wear any underwear that had been used by somebody else," she would say. "So no man wants a woman who has already been used. A woman should see herself as an oyster and only yield up her pearl in the right circumstances to the right man." This stuff about pearls and oysters totally confused poor Maia who had to be reassured that what we had told her was in fact accurate. As for Cornelia I rather suspect that she cast her pearl before swine long ago. She and Walter seem to have got very close when they were both in Paris according to the hints she has dropped. Now that she is married I don't suppose I'll hear any more about it.

We are back in London and Father is putting his heart and soul into the business and has vowed that he will give up gadding about the country preaching in Methodist halls like he did in the past. Besides bringing on his turns the visits distressed him with the condition of the poor people, especially in Wales and in the coal mining districts in the north. The only visit that cheered him up was when he went off to Grimsby and stayed with Harry Kirman. "What wonderful people," he said to me afterwards. "Pure gold. And do you know there are as many as four chapels in the town. Four!"

Whistler arrives this week as well, which has cheered him even more. The Prince of Wales was delighted with the double portrait that he did of the Princes. It was such a shame that Albert, the elder one, died so young. So Whistler had to do two more portraits, one of each of the Princes. They say that Princess Alix keeps the one of Prince Albert in her bedroom. The old Queen is ailing badly and looks like she cannot last much longer, and a good job too if you ask me. I've heard that the Prince has already set about ordering his coronation robes on the quiet. Whistler obviously thinks that he will be asked to do the paintings of the coronation and of the new King. Quite a feather in his cap if he can land that one. Father and Mama are looking forward to it as well; they made quite a killing in France selling his paintings of the Jubilee.

The real reason that Whistler is coming over, though he doesn't know it yet, is to give me drawing lessons. I am to enter the Slade School of Fine Art in the autumn and I want to be properly prepared. It will be full of posh girls who have their own private drawing masters but I intend to have the best master of all and to be the best in the class. Father has helped me a lot. I hadn't realised that he is so talented, though he denies it and says that he lacks both practice and application. "But don't ask Harry for any help," he says. "He draws like a mule. He paints better than anybody else in England, but he still can't draw and he knows it!" Cornelia says that she will set up a drawing class for women in the cutting room at her business. Maia and I will be the first pupils with Father as the instructor. Father says that he knows a professional model by the name of Seamus who will come and sit for us. I suspect that this is one of his old drinking pals, so let's hope he stays sober. In could be rather fun. So could the Slade, which I'm told is full of the most scrumptious young men.

*Hat 4*

# London

## *Early summer 1900*

Late spring in Paris has been the worst in living memory: cold snow-wet winds howling in from the Russian steppes interspersed with rain-wet gales, the aftermath of Caribbean hurricanes, howling in from the west. London is enjoying a glorious early summer. Cherries are in full bloom, candles have appeared early on the chestnuts, birds are contentedly sitting on eggs which they are sure will hatch well ahead of time. Ladies protected by their parasols stroll arm in arm with their husbands or admirers in the royal parks. Even the old Queen has been seen out and about in an open carriage from time to time, the populace amazed to see 'Mrs Brown' down from her hermit's cave at Balmoral at this time of year. "Having a last look at the old place," mutter the sceptics.

Pablo gazes around in wonder. Open parks with verdant green grass upon which all can wander at will. The beauty of Prince Albert's memorial, the splendours of Westminster Abbey, the magnificent houses of the Strand and Piccadilly. Beautiful women in their finery, their strong white arms carefully shaded from the sun, their rosy cheeks toned down by powder or toned up by rouge depending on the user's preference. To save money he has been sleeping under the railway arches in Camberwell. He would have preferred King's Cross or St Pancras but the police there are too officious and kept moving him on. Fortunately it is a relatively short walk from there to the new Tate Gallery where he wanders for hours gazing in wonder at the collection of Gainsborough, Constable and Turner. How wonderful!

Night times are more difficult. He has enough money for a meal once a day, followed by a convivial time in one of the public houses. What to drink is a problem. The beer he would not feed to a horse, absinthe is unheard of, wine is good but expensive. He compromises on gin, which has the advantage of being cheap and not requiring him to relieve himself in the middle of the night. At one stage he has stumbled across the Goupil and Sons gallery in the Strand and been summarily ejected with the comment 'we want no tramps in here'. This has put him off trying the address given him by Casas just before he left Paris. "That's the place to go, my boy. They will expect you there. Mention my name and for God's sake make sure you are clean and tidy." Money is now running short. Although he has made vast numbers of sketches, Pablo has not been able to paint. He must regularise his life in some manner.

First step is to locate the address. Not difficult; Southampton Street is only a short step from the Strand. The building itself is not as grand as Goupil, though it is made more exciting by the colourful arabesques down the door jambs and the rich colours of the paintwork. The interior is blacked out by a substantial curtain, only allowing a view of the single painting displayed in the window. Pablo's heart soars. He recognises the painting immediately. It shows a woman in a red blouse, flowing cream skirt and tiered hat seated on a green chair, staring pensively into the distance. Not only does he recognise her as Gabrielle but also the paintwork and pose as typical of Casas! He must be cautious. Rather than rushing in immediately he takes himself off to Camberwell and treats himself to a good meal before bedding down for the night. Being young and never having had any trouble sleeping he awakes next morning totally refreshed and eager to get on with the next phase of his life. First he must go to the public baths where he washes and scrubs himself until his skin is bright red. Then to the barber, who combs and cuts his shaggy hair before setting to work with the razor. Pablo insists on keeping his moustache despite the barber's protestations. "Looks like cat scratchings," grumbles the barber, a comment too subtle for Pablo's elementary English gleaned from art magazines.

Pablo now looks like a respectable working man and less like a tramp. He is ready to try his luck with the Outland Gallery. He enters. And finds that he could be back in Paris! Two paintings by Nonell, a

Manolo sculpture, countless paintings and drawings by Casas, one of Gauguin's views of Pont Aven, two Degas pastels of ballet dancers and, hung in the most obscure corner of the gallery, a view of the Moulin de la Galette by Pablo Ruiz. He gazes at it in rapture. He is known even in England. He cannot tear himself away, stands there for nearly five minutes considering the scene making mental notes. The drawing is a trifle sketchy, the colours raw in places though he has caught the blue tinge of the artificial lighting quite well. Why does it fit in with the rest of the exhibition? Of course it could almost be a Casas, so heavily is it influenced by the older man. Joy is replaced by disappointment.

"You are obviously intrigued by this painting." This is the smartly dressed man who had been sitting at a desk in the corner writing when Pablo entered. His hair is vaguely ginger, now strongly mixed with grey and beginning to recede, though his beard and moustache retain their original brightness. His eyes are sunken, his cheeks gaunt as one who has recently endured a sustained and painful illness. This draws attention to his prominent nose, which sweeps in two waves down his face, as if the designer had changed his mind half way about where it should end. His lips are thin and drawn down at the end in an expression of sadness and disappointment.

"C'est moi!" exclaims Pablo, momentarily forgetting his English in his excitement. "Me, it's me!"

"Do you mean that you are one of the figures in the painting? Show me. Which one?"

"No, it is me. My painting. I did the painting. It is mine. But how did it get here and why doesn't it have my full name, Pablo Ruiz y Picasso?"

"My dear chap, welcome. Come and sit for a moment. I had expected you earlier. Casas wrote to say that you had left Paris in a huff and that he thought you might be coming to London. That was nearly a week ago. I thought Casas had got it wrong and you had gone back to Barcelona instead. You should thank Casas, he has been a wonderful friend and supporter of yours. He sent us this painting and another one that we have downstairs with a selection of his own work. I'm not too happy about the other one; it is too dreary for my tastes, it will never sell. The one here is much more interesting, even if it is too close to Lautrec and to Casas himself. Definitely a young man's work. How old are you, by the way?"

"I shall be nineteen in October."

"Well, I thought you were much older than that. Where are you staying? Do you have a studio arranged yet?"

Unwilling to admit his situation, Pablo merely shrugs. "Fine. You have some money? Yes? I have to sit the gallery until closing time then we will have a chance to talk further. Go across the road to that café and wait for me there. I will be some time so be patient. You have your sketchbook! Good, that will help to pass the time."

As Pablo crosses the road Vincent whistles to one of the street urchins that are always hanging about in the hope of an errand or a poorly guarded purse. "Go to this address with this note. Wait for a reply. Be back here before dark with that reply. If you do that I will give you a florin."

"I want the florin now."

"If I give it to you now I'll never see you again. Here's thruppence and be off with you."

"I can see Jen-Jen giving me hell for this."

*The Strand*

# London

## Summer 1900

On the contrary, Eugenie is delighted. She has heard much about this young Spaniard with the delicate hands and the deep black eyes. *Needs a proper wash, a decent hair cut and to get rid of that horrid moustache. Apart from that he's rather a nice looking boy. With Cornelia gone we have a spare room. He can have the one that Vincent had when he first came here. I'll send Maia down to the market for some fresh flowers and Rose upstairs to find some of her father's old underwear that the lad can have. His will need a good wash. I might even just throw it away. A good job the weather is fine, those shoes of his don't look up to much. Oh, and Rose will need to bring him some socks, it doesn't look like he has any at all. Then there's supper. He can just muck in with us. I hope he likes pickled cabbage.*

A nervous Vincent has brought Pablo home with him. To be greeted by a flurry of skirts, a making of beds and complete indifference to himself. As the nominal master of the house he finds this disturbing. Seeking an excuse to escape, an idea strikes him. "You ladies need some time to get everything in order. All this excitement is too much for poor Pablo who I can see is confused by everything, especially since he hasn't settled down to hearing all this English coming at him at once. I remember what it was like for me when I first arrived, having spent the previous few months speaking French all the time. I'll just take him off somewhere quiet so we can chat. We'll come back when everything has settled down." A by-now well practised 'humph' from Eugenie who is well aware of where this 'somewhere quiet' is likely to be. Never mind, order can be restored once the men are safely out of the way.

213

The White Horse has not improved with age. Twenty-five years' more tobacco smoke has impregnated its walls. The tables and chairs have not been replaced, nor have the windows been washed in all that time. A steady accretion of death, debt and prison has led to a turnover of clientele who still sit at the same tables as their predecessors playing the same games of cards and dominoes. Some of these are the same boys who used to run errands for the bookmakers and pimps in the old days, now bookmakers and pimps in their own right. One constant is Seamus, still propping up the bar in front of his pint of porter. Time has not been kind to Seamus. Age, prison and alcohol have taken their toll on his physique and never-too-outstanding mental capabilities. In his late sixties he is no longer able to supply the muscle required to keep the tarts in order or to encourage the tardy to pay their bills. Instead he is an information exchange, detailing who has what skills, where a person can be found or who is due for release on what date. The small amount that he receives from Cornelia for his life modelling goes from her directly to his landlady in an effort to prevent him drinking it away before he gets home.

Although the language is different and the furniture unusual the general ambience of the pub is familiar to Pablo. This is a drinking den such as he has frequented in Barcelona, Madrid and Paris since he was fifteen. The girls who come in to pay over money to the card players are also familiar, if not as flamboyantly dressed. *Brixton could be my home*, he thinks. *I could enjoy it here.* One thing he does not enjoy is the horse piss called porter. He would much prefer an absinthe or a gin. Not that he can complain. It is free and bought for him by the man who is his landlord, benefactor and picture dealer. Besides which, he is not a poof like Manyac.

"You asked me," begins Vincent, "why I did not put your full name on your painting. There are several reasons. First of all, my clients would not recognise a double name; Ruiz y Picasso would just be too much for them to handle. So I had to decide on one or the other. Picasso is a problem, being unfamiliar to the English ear. It has the other problem of sounding too much like Pissarro, which would cause confusion. Nobody would ever remember an artist called Picasso. I therefore decided on Ruiz which, after all, is your father's name."

"But Ruiz is such a common name in Spain. It is like Smith or Brown in England."

"This isn't Spain. There are no artists called Ruiz in England. Trust me, Picasso just isn't right or euphonious enough. Ruiz is the name that will catch on. Now, what we have to do is to find you a studio. There is no way that you can paint in the house; even Rose is not allowed to paint in the house. I will talk to Cornelia. She rents a warehouse on the South Bank; perhaps we can find you a corner in there where you can paint. You'll need some brushes and canvas. Rose can see to that; I'll give her some money or she can get it from Cornellisons and I'll pay them later. You can stay at ours for a short time until you get settled. Have you got any money?"

"About ten francs. I don't know how much that is in English pounds."

"Not enough. You can do some posing for the girls at the warehouse if you like. Whistler should be here the day after tomorrow. He'll need an assistant until Walter can join him. I assume you can mix paint and prime a canvas. Can you paint butterflies?"

"I suppose so, I've never tried."

"Whistler's signature is butterflies. He has them painted all over the frames of his paintings. You will have to do the butterflies for him. Working with Whistler will be good for you. He was a great friend of Manet. Many people see him as Manet's heir; much more considered and solid in his work than Monet, who seems to have gone gaga in his old age. You will learn a lot from Whistler. Not that he will teach you anything. You will just have to watch him and see what he does and how he does it. Another pint of porter? There's just about time for one more. It's so long since I've been in here I've almost forgotten the taste. Come with me and I'll introduce you to Seamus. He knows everybody here. If you need something or if you are in trouble, just ask Seamus."

"That's right," says Seamus, "I knows everyone, even a few coppers.

215

You look a likely lad. Any good with your fists? No? I'll show you a few things; you could be quite useful once you fill out a little bit. If you want I'll get you a job looking after the girls. You might like that. The money's not that great, but the extra perks can be tasty. Come down the warehouse with me Thursday and I'll show you round and where we do our posing for the young ladies."

Pablo is even more confused by this encounter than he was by the excitement at Hackford Road. Tomorrow he will have more leisure to consider these strange new surroundings and appraise the nature of the English.

*Cornellisons*

# Brixton

## *Summer 1900*

Maia has been pestering Mama for weeks to get her a new kitten. Instead of which we now have Pablo! He is just like a kitten: skittish, fearful and desperate to be stroked. Besides which, he has such funny hands, like a puppy that hasn't grown into its paws yet. Father has taken to him whilst Mama just pretends he is her long-lost son, she spoils him so much. Cornelia has decided that he needs taking in hand so she has given him a pile of art books to read. He doesn't make much progress. I suspect that he may be illiterate or at least very slow. He says that he had to cheat on his entry exam for secondary school, which doesn't sound promising. Cornelia says that he might be an 'idiot savant'. She says there are some people who are mentally defective in some way who have an amazing ability in one specific area, such as drawing. Not that I think Pablo is like that. He draws a lot and has studied assiduously but I don't think he is quite the amazing draughtsman that he considers himself to be. Nor is he quite as dumb as Cornelia implies; he is picking up English quite well, joining in the family conversation whenever Maia lets anyone else get a word in edgeways.

Cornelia has set him up with studio space at the warehouse. Last Thursday we took him along to the drawing class to be our model. What a scream that was! Pablo has never posed before so he didn't know what to expect. As well as Father there was us three, Lizzie Kirman's second daughter Laura and the Misses Needham. Cornelia had decided on a simple pose on the chair first thing, so she set that up and sent Pablo away to take his clothes off. He came back wearing just his trousers. Father asked him what was going on. It turned out that Seamus had told him that he would leave a posing pouch for him to use. Good old Seamus, he did no such thing, not possessing one himself. So Pablo went off into the corner to take his trousers off. He came slinking back like a puppy that had been told off for wetting the carpet, trying not to show his bits. Well, he had to in the end, you can't pose without doing that. We girls all had a good titter before we got down to work. I think Father was quite amused. Afterwards Cornelia and I had to explain to Maia why Seamus's thing is always white and flaccid whilst Pablo's was quite upstanding. She was very amused. I'm sure that she will go back to school and tell the other girls all about it in graphic detail. I must make sure that she doesn't take her sketchbook with her.

While we were getting our things I came upon Pablo and Cornelia on the back stairs. And she was kissing him! I saw him put his hand on her bottom. She pushed him away furiously. "You said I could have a kiss as payment," he said. "I said a kiss only," whispered Cornelia like a snake about to strike. "One kiss, not taking liberties. Any more of that and I'll have Father throw you out of the house and bar you from the gallery. Any more trouble from you I'll burn all of the drawings and paintings in the studio and you with them." I don't think Pablo is used to that kind of treatment, he was so confused. On the one hand he was cowed and ashamed. On the other you could see how much he loved it. Cornelia is like Boadicea when she gets angry; enough to impress any man, especially a youngster like him. "Do I get another kiss if I pose again?"

"I don't know, I'll think about it."

That could be quite fun.

Laura stopped off here afterwards for a gossip while Father was down the White Horse with Pablo. Laura's brothers are just about to go to South Africa. Charles and Walter have joined up, leaving just Laura at home. Lizzie is pleased to get the boys out of the house at last, though I rather think that she would have been happier if they had done something less dangerous. Mama did not help, telling us how her uncle had gone off to the last war, contracted a disease and died. "More of them die of disease than enemy action," she said. Poor Laura went deathly pale. A good job that Lizzie wasn't there. Young Harry is still in Grimsby with his father. He is married now with a two-year-old and another on the way. Mr Ross has promoted him to full deck hand and he is working towards his bosun's ticket, whatever that is. Harry is pleased with him and delighted to have at least one of his family within easy reach. We have to call him Old Harry now, I expect, since Young Harry's son is Harry as well. 'Little Harry', I suppose. That's Harry's second grandchild. Doris's son is nearly four now and a bonny child; he comes round here whenever he can to see Father, who plays with him as well as teaching him how to read. Harry says he is not going to sea any more. He has become what they call a 'lumper', carrying the fish off the trawlers then cleaning up the boat from top to tail afterwards. He seems to like the life, especially when there is an early morning start, so he gets the end of the day free for his painting while it is still light. Father seems to think that Harry has become a great painter. The ones of his I have seen are somewhat strange: stripes of paint and objects with odd angles. Perhaps I will understand them more once I start at the Slade. When Father tells Lizzie what a good painter Harry has become she just sneers. "Yes, a great painter, but a lousy husband."

# Brixton

## *Summer 1900*

*Dear Father and Mother*

*I am sorry I have not written to you for such a long time. You know that when I have a pencil in my hand I would rather draw with it than write. If I could explain all that has happened to me in a painting, I would rather do that than have to set it down in words.*

*First of all, Father, thank you for the money you sent me in Paris. I know that you expected me to use it to return to Barcelona. For a while I considered doing just that. To do so would have been a retreat, an admission of failure. And I did not fail! I had friends and supporters. I sold paintings and Gauguin's dealer was interested in my work. Despite the love both of us have for England I would have happily stayed in Paris despite its squalor and terrible weather. Leaving Paris was no admission of artistic failure but a determination to avoid people who wanted to lead me down paths that I had determined never to tread. My main patron was someone you may know as the black sheep of his family: one Manyac, a notorious homosexual. Not only did he buy my paintings, he also worked as an unpaid agent with gallery owners. However, it was evident to me that his support was not purely disinterested but was also of the amorous kind. After Casagemas's suicide he even arranged to move into my studio.*

*Now, I can deal with such people. I am young, determined and strong; I can fight them off if necessary. My other companion in Paris was an excellent man, Max Jacob, who Father would love. So intelligent, well read, with such perfect manners. Also a homosexual but the soul of discretion; never one to force or to insinuate himself upon* you, quite unlike Manyac. You know how people talk and jump to conclusions! Because I was associated with these two men it was assumed that I too am like them. Manolo even began to refer to me as his 'little sister'. After Casagemas's death perhaps I had become more highly strung; you know how we Spaniards can fall prey to fits of depression. Carlos's funeral was certainly depressing. I saw a beautiful woman turn from me in disgust because she thought that I was the lover of these two men or, even worse, that I sold my favours to such men. I had to leave Paris for somewhere that such aspersions could not be made on my character. Rumours could well have already reached Barcelona, so I determined that London should be my destination.

And here I am! I beg of you, when next you see Casas on one of his rare visits, to give him all of my thanks and to heap upon him all of the hospitality at your disposal. There is an art gallery in London called the Outland Gallery, run by a couple called van Gogh. He used to work in Paris for Goupil and they both travel to Paris a lot to visit the salons and the studios. Casas mentioned my painting to Madame van Gogh. Besides that, he also sent her a couple of my paintings and told her that I was no doubt headed for London. Not only did I find my painting on display, albeit in the worst position in the room, but I also found myself a friend and a lodging. The van Goghs have set me up in a clean, charming room in their house until I can find somewhere of my own. They live in a district called Brixton, an astounding area which has streets lit by electricity! A lot of the people here are in trade, as well as many artisans of the more respectable type. Hackford Road, where I live, is a very pleasant street with solid houses, apparently built by Madame van Gogh's father.

Mr van Gogh's eldest daughter, Cornelia, owns a couture house in Mayfair. Her workshop is in a large warehouse near the Thames, which used to be used for tea at one time. Part of it is not being used for anything so she has allowed me to have this as my studio. The light is not very good but there is a small gas lamp, which helps on dim days. A couple of nights a week the cutting room is cleared and used as a life studio for the van Gogh daughters and some other young

221

ladies. Mr van Gogh is in charge of this as the tutor as well as doing some drawing himself. He could have been very good if he had applied himself earlier. I pose one night a week, which gives me some money in my pocket. I am not very good at it, never having been one for sitting still. The other night I am allowed to draw with the ladies. The model is an old Irish man of around seventy. At one time he must have had excellent muscles. Now they have all gone to flab and fat. I am thinking of doing a painting of him with one of his nieces and her dog. They would make a charming scene, like a set of vagabonds on the road or circus performers, perhaps.

At Mr van Gogh's suggestion I have been doing some drawing in an area called the East End. This is the immigrant and Jewish quarter. It is full of Russians and Poles who have fled here to avoid the pogroms in their own countries. They have wonderful faces, especially the old men, which I have tried to capture in paint. I have used a blue palette to give an otherworldly feel to them as if they are caught between two countries and two cultures. One of the paintings has the two Jews facing one another. The two heads almost completely fill the canvas so that they almost blend together into one person, so close is their conversation. For the other I cheated a little bit. Madame van Gogh's grandfather Elisha is nearly ninety. He has a wonderful old face, so I used him as a model, just adding a Jewish beard. He looks magnificent. You wouldn't know that he is more gypsy than Jew!

Perhaps that is where the van Gogh ladies get their looks from; they are certainly not typically English. Madame van Gogh must be over forty, though at first sight you would think her no more than thirty-five or so. She has a light complexion with those 'English rose' cheeks, which is very strange given her jet black hair, which is almost Spanish in its lustre. Her figure, too, is more Spanish than English, being very full and in excellent proportion. Her eyes are the most peculiar colour I have ever seen. They are of a dark blue bordering on grey. Each eye has flecks of green and yellow as if there are a dozen cats hidden behind them gazing out through thin slits. Cornelia, the eldest daughter, has her mother's full figure. She appears slenderer because of her greater height, with a darker complexion. No doubt her business acumen is inherited from her mother who is the driving force behind the gallery, her husband far more interested in the art and the artists than in making money. Cornelia's business is very successful, so much so that she has trouble keeping pace with her orders. She is taking on extra workers in anticipation of a flood of orders for the coronation, which she claims cannot be far off, the Queen being so antiquated.

The other two girls look much more like their father. Rose is a charming girl with copper hair like someone out of a Titian painting. Her nose has the same double-dip feature as her father's, which on her is absolutely charming. Like her mother she bustles around, being light on her feet and full of enthusiasm. In September she enters art college, which she is most happy about. The youngest daughter, Maia, is just fourteen and neither her person nor her figure is yet fully formed. From things I have seen I believe that she is a determined character, quite unlike her father who is soft and yielding, the sort of person who would give ten pesetas to any beggar he saw in the street. The girls obviously dote on him, he is so kind and gentle with them and can deny them nothing. Their mother is the disciplinarian in the family, which they respect even when loving their father.

The Grand Opéra de France have been playing Bizet's 'Carmen' in London for the last three months. They sell out every night. Such is the excitement that there is now a vogue for all things Spanish and for bullfights in particular. I have already sold several drawings and a painting based on the corrida. Mr van Gogh has put on a new Spanish exhibition with as many bullfight paintings as he could find. I have four paintings and three drawings in the show, more even than Casas. His paintings could be anything, except that he has given them careful titles to fit in with the general theme. His 'Carmen', for example, could be any grieving woman in a bourgeois interior. He seems to have borrowed a suit of lights from somewhere because he also has a painting of the same model wearing the jacket. Mr van Gogh does not care as long as the show sells out! I'm much

223

*the same. A couple more sales should enable me to get my own place
and to give up the modelling, which really does not suit me at all.*

*By the way, something which I think will please Father very
much: in Paris I signed all of my paintings 'Picasso', since every other
Spanish painter in Paris seemed to be called Ruiz. However, Mr van
Gogh has decided that this is not a consideration in London and that
I should sign them with my family name, so I am back to being plain
'Ruiz' and proud to be so.*

*Your loving son*
*Pablo Ruiz y Picasso*

*Here Lane*

# Chelsea

## *Winter 1900*

Pablo has just finished his fourth butterfly. This one is a trifle different with a yellow tinge to the edge of its wings instead of the deep blue of the others. Despite his misgivings Whistler has allowed him to take designs from an entomology book borrowed from Brixton library instead of using the standard signature butterfly as his previous assistants had done. In return Pablo has been able to watch him apply a series of glazes to his latest paintings. "This is an ancient technique," explains Whistler. "Leonardo would have done this. The academic artists still use glazes, but not in this manner. The way I do it gives you a deeper and more expressive colour, especially if you use glaze over glaze. Be careful to make sure the previous layer is dry first or you will get all sorts of funny results." Pablo is much taken with the idea of achieving 'funny results'.

A thunderous rapping on the studio door. Pablo opens it to two military-looking young men with magnificent moustaches and smoothly shaven chins. *Madame van Gogh was right about shaving mine off*, he thinks. Behind the two guardsmen stands a portly but erect figure and an imposing woman whose double chins are still solid enough not to wobble unless she runs, which, given her advancing weight, she is hardly likely to do. "Ah, Monsieur le Duc de Lancaster," says Whistler.

"No, my dear chap, this is England, I fly under my own colours here. Mr Whistler, may I introduce Mrs Keppel? Mrs Keppel was on her way to a fitting and I asked her to accompany me. And I assume that this young fellow is one of your assistants?"

"Yes, Your Highness, he is one of van Gogh's *protégés*, a young Spaniard. Quite talented, very eager to learn. I believe that Your Royal Highness would like to look at the sketches for the forthcoming portrait? You see that I have made several of the head and made suggestions as to the background, based on the interiors at Marlborough House. Obviously we cannot go much further until the robes have been made up. Which reminds me, how is Her Majesty? They say she took the air in Hyde Park several times over the summer."

"Fading, alas. It will be a shock to the nation when she finally goes. Her doctors say that it cannot be long: a year or two at most. The winters in Scotland cannot be doing her any good. I suspect this one could be her last. The ministers are already making plans for the state funeral, depending upon at which time of the year it may fall. The coronation will have to be delayed for a decent period of mourning. Can't say I fancy sitting in that draughty old cathedral in the middle of December. Don't think you'd be too keen would you, Alice old girl?"

"Would I be invited? Princess Alix might not be too happy."

"Well, it's my coronation! Anyway, she is quite happy as long as you and I are discrete. At least she knows where I am when I'm with you and not getting up to any mischief."

"I'm not too sure about that!" Mrs Keppel grins slyly and hugs the Prince's arm. "Now I have to be off, my fitting was three hours ago. How do I get to Lambeth? She said to go there rather than to Mayfair to avoid being seen, especially since the dress is for the event we were just discussing."

"You can't very well take my carriage, it's the one with the coat of arms on it. You'll have to take a Hansom. Do you know the way to this place? Cab drivers are useless on directions once they get south of the river."

"Are you going to Miss Cornelia's, Madam? I know the way there. My studio is in the same building. If you don't mind me travelling with you, of course."

"You young scallywag, you're just after a free ride! If Mr Whistler can spare you I'm sure that Mrs Keppel would be happy for you to accompany her, you seem clean and presentable enough. Alice, do you have money? Carruthers, give Mrs Keppel some cash will you? Make sure there is enough for her cab fare home as well. Or rather, meet me at the Savoy. Shall we say around seven? Excellent! Goodbye my dear. Look after her well, young man, or you will have me to answer to."

Pablo bows his way out of the room, tripping over the edge of an easel as he does so. The journey to Lambeth is achieved in silence, both parties being unable to think of a topic of conversation. Mrs Keppel is unimpressed with the warehouse and even less so when she discovers that Cornelia is no longer there. "Madame Cornelia waited for Madam for nearly two hours, then she had to return to town to assist with a fitting for Lady Camberley. However, her assistant Doris Kirman will be able to help Madam. She is well versed in the design and has done the initial cutting instructions herself."

If anything, Doris knows more about the physical construction of the clothes than Cornelia, and is more pragmatic about the variability of an individual woman's shape and size over a month or over years. For Mrs Keppel pragmatism is essential. The expected event may be over a year ahead; a year in the life of Mrs Keppel can mean many pounds and several inches on her already considerable frame. Designing a garment for such eventualities without it looking like a tent is Cornelia's responsibility. Doris's job is to manage the final make up of the garment in such a way that it can be future proofed without too much effort by the couturier or too much embarrassment on behalf of the client.

Pablo sits quietly in a corner whilst the fitting progresses. None of the women pay him or his sketchbook any attention, for men in a fitting room are a mere disregarded trifle to be turned to only when a chequebook is required. The dress is taken for a few nips and tucks to be made (in truth for it to be let out even more than expected), leaving Mrs Keppel at a loose end to browse around the fitting room. "What a charming painting! Who is this?"

"My little boy, Michael," says Doris. "He is always playing with that ball, it's his favourite toy. I love that painting, I bought it as soon as I saw it. It's just waiting there for me to take it home."

"Lovely! And clever of the artist to have cut out all of the detail from the background so that you have to concentrate on the child. Who is the artist, by the way?"

"I am, Miss. Cornelia lets me have a room downstairs as a studio and I did it one day when Doris asked me to mind Michael for her. It took ages getting it down at first. All he wanted was for me to play ball with him, but once he had gone home it was simple to finish it off. I can't afford to pay for a model so it was lovely to have him here."

"Is that why you were drawing me all the time?"

Pablo blushes. He believed that his sketching had gone unremarked. "I hope you don't mind, Miss. You looked so regal standing there that I couldn't resist."

"I think you should avoid the adjective 'regal' in this case. His Royal Highness would not approve. I believe that you pose for the young ladies of an evening? And are you paid? Well, I too wish to be paid. I shall accept one of your drawings as payment, if that is not too much?"

Pablo is delighted. One out of the several drawings he has made is not too high a price. The rest will serve well as a basis for a painting at some later date. He carefully chooses one from his pad. Not the best one or the most finished. A simple head that shows Alice Keppel as she might have been five years and three stones ago. Mrs Keppel is also delighted, vowing to show it to the Prince that evening at the Savoy. Her business done, she departs in a Hansom leaving Pablo to work up the rest of the sketches before he in turn is called upon to pose.

Posing has become somewhat of a chore since Whistler's return from France. At first, working at his Chelsea studio had been almost peaceful, a rest from the demands of his own studio and the incessant female chatter of Hackford Road and of the Lambeth fitting room. For a couple of weeks he worked there on his own, preparing canvases, grinding paints, painting butterflies on picture frames. The arrival of Whistler's regular assistant, Walter, brought an end to his sheltered existence. Walter was a harder task master than Whistler had ever been and demanded regular hours and close concentration on the work rather than the lax attendance and constant daydreaming of great paintings to be executed, which up until then had been the norm.

Changes were made at the life classes as well. Pablo had continued to insist on the extra payment of a kiss from Cornelia for his attendance. In an attempt to extract further favours he had begun to demand his payment whilst still naked from the pose. Cornelia was not distracted. Her kiss was not a mere token; she donated it with a great deal of enthusiasm and skill, the result of long practice. What she would not allow were any liberties with her person or any further displays of affection. Pablo's expectation that she would at some point take hold of his erect member, after the fashion of any alert Parisian streetwalker, was never realised. Worse was to follow. Once Walter appeared, his wages were immediately cut. The money was the same, the kiss was no longer offered.

At first he had enjoyed Walter's company, going with him to the music hall where he saw the great Dan Leno and made friends with the ageing singer Charles Chaplin and his young son Charlie. Then the regimentation at Whistler's began to get on his nerves, as did the older man's confidence and constant reminder that he was well regarded in the Parisian art world, being friends with Seurat and young lions like Marquet and Matisse, as well as championing the strange cube-like art of the reclusive Paul Cézanne. And no more kisses from Cornelia! Pablo hated the way Walter slapped on paint in thick *impasto*, he hated the squalid realism of his interior scenes, he hated Walter's confidence and the way he refused to regard him as an equal in artistic terms. So he also hated Matisse and Marquet, Seurat and Cézanne and would outpaint the lot of them, see them bow down to his genius.

# Brixton

## *January 1901*

Every other day at least one person in Hackford Road mentions Pablo moving out to his own lodging and studio. Every day nobody does anything about it. Vincent and Eugenie have a son at last, Rose and Maia have both a brother and their very own puppy. Pablo is happy to be back with a close family, especially to have three women to dote on him. Today is no exception; he is being smartened up. He has received a summons to attend Mrs Keppel at her house in Kensington. Eugenie demands that he looks his best for what she considers a royal appointment. The Prince's mistress is only two steps away from being a queen.

She has prepared his best suit for the occasion: a dark grey with sewn-in turn ups, an old one of Vincent's which has been adjusted to fit. The trousers have been shortened, the jacket taken in a trifle. Maturity and good food have seen Pablo broaden out to rival Vincent in chest and shoulder, though he will never attain any great height. "Your hair is a mess again," Eugenie tells him. "Sit down." Snip, snip. Some areas at least are tamed. Out comes the hairbrush. Every hair is brushed into its allotted place then Eugenie smooths it all down before kissing the crown of his head. "That's it, all done. Coat and scarf on. You look a proper gentleman." Eugenie moves to give Pablo a quick kiss on the cheek, misses and finds his lips instead. Which turns into something else: a long lingering embrace. She detaches herself at last and, scarlet with embarrassment, ushers him out of the door.

Rose, who has been the inadvertent and unseen spectator of the later events, is astonished. Admittedly her mother is a flirt, but surely

230

this is taking things too far? When puzzled her normal reaction is to discuss the matter with her father, certainly not something she could contemplate doing in this situation. Maia is too young, Lizzie Kirman too much of a gossip, which leaves Cornelia. A good idea. She will take a cab to Mayfair after the drawing class at the Slade on Monday. She winces at the thought of the drawing class. Could anything be more dull? Hours spent copying plaster casts of hands and feet, carefully shading them with variations of cross hatching when a charcoal smudge would be so much more aesthetic and take a tenth of the time. They have been promised life drawing in two years, something at which she is already highly proficient.

*The Slade is not all it is cracked up to be*, she thinks. The girls are snooty and the young men either effete or socially incompetent when faced with young women. Effeminacy holds no problems for her; at least these types are willing to talk about art and poetry instead of rugger and fox hunting. As for the 'normal' young men, their normality has been bred out of them by their upbringing. Off to a boys-only school at seven then to a men's college at university, the only girls they have ever met have been their sisters and their sisters' friends, usually in the company of their mama. Meeting unattached, unchaperoned modern women must be such a shock to their systems, poor things! Rose has considered leaving the college completely but knows that her father would not approve. A diploma from the Slade gives her an *entrée* to the wider art world, to opportunities in salons and other competitions and introductions to buyers and dealers who visit the studios every now and then. But she must progress, which she will not do tied to plaster casts of Roman feet. Something else, then, to ask Cornelia. Some studio space in the warehouse where she can paint. And keep an eye on Pablo.

Who at that moment is standing before the address he has been given in Kensington. An imposing Georgian frontage with white stucco Corinthian pillars holding the solid porch. *Caryatids would be better*, he thinks before taking hold of the huge knocker and announcing his presence to the whole house. A uniformed flunky opens the door and leads him silently into the drawing room. To Pablo's surprise he is met, not by the lady of the house, but by the royal personage himself. "Welcome, my boy. No need to bow so much, you will do yourself an injury. I believe you are Spanish, are you not? Never been there. All the relatives are in the north, don't you know? Met some Spaniards in Paris. One Casas. Nice chap despite looking like a blasted anarchist. Anyway, did you do this?" The Prince holds up the drawing Pablo had given to Mrs Keppel. "Damn fine drawing. Too kind, taken a lot off her, if you know what I mean? I do not pretend to know much about art, I leave that to van Gogh to advise me, but I do know what a good looking lady looks like, particularly this lady, and I say this is a damn fine drawing. Much better than those French chappies. Now, what I want you to do is to work this up into a portrait. You know, full-length thing like Whistler did for Lady Campbell. Not as dark as that, you understand. Her family said it looked like a streetwalker on a dark night. I want it bright and shining, like the lady herself. You work at the same place where they are making her coronation dress? Good, you can use that as a model so she doesn't have to spend a thousand hours posing for you. Got it? Good. I think 200 guineas should be sufficient, don't you? Well, good day to you. I will send Mrs Keppel round to you when you are ready with a suitable canvas." The Prince hurries off in his habitual jaunty manner, uninhibited by his growing girth.

A dazed Pablo is shown out by yet another flunky. He heads off towards Southampton Street, hoping to find Vincent at the gallery. Vincent is busy selling a Burne-Jones painting of ethereal etiolated young girls arrayed as angels to a gaunt, aged aristocrat whose choice of painting is determined by lust rather than aesthetics. Vincent houses the cheque in his desk drawer before seeing the customer out. "Nasty chap. I wouldn't want him near any of my girls. Eugenie usually deals with him. She's safe enough, a good thirty years too old for him. Now, Pablo dear boy, how have you been getting on? What are you doing here at such a time?"

"Please, Mr Vincent, what is a guinea?"

"You mean a guinea fowl. It is a bird, a bit smaller than a chicken. More gamey to the taste. Excellent with onions and gravy."

"Why would someone offer me a flock of birds for a painting? Where would I keep them?"

"What do you mean, a flock of birds?"

"I've just seen the Prince and he wants me to paint a portrait of Mrs Keppel. He said he would give me 200 guineas for it. What would I do with 200 chickens? Where would I keep them? Mrs van Gogh would be furious."

"Mrs van Gogh would be absolutely delighted, as you should be. A guinea is money! One guinea is one pound and a shilling, so he is offering you 220 pounds. That's a fortune for a young lad like you; it's as much as Whistler himself gets. And he has offered you guineas; that's a payment to a gentleman. I remember Whistler being furious when offered payment in pounds 'like a mere artisan'. You could buy yourself a new suit instead of wearing my cast-offs! I think we should celebrate. There's a little drinking den in Bethnal Green run by a Dutchman who always has a bottle of the best *genever* hidden under the counter for special customers. I'll put this cheque into the bank on the way. The gallery can look after itself for one day."

# Grimsby

## *January 1901*

Harry, too, has had a commission. The owners of the new Scunthorpe steelworks wish to donate a large painting, six feet by four feet, to the local town hall to display in a prominent position on their stairwell. Mr Ross has put forward his man Harry as a prime candidate. Nobody likes to offend Mr Ross. The commission is for the princely sum of ten pounds plus the cost of the bare canvas. Any sensible man would reckon for how long he could live on the profit after the cost of materials. Being an artist, Harry approaches it from a different angle. He could order two sets of canvas, paying for one of them himself. They could be set up in one of the drier fish sheds to be worked on at the same time. One version would be for Scunthorpe town hall, the other sent to Vincent, to be entered in the Royal Academy.

He hitches a ride from a carter taking a load of cod off to Doncaster, arriving in Scunthorpe just as it is getting dark. Leaving his bag at a cheap lodging house he sets off with his sketchbook for the steelworks, visible from miles around, the flames erupting against the heavy winter clouds. Harry has seen John Martin's enormous paintings of the Last Judgement, which have been touring the country. The Last Judgement is tame against the light, heat and horror of the steelworks with its huge black buildings thrusting skywards, silhouetted against the fires of the blast furnaces. Bent stick figures wander between the buildings like angels still amazed from their fall. For a while Harry is dumbstruck; then his charcoal stick takes charge, carving its way across the paper. Then another drawing and another. These will smudge and blur by the time he returns to his lodging. No matter, the ideas are there, the impression is made. Hands and feet frozen he returns to town, mind awhirl with possibilities.

The fish shed is freezing. Deliberately so, it is designed to keep fish chilled and looking their best before they can be sold. A cold north-easterly blows under and round the doors, the odd flake of snow insinuates its way across the floor. Harry is wearing every item of clothing he possesses: both sets of long underwear, his working trousers over his Sunday best, pullovers, pea jacket, fur hat with ear flaps, fingerless gloves. He is still cold. The paint has to be worked on the palette with his knife before it is pliable enough to be applied. Once on, it does not go off for days so that it cannot be worked over. Harry is pleased with his foresight in using two canvases; he can work on one while the other dries. Progress has been slow at first, partly the result of covering both with a white ground in order to produce more radiance in the overpainting. This is a technique picked up from Whistler, one of the things that the older man learnt in Paris, which allows him to get away with a much darker surface than the academics who are still using pitch as a ground.

Each canvas is divided into three horizontal layers, which Harry thinks of as foreground, background and sky. The colours do not correspond to the normal conception of those definitions. Foreground begins with a cerulean blue, fading upwards into a heavy Prussian, moderated by a gentle addition of chalk white. A sharp division is marked by a deep grey line, almost black to the casual eye, into a cobalt green background which in turn fades away through lighter greens and yellows to the palest of Naples yellow. Again a heavy deep grey line to the sky, alizarin at first, seguing to scarlet, then abruptly to Prussian blue along the canvas's upper edge. Harry tries out variations. Takes off paint here, increases the tones there, allows light *impasto* or scrapes down to the thinnest of layers. The two canvases stare at one another, so much alike in conception, so different in execution.

Theory says that there needs to be a centre to the painting, or if not a centre at least a focal point which corresponds to the golden section in its placing. Theory also says that the painting should be planned in its structure with the colours brushed in as underpainting many shades lighter than the end result. Underpainting has already gone by the board, the final layer having been laid straight on the ground. Besides, it has been changed and scraped off so often that the painting has little or no relation to its original format. Instead of either a central object or one within the golden section, Harry adds the steelworks buildings themselves hard up against the left edge of the painting. He is caught in two minds as to how to render them, as totally flat objects or as cubic masses. The idea of a strictly representational set of structures never even enters his head. At last he opts for the flat solution, an overlapping series of squares and rectangles which he composes using a colour scheme and theory unique to himself. The effect is to imply that all the colours emanate from the interior of the steelworks, a sun shooting its rays across the sky and the firmament. There are no people; steel is the hero and the source of all wealth and joy.

To his surprise both Scunthorpe town and the general population, led by the *Scunthorpe Evening Telegraph*, accept the symbolism and the painting itself, declaring it to be a "Glittering, joyous celebration of modern industry and the glory and wealth it has brought to the town. An aesthetic achievement of which we can all be proud. Mr Kirman is to be congratulated on a painting which will be long remembered and appreciated through the length and breadth of Great Britain." On the other hand its fraternal counterpart did not meet with such an understanding welcome. Only through Vincent's influence and contacts was it accepted into the Royal Academy. *The Times* was, as usual, in fine form, describing it as "A painting that sang colour and screamed light, met with jeers, angry babble and screaming laughter." A prophet has no honour in his own country.

# London

## *2 February 1901*

L ondon stands still. There is not a street crier to be heard, even the pigeons have deserted the capital for the day. All that can be heard is the soft shuffle of marching feet, the creak of the gun carriage and the sound of weeping women. The old Queen is being laid to rest, carried on her last long journey from the royal palace to Windsor to lie in state. Old Elisha is one of the few who can remember what it was like not to have Victoria on the throne. Only those over seventy can remember King William, the haziest of kings now fading from their hazier receding memories.

The Queen is dead, long live the King. King Edward VII accompanies his mother in a white open carriage despite the freezing January weather. Naturally he is sad at his mother's death. In truth they were never close. She did not trust him with any affairs of state or allow him to undertake official functions abroad. A successful visit to India was dismissed as a mere holiday, his attempts to reconcile Germany and France an undermining of her legitimate government. Not that Bertie did much to arouse enthusiasm in his mother. Affairs with married women, gambling, involvement in scandals and divorce cases showed him as lacking in any moral compass, a worry to both her and her late lamented Prince Albert.

Now he is King. Victoria's Bertie is no more. Susan Pelham-Clinton's Eddie is Emperor of India and King of Great Britain, Ireland and the Empire on which the sun never sets. Whistler, Pablo and Walter watch the procession from a privileged post high up in a government building, arranged by the equerry of the new King. Whistler is taken by the design of the procession, Walter by the clothing and postures of the crowd, Pablo by the sheer stately glory of the procession, the busbies of the soldiers, Her Majesty's horse caparisoned in a white blanket, the new King in military uniform with the Star of the Garter on his left breast. Like the new King he is already looking forward to the coronation. How glorious that will be! Edward himself can only feel relief. The relief that comes when a long wait is over and real life can begin at last, setting out a new Britain in this glorious century for his son to inherit and carry forward the new line of Saxe-Coburg-Gotha.

The wake is unlike any other. There are no fights, nobody gets drunk, or very few. London's police have the quietest night they have ever had, not a domestic or a burglary in sight. Life is similarly subdued in Hackford Road. As a sign of respect the gallery has been closed for the last week since the Queen's death. Eugenie has set about those little jobs put off until another day, the cleaning out of cupboards, the sewing up of tablecloths, the mending of long-forgotten underwear. Vincent has surreptitiously slipped out to the Lambeth warehouse to spend time with Pablo in his studio, painting the few flowers that are to be found at that time of year and starting on a series of portraits of the family. Pablo has his own portrait to get on with and has no interest in or respect for crown heads, be they Spanish or English. He has his portrait of Mrs Keppel to complete, which keeps him in a state of constant excitement. Since the Slade is also closed Rose has had time to set up an easel in a far corner on which she has sketched out a composite figure of Seamus and Pablo, with Seamus's hoary old head superimposed on Pablo's previously scrawny body. To complete the composition she has added a begging bowl. Pablo has suggested adding a guitar, which has caused her a myriad of problems with its placement and complicated shape. Fed up with listening to her furious imprecations to herself, Pablo has strolled over and drawn it in for her. "Any Spanish child knows how to draw a guitar," he says. Rose is spitting blood, mute in her anger. But she leaves the guitar perfectly placed and drawn, where it is.

Maia is alone in her room with a set of gouache paints bought with her own money. She is practising painting butterflies, which she is copying from the same book that Pablo had previously borrowed from Brixton library. Copying is a good exercise, she knows, and now that Pablo has grown too proud to decorate Whistler's frames, if she becomes skilled enough she might be allowed to replace him in the Chelsea studio alongside Walter. Not that either Whistler or Walter notice her existence. Cornelia is so bossy, Rose so exuberant, that no-one pays any attention to little Maia. That's not true, her father is always free with his time, treating all three of the girls equally, giving them all the time that they need, however busy he may be. Maia realises Vincent is able to do this because Eugenie will always step into the social or business space that he leaves behind. Still, much as she respects her mother she absolutely adores her father. It is he who has allowed her to attend the evening life-drawing sessions and taught her how to use gouache and watercolours. Once she has progressed on to oils she will paint much better than Pablo or Rose, or even than Mr Whistler himself.

Today is a quiet day, a day of mourning, a day when the country takes breath before launching itself upon a bright new unknown world. Lovers dream of a sunny future, youngsters contemplate a successful career, artists plan the paintings that will make them famous. Those in the middle wonder how life has passed them by and wonder what dreary and desolate end is to come.

# London

## *June 1901*

The Royal Academy open exhibition this year has five paintings labelled 'by courtesy of the Outland Gallery', far more than any other London gallery. A small pastel of a bunch of alstroemerias by V.V. Governor has already sold for fifteen pounds. Harry's steelworks painting has attracted much more attention as visitors come to point and jeer and write letters to *The Times* complaining about the deteriorating quality of the Academy's choice of paintings. Only a few spend any time in front of a painting of an old beggar with a guitar, presumably viewed through a poor quality window which has covered the painting in an overall blue tinge. Of that few, one or two note the painter 'R.V. G.' as someone to watch in the future.

These are mere sideshows for the main event: King Edward VII in his full coronation robes painted by the eminent and, at last, loved and famous American painter, James McNeill Whistler. *The Times* describes it as 'a triumph', *The Daily Herald* as 'a tribute to a much maligned but increasingly loved monarch'. The King's advisers see it as the first step in the process of making the public forget his past indiscretions and recognising his solidity, his peacekeeping, his role as a British bulldog.

On hanging day, the committee had hung to the left of the King a portrait of Mrs Keppel, given the stylistic similarities of the two paintings. The morning of varnishing day was reserved for a private visit by the King and Queen. True to form, the Queen was an hour late in her preparations and artists were already waiting, brushes and varnish in hand, in the lobby when the royal couple arrived. All was well for half an hour or so as they made a leisurely tour of the gallery, accompanied by a pick of the academicians, who were struck to silence by the torrent of words in both Danish and English from the Queen as they reached the King's portrait. Being deaf, the Queen was unable to judge her volume, which was loud enough to bring a host of minions running, convinced that something untoward had happened to the Queen or that the King himself had suffered a heart attack. "You cannot do that. It is an insult. Have it removed immediately. I will not stand for it. Get it out of here this moment. No, you fools. Not that one. That is the King. You cannot remove the King. That one. That woman. She cannot stay. Throw her out. I do not wish to stand here to be insulted by the sight of her. Get her out." The royal visit was cut short. The throng of artists had to wait another two hours while the hanging committee was recalled to make a decision as to where Mrs Keppel's portrait might safely be hung and which innocuous painting should replace it.

Much as Whistler's portrait is admired by the visitors notoriety is more influential than quality or fame, so it is that Mrs Keppel is the painting which attracts the most attention, 'Pablo Ruiz' the name that is lodged in people's minds. Surely a famous artist from the court of the Spanish king, someone to be sought after when portraits and formal paintings are required. How strange that he should be associated with the Outland Gallery, the outlandish gallery which shows such astonishingly bad paintings. Though they are, of course, known for their attachment to modern Spanish artists. The gallery is quite happy to arrange for the artist to undertake commissions for his normal fee of 250 guineas plus a twenty-five guinea commission for the gallery. Madame Van Gogh explains this so charmingly that no-one ever seeks to question what right she may have to an arrangement fee when she has done nothing but invite them into her gallery. If she can sell them a painting by Governor or Casas at the same time, so much the better. Even she totally fails to sell anything at all by H. Kirman.

Discreet and fawning as ever, the newspapers fail to mention the Queen's outburst and the rapid rehang of the exhibition. Nevertheless the word circulates rapidly in fashionable circles, becoming the first scandal of the new reign. The royal couple escape the gossip by departing to the South of France to prepare themselves for the ordeal of the coronation ahead. Edward ponders the wisdom of having a portrait of Alix done by Señor Ruiz. Instead he takes his son George aside and proposes a formal portrait of George's two eldest sons, Albert and Edward, Henry as a mere baby being too young to be included whilst Mary as a girl is too insignificant. Upon George's agreement a royal command is issued, which is to whisk Pablo away to rural Norfolk for a month in the autumn, to the relief of all at Hackford Road.

*Fleet Street*

# Brixton

## *Autumn 1901*

Pablo is now himself a butterfly. His old black suit has been discarded in favour of a royal blue with paisley pattern waistcoat. Smart button-up boots replace his worn-out shoes; there are matching blue silk socks underneath. By the front door is his silver-topped cane and top hat, this one new and shiny, worn in memory of Carlos. Although it is not strictly necessary today he will call at the Royal Academy to collect his painting of Alice Keppel. Then he will deliver it in person to the lady, who may also be in the company of the purchaser. Pablo is fraught with confidence and excitement, which might explain what happens next.

Eugenie has had a fit of cleanliness. As happens now and then she has decided that the maid has not cleaned some areas of the house sufficiently well, or not at all. Armed with a feather duster she is cleaning the pelmets and the picture rails, reaching as high as she can, delicately balanced on tiptoes. She is only dimly aware of Pablo in the passageway until he walks up behind her, slips his hands around and holds one of her breasts in each hand. Eugenie counts to five, enough time for her nipples to harden, before she turns round to remonstrate with the young man. "You really shouldn't..." to be cut short by his embrace and kiss. She draws him to her strongly enough to feel his emergent erection through her dress and for him to feel the softness of her breasts against his chest.

This time she is more determined. "That was very naughty of you. Look, here is your cane. Be off or you will be late for Mrs Keppel." Pablo is tempted to linger, but realises that to do so would only cause embarrassment all round and recriminations on the lady's part. He bows slightly and exits through the front door as rapidly as his top hat allows. Eugenie places her duster on the hall table, adjusts her blouse, refastens her hair, sits down on the stairs. *I really must stop doing that*, she thinks. *It's all very well carrying on with Casas in Paris where nobody knows me. Doing the same thing in my own house with so many little pairs of eyes around is crazy. I know the girls think I am a flirt, which is true in part. Men are so susceptible; if they will buy a painting on the basis of a pair of pretty eyes and a sly smile why should I care? Nevertheless, I am responsible for the girls and Vincent has always been so good to me. Not his fault that his illness has left him unenthusiastic in physical terms. I should try to rouse him more, I suppose. Yes, that's what I will do. We will go to bed an hour earlier and wake up at dawn. If I can't rouse him in the evening I shall just have to try harder the next morning. Perhaps then I won't let things like this catch me out. I shall be the best-behaved wife south of the river.*

Eugenie is right about the existence of little eyes. Maia, unnoticed as usual, has been watching this scene from the top of the stairs. The sight of men and women embracing, sometimes even more, is not unknown to her. Cornelia and Rose have been at pains to ensure that she knows about what such actions mean and their general consequences. Since seeing Pablo posing she now understands why women make such peculiar noises when enveloped by a man and what the strange sounds are that emanate from her parents' bedroom occasionally. What she has not seen until today is either of her parents kissing or fondling anyone else. Perhaps there are different rules for people who share a house, it is not just mothers and fathers? For what she might term 'low-level' questions about relationships between men and women she would normally consult her father. This particular question does not seem to be low level. It appears to be complicated and subtle. Cornelia is the one for subtlety, she had better ask her.

Cornelia is found in the cutting room, directing two of the women to make up sashes in purple, white and green stripes embroidered with the slogan 'Votes for Women'. "I don't think Mrs Fawcett would approve of that," says Maia. "And who said they were the right colours?"

"We are leaving Mrs Fawcett," explains Cornelia. "Mrs Pankhurst and I have finally given up on that soppy load of mummy's girls. We want some real action, votes for all women, not just the rich ones. Simon agrees that the only way forward is direct action. He's not so happy about us joining with those socialists in the ILP but he has enough sense to know that any support we can gather will help further the cause. I'd even join with the Irish or the anarchists if I thought they would help us." Maia is shocked. This is her cool, calm and collected elder sister speaking about taking cause with anarchists! Perhaps now is not a good time to ask her about her mother's actions?

"Well, squib, what are you doing here? Don't see you sewing for the cause or ordering a fashionable new dress to show off to your young man."

"I don't have a young man and I don't want one, thank you. I've come to ask you something about Mother."

"Well, if we are going to talk about our mother behind her back we had better all do it together and in private. I don't know if Pablo is about but Rose is in the studio. If she is on her own we can lock the door and be as bitchy as we like."

Rose knows full well that Pablo is not likely to be in the studio. She says nothing and follows Cornelia to the other end of the building, which smells of turps and oil paints. "Rose, good you are here. Squib wants to have a bitching session and I thought we could all join in. Watch out where you sit, girl, those chalks have left powder everywhere. Now, what do you want to say?"

Maia tells her sisters about the scene she has just witnessed. Rose adds her experience of seeing an earlier kiss. Silence. "There is something about that Pablo," says Cornelia. "I really enjoyed kissing him as well, I must admit."

"As much as you enjoyed Walter?"

"Walter and I are just good friends. There was a time in Paris when we both thought that we might become more than that. We agreed it was not going to work and there was no future in our relationship. Simon and I are very happy together, except when we are apart, that

245

is. I hate him going off back to Leeds all of the time, but I know that's his job, just as he accepts me being in town until late sometimes."

"So why did you stop kissing Pablo when Walter arrived from Paris," asks Maia.

"My, we are a sharp little squib, aren't we! I made a decision. Much as I enjoyed kissing Pablo it wasn't fair on Simon. Walter's arrival reminded me that my single days were over and that I should be more respectable. Anyway it was getting to be annoying having to control his hands all the time. Anyone would think his father was an octopus the number of hands he seemed to have."

"Come on girls. We are not here to discuss Cornelia's indiscretions but to decide what we do about Mother. Since Father's illness she has turned into a total flirt. I don't suppose we can do anything about that. What we have to do is to stop it going any further. There is no use talking to Father about it. He wouldn't do anything, even if he believed us. What I think we should do is quietly let Mother know that we have seen her misbehaving, just drop a hint. And keep an eye on her, especially when Pablo is around. He's a real jackdaw in every sense. Watch him around Whistler, he grabs any idea or technique he can from him. He gobbles up commissions like he gobbles up women, as Cornelia should know."

"Now don't start that again, our Rose. That's a good plan. You and Maia can put it into operation at home. The two of us will look out for Pablo when he's here. I don't want him bothering any of my ladies, they are quick enough to get themselves into trouble as it is. A good job I know a woman who is clever with such things or I would have no workforce at all. Right, musketeers! All for one and one for all!"

# London's East End

## *Autumn 1901*

Rose has dressed carefully for her excursion to the East End. Her clothes are no different to those of an ordinary working woman, if a trifle cleaner. She might be a kitchen maid sent out on an errand or an assistant in one of the better local shops. In her bag she carries a sketchbook, pencils and charcoal together with a sharp knife which has the dual purpose of keeping the pencils trim and warning off any potential predators. The canyons of Brick Lane and its surrounding streets can be dangerous for an unaccompanied young woman. Presenting as she does a confident air and a sharp tongue, Rose has managed to keep off any unwanted attentions. As a regular visitor she is now accepted into the community. Old men nod and smile at her as she passes, young women check out her hat and clothes, looking for tips that they can copy. Forever on the lookout for interesting scenes she spies an emaciated woman feeding her child in the doorway of an empty shop. Two children lurk around a market stall waiting for the stall holder's attention to be distracted so that they can make off with some fruit for themselves or vegetables to be cooked at home. An ancient Jew boils bread rings in an old boiler. Watch out! A dray pulled by two huge horses comes thundering down the road to pull into the brewery. The driver has been sampling his own wares at each pub to which he has delivered and is now barely in charge of his horses, who at least have the good sense to return to their stable.

She ventures as far north as Columbia Road before turning back. In a quiet side street she leans against a wall, pulls out her sketchpad and makes as many drawings as she can in the few minutes she allows herself. These are jottings, a reminder of what she has seen. The mother and baby are five clean lines, the dray horses scumbled charcoal, the bread seller a stick figure with scratched beard and yarmulke, a cat under the market stall, an exceptionally tall policeman. That done, she turns back down Brick Lane, desperate for a rest and somewhere to sit. The obvious choice would be one of the local pubs, which is impossible. Those which she would naturally choose would not admit an unaccompanied woman, however well dressed. A few would not admit a woman at all. The others would allow her in and even serve her a large gin should she require but it would always be assumed that she was plying her trade, so there would be no peace until she left with the highest bidder. Instead she has to settle for a pie shop, dense with meat fumes and tobacco smoke. The tobacco makes her gag at first, only to be settled by the first bite of her gristly pie. A couple of the women she has met before greet her. They do not have time to talk, needing to rush back home with a pie for their husband's dinner. Fortified, Rose rises and makes her way back across the river to Lambeth.

Today Pablo has been summoned to an address in Kensington Square, one of the large Georgian houses rented by men of quality when they are in town for the season. He has been here before, so steps confidently past the convent of St Maria Assumpta to the most imposing house in the square. He is expected and is admitted immediately by a flunky in a costume that reminds him of Whistler's butterflies. Mrs Keppel and the King are just finishing breakfast, the porridge and kidneys being removed from the table whilst the King enjoys his first cigar of the day. "Come in, my boy. Now, my people have arranged for you to go up to Norfolk by train tomorrow. You will be staying with a family called Kett, one of the gamekeepers on the estate. They will meet you at the station and see you settled in. Their cottage is easy walking distance from York House. Prince George will be expecting you the day after tomorrow at nine o'clock sharp. As a navy man he is quite particular about punctuality so make sure you are on time. There is no need to keep clocks an hour fast in that house, eh, Alice? Now, we want a smart portrait, like the one you did of Mrs Keppel. Remember that young Edward will be King Emperor himself one day so you are producing an historical document, something that will be hung in the gallery at Buckingham Palace eventually, so do your best. Keep it formal. Make sure that the clothes are correct and tell George that if the boys wear any decorations they must be the right ones and worn in the correct manner. You've got that? Good. Off you go my boy. If you need any money up there, just ask George's people and they will see you all right. Fine? Off you go, then."

Pablo bows his way out, a bit annoyed at having been dismissed so cavalierly. Never mind, this commission will make his fortune. He sees himself as Holbein or Van Dyke or even Velásquez. Court painter to the King of England! That's better than living in a rat hole in Paris surrounded by poofs and tarts. Walking back to Lambeth he has time to reflect on the paintings he will not paint. Developing themes from El Greco or charting street life are no longer options. Instead he will be a poodle for the great and the good; better than being a mangy mongrel in the gutters of Montmartre. Walking across Vauxhall Bridge he spies a figure on the other side of the road working away at his easel, a figure who could well be Monet trying to catch the reflections of the scudding clouds against the gloom of the Parliament building in the distance. *One day*, thinks Pablo, *I will be as famous as Monet. No, one day I will be even more famous than Monet, the King will see to that.*

Nevertheless he is not in the best of moods when he arrives at the warehouse, especially as Rose appears to be intent on a large canvas in the corner. For the moment she is studying a mass of black feathers on a table in front of her. On closer inspection it turns out to be a dead jackdaw in the first stages of decomposition. "That smells disgusting."

"Yes, I know. But it's only for a couple more days. I've got the positioning right, all I have to do now is to get the detail of the feathers down and I've finished with it."

"Is the girl holding the bird meant to be Maia? I can't believe that she is that scrawny, she looks like a puff of wind would blow her away."

"It's only based on Maia. I needed someone to hold the pose for me then I thought that her face was interesting in its own right so I put her face in as well. Really it's a girl I saw up in Hackney looking at a dead bird. I couldn't decide whether it was her pet that had died or if she had found it dead in the street and was thinking about taking it home to eat it. Then again, it's neither of those things, it's a meditation on life and death. The bird is dead and the girl looks like she needs to eat or she will go the same way in a few days."

"So why is it all in blue?"

"Blue is a very sad colour. It is the colour of the sky, the colour of the Virgin Mary's gown. It symbolises heaven, where we will go when we die. It is a poor woman's colour because poor women are always so close to death from starvation or childbirth or a thousand other misfortunes and diseases that afflict the poor."

"Very fine, I'm sure! You'll never sell it, of course, so I don't know why you bother!"

"You never sold your Carlos painting but you still did it. All you do now is fat old women in posh dresses or aristocrats' mistresses. They sell, but they are not art. Just advertising for the rich to see how much money they have and what expensive women they can afford."

Pablo and Rose are now virtually eye to eye. He knows in his heart that Rose is right. At the same time he is conscious of his smart clothes and silver-topped cane, things he has no wish to give up. He settles the argument by taking Rose in his arms and kissing her passionately. Rose is not altogether taken by surprise. She has been aware for some time that their discussion has had more to do with sex than with art. Within moments Pablo has one of her naked breasts in one hand whilst his mouth is glued to the nipple of the other. His spare hand searches unavailingly for the fastening on her skirt. Rose contemplates this for a moment. There are hot wires shooting down through her belly from her nipples, an electricity which seems to hypnotise the rest of her body, causing an increasing dampness between her legs.

"That's quite enough now. Off you go and pack your bags. A good job we will not be seeing you for a month or two." Rose adjusts her chemise, refastens her blouse. Turns away towards the door to the cutting room. *No wonder Mother lets herself go now and then,* she thinks as she rearranges her hair.

Pablo is left feeling desolate and foolish on one knee on the dusty floor, still wondering why he could not find that damn skirt fastening. *English women are wonderful but very strange,"* he thinks. *"One moment they have surrendered, the next reinforcements have arrived and they fight you off, just like Wellington at Badajoz."* He slinks off back to Hackford Road to pack his bag in preparation for the journey to the depths of rural Norfolk.

Like Wellington at Badajoz, Rose thinks it was 'a damn close run thing.'

# Brixton

## *Spring 1902*

Pablo is back from Norfolk and the new year festivities are well over. If he never sees Norfolk again he will be pleased. A landscape as flat as a table top, unrelieved by field upon field of beets and cows. A population given to monosyllabic utterances in an incomprehensible dialect, the women correctly referred to as 'Norfolk dumplings'. A wonder that the population ever increases with such ugly women. Maybe it is the boredom of those long, flat winter nights? It certainly cannot be the beer, which tastes like it has been brewed with the mud from the fields, giving him terrible stomach pains and an irritable bladder.

Nor is he sure that Hackford Road is much better. There seems to be a conspiracy to tantalise him to death. Cornelia is the most straightforward. Pablo has been readmitted to the life classes on the evenings when there is a male model. As back payment for his previous posing, on such occasions Pablo is allowed one of Cornelia's long, lingering, frustrating kisses, now with his arms firmly pinioned to his sides. The weeks when Simon is away are the most frustrating, as Cornelia compensates for his absence with longer embraces than usual. Eugenie pretends that she is just being motherly. Motherly in this context translates as much brushing and stroking, a sidling past which allows her breasts to range along the back of his shirt. Even a full kiss to celebrate special occasions such as a new commission or a particularly remunerative sale from the gallery. Although she does not shrink from contact, when it comes along she tries to avoid times when he might come round behind her when they are alone to cup her breasts in his hands once more. Rose is the most infuriating of all. She has not firmly decided what her tactics are to be and as a consequence swings from utter disdain to the broadest liberality, though Pablo has not yet found that elusive skirt fastening.

The atmosphere in Hackford Road is one of barely contained concupiscence. Even Vincent is a party to this. Eugenie has kept her promise to herself and embarked on a steady siege upon Vincent's manhood. He does not know what to make of it. On the one hand he is delighted to have a wife so devoted to him that she finds it difficult to keep her hands off him. On the other he does find it rather wearing. After all, he will be fifty in a few months' time and not quite as vigorous as he once was. To escape the febrile atmosphere in the house he has taken to long walks in the new Dulwich Park where he tries to make sense of all that is happening around him. Eugenie, as well as becoming increasingly amorous towards him, is even more flirtatious than usual. This may be a reason why sales are up but still does not explain her behaviour at home. All he can think of is that his lack of attention to her during his long-drawn-out illness has left her with a sexual deficit which she needs to fill. He is aware of her dalliance with Casas in Paris, where he knows a large number of people of all social classes, most of them all too happy to pass on gossip and observations to him. But that was some time ago now. He is also aware that Eugenie is taking her maternal affection for Pablo too far at times, though he is confident that this will wear off.

Quite what he needs to say to Cornelia he is unsure. She who is always so strict and proper is quite prepared to kiss Pablo in public, though not in the manner of brother and sister. To reproach Cornelia about this would be akin to running blindfold into a minefield. Best to keep quiet and say nothing. Rose is less of a problem in that respect. She treats Pablo with barely restrained contempt as befits a lackey of the aristocracy. Vincent has tried explaining to her that, as an art dealer, he too is a lackey of the aristocracy and as one of his dependants, so is she. Her attendance at the Slade has been poor of late, which does not bother him overly much. The girl can draw at least as well as Pablo, whilst her painting has got a much finer and sharper edge to it. Vincent is much happier displaying the paintings of R. V. G. in his gallery than the glittering finished paintings of Pablo Ruiz. Without Rose's knowledge he has already organised an exhibition for her with Ambroise Vollard in Paris in the new year as part of a deal to take Vollard's collection of the latest Gauguin paintings, which he is finding increasingly difficult to sell. Despite his dislike for the man Vincent has a deep regard for Gauguin's painting, far removed as it is from the fashionable forms of divisionism among the younger French painters. "Mere colour-splatterers," he grumbles. Gauguin, he feels, uses his non-naturalistic colour to express emotion, to get close to the inner life, to elucidate God's purpose to an increasingly materialistic world.

The walk has done him good, helped him clear his mind and bear the peculiar atmosphere at home. Perhaps this afternoon he will pick some flowers on the way home that he can paint downstairs in the kitchen while Eugenie is at the gallery. He is not prepared for what he sees in the kitchen. Propped up against one of the chairs is a large painting, some five feet tall, of a girl contemplating a dead jackdaw. This he believes to be Maia contemplating her own death. He is struck with horror. Then amazement. What has he bred that can so disturb him? He draws up another chair and sits for an hour studying the painting in all its details and implications. This is more than all of his sermons, sharper and more direct than Gauguin. A commentary upon hardship, a confirmation that in the midst of life we are in death.

Rose is in the sitting room. "Is that painting yours?" demands Vincent.

"Yes, Father, of course. What do you think of it?"

Vincent goes back into the kitchen, gathers up his charcoal, paints and brushes into a convenient box. Returns to Rose. Presents her with the box. Leaves her without a word.

# Westminster

## *June 1902*

Cornelia is exceptionally busy. Every peeress wants a new dress for the coronation. Even the smallest couture houses are overwhelmed. As one of the most fashionable, Cornelia's emporium is beset at all hours by importunate matrons. Simon has been a great help, setting up a subsidiary cutting room in Bramley to do the basic work on the dresses before they are shipped back to London by train for finishing. If Cornelia were never to design or make another dress in her life she would still be a rich woman.

Pablo is similarly harried from pillar to post by peers and their wives and daughters. Acting on Eugenie's advice he has quadrupled his prices. Even then, he has more work than he can cope with. Two of Rose's classmates from the Slade have been co-opted to brush in the base colour over his initial drawings while Maia transfers his sketches of furniture onto the canvas for correction later. For larger paintings she draws indications of background objects onto card, which can be pinned onto the painting and moved around until a correct balance is achieved.

Rose views this with disdain. She is immersed in her drawings from the East End, turning them into a series of finished paintings that both disturb and excite her father. The starving woman feeding her baby is a huge success; Vincent can hardly bear to look at it, it is so poignant. The Jewish bread man looks equally near to God, is perhaps even God himself. She has combined a life drawing of Pablo with a female model to give a naked young couple sadly clinging to one another. For a while she is oblivious to all of the excitement around her. Then two days before the coronation she disappears, not to resurface until all is over. Dressed in one of her father's old suits, since cut down to accommodate Pablo's lesser height, she cruises the pavements of London, sketchbook in hand. Hair hidden under a flat cap, she could be any young man from the Slade trying to capture the event for posterity. But her gaze is not towards where the procession will be, it is directed to those who have gathered from the four corners of the country, even from the bogs of Ireland, to see the first coronation in over sixty years. Who knows when there will be another? Many of them have nowhere to stay, both inns and stables being full to capacity. Nor do many of them have enough money in their pockets, even if they could find a lodging. These are the people that Rose is looking for, the ones who are sleeping, often in family groups, in doorways and under archways.

Among the crowds are several musicians and singers rattling tin cups and calling on the passers-by to be generous. One in particular takes Rose's eye, a strongly built man with only one leg bellowing out a popular song at the top of his tuneless voice. Always ready to help a sufferer Rose joins in with her own, clear voice. After one verse the man stops singing and approaches her. "Don't do that, matey, don't join in."

"Why not? It makes it all the more pleasant and tuneful."

"Exactly. We don't want it to be tuneful. There are plenty of real musicians who can be tuneful. What we want is to be heard and as off-key as possible. That way people just get irritated and give you money so that you move on. You gets a lot more that way than with the pretty stuff. Then people just gather round and listen instead of dipping into their pockets."

"I wonder if that's what they do with my paintings," muses Rose as she struts away down Whitehall where she is observed by her father and Pablo, both of whom immediately recognise the suit even if it takes them some time to realise who is wearing it. They are high above the crowds, sharing two windows with Whistler who is back from Paris for the occasion. While Pablo is seeing to the aristocratic portraits

256

it is Whistler's job to capture the scene as a whole. Both are madly sketching away as the procession passes, before Whistler hurries away to be admitted through a side door in the abbey so that he can ascend to the high balcony in order to catch the service and the crowning ceremony below. At his age he would rather have left this part to Pablo or to Walter, the hustle and bustle followed by the stairs not being kind either to his ageing legs or to his cigar-damaged lungs. Walter is left clinging to the railings of the Houses of Parliament, desperately trying to generate enough sketches for the master to work up into a usable form at some later date.

Unlike the state funeral, the coronation leaves everyone tired and grumpy. Many did not see as much as they had hoped. Perhaps the King had turned away at the wrong moment or someone in front had jumped up to see what was happening. Those who had camped out over night are exhausted, most are hungry and thirsty, the latter to be assuaged by copious draughts of ale and porter. Inevitably excess on an empty stomach leads to irritability and disagreements which spill over into fisticuffs. Men scuffle, women shriek and children wail. Nor are the King and Queen immune; they too are irritable and take it out on their various minions.

Rose is particularly tired having gone forty-eight hours without sleep. Fearing a raucous party back in Brixton she heads for the warehouse, which she hopes will be empty. Which it is, for a while. Pablo strolls in, throws his sketchpad onto a chair and waxes enthusiastic about the colour and the pageantry he has just witnessed. "Only in England could one see such a wonderful display. Didn't the King look marvellous? Even better than in Whistler's portrait. What a great king he will make."

"Listen, he's no more than a fat old *roué*: eats too much, drinks too much, gambles too much, goes off with every woman who offers herself, and God knows there are plenty of those. He's just typical of those crumbling, bumbling old aristos you are so fond of. The sooner we get rid of them the better. Once we get the vote and have some women in Parliament, the whole lot of them will be swept away: kings, queens, dukes, princes, all." Tiredness and excitement have combined to raise Rose's colour to a brilliant red. At some later date the memory of her will serve as a model for Pablo's sculpture of Boadicea. Now he has other interests. He pulls Rose to him and pulls up her shirtfront, diving down to devour her breasts. Because of his familiarity he has no problem finding the fastening of her trousers, which he drops to the floor alongside his own. A sleep-deprived Rose has no defence; those bursts of electricity from her nipples engulf her and she loses her virginity on the painting table, to emerge, her back covered in chalk dust, her front with bites and bruises from Pablo's ravishing lips and teeth. *Well*, she thinks, *that wasn't too bad after all. I will need a wash in all sorts of places after that. I wonder if he can manage it again?*

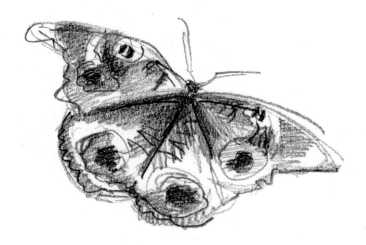

# Grimsby

## *Autumn 1902*

*Dear Vince*

*I imagine you and the girls had a rare old time over the coronation. The pictures in the papers here are very impressive. I've never seen Grimsby like it: flags and bunting everywhere, dancing in the streets and so on. It was as if a huge weight had been lifted off the town now that the old Queen has gone. The sketches on the music hall are even broader than usual, as are the insults from the crowd. We had a grand time there last week, even met a couple of the turns: a singer and his son. Do you remember the Wine Pipe? We had gone there after the show when this chap turns up who sings the sort of soggy song that I hate, all grieving mothers and unrequited love. Anyway he was well gone before he even got there. Charlie, his name was. With him was his son, about ten or twelve, one of the clog dancers who dances a lot better than his father sings. Had a nice long chat, with Charlie getting even more pie-eyed; could only just manage to get up to take a piss. When he comes back the lad gets up to take a piss as well. Except he is the dead spit of his father, rolling about all over the place, three staggered steps forward and two steps back. Picks up somebody's cigarette, tries to light it. Misses, shrugs, puts it behind his ear. Misses. Can't find it on the floor. Then walks off to the jakes absolutely stone cold sober. The whole pub erupted. Hilarious! Young Harry, who as you know was on the boards himself for some time, thought it was the funniest act he had ever seen. I don't think the father was particularly amused, since in the end we were all laughing at him.*

*Well, I know I've been saying 'we' all the way through this. I've*

*just moved in with a widow who lives down the street called Saranne.*
*She is a smart body, full of fun and ready to tolerate an artist who can*
*be up at all hours and disappear down the beach whenever he feels*
*like it. She has her own house, just a terrace, like, and three sons. Her*
*husband was a skipper on the boats, went missing somewhere off*
*Iceland a couple of years ago. I've told her about still being married to*
*Lizzie and about how I upped and left. She was a bit dubious at*
*first, which is why it was some time before I moved in. Young Harry*
*gets on very well with her. Little Harry has even started calling her*
*'Grandma', even though I try to discourage him. I thought that my*
*Harry would be upset at that but he doesn't seem to mind.*

*The other boys called in last week on their way back to London*
*from Richmond. Walter is going to take his discharge, which is a relief.*
*Charles has decided to stay on, even though he was wounded quite*
*badly in Africa. I'm sure that Lizzie will be as delighted to see them*
*as I was; they have grown into such big, strong lads. And can't they*
*drink! You'd think that the African sun had dried them up so that*
*there's a parched desert inside. "You've no idea what it's like, Dad,"*
*Walter said to me. "Marching along through the veldt day after day*
*in that blazing sun, over a hundred degrees most of the time, with*
*nothing but a tiny canteen of water to last you until the next water*
*hole, which for all you know has been poisoned by the Boers anyway."*
*Sooner him than me.*

*Well, what you really want to know is, what have I been painting?*
*Apart from the ones I sent you last week, that is. Old man Ross can*
*be a grumpy so-and-so and very tight when it comes to forking out his*
*own money but he is great at getting other people to shell out theirs.*
*His last trick was to get the City Council to commission a painting to*
*go in the council chamber. There was quite a to-do about it and the*
*appropriation for it had to go to the full committee. The three ILP chaps*
*thought it was a complete waste of money, which could be better spent*
*on the local schools. On the other hand they didn't want to be seen as*
*'anti-culture' so they abstained. The Conservatives voted for it in*
*principal, with the proviso that it shouldn't be 'any of this modern*

muck'. Just to annoy them the Liberals voted for it as long as it was 'in the spirit of the times', so that in the end it got through quite comfortably. As usual the appropriation won't see me on easy street for the rest of my life. Still, it will do; it gave me enough cash and time to finish off the four that I sent you.

The painting itself is already up in the council chamber. I'm inordinately proud of it, especially since the Conservatives are spitting blood and threatening to tear it down. What I've tried to do is to carry the three divisions idea that little bit further, getting rid of the lines between the areas so that the painting is seen as a whole instead of the old foreground-background division. Each third shades evenly from light to dark across the painting before moving back again. That's exactly what happens with the evening light here. Sand becomes sea and sea becomes sky so that you don't really know what is what. Now, this was meant to be a celebration of the fishing industry, which is how come they wanted it in the first place. I think even the Liberals were expecting nice paintings of trawlers. Instead of that I have put in rectangles of colour to represent the trawler funnels, most of which I had painted myself in the first place. Then I painted each one with a different company colour. The trawler owners love that, they find it much better than having just a painting of one trawler with one company's colours on it (they know full well it would have been Mr Ross's colours, too). So there it is, twelve feet wide and five feet high, the best thing I have ever done, as I'm sure you would agree if you were to see it.

Do you remember you gave me an introduction to some painters in Holland when I went over there on the boats in the summer? I met a grand chap called Pieter, a landscape painter. We got on like a house on fire and exchanged ideas and addresses. I sent him a copy of the local paper with a reproduction of my painting in it. Spread it right across the inside page, they did. Well, he thought it was grand and showed it to some of his friends in Brussels. So now they've invited me to send them six paintings for their annual exhibition. 'Les XX' they call themselves, which I suppose you will recognise as being 'Twenty', except they say it in French, of course. I don't have enough cash to do that, though. Could you arrange for some of the paintings of mine that you have to go over with one of your shipments? A commission if we sell anything, as you might expect.

My best wishes to you and the girls and to Eugenie.

Your indebted friend

Harry

Harry

# Lambeth

## *Autumn 1902*

Like Harry, Pablo is hard at work on a massive new painting twelve feet wide and five feet high. The difference is that he has assistants to help him with it. The girls from the Slade have finished their basic drawing and underpainting and gone back to their studies, so that the full structure of the subject is now revealed. Based on several of Pablo's drawings and a few that he has 'borrowed' from Walter's collection, the painting shows the open coronation coach, drawn by magnificent plumed horses accompanied by horsemen of the various guards' regiments in their full shiny regalia. King Edward sits erect in the carriage, plumed hat bending in a gentle breeze. Pablo is trying hard not to be too meticulous; he is seeking a mobile effect to mirror the kinomatograph impression that is currently being shown in several of the metropolitan theatres. His paint flows gently along in a vaguely impressionist manner, something which has by now become accepted even by *The Times*' art critics. He is glorying in the colours, loving the opportunity to be free with his paint application.

He can by now draw the King almost from memory, remembering always to deduct a couple of stones in weight and several inches in girth. The King's hands, one resting on the side of the carriage, the other waving regally, are rendered to perfection. He has been drawing horses since he was ten and glories in the opportunity to paint them larger than he has ever done before. Where the general populace is to be seen it is as an indistinct mass as if through frosted glass. Which leaves the coach itself, a horrible lump in the centre of the painting, which is also dull and time consuming to paint. The problem is solved by Maia, his last remaining assistant, who is employed to cover it with gold leaf, a task which she undertakes with infinite patience and the steadiest of hands.

Eugenie has plans for this painting. It will be shown for public exhibition at the gallery, admission fee one shilling per person. Two of Seamus's illegitimate sons have been engaged to police the huge crowds that are expected. Once the excitement has died down a public subscription will be opened to purchase the painting for the nation. Expectations here are for thousands of pounds rather than a mere few hundred guineas. One must eat. Vincent is not so happy. He would prefer to put on an exhibition of Roualt, a dedicated artist he met some years ago at Moreau's *atelier*. Eugenie points out to him that even if they were to sell every one of Roualt's tiny paintings, it would only fetch a half of the admission fees to see the Ruiz 'Coronation'. Vincent retires, unhappily defeated. He can always show Roualt at a later date.

Outwardly calm and unflustered, Pablo is still beset by waves of Spanish depression, uncertain if his fame will last or whether he wants fame and fortune at all. Rose's paintings bother him; they are going in a direction that he finds both repulsive and attractive, taking him back to the Paris of the Moulin de la Galette and the Barcelona of Els Quatre Gats. To compensate he spends every evening he can at the Canterbury Music Hall in Lambeth, compulsively drawing the stars and drinking with the performers in low bars afterwards. His favourite is Charlie, a young clog dancer with an alcoholic father and a mother in a lunatic asylum. Charlie is fond of borrowing Pablo's top hat for his impression of Champagne Charlie and the grossly insulting imitation of his father's alcoholic stumblings. *This is what you are like,* thinks Pablo. *Just like this lad, determined never to do like others. I would love to be a revolutionary, overturning all of the past traditions. On the other hand, look what I have achieved already, paintings as big as church frescoes loved and admired by thousands, invited to show at all the major international exhibitions. Do I really want to go back to sleeping under railway arches and being the paid toy boy of a poof like Manyac?*

Nor are his feelings of instability reduced by his relationship with

Rose. Her attitude to him is less abrasive than it has been before, whilst still keeping him on tenterhooks waiting for an explosion. As a sensible girl she refuses him any sexual favours except for her perceived safe time either side of her period. She has discussed this with Cornelia who has assured her that, whilst not infallible, this is the safest course she can adopt which does not require that ever-variable commodity, male co-operation. "A girl must look after herself," declares Cornelia, "and not rely on some rutting male to do it for her." The periods of abstinence drive Pablo wild, which is just as well since within the four-day window that Rose allows herself she is completely insatiable. "If I'm going to have to go on a diet the majority of the time, I might as well stoke up and get my fill on the few days that I'm allowed," she tells the confused Pablo.

He is also jealous of Rose. There seem to be no limits to the subject matter of her painting – harlots, virgins, saints, sinners, beggars, artisans, dying children, happy children – or to her means of expressing her feelings about them through paint. Pablo's father has sent him postcards of Catalan altar paintings and mosaics. She has combined the naïve figures with a sensibility that she has imbibed from reproductions of El Greco, who she regards as the big brother of the church painters. Her figures are distorted, elongated, simplified in such a way as to fire their emotions at the viewer, who is also fixed by their enormous eyes, like those of a starving child. Pablo knows full well that if released from his financial and aesthetic bondage, he too could paint like that but now he is as much in bondage to the thousands of guineas poured on him by the British aristocracy as he once was to the 150 francs that Manyac gave him every month. *One day*, he says, *I shall be so rich that I will be able to paint whatever I like. I will make the world sit up. I just hope that I will still remember what it is to paint like that.*

# Shipley

## *Autumn 1902*

*Dear Papa*

*I feel strange writing to you, we who have been living in the same house for so many years. My fortunes having changed so much we may not meet for some time to come. I have gone north to be with Simon for my laying-in now that the birth is not too far away. I know Mother would have liked me to go to Hackford Road or for her to move in with us in Kensington, but coming up here is much more convenient all round. Perhaps she can come up for a week or two once the baby is born, and you as well, dear Papa.*

*It is the baby that I need to talk to you about and of myself as well. You know that we had agreed to have the children raised in the two religions so that they can decide where they worship once they are adults? I have been thinking about that. What happens if the baby is a boy? Should he be circumcised or not? Do I have to be churched after the birth? All sorts of problems. Also, I've been talking to the rabbi here as well as with Simon's mother. Our family life in Brixton has been so close and loving I want my children to have the same. Once we are settled here we would be part of Simon's family, with all their habits and observances. How could I deny that to the children?*

*Dear Papa, you have always brought us up to be good Christians in the Methodist tradition. How could I desert that now, be a mere apostate? What will happen to my eternal soul? Will I be damned forever for denying Christ? Perhaps it is the price that I will have to pay for giving myself so completely to my children? Please guide me on this and on another matter that I have been considering.*

*I am now very well off. The old Queen's funeral followed by the coronation has made mine the best-known couture house in London. Women come to me now rather than going to Paris. Part of my success has been due to the help of Doris and Laura Kirman, both with their eye for design and their skill in the cutting shop. I would like to give the business over to them in some manner so that I can devote myself to the children (there I go, I've not had this one yet and I'm already projecting a huge brood!). My problem is that two thirds of the money used to set up the company comes from Rose and Maia so I don't feel in a position to do anything without talking to them first. Perhaps I could buy them out in some way (I'm sure I have easily enough money to do that), with some extra to recognise the profit we have made over the last few years. This all sounds terribly commercial, which I don't mind usually but it is more difficult when it is family. Papa, could you talk to them for me, please, to prepare the ground for me? I'm sure it will come as a shock to them and I don't want it all to be done by letter.*

*The pregnancy is progressing very well. I have been a trifle nauseous but that is over now and I am feeling fine. Simon and I have been for walks on the moors, which are most handsome at this time of year. These are becoming shorter and less frequent as the winter draws closer and I grow larger. The air here is so much fresher and healthier than down in London, the wind off the Pennines clears away any fog besides completely disarranging my coiffure.*

*Your loving daughter*
*Cornelia*

# Lambeth

## *Autumn 1902*

*Dearest Cornelia*

*Of all my children you are the most organised and careful, so it is no surprise to me that you are seeking my advice on these momentous matters. Quite rightly you have put the salvation of your eternal soul ahead of mere earthly considerations, though your attitude to those and to the people around you does you credit, suggesting that your soul is in no danger from that direction.*

*As for your intention to convert to Judaism, this is a matter that you should consider most carefully. There will be people in both communities who will reproach you and 'spit on your Jewish gaberdine'. This is a cross that you should be prepared to bear. From my point of view as a lay preacher within the church I believe that your conversion will find favour in the eyes of God, who is the one to whom we must all answer. You should remember that Jesus Christ himself was a Jew, as were his disciples and Saint Paul. We are all people of the Book, who have been chosen to worship the one true God. He sent his son to us to lead us back into the path of righteousness, to bring a new gentler form of belief now that the tribes of Israel have moved out of the desert and into the city. Some choose to accept that the message was from the son of God, others that Christ was a prophet among many. We Christians believe that those latter people are wrong and they are harming themselves by failing to accept the message. But we do not condemn them for it because we know that they do this out of their love and devotion to the God that we all worship, who will one day come to judge us* all for the sincerity of our belief and the goodness of our actions in this life. Neither faith nor good works are sufficient; we must have both.

I am sorry, I feel as if I am writing one of my sermons! What I want to say is that as long as you believe firmly in God he will understand that any path you choose is one that will lead you to Him. Does God really care if you worship Him on Saturday or on Sunday? What are our forms and ceremonies to Him? What he cares for is what is in men's hearts. By all means adopt your husband's religion, my dear, and may my blessing go with you.

Now to more earthly matters. I can quite see that a move to Yorkshire would be good for you and your new family, as long as you do not neglect your old one! Of course Mama will come up for a few weeks after the birth. I think your problem will be trying to get rid of her! Simon will doubtless be taking a greater role in managing the manufacturing business so will not expect to be in London dealing with sales very often. For him to be living in Yorkshire while you and the children (there I go as well, multiplying your offspring) are in London would be a recipe for disaster. We will all miss you, me more than anyone.

I have talked to your sisters about what to do about reimbursing them from the couture house. Rose is very happy to take whatever settlement you decide to make. She says that she has plans for next year, which will be made much easier with extra money to support them. Maia is more complicated. She is sixteen now and wants to begin a serious life of her own. For the last year she has been spending some time in the cutting room and with Lizzie Kirman helping her with her hats. You know how quiet Maia is, so I had no idea that this is what she has been doing. We had a long talk about it and how we could reconcile her wishes with your giving the company to Doris and Laura. In the end we decided that the best plan would be for Maia to enter the company itself as what I might call 'the hat department', designing and selling hats to complement the dresses. The best way of doing that, we decided, would be for

Doris, Laura and Maia to have one-third share each in the company. They can decide what wages they pay themselves once they are sure of their income. What do you think?

Your loving father,

Vincent

# Brixton

## *Autumn 1902*

Father is such a sweetie! Quite how he manages to keep four fractious females in order and content with their lives I cannot imagine. Cornelia started it all with her disappearance up to the wilds of Yorkshire, leaving fame and fortune behind for the sake of filling the world with a menagerie of children. I'm sure I will love them all when they arrive but babies are far from my mind at the moment. She asked Father to sort out the finances from her company, which she wants to pass on to Laura and Doris. Since Maia and I put our money into it in the first place, Cornelia felt she needed to recompense us in some way.

Father wanted to know what I planned to do, which was very awkward. In the end I had to tell him that what I really wanted to do was to leave the Slade and go and study in Paris. I'd originally intended to go to the Académie Carmen, but Whistler has closed it since he became ill so I would have to look elsewhere, preferably for one that is not full of soppy English art students. God, those men are so boring! What they need is a good war to shake them up. Anyway wherever I go I will need some money to support myself. Then Father tells me that he has arranged a show for me at Vollard's next year! What a surprise that was! Maybe he thought the news would make me change my plans; instead it made me all the more determined. Think of all the work I could do in my own studio in Paris!

We talked about this for some time. Father said that he would find me a studio in a respectable area. He mentioned a couple of complexes to keep away from – Le Bateau-Lavoir and La Ruche – as both are disreputable and insanitary. (I mentioned them to Mama afterwards. She just shuddered and said that no daughter of hers was ever going to live there.) Then he really shook me. He asked me what I was going to do about my affair with Pablo. How on earth did he know about that? We have been so discrete. Only Cornelia knows anything about it and she wouldn't tell. I don't put it past Maia to have gone nosing around, she is so sharp and so quiet, but she keeps things severely to herself. However he found out, giving him a straight answer was most embarrassing. I've certainly no intention of taking Pablo to Paris with me, even if he wanted to go. The sex has been great, especially since, as he tells me, he has had so much experience, having been in and out of brothels since he was fifteen. Can't imagine it would be half as much fun with any of those twerps at the Slade. But I'm not in love with him or anything, it could almost be anyone, except that Pablo is virtually part of the family so it doesn't seem so naughty somehow.

As I say, trying to explain this to Father was very difficult, him being so religious and all. Strangely it didn't seem to upset him one little bit. In fact he seemed quite glad. "I love Pablo as a son," he said. "He is charming, well brought up and devoted to art. On the other hand I would hate to have him as a son-in-law. He is completely morally unreliable, especially where women are concerned. I would spend all my time spying on him just to make sure he was behaving himself. Not something I would ever want to do. I'm glad that your first experiences have been satisfactory and I thank Pablo for that. From now on you need to consider your actions more carefully, especially in Paris where an attractive young woman like you can find so many pitfalls to tumble in to." Then he gave me a big hug before sitting down with me to write a letter to Cornelia.

What I have to do now is to settle down to complete as many paintings as I can so that I have plenty ready for Vollard when I get to Paris. Then I have to tell Pablo that I am leaving and he is not coming with me. And, oh dear yes, I have to talk to Mother. Now that will be difficult. I'm sure she will not approve of me going at all, especially going on my own. Also, I suspect that she will not want to have another member of the family living permanently in Paris. Cornelia and I have discussed this and we are both fairly sure that Mother likes to let her hair down a bit on her trips over there. She's unlikely to relish the idea of 'little eyes' peeking at her as she does so. I will do my best to be polite but firm with her. Telling her that Father is all in favour should swing the argument and Cornelia will help. The other question is, who will look after Maia? Maia would say that she is old enough to look after herself. Sixteen is a tricky age, just the easiest time to get yourself into trouble. Working with Doris and Laura will be good for her; they will keep a weather eye open. With luck all the advice Cornelia and I have given her will make her wiser than most girls her age.

# Brixton

## *January 1903*

Rose's trunk is in the hallway waiting to be taken to the station. Rose is tidying herself after emotional farewells with her mother and pinning on her new hat, a present from Maia. This is a flamboyant creation with peacock feathers and wax flowers. Whether it will stand up to the journey is a moot point. Rose vows not to try promenading on the deck of the ferry just in case. She has said her goodbyes to Pablo the previous night. He is now hiding away from her in his room. "Sulking," she says. Even on this night, the last on which they will be together, Rose has refused to break her 'two-day' rule, much to Pablo's annoyance and frustration. Rose is adamant that she is now turning over a new leaf, despite all the temptations of Paris and a room of her own. She has had enough of men and now only thinks about the wonderful paintings that she will paint over the coming year.

A loud hammering on the door announces the arrival of the cab. Vincent and the cabbie manoeuvre the trunk onto the boot rack, leaving Rose and Maia to take the forward-facing seats inside. Eugenie watches in tears as Vincent joins his daughters, waves her sodden handkerchief as they drive off. She is still hoping that Rose will change her mind, that Vincent will convince her that to go off alone like this is too dangerous. It is bad enough having one daughter struggling with the pains of childbirth in the wastes of Yorkshire without having another taking herself off to the fleshpots of Paris. Not that her emotions are quite that simple. She is angry with Vincent for not putting his foot down and forbidding Rose to go. Besides that, she could do with visiting a few fleshpots herself; life in South London is so dull with nothing but housework and looking after the gallery. At least the gallery is closed for this, the quietest month of the year. An unseasonal warmth does nothing to lift Eugenie's mood. She will sublimate her sadness and anger by giving the kitchen a good clean.

Half an hour later she is hard at work removing some stubborn stains from the sink, oblivious to all around her. Pablo has emerged from his room in search of breakfast. Spying Eugenie at the sink he seizes his chance, encircling her breasts with his hands. This time he meets no resistance, his suit reinforced by a combination of resentment and envy. *Just a little*, she thinks, *then I will tell him to behave himself and go away*. She has failed to take into account Pablo's frustration and undoubted expertise in this field of action, his ability to manipulate with his hands equal only to his ability to paint with them. By this time, all thoughts of clean sinks and matronly resistance have disappeared to be replaced by an overwhelming lust such as Eugenie has not experienced in several years.

Her passion takes Pablo totally by surprise. Before he knows it he is flat on his back on the kitchen floor while Eugenie rides him as expertly as any whore. She lifts his head to hold it to her engorged nipple. Unable to contain himself, the result of abstinence caused by Rose's 'two-day' rule, he ejaculates, almost to his own surprise. Eugenie takes no notice; she is set upon her own pleasure, which she achieves at last. Only just in time as Pablo's member is giving up the task, flopping out of her like a limp asparagus. "Oh Paul, oh my darling Paul," she gasps into his neck.

Eugenie gathers up her clothes and Pablo, taking them upstairs to his room. To use the marital bed would be unacceptable. Besides, only a single space will be required for the activity she has in mind. Pablo's mind is still reeling from his sudden good fortune. Eugenie is not as firm or svelte as Rose but she is still a well kept woman. Her breasts are larger as are her hips, the result of three children. Her limbs are fleshier, though not grossly so, while her complexion has been kept young by all of the creams and unguents that London and Paris can supply. They are both looking forward to a long and pleasant morning to assuage their various pains and regrets.

# Paris

## *Summer 1903*

This being summer there have, of course, been storms in the Channel, which have prevented sailings for several days. As a result, after two weeks of drought Rose's letters have arrived in a rush. Ignoring the smell, Rose has found herself a bench by the Seine to indulge herself in reading about home.

*Dear Rose*

*Only a quick line from Southampton Street where trade is horribly dull at the moment. People do not know whether to wear their summer best or their winter overcoats, the weather is so changeable. I have finally managed to put on my Roualt show, more for myself than in the expectation of any great sales. One must do things to please oneself from time to time. Lady Ottoline came in this morning with Mr Russell, each persuading the other to make a purchase. Apart from that I have sold only two others. I have managed to sell one of your 'blind beggar' paintings and I will send you the money soon.*

*The house feels so empty without you. It was bad enough when Cornelia left. Now it is like a desert. Maia is a little mouse; one can so easily forget that she is there. For most of the day she is at the warehouse with Doris, so we hardly see her. This is the first time your mother and I have been alone together here since we married. First there was your grandmother, then you three came along. Pablo is still here, of course, but he is always off at posh houses painting his clients or down at the music hall. He has developed a fascination for this lad Charlie who does funny sketches now he has left the dancing troupe.*

Pablo spends hours up in the gods drawing him and the other acts. Yesterday he amused us with a flipbook he has made of Charlie as a drunken tramp. As you flip the pages it looks like he is staggering all over the place; much more fun than the kinematograph.

Ah, looks like a customer at last. Write soon my darling.

Your loving father

Vincent

★

Dear Rose

At long last the winter up here is over and I am able to go out and about with baby. He is quite adorable, except when he wakes in the middle of the night. Simon is annoyed by that because I have refused to have a nursemaid and because I feed the baby myself. It is such a wonderful feeling! Mother suggested that I do it. She has never got used to this thing about having servants, especially when it comes to looking after the children. "Who do you want the child to learn from?" she says. "From you or from some drab off the streets?" I hardly think that Simon or his mother would engage 'some drab off the streets' but I take her point; if I want the child to be like me then I have to be around to be the exemplar.

He is trying to lift his head up and looks around him all of the time with his great big black eyes. They say that babies don't recognise different people, yet when I go anywhere near him he starts to gurgle. Perhaps it's the milky smell? Mother can't keep her hands off him, which is getting a trifle frustrating now. She says that she is going back to London 'sometime soon'. She has been saying that for the last couple of weeks then changes her mind once she sees the baby. Oops! Feeding time, better go or I will leak all over this blouse.

Enjoy yourself in Paris, my sweet. Have lots of nice men, but only at the right time.

Your sleepy sister

Cornelia

Dear Rose

I take time out from my packing to send you this little note. I have had a wonderful time here with Cornelia, Simon and little Aaron, who is the most beautiful little boy. Given the chance I would stay here forever. However, I have the feeling that I may have outstayed my welcome and like a good mother-in-law I am beating a retreat before I am asked to leave. One day I hope to be making the same exit from your house and baby. I still worry about you, my dear, alone in Paris. When I was there I always tried to have someone accompany me, especially since artists live in such awful areas. Señor Casas was always very helpful in this respect. Please give him my regards should you run into him. I'm told he wants to marry this little Julia of his. The family are kicking up a stink about it. Since they hold the purse strings he is afraid to take the plunge until he can get them to agree. I can understand their reluctance; she is over twenty years younger than he is. Like all models she hardly has an unblemished reputation.

Speaking of Casas, he sent me a cutting last week from a Paris newspaper. Simon was kind enough to translate it for me. It was a sort of general overview of the coming artists in France by Señor Rusinol. He mentions you and says that your painting is 'mystic, sensual, refined and barbarous, medieval and modern'. I suppose that is meant to be a compliment? I'm not too sure what he means about the 'medieval' bit, unless he's talking about those funny Catalan church paintings you are so fond of. Please let us know how the exhibition at Vollard's goes. We were hoping to get over to see it earlier, though this may mean closing the gallery for a while and I have been so tied up with little Aaron. Cornelia is talking of having a photograph taken of him, which seems like an extravagance to me.

Best wishes from your loving mother,
Eugenie van Gogh

*Dearest darling Rose*

*You cannot imagine how much I have missed you since you have been away. (I know exactly what he has been missing, grunts Rose.) All day long I slave at my canvases, trying to breathe life into the pudgy faces of the English upper classes. These people are so boring, I cannot believe that you have put up with them so long. The French had the right idea: bring in the guillotine! As much as I try and sharpen up the paintwork to bring in some idea of complementary colour or to make the composition more expressive, I am defeated by the subject and the client's determination to have a photographic image. That bloody camera!*

*Hackford Road is so dull without you there. Maia is at the warehouse all day, your father is at the gallery and your mother in Yorkshire with her grandson. I spend my evenings at the music hall drawing as much as I can so that I have rows of notebooks full of sketches. I just wish I had the time to work them up into an interesting painting. Even something like a Whistler or even a Frans Hals would satisfy me at this point. The Spaniards in Paris keep me abreast of your work. They are most complimentary, using it as an excuse to sneer at what I am doing. Never mind, let them stink in their rat holes and empty their night buckets out of their windows onto the bourgeoisie as they see fit. One cannot live like that all one's life; the aristocracy keep me in good shoes and warm clothes. If I can't paint everything that I like, why bother?*

*Anyway, my darling, look after yourself. I look forward every minute to seeing you again.*

*Pablo Ruiz*

*Dear Rose*

*Just a quick line to introduce a new friend of mine who will be moving to Paris soon. He is a Dutchman called Pieter Mondrian who*

I met last year. He speaks good English so you won't need to drag out whatever Dutch you might have picked up from Vincent. He introduced me to a group in Brussels called Les XX. We both showed there in their annual exhibition last year. He was extremely kind about my painting (so much so that I suspect that he might be moving in the same direction himself now). The upshot was that I actually sold a painting for the first time outside sleepy old Lincolnshire. Not that it was very expensive; just about paid for me to get over to Belgium on my boy Harry's boat and stay for a few days. Piet is a good lad. Please look after him and show him around since he could be lonely in the big city for the first time.

Best wishes
Harry

★

Dear Rose

Wish you were here. No. Wish I was there. London is the same as ever. I am working hard making hats. Mother is away and Father is most kind whenever he notices me. Paint well.

Maia

# Montmartre

## *Summer 1903*

*Dear Cornelia*

*Here I am, sweltering in the French summer, wearing nothing but my chemise with the windows wide open. The studio is overlooked by the windows opposite but I don't care. I have been trying to work on a new painting of a sick girl in hospital attended by a nun. The composition is fine but the hot weather is drying the paint too quickly so that I can't move it around as much as I'd like to.*

*The studio itself is grand, on the top floor of an old building, which the neighbours claim is about to be pulled down, hence the low rent. They also say that the demolition has been scheduled for the last ten years, so I am not that worried about it. More likely it will fall down around my ears first. I've plugged the worst leaks in the roof and managed to get the gaslights working, which particularly emphasise the blues on my palette. Apart from the problems with the weather, the painting is going extremely well, especially after the show at Vollard's, of which more later. Moving to Paris threw me when I arrived. It seemed wrong somehow to go on using my London sketches so I had to go walking about the streets here first. Using Father's old suit is a great disguise. Nobody bothers me except the streetwalkers until they realise I'm not some young lad. I've made friends with a few of them, who are really good company. They have taught me the sort of French that you don't learn at school.*

*Vollard's exhibition was a bit of a mixed bag. He sold three large paintings, which gave me enough money to buy as much paint and canvas as I like and was a good enough incentive for him to offer me* another show late next year, as long as he approves of the work that I do in the meantime. As you know I've still got plenty of money in the bank at home. I'm determined not to touch that except in an emergency, so I've taken a couple of extra jobs to help me along. First of all, I've been doing some modelling. Completely immodest of me, I know, though we all got plenty of practice at the warehouse on those nights when the life model failed to turn up. Some of the artists assume that their models will automatically sleep with them. They are very disappointed when I turn them down and swear that I will never sit for them again. Then they change their minds because I know how to sit still and hold a pose and because I'm reliable. I've even done some modelling for Señor Casas (don't tell Mother, she would be furious). He's very sweet and so much in love with his Julia. I can understand why Mother was so keen on him, especially with his great big anarchist beard.

My other job is far more regular, as a studio assistant for Monsieur Rodin. I have to measure up his maquettes and transfer the measurements to the full-sized sculpture before helping to supply him with clay and cleaning up the scrapings from the floor. Here I have a confession to make, in that I have to admit that I have quite taken to him despite his age and have even slept with him a couple of times. Isn't that terrible of me! He has a lady at home who he refers to as his wife – though I don't think they are actually married – who is as old as he is. Perhaps they don't have those sort of feelings for one another any more? Anyway he is kind and thoughtful besides being as randy as a goat. Mind, I'm hardly one to talk, am I?

I've made a couple of interesting friends, both poets. Max says that he knew Pablo when he was here three years ago. "A most promising painter and a lovely boy," he says of him. The Spaniards nod and wink knowingly when Max says things like this, since he is known to prefer young boys. They insinuate that Pablo and Max were more than just good friends. I can't believe that, can you? I don't completely understand his poetry; French people tell me it is exciting and very advanced. The other poet is a huge man I just call Bill. He is some sort of Polish count, or would be if he were at all sure who his *father is.* His family name is Kostrowicki, which I can spell but not pronounce. His poetry has words all over the place, something that he picked up from Whistler's friend Mallarmé. He is quite keen on me. I think I will pause a little and get to know him a bit more. Besides, I have to make a decision on what to do about the Rodin situation.

Talking of beards, one of Harry's friends turned up this week: a Dutchman called Piet who speaks reasonable English and a little French. He is a great admirer of Harry's, describes him as one of Britain's finest artists. His paintings are quite minimal, based on Dutch landscape with a touch of Harry's blocks of colour. Casas set him up in a dingy studio in Le Bateau-Lavoir, which is all he can afford. Piet has made friends with a Frenchman from Le Havre called Georges Braque. They have really taken to one another, in and out of one another's studios all of the time. At some point they are talking of going over to visit Harry in Grimsby to set up an artistic circle. Better than St Ives, I suppose.

Just to finish, I did get one review of my exhibition in the *Mercure de France*, which I am proud of, even though it does paint me in a rather dreary light. I enclose it with this missive from your loving sister

Rose


"It is extraordinary, this sterile sadness which weighs down the entire work of this very young woman. Her world is no more habitable than the lepers' houses. And her painting itself is sick, the negative sense of living, the illness from which she, more than anyone else, seems to be suffering."

# Brixton

## *Summer 1903*

The journey down from Yorkshire is long and tiring. Despite the hot summer sun the other passengers in the compartment insist that the windows be kept closed 'to avoid chills and the dirt from the engine'. The gentlemen refrain from smoking but the heat inside the compartment and from inside their tweeds combine to produce an ambient atmosphere of old tobacco. By the time the train arrives at King's Cross Eugenie is exhausted and perspiring freely. The onset of one of her sweats – a new sensation totally unwelcome at the best of times but completely enervating in this summer heat – has made her incapable of even lifting her bag from the train. Some silver and a busy porter solve the problem, escorting her to the cab rank where she engages a Hansom for Southampton Street. The thought of trying to make it all the way to Brixton in one go is just too much for her.

Vincent is sympathetic as usual. He sends out for a glass of brandy and a currant bun to revive his ailing wife. Eugenie downs the brandy gratefully; the bun goes largely uneaten. After some discussion it is decided that the gallery should be closed for the day whilst Vincent takes Eugenie home in a cab. Finding one willing to go south of the river is not that easy. Yet again, copious amounts of silver make the impossible possible. Perhaps because of the hot weather the streets are clearer than usual, allowing them to arrive home in double-quick time. Vincent pays off the driver and carries the bag into the sitting room. Eugenie announces that she cannot stand up any longer and will go and lie down on her bed for a while. Leaving her hat behind she climbs the stairs slowly and gingerly.

Vincent is aroused by a huge shriek from their bedroom, rushes upstairs expecting to find his wife having a heat-induced fit. Instead he finds an incandescent Eugenie standing at the foot of the bed screaming at the naked couple within it. "You louse, you dirty squirming Spanish bedbug. How dare you defile my marriage bed like this. Get out, get out. I never want to see you ever again. Never, not ever. Don't you dare set foot in this house. Get out and take all your things with you." Eugenie opens the window and begins throwing Pablo's clothes onto the street below, taking care to tear off the brim of his beloved top hat before it too follows his shoes onto the pavement. "Get out, now. Get out. Don't come into my sight again. Never, not ever." Pablo snatches up a sheet, which he wraps around himself, narrowly dodging flailing nails as he scrambles out of the door.

"As for you, you hussy, I'll beat you black and blue. I'll knock you into the middle of next week. Let me get at you, I'll tear you to shreds." Maia is careful to get out of the bed as far away from her mother as she can. She still does not move in any other than her quiet and considered manner, taking care not to crease her clothes as she picks them from the floor. Eugenie lunges at her with fists flying, getting in some mighty blows before Vincent can intercede. Only then does Maia take flight, making her bedroom slightly ahead of her enraged mother whose progress is impeded by Vincent's arms. Finding the door locked Eugenie makes instead for Pablo's room. Here are piles of new clothes, some fresh from the makers. Out of the window they go: trousers, coats, shoes, even tie pins and cufflinks, which roll away down the nearby drain.

Pablo tries to collect and stack as much as he can, encumbered as he is by the uncomfortable sheet, which insists on getting between his legs and tripping him up. The neighbours have poured out of their houses to view the entertainment.

"Listen to her, always so high and mighty. Not so posh now, is she? Giving herself airs. Her father was just a brickie, you know, picked her mother up in some shop or other. We all know what kind of shop that was, don't we?"

"That's the trouble with that house, always full of bloody foreigners. He tries to pretend he's English but it's obvious he's German or something. Bloody foreigners coming over here stealing our jobs and seducing our girls. Ought to be against the law, it should. Serves her right for letting them into her house in the first place. I never trusted them, me. Dirty, greasy dagos and nasty fritzes. We'd be well rid of them."

Children are making off with whatever garments they can find. It is impossible for the encumbered Pablo to protect them all. "Put some knickers on, love," shouts a spectator. "We don't want to see your bits." Pablo does so under the cover of his sheet. This allows greater child predations but allows him at last to gather together a coherent pile with which he heads off down towards the high street. To be followed ten minutes later by Maia, suitcase in hand, and more violent imprecations from her mother of which 'tart' and 'whore' are the kindest.

The spectators drift back in groups to one another's houses to discuss at length the events of the afternoon and the inadvisability of allowing foreigners into one's house, especially when there are young girls around.

Eugenie has collapsed in tears on the lounge divan. More brandy is demanded, which Vincent supplies in copious amounts. He is as much in need of fortification as his wife, having just lost both a son and a daughter. To some extent he has learnt to control his fits by a combination of controlled breathing and a mental contemplation of one of his many Biblical aphorisms. At present this has the advantage of shutting out Eugenie's continuing tirade against the errant pair, which continues unabated.

The front door is still wide open so that Doris Kirman's entry goes unremarked for the moment. Given the amount of chaos and the explosions of tears, Doris is convinced that the van Goghs have already heard her news. "Isn't it terrible," she says, "but not really that unexpected, was it? We were all just waiting to hear that it had happened." Eugenie ceases her cries and wails, amazed that the goings-on in her house had been such public knowledge whilst she was left in ignorance. "Why did nobody tell me?" she asks. "Am I always to be the last person to know?"

"But we talked about it only last week," replies Doris. "You said yourself that it would not be long before he went."

Vincent is forced out of his semi-trance. Aware that there must be some confusion he tries to clarify the situation. "What are you talking about? Doris, who has gone? Gone where?"

"It is Mr Whistler. He died. This morning. We've just heard."

All this is too much for Vincent. Neither breathing nor Biblical knowledge is sufficient for him this time. He collapses in a fit so prolonged that Eugenie and Doris fear for his life. They hold him down as much as they can, aided by a passing neighbour whose brawny arms added to theirs finally subdue the patient and assist in getting him to bed, denuded of sheets as it is. A doctor is called, who looks glum and shakes his head. He continues to do this for nearly four weeks as Vincent thrashes around in response to dreams where he sees the Devil coming at him in the guise of Mr Worldly Wise to punish him for his financial success. He blames his desertion by all three of his daughters on his love of his gallery, which they must feel has left no room for his love of them.

After four weeks he recovers. Sits up. Talks sensibly and coherently. His hair has turned completely white and he will never walk again.

# Montmartre

## Summer 1908

Dear Cornelia

*You know how jealous I am of you with your three boys, so much more civilised than we three girls. So I'm planning the big step myself, except that Bill doesn't know that yet. Thirty seems a late age at which to start but since I'm only planning on the one, that shouldn't be too bad. Look at you, still producing at getting on for forty! In preparation I've formally taken Bill's name, even though we are not officially married. He has been tempted recently by this fluttery butterfly Marie but I've put an end to that and sent her packing. She is just as sticky as that Gwen girl is around Rodin but a lot prettier in her soggy way. She's terribly short sighted, which makes her look vague and appealing so she never wears her glasses. What I really can't stand about her is her pictures which are not worth the cheap canvas they are painted on. Soggy rubbish. Burne-Jones seen through a romantic fog.*

*I've been working with Harry's friend Georges on some new techniques. Georges used to be a house painter like Harry — which is why they get on together so well — so he knows about all these ways of faking wood finishes and so on, which we are trying to incorporate in our paintings. In return I've shown him how to use real dress materials on the picture surface instead of painting it in and tearing up bits of paper and card to represent various objects and ideas. Some of the things we have come up with are totally wild, enough to give poor old Vollard a rolling fit. Braque introduced me to a new dealer in town, a German called Kahnweiller who thinks what we are doing is absolutely wonderful. A good job too because both John Quinn and*

Leo Stein think they are rubbish. I had a go at Leo about that and the way he always seems to prefer Matisse's paintings to mine. Leo took it in good heart until his sister butted in. She's a huge lumpy lesbian who lives with this ferocious lover of hers called Alice. Anyway, Gertrude, that's the sister, started to defend Leo and call my painting 'academic and boring'. Now boring it may be, but academic never, not ever. So we had a huge row in the middle of the street. I don't suppose I'll see them again. With luck Kahnweiller's Russian contacts will pour in to fill the gap.

Now and then I get such wonderful letters from Father, who keeps me abreast of all the news from home. I suspect that he also sees Maia from time to time but he never tells me directly. The wonderful thing about Father is that when he is talking to you or writing to you he convinces you that you are his favourite daughter of all. At the same time we each think that one of the others is his favourite. Which means, I suppose, that he treats us all equally whatever we get up to.

Speaking of which... I see Mama sometimes on her visits to Paris. She makes a point of dropping in now and then when she knows that Bill is not around. Still as flirty as ever, and she keeps in touch with the Spanish artists in particular. She seems to have added a new one to her entourage called Juan, who I always refer to as 'Mother's grey Spaniard'. He seems pleasant enough and I think Mother is rather taken with him, though she ensures that I never see them together. Juan is a bit of a magpie when it comes to ideas and techniques, so Georges and I tend to keep him at a distance. I'd be surprised if Mother hasn't abandoned the idea of distance altogether when it comes to this young man.

Enough of gossip, at least until you send me some in your eagerly awaited next letter.

Your broody sister

Rose

(Madame Wilhelm Kostrowicki!)

# Shipley

## *Autumn 1908*

*Dear Madame Kostrowicki*

*How strange to call you that! Does Bill know about your interesting condition yet, or is he, like most men, unable to count up to twenty-eight? That is one of Mother's favourite phrases, if you remember. As far as I can make out from Doris Mother is relatively well behaved in London. Perhaps she reserves all her misdemeanours for Paris. To be fair, she looks after Father very well; keeps him clean and tidy and makes sure that he goes out and about in his wheelchair. He's the one who sits the gallery most of the time, even manages to get himself tiddly of an evening with his friends from time to time. The doctor that Simon engaged for him is mystified. He says that there is nothing physically wrong with Father at all, it is just that he cannot walk. He can stand up as long as he holds on to something. From hints that Mother drops it appears that he is able to perform his husbandly duties quite adequately. Knowing Mother, he is not as enthusiastic or as frequent as she would like. Simon is talking about consulting some mind doctor in Vienna but Father won't hear of it.*

*Guess who I met in London last week? Maia! I went down for the big demonstration in Hyde Park. Doris had made all of the sashes for the Yorkshire contingent and brought them up to King's Cross for us. When we got to the park there was Maia acting as a steward and shepherding us about to our allotted places. She's not as quiet as she used to be but twice as sharp and a real sergeant-major, as you might expect. She is living with Pablo now in a big house near the new science museum. From what I could gather she has quite a time* keeping Pablo in check, especially when he goes off for weeks away at those posh house parties in the country, supposedly painting his host or hostess. We had quite a long chat before the speeches and the march itself. I didn't know it at the time but it transpires that after the march to the Houses of Parliament Maia got herself arrested. Something to do with assaulting a policeman. Anyway Pablo bailed her out, though I don't think that he was best pleased.

Pablo himself has got quite chubby. Given that he is not very tall it does not sit well on him. He has also got snobby and pretentious. It's all the fault of the Princes' portrait, of course. It was meant to be shown in our gallery but Mother refused to have anything to do with it after he went off with Maia, so it was shown at the Grosvenor instead. Two shillings' admission! Can you imagine? So a great hoo-hah, articles in The Times. Then the King donated the portrait to the Tate Gallery much to the Queen's annoyance, which caused another scandal. On top of that the King decided he was going to make Pablo a knight. Mr Asquith kicked up a fuss at that because Pablo is a foreign national so can't be a Knight of the Realm. In the end they got round it with some sleight of hand, so that Pablo is now Sir Pablo Ruiz. Quite a move up from that scruffy boy with unwashed hair, dying shoes and no socks that we first came across those years ago.

Despite his rise through the ranks Mother still refuses to have anything to do with him, or with Maia either. Doris tells me that Maia makes a point of going to the gallery at least once a week when she knows that Father is there on his own. They are closer than they ever were, even if he and Pablo are only on nodding terms nowadays. You know that Father always wanted a son, so the loss of Pablo to him is particularly painful.

I don't know what it is like in Paris but everyone here is crazy for war except that they can't make up their minds who they want to go to war with. Up here in Yorkshire the feeling is anti-French, partly because the French are the ones we have always gone to war with, partly because the Germans are such good customers for the wool trade. London is different. Everyone there keeps on about the navy and how *we should be building more dreadnoughts to keep pace with the Germans. I don't see it myself. Why should we want to fight the Germans, or even the French for that matter? Can you see the Germans trying to invade Ramsgate? They would die of food poisoning from the jellied eels! Seriously, I am worried. Harry's boys had a hard time in South Africa in the last lot and I don't want to see my boys sent off to fight, even if it is only across the Channel in France. Once you are a mother you will understand these anxieties.*

*Your loving sister*
*Cornelia*

Tottenham Court Road

# Lambeth

## Summer 1913

*Dear Rose*

*Congratulations on the new baby. Cornelia had said to me that you had sworn you would stop at one. I expect you changed your mind, unless there was an accident at some point. It is so easy to get carried away after a few glasses of gin. One of each, Cornelia tells me, which is quite a change for your family where it is always all boys or all girls. After what we saw the other week I don't think that we will be looking to Maia to continue the trend with her, one way or the other.*

*Pablo still uses the room in the warehouse occasionally for what he terms his 'real painting'. Maia likes him to do that because his 'real painting' makes him happy and because he is only a couple of rooms away and she can keep an eye on him. She is like a volcano at the moment, what with working for the movement and starting two new girls in the hat business. I rather suspect that she had some sort of involvement with Miss Davison's horrific stunt at Epsom that so upset us all. We were all shocked by it, whilst Maia acted as if she had known about it all along. I suspect that she was the one who had run up the banner that Miss Davison was trying to pin onto the King's horse. They say that a group of them chose lots as to who would do it. Probably Maia was one of them. A pity; she would never have let herself get run over.*

*Anyway she has started using interesting paper decorations on the hats twisted into weird shapes, just like some of Dad's latest paintings and was anxious to show them off to Pablo. We all put one on and went off to the studio wearing them. Pablo didn't seem too*

293

pleased to see us and wasn't quite as complimentary of the hats as Maia was expecting. There was a new painting on the easel, which we all asked to see. I must say it was rather fine: the back view of a female nude in luscious flesh colours, perhaps a trifle overdone but a real eye-grabber. She must be luscious herself with all those soft curves and elegant lines. I don't always like Pablo's paintings; even I have to admit that he certainly can draw. In the corner of the painting he had written something: 'Ma jolie'. "I don't think that 'ma jolie' is Maia," Laura whispered to me. You should have seen Maia's face, as sharp as the cutting edge of the guillotine and twice as hard.

That night the police were called to their house in south Kensington. By all accounts Maia was throwing Pablo's clothes out of an upstairs window. When they arrived she gave them a load of abuse and even hit one of them with a suitcase. Whether it was deliberate or not, I don't know but when they found her WSPU sash the police decided that it must be another stunt, so they arrested her and took her down the local station. Once they found out that she had been arrested before for attacking the police they charged her and locked her up. It was lucky for her that the magistrate understood that this was only a domestic dispute and that the policeman had been struck by accident (though I'm not totally convinced that was the case). By the time she got back to the house her cases were in the hallway and two heavies were on duty to stop her going in. Laura and I have put her up for a while at Mother's. Your father wanted her to go back to Hackford Road but your mother wasn't having it. "She's made her bed, now she must lie in it," she said, though by all accounts it wasn't her bed that she made, or unmade, in the first place.

Well, that's how it is. Cornelia is on her way down from Yorkshire. I guess that she will be taking Maia back with her for a while. I'm sure she will write and let you know what is happening.

Best wishes

Doris Kirman

# London

## *Spring 1919*

The war is over. The boys are coming home, those of them that are left.

Harry does not know whether to laugh or cry. Charles and Walter had both re-enlisted at the outbreak of the war in 1914. Charles was wounded soon after, spending three months with his father convalescing. Walter was listed as 'missing in action, presumed dead' after the great attack of 1916. Soon after, Charles turned up in Grimsby in civvies, still weeping for his dead brother, moving from house to house before being arrested by military police, tried by a military tribunal and shot for desertion. Now Walter has turned up. Not dead at all but wounded and taken prisoner. Drinking even more than after South Africa, telling anyone who would listen the idiocies of the British high command. "Should be lined up against a wall and shot, the lot of them."

Cornelia has not been so fortunate. Despite being only sixteen Aaron had lied about his age to join up with one of the local pals' battalions just in time to catch the second battle of the Somme, from which he never returned. Her other two boys are young enough to feel disappointed at 'missing the show'. Whilst desolated at the loss of Aaron Cornelia is still able to face her God and thank him for bringing an end to the war before the others were old enough to join up. It will be some years before she dresses in anything other than black, except for one special occasion…

Maia has spent the war working in a field hospital in Picardy where she is acknowledged as a highly efficient if unsympathetic nurse.

The lack of sympathy is a front, a mask to cut her off from the horrors that she is confronted with every day. Amputations, disfigurements, even drownings as a result of lungs poisoned with mustard gas, are part of her normal life. Early in 1915 a casualty was brought in who she recognised as one of Rose's contemporaries from the Slade. On the odd quiet afternoon the two of them spent time together discussing design, painting and the women question, on which the Captain was totally in agreement. Upon his temporary discharge Maia took leave of absence, leaving with him for their formal wedding and extended honeymoon in Cornwall. Both returned to duty later in the year on different parts of the front. Despite no longer being able to see her husband any longer on his short leaves, Maia was delighted when he was withdrawn from the dangers of the Western Front to be posted to Macedonia. Where he died of dysentery.

Sales of paintings in Paris have been brought to a halt by the war. Rose has managed to keep herself and the two children on Bill's army pay, supplemented from time to time with subventions on her funds in England and regular presents from her father. Bill has been good to keep his head down and fortunate to be assigned to a quiet part of the front. One night he fails to keep his head down quite far enough, catching a lump of shrapnel on the side of his skull. In itself the wound is not a dangerous one. The shock of the shrapnel causes a haemorrhage in the brain and a disruption of the meninga. To save his life he is trepanned, the skull cut off to relieve the internal pressure. Rose is shocked to see him but delighted that he is still alive and no longer fit for service. She begins to paint again. Bill writes as if his life depends upon it. Intimations of mortality, perhaps? The official cause of his death in 1918 is registered as pneumonia. Whether this is the result of his wound or of some other illness working on his enfeebled physical constitution is impossible to tell.

As for Pablo, he has had what is sometimes referred to as 'a good war'. Its first year did not start well. Eva, who had moved into south Kensington the week that Maia moved out, died of consumption the same August that the war began and only a week after Pablo had been elected to membership of the Royal Academy in acknowledgement of over ten years of showing the prime exhibit at the annual open exhibition. Nothing daunted, Pablo spent the rest of the year painting imaginary impressions of brave Allied soldiers capturing enemy trenches and rescuing endangered nuns from the depredations of the Hun, before taking ship to visit his young friend Charlie in California. Charlie has endured some opprobrium for hiding away in America rather than rushing off to the front. As a Spaniard and therefore a neutral, Sir Pablo can voice his support for the cause, as well as undertaking some fundraising in America without fear of criticism. Indeed *The Times*, subservient as usual, is full of praise for his efforts. His arrival back in Southampton with his screen actress wife is greeted with loud applause from the assembled spectators and commissions for war memorials from a grateful government, which survive to this day. A series of paintings used to advertise motor cars in Europe and the United States cements both his popularity and his bank balance in a manner unknown since 'Bubbles' was used to advertise soap. A career which began with advertising for Els Quatre Gats in Barcelona has reached its pinnacle with the new Packard convertible in Croydon.

# Brixton

## *Spring 1919*

The spring is late this year. Despite coats and blankets, Vincent finds life in his wheelchair cold as well as frustrating. Over the years his shoulders have broadened and his arm muscles solidified and filled out from the effort of moving himself around. As befits a borough which will soon become South London's prime shopping area, Brixton has good smooth pavements. Southampton Street is the same, giving Vincent plenty of opportunities to be self-sufficient, to keep up an interesting working and social life. All the same, his health is suffering. Sitting all day has given him piles and constipation, an embarrassing and painful combination. Nor has the sedentary life been good for his heart, grown lazy for lack of exercise, or his corporation, steadily increasing for the same reason.

Undaunted, he has turned into a prolific letter writer. Each of his daughters receives at least two letters a week from him, full of advice and consolation. He is still the same pilgrim, still the same devoted follower of Jesus Christ, yet he refuses to condemn their lives or any of their actions on moral or religious grounds. Actions are only condemned if they are likely to impair the actor's happiness or to harm others. A new lover is to be treated kindly, the old one cast off in the gentlest possible manner. Business is to be transacted fairly, children to be friends who need guidance, neighbours assisted when in need. By this time in 1919 he has sent over 2000 letters, including nearly fifty to Pablo.[1]

---

[1] Published by the Society of Friends as *The Collected Letters of Vincent van Gogh* (1961) to 'bring comfort to all those in spiritual need'. The book enjoyed a vogue in the sixties, including a brief appearance in *The Sunday Times* best-seller list and a recommendation by the Archbishop of Canterbury.

The inclement weather, a weak heart and a spring cold have finally laid him low, making him subject to an increasing number of fits, which have made him all the more susceptible to illness. Towards the end of April they all culminate in a severe bout of pneumonia, from which he never recovers. On the first day of May Vincent dies in the company of Eugenie and Cornelia, Rose still being en route from France.

His funeral takes place beneath glorious May skies, a day for celebration rather than for sadness. Rose and Cornelia are dressed in their brightest colours, alongside Doris and Laura Kirman. Harry has come down from Grimsby with young Harry and Walter, the three of them incongruous in their corduroy trousers and cotton shirts. Eugenie looks the part of the grieving widow in her black mourning and lacy veil. Pointedly she ignores Maia, who seems happy to return the compliment. Besides the family the chapel is crammed full with those who have met and admired Vincent for his human qualities as well as his correct and devout manner. Most have forgone a day's pay to be here to pay their respects. 'To be a Pilgrim' is sung louder and more fervently than at any ordinary Sunday service.

Pablo is not there. As yet, he knows nothing of Vincent's death, having taken his American wife off to Cannes at the invitation of David Windsor who has a soft spot for the aristocracy of Hollywood. The news reaches him some days after the funeral, moving him to write a letter of condolence to the widowed Eugenie.

# Cannes

## *Spring 1919*

*My dearest Eugenie*

*How can I ever forget the kindness of your family in taking in a waif from off the street, feeding and sheltering him in his hour of need? Not only was I fed and clothed but also loved and cosseted, provided with somewhere to paint, introduced to some of the leading painters of our age and the leading patrons of the arts extending as far as the Royal Family itself. Vincent was wonderful. I could have been his son for all the care he lavished on me and the good advice he gave. Even when all others had cast me out he still treated me to the fruits of his good sense, as if I were a lost sheep or the prodigal son considering returning home.*

*Above all, it was your love and care that held me in the bosom of the family, giving me a calm ecstasy that I had never experienced before, something which has driven my life and my art ever since. Vincent often told me that there is in fact only love that matters. Whatever it may be. And they should put out the eyes of painters as they do of goldfinches to make them sing better. Only the love of a wonderful woman like you is worthy of an artist. Your love has blinded my eyes to all else, causing me to sing and to paint all the more brilliantly.*

*My dearest Eugenie...*

★

Pablo continues in this vein for another four pages, a paean of praise that would turn any woman's head, except that Eugenie looks at the postmark, realises who the letter is from and promptly burns it unread.

Cornelia and Rose both receive virtually the same letter ("dictated to some minion" suggests Cornelia), which they compare before Cornelia throws hers in the rubbish. Rose decorates hers with obscene drawings and scatological comments before hurling it into one of her folders among a group of drawings.[2]

Maia has opened hers and reads it carefully. She takes a pair of scissors, cuts each sheet into precise rectangles, which she impales on the spike next to the toilet in her outside privy.

Harry, Walter and Young Harry have a few pints of porter in the White Horse for old times' sake before making off for their train. Eugenie sits in the kitchen at Hackford Road wondering when she will be able to make her next trip to Paris and whether she will still have to wear mourning when she does so.

---

[2] This is now in the Kostrowicki archive of the University of Texas. The one on display at the Kostrowicki Museum in Nagasaki is in fact a copy.

# The Times

## November 1937

# R

## A. President denounces excesses of modern art.

Last evening saw the installation of the new President of the Royal Academy of Art at Burlington House in Piccadilly. The banquet was attended by over one hundred academicians, gallery owners, noted art collectors and tutors from the Royal Academy schools who had assembled to honour the President elect, Sir Pablo Ruiz.

Sir Pablo is well known among the general public for his royal portraits, notably the double portrait of HRH the Prince of Wales and HRH the Duke of York as were, and the recent portrait of the two Princesses Elizabeth and Margaret. They have been likened to the great Renaissance portraits of Titian, Da Vinci and del Sarto, although some critics have felt that, while the colours have been entirely naturalistic, the features of the subjects have been rendered in an overly aggressive and simplistic manner. Sir Pablo himself refers viewers back to Catalan church art with its almost naive feel to its subjects and heightened colour scales.

In his speech to the guests, Sir Pablo was forthright in his opinions on much of continental art. 'This is the art of decadence,' he declared, 'from the communist anarchy that we see in Russia to the art of the gutter in Paris. Hopefully Russian art is merely an experiment brought on by the exuberance of revolutionary times. The art of Paris and Munich has no such excuse. It is the culmination of a series of disastrous experiments, of talentless artists throwing themselves before the public in a spirit of notoriety. Men, and even women, gaining notice for their decadent lifestyles and talentless daubs rather than for any article of beauty that they may accidentally produce.'

Sir Pablo went on to attack some of the leading lights of the Parisian art world by name. 'Perhaps the least obnoxious in his actual production is Monsieur Matisse. After the first shock we can recognise his paintings as being landscapes or interiors or even a portrait. But what portraits! Bright green stripes down a face, paint applied straight from the palette with no relation to anything seen in nature. He takes a charming Catalan fishing village and turns it into a vision of hell, all heavy reds and blues applied not with a palette knife but with a trowel or the back of his thumb.'

'Matisse has had an unfortunate influence on younger artists within France and throughout Europe, as has the English artist Harry Kirman. One deluded Dutchman has spent his time painting mere blocks of colour in imitation of a child's toy, one may suggest. Even before the war German artists vied with one another to produce the most garish possible paintings, even of the most respectable social gatherings. But, then what can one expect from Germans?' ('Hear, hear' from the audience.) 'Even now, some talented German draughtsmen are deluded enough to destroy the impact of their work by overlaying it with Matisse's crazy colour combinations. Acceptable as they are in some quarters, Matisse and Kirman are the leading figures in the destruction of real art. Even when trying to imitate the glorious Ingres, Matisse still cannot resist smearing on the first tube of paint that comes by accident to his hand.'

'But,' he continued, 'even that pales by comparison with this fellow Braque, a failed house painter by all accounts. All he has is lines and cubes and triangles. A sort of triangulism, with scratchy colours and complete disregard for the laws of perspective. Even a skilled artist or a dedicated connoisseur could take weeks puzzling over what could possibly be the subject of these daubs. Can this be art, I ask you?' (Loud applause.)

'We in Britain and, I hope, in my native Spain as well once the disease of socialism has been banished from it, will not be sucked into this morass of wishy-washy emotionalism. We will continue to cherish the skills of the great artists, the moral imperatives of uplifting narrative painting, the verisimilitude of the portrait which gives us both the likeness and the character of the subject, the perfect proportions of both building and landscape; in fine, the colours and perfections of God's creation.' (Loud applause.)

'My friends, I call upon you to eschew the temptations of the simple and the appeals of the so-called avant-garde but to work hard upon your craft. You will be rewarded by a lasting reputation long after the likes of Matisse, Braque, Kostrowicki and Kirman have been forgotten. Work in the tradition of Holbein, van Dyke and Alma-Tadema so that the British art of the first half of the twentieth century will be remembered forever.'

Sir Pablo sat down to renewed thunderous applause from his audience, the approbation of whom is shared by this newspaper."

# Modern Art in Europe

## Phaidon, 1950

### France

(p.17) **Rose Kostrowicki** (b.1880) Studied for a short time at the Slade, exhibiting early work at the Outland Gallery in London. Influenced by the symbolism of Gauguin, this concentrated on views of the poor and the dispossessed, her figures elongated and stylised to achieve greater expression. Although increasingly popular nowadays, especially among the young, these early paintings are disfigured by an excess of sentimentality. Moved to Paris in 1903, where she worked for the sculptor Rodin, whose mistress she was for a short period before meeting the poet Wilhelm Kostrowicki who she lived with until his death in 1919. Her collaboration with Georges Braque led to one of the great periods in modern art, with an explosion of techniques and approaches, including collage, advanced abstraction and the beginnings of automatic writing. Although Braque withdrew into a more representational framework, Kostrowicki continued her researches. Her series 'Calligrammes' (named after Wilhelm's finest collection) is a classic of modernism with examples fetching the highest prices at auction. She returned to Britain in 1940 on the German invasion of France. Created a Dame of the British Empire in 1947.

### England

(p.389) **Henry Kirman** (1853–1933) Began life as a house painter in South London. Studied life drawing at Borough Road College before abandoning his family and moving to Grimsby, Lincolnshire. While working as a fisherman and dockside labourer started to paint landscapes and portraits of his neighbours. His work moved steadily towards abstraction, epitomised by his famous 'Trawlers returning with their catch' for Grimsby Borough Council (now in the Tate Gallery). Collaborated with Georges Braque and Piet Mondrian, briefly forming the 'Triumvirate' group, which was highly influential in Holland and Belgium down to the formation since the war of the COBRA group. Kirman is credited with pushing both Braque and Mondrian towards full abstraction at a time when even Kostrowicki was still dependent on the figure. The news that two of his sons were killed during the first war saw the production of his finest painting, the black-on-black 'Memorial' (now in the Guggenheim Museum, New York), which had such an influence on Russian revolutionary art and Malevich in particular. His influence is still felt today in Britain and in the USA among the 'colour field' painters. Strangely he was unable to sell anything other than his early paintings of trawlers to private patrons in Britain until after the Great War, despite the continued support of the Outland Gallery.

(p.402) **V. V. Governor** (dates unknown) Painter of small-scale landscapes and flowers. Exhibited regularly at the Outland Gallery to 1914. Presumed killed in the war. Otherwise little is known.

(p.404) **Vincent van Gogh** (dates unknown) Manager of the Goupil Gallery in London. Credited with introducing Impressionist painters to London and encouraging the taste of the English upper classes for the modern art of their time. Presumed to have moved back to Paris on the sale of the Southampton Street Gallery to the Outland Gallery around 1903.

(p.405) **Eugenie Gough** (1858-1941) Owner and manager of the Outland Gallery, London. Best known for its support for Spanish artists, particularly Juan Gris and Ramon Casas, the Outland Gallery also brought the paintings of Harry Kirman to a wider British public, despite his lack of commercial success. For many years Mrs Gough bought in Kirmans even though she knew it was impossible to sell them, in order to support the artist. The gallery also began the career of Pablo Ruiz, who Mrs Gough rescued from abject poverty, even giving him free lodging at her own home despite the opposition of her husband and daughters. After the war was the first to show the paintings of Miró and to a lesser extent Dalí. It is said that she part-financed the Dalí/Buñuel film *Un Chien Andalou*, supplying the idea for the initial sequence. Until its closure in 1928 the Outland Gallery remained at the cutting edge of modernist art in Britain, a project which fell into disarray after its closure.

(p.408) **Sir Pablo Ruiz** (b. 1881) Reactionary academic painter. Originally from Malaga by way of Barcelona and Paris, Ruiz was taken up by Eugenie Gough of the Outland Gallery on his arrival in Britain. Initially working in a rather puerile symbolist strain with some influence from El Greco, patronage from the Prince of Wales (later Edward VII) and the support of J. McN. Whistler brought him to the attention of the British aristocracy. His painting of Mrs Keppel at the Royal Academy caused a public scandal because of its subject matter. By contrast the painting of the two sons of the later King George V was an instant sensation. That and the 'Coronation' series cemented his fame, leading to a deluge of commissions. On return from the USA in 1919 he designed around thirty war memorials, the majority in a turgid and *retardaire* style. Between the wars he continued with portraiture though in a more informal setting, reflecting the life of the upper classes on the Côte d'Azur in particular. Elected President of the Royal Academy in 1937, from which post-leftist artists tried to have him deposed following the exhibition there in 1939 of his painting 'Franco Liberating Barcelona'. Moved to Spain in 1941 to escape the bombing in London. In 1946 emigrated to the USA to avoid British super-tax, taking a financial interest in Charlie Chaplin's United Artists film company. Saw himself as a breakwater against the tides of modernism, which he deplored; his influence was a major factor in the insular and backward nature of British art between the wars. Currently lives a reclusive life in California where his portraits are still in demand among a certain coterie of filmmakers. Otherwise the paintings of Sir Pablo Ruiz are nowadays either ignored or forgotten.

*Joanna's Prophecy*

"*There is one among us who comes to a forking of the ways. One way is to heat, pain and dissolution. A falling. A divorce from God. Belief in himself as a supernatural being. Great unhappiness. A descent for his soul while his memory rises to unknown heights.*

*The other path is that of the good Samaritan. Of rescuing the fallen for God. Of carrying the Word. He may weaken, leave the struggle but he must return to lift up sinners, to rescue from evil those who have fallen. Alleluia.*"

*Irises*